CW00724170

HELLER VERLAG / HELLER PUBLISHING Co.

Max Claro

Code Peking Duck

A novel based on actual events

Translated from the German
by Nicholas Corwin

HELLER VERLAG / HELLER PUBLISHING Co.

Code Peking Duck
by Max Claro

Originally published in Germany as
Der Rausholer by
HELLER VERLAG / HELLER PUBLISHING Co.
P.O. Box 1204, D-82024 Taufkirchen, Germany

This novel is based on true events!

Translated from the German by Nicholas Corwin
(as authorized by Max Claro)

Cover design and layout by Sigrid Kowalewski, Munich, Germany
(*sidko.de*), with images from 123RF and photos by the author.

Paperback ISBN 978-3-929403-95-4
Printed in the EU
eBook ISBN 978-3-929403-66-4

Contents

Prologue

Today, in the era of Julian Paul Assange and Edward Joseph Snowden—two men whose activities have cost the lives of countless unnamed agents and caused many more to forfeit their freedom—nothing could motivate me to reenter the world of the intelligence community. All the same: I regret nothing. And I would do it all again, exactly as before.

Everything I did, I reconciled with my conscience. Even today, I'm occasionally agonized by uncertainty about whether—as a result or consequence of my actions—people might have come into harm's way. But to the extent that any human being's life can even be offset against that of another, one thing is certain: I saved far more lives—lives that were confronted with the utmost peril—than I ever jeopardized or destroyed.

The events in this novel took place between 1971 and 1979. They are based on true occurrences.

In the Vietnam War, a proxy war among three super-powers—the United States, the Soviet Union and China—millions of people lost their lives. The Vietnam conflict ended in 1975 with the victory of the Communist Viet Cong.

Mohammed Zahir Shah peaceably ruled the Kingdom of Afghanistan for nearly forty years, until 1973. Shah Mohammed Reza Pahlavi autocratically ruled Persia—Iran—until he was expelled by his people in January 1979. A month later, Ayatollah Ruhollah Khomeini installed the regime of the mullahs and proclaimed the Islamic Republic of Iran on 1 April 1979. At this time, a Siemens subsidiary, Kraftwerk Union AG, had been constructing a nuclear power plant in Bushehr, on the Persian Gulf. Block 1 was 85% complete; Block 2 was half finished.

In those days, things were different than they are today; some were simpler, others more difficult. It was commonplace and legal for companies to bribe foreign politicians and to deduct the bribe payments from their taxes. You could still take fluids, scissors, and knives aboard commercial airliners, and smoking during the flight was allowed. The digital age still lay in the distant future. We had neither the internet nor emails, nor cellphones, apps, GPS, nor DNA analysis. From a technological perspective, video surveillance of train stations, airports, border crossings, public spaces, and dwellings was no more feasible than a worldwide data exchange. Cameras still had to be loaded with emulsion film; the most popular spy camera was the Minox C, a masterpiece of German engineering. It was an easy matter to forge passports by swapping the photographs and making the official seal look genuine using a hand-cut rubber stamp. In most countries, including Germany and the United States, a caller's telephone number was never displayed, and you could place anonymous phone calls from any telephone booth. As for the calls themselves, it was a breeze to eavesdrop on them using swapped-out mouthpiece microphones or induction coils, or by tapping the lines. Vehicles, regardless of make, manufacturer, and size, could be easily repaired, manipulated, and hotwired using simple tools. Door locks could be opened with a master key, and safety locks could be picked using two staples or hairpins. The most greatly feared alarm system was a dog.

The Cold War prevailed between the Western powers, led by the United States, and the Eastern Bloc, led by the Soviet Union. The Iron Curtain, as Churchill famously called it, divided Germany and separated the West from the Soviet Union and its satellite Eastern Bloc countries—Poland, Czechoslovakia (then a single country), Hungary, Rumania, and Bulgaria. Citizens of the Western powers were allowed to travel to the Eastern Bloc, but citizens of the latter were not permitted to travel to the West. Borders were secured with live ammunition and appeared simply impenetrable. Nevertheless, thousands of people succeeded, for political, personal, or economic reasons, in fleeing to the West. Assisting and aiding escapes proved a lucrative business. Intelligence services also participated in it, primarily whenever they were able to extract strategic, scientific, or technological know-how from the opposing side. This might happen, for instance, if a highly decorated general or a brilliant nuclear scientist were to switch sides, or if the life of one's own agents operating on hostile territory was in jeopardy. Nowadays, borders are open; hence, a virus was able to rapidly spread worldwide, claiming many times more victims in the first year of the pandemic than did the Iron Curtain in the several decades of its existence.

CHAPTER 1

Motherly Love

It hadn't been easy, using a dull tin knife to cut down roses. I had swiped the knife a couple of days earlier from the dinner service on Pan Am's Flight 3748 from Los Angeles to Munich. After hacking away at a rosebush in a municipal park, I removed the bottom third of the stems and decorated them with bits of grass to spruce up the whole arrangement like an ikebana. But a special occasion simply demands a special effort. Was it forbidden? Well, in any event, the Böhmerwaldplatz, a Munich park, didn't boast any sign reading *Cutting Roses Prohibited*. And whatever wasn't forbidden had to be allowed, right?

I was surprised at the kind of thoughts that were coursing through my head, because in recent months, the last thing I had cared about was the question of what was forbidden or allowed. And there had been a lot more at stake than a couple of red roses!

So now I was standing before the fateful apartment building where I had grown up, on Lisztstrasse in the Munich neighborhood of Bogenhausen. It was a sunny day in August 1972. I took a deep breath, hesitating before finally ringing the front doorbell. Then the door to the building suddenly opened, and a somewhat stocky lady with a round head and alert eyes invited me inside. It was Mrs. Angermeier, who lived in the janitor's apartment on the ground floor. She eyed me curiously.

"Dear me, Michael! We haven't seen you in such a long time. I almost didn't recognize you with the short hair. How's medical school in Hamburg?"

"Just great!" I lied, somewhat distractedly making my way to the second floor, where I rang at the Müller apartment.

Now the door was opened by a slender, unprepossessing woman with brown locks of hair and chiseled features. How often had I glowingly imagined this moment of reunion and reconciliation! My mother would rejoice at her prodigal son's return, and I would forgive her for everything she had ever done to me.

I opened my arms to warmly hug and embrace the woman who had brought me into the world twenty years before. But all my mother did was take the roses, retreat a couple of steps, and toss the bouquet in the kitchen sink, right next to the hallway. Then, with a stony gaze, she threw four letters at my feet and said, "Here's the mail that's come for you." I closed the apartment door behind me.

Had I been able to shed tears, that moment would have surely been the right one. But as a small child I had been broken of the habit of crying. Even when I was very young, my mother had yelled at me whenever I had dared to cry, holding my mouth and nose until I blacked out. Sometimes, when tears rolled down my cheeks, she would strike me in the face with her open palm so powerfully that blood squirted out of my nose. That's how I learned to avoid tears and, with every bit of force I could summon, to displace feelings that would have occasioned any bawling—until, finally, I could no longer cry. It has remained like that right down to the present day.

After composing myself a little, I asked softly, "How did Mrs. Angermeier get the idea that I was attending medical school in Hamburg?"

"I had to tell her that, and the neighbors, too, because otherwise I couldn't have stood the shame!" my mother hissed back.

"What shame?" I asked innocently, although I could well imagine the tirade that would now follow.

"You've still got to ask? You? Someone who dropped out of high school right before graduation? You? The son of a teacher and the grandson of a senior civil servant!"

Now my mother's face was flush with rage; her features seemed to be mutating into some kind of demonic grimace. She inhaled deeply, and with all her might screamed, "*You failure! You idiot. You sniveling coward. Good-for-nothing bum! Mooch! Dropout!*"

After taking another deep breath, she spat out another sentence, one I had also heard from her hundreds of times:

"You aren't even worth the dirt under my fingernails!"

I bent down and picked up the letters she had thrown at my feet, while she added for good measure, "Get out of my house! Get out! You goddamned son of a bitch!"

"But Mom, that would mean—" Somehow, the wisecrack spontaneously popped out.

"You know perfectly well what I meant! Get out! Now! Don't ever show your face around here again!"

The humiliating things she was spewing were exactly what she had said, word for word, while giving me the boot fifteen months earlier. Mom was a teacher. She had gotten divorced shortly after I was born. As a child and teenager, I had submitted to her emotional and physical abuse—right up to the moment when I botched my last round of final exams in high school. Then I simply left. Exactly like I did now.

Why was my mother that way? Why did she torment me, as only she could do, accusing me of being just like my father, whom I had neither chosen nor ever been permitted to meet? She always reproached me by saying that my father had simply left her with a mountain of debt without paying even for a single diaper. Much later on, on my own, I discovered an explanation for the hostility of the most important person of my childhood: my mother had presumably projected onto me the entirety of the hatred she harbored towards my father. But that was no excuse.

I set off to see Boris, an old school friend who had offered to put me up for a couple of days. I shoved the letters into my jeans pocket, but not before glancing at the sender: three of them were from the *Kreiswehrersatzamt*—the district recruiting office in charge of conscripts for the Bundeswehr, that is, the German Army. The fourth one was a blue Air Mail envelope, adorned with the characteristic slanted, green-and-white stripes along the edge. It had arrived from Tehran, thousands of miles away.

CHAPTER 2

Uncle Sam Wants You!

Fifteen months earlier

It was an exciting, and—in the truest sense of the word, uplifting—feeling to peer out the window of the brand-new Pan Am Boeing 747 and gaze at the world from a bird's-eye view for the first time: forests, meadows, church towers, cemeteries, houses, streets, and colorful vehicles smaller than toys. It was a couple of weeks before my 19th birthday. After we had left the world below us and the pilot switched off the no-smoking and fasten-seatbelt signs, I promptly ordered a glass of bourbon. Nobody thought twice about checking the age of some long-haired hippie with a full beard. Even the passport inspector at the airport had been rather lax. I probably could have traveled using nothing more than my school identification.

I lit up a cigarette while mulling over the past few months and dreaming of my golden future. After getting kicked out by my mother, I had only a single goal: America! The land of unlimited opportunity—it was true. The country of Elvis and the Beach Boys! But first, the airfare had to be earned the hard way. A school friend's father owned the Würth laundry and dry cleaners on Wagenbauer Street, and he hired me as a jack-of-all-trades at a weekly wage. I sorted hangers and laundry of every description, loaded and unloaded the washing machines, steamed blouses, and ironed shirts until I had finally saved up 630 Deutschmarks for the flight, plus an extra 200 for spending money.

It was a breathtaking feeling, soaring high above the clouds in this enormous metallic bird, flying from one continent to another. As we descended, looking out the window I could see the Statue of Liberty, the symbol for the promised land.

How did that old song go? *New York, New York—if you can make it there, you can make it anywhere!*

In this country, anyone could go from rags to riches. Surely it was worth a try, at least!

Just a couple of hours after we landed, I found myself overwhelmed by the Big Apple. I wandered a few blocks eastward from Times Square to the Empire State Building, up to Rockefeller Center, back to Times Square, and all the way up Broadway. Then I walked eastward again along 54th Street, doubling back to Seventh Avenue, and continued north until I reached Central Park. After intensively comparing the rates at the numerous currency exchange booths on Broadway, I finally chose one and traded my hard-earned 200 Deutschmarks for the princely sum of $57.25.

People here were different than Germans. Friendlier, more talkative, and, above all, more outgoing! People I had never seen before in my life simply asked me—right on the street, or while waiting in line at the currency exchange booth, or even in the middle of Times Square—how my day was, how I was doing, where I was from, or where I was headed.

The sun was setting in the horizon as I began getting tired and sat down on a bench in Central Park. Hendrix, who resembled Bob Marley, joined me. He offered me a joint and gave me a couple of tips for surviving the concrete jungle—in which, he was absolutely convinced, I wouldn't survive very long without him. He said he was now my brother, I could tell him everything, and he would personally protect me for the next few days. It sounded as though the Godfather of Upper Manhattan was extending a protective hand over me—a most reassuring feeling!

Hendrix advised me to distribute my money by putting $20 into each shoe—that, he said, was the most secure hiding place—while keeping the rest in my left and right jeans pockets. Then he showed me the safest place to sleep in Central Park, one that had a "built-in alarm system." This consisted of birds that were nesting in a nearby bush and would start shrieking if anyone approached at night. Oh, man, was I glad to have met Hendrix. He was a true pro who was familiar with every angle and really knew his way around.

The next morning, my shoes had disappeared. With all the money, naturally. Two huge globs of bird shit had landed on my jacket. Luckily, there were enough water fountains in the park for me to clean the jacket and freshen myself up a bit.

I resolved to apply for a job in a restaurant, more precisely, as a busboy and dishwasher—since in German, we use the expression "from dishwasher to millionaire" to describe the journey from rags to riches. For two long days, I offered my services in literally every restaurant between East Harlem and the East Village for a miserable $2.00 per hour—unfortunately, without success. I wondered whether it was due to my rather shabby appearance? Or the fact the competition, which was overwhelmingly African-American, worked for perhaps even less money?

In Times Square, I struck up an acquaintance with Jimmy, a tall, athletic guy from Texas. He spontaneously invited me for a beer, and in his peculiar yet pleas-ant-sounding Southern drawl, regaled me with stories about the great life in his hometown: cattle, cowboys, the romantic Wild West in real life. I simply had to go there, he said. After our beer, he told me to wait a few moments; he had to quickly get hold of some money. He then walked about fifteen yards down the street, to the corner of West 46th, and spoke with a prostitute who slipped him something. Then there was a brief quarrel of some kind. Suddenly, Jimmy threw the woman on the ground, grabbed her head with both hands, and kept slamming it against the curb until she stopped moving. I figured that he was her pimp and that she must have been earning too little. A cop, who had been standing even closer, had witnessed the whole scene. But he crossed the street and calmly walked away as if nothing had happened. I felt sick. But what was I supposed to do? Confront Jimmy, who was physically stronger than I was? Offer first aid—without a clue as to how to do so—to a severely injured woman who might have just been murdered?

Suddenly, I just wanted to get out of this sick city. Anywhere but here! The Port Authority bus terminal was just ten minutes away on foot. How far would I get with the $6.45 I had left? San Francisco? Los Angeles? Chicago?

The money was enough to get just as far as Detroit—and even that was possible only because the friendly, dark-skinned lady at the ticket window took pity on me and spotted me five cents, since I was a nickel short of the full fare.

The trip in the Greyhound bus lasted around fifteen hours. Despite the comfortable reclining seat and the quiet overnight ride, I hardly slept. In my mind's eye, I kept seeing the prostitute, likely murdered, the indifferent cop, and the megalopolis of New York, with its skyscraper canyons and teeming masses of people. Not to mention the wailing of police, fire, and ambulance sirens, more or less nonstop, day and night.

In Detroit, the street leading from the bus station into the city was lined with tire dealers. Faced with utterly empty pockets, I went to the first one I could find, to inquire whether they had a job for me and what they would pay. I actually found some work at a place called "Rudy K." For $1.60 an hour, I was to sort out the tires with minor defects. I was also offered room and board in the tire warehouse. Rudy, an immigrant from Czechoslovakia, gave me a pair of worn-out work shoes, so I didn't have to walk barefoot over the hot tar.

After two weeks, I had saved enough for a pair of sandals, a Greyhound bus ticket to Los Angeles, and a small financial reserve at my new destination. The journey to Los Angeles, which took two and a half days, made countless stops through the most diverse landscapes in several states—Michigan, Illinois, Iowa, Nebraska, Colorado, Utah, and Nevada, culminating in sunny California. I regained my courage, optimism, and self-confidence. This bus trip alone was already worth the entire journey to the United States! And on top of that, there were all the people and their stories that I was privileged to hear.

Along the side of the road, I kept noticing enormous billboards showing an old man with a white goatee and a top hat colored like the American flag. He had a long, pointy nose and gazed right into my eyes with a fierce, hypnotic look, pointing directly at me with his right index finger. Underneath the picture, in enormous letters, was the caption:

Uncle Sam wants YOU!

What a bunch of crap, I thought. Why does Uncle Sam want me? Or anyone else driving past? Is he gay? If so, is he even allowed to advertise that? Had I missed something in English class? And if he wants me or someone else, then maybe he shouldn't look so fierce. He looks like the devil inviting me to join him in hell or something.

I couldn't ask the man sitting next to me, an overweight, somewhat scruffy-looking Mexican. He spoke only Spanish and probably wouldn't have known the answer anyway.

Somewhere in the middle of Iowa, though, I acquired a new seat neighbor, a neatly groomed, older man wearing flannel pants and metal-rimmed glasses. He gave me a friendly greeting and immediately wanted to know how my day had been going so far, how I was doing, where I came from, and where I was heading. After some small talk, I pointed to one of these enormous billboards and asked him, "Who is Uncle Sam?"

"Ha ha," he replied, laughing. "You're not familiar with Uncle Sam?"

"Sorry, I'm afraid not."

"Uncle Sam personifies America. You know, I was stationed in Augsburg once. I think you've also got some kind of symbolic figure like that over there in Germany. Isn't he called 'German Michael' or something like that?"

"That's right," I said. "It's actually called 'Deutscher Michel.' But that's really more of a simpleton who doesn't exactly represent the typical German."

"Uncle Sam doesn't represent the typical American either," the man explained. "He symbolizes the American government."

"And just who is it that Uncle Sam wants? And why?" I pressed the man further.

"The United States of America is at war," the elderly man intoned solemnly.

"You mean the war in Vietnam," I added, hoping to avoid coming across like an idiot who wasn't living in the real world.

"That's right, my boy. And whenever the United States of America is at war, Uncle Sam seeks volunteers who will fight for their country."

"But you do have the draft here. So doesn't every young guy still have to fight in the war, whether or not he wants to go?"

"That isn't enough for Uncle Sam," explained the old man. "A lot of guys are buying their way out, or they're getting medical exemptions. Besides, Uncle Sam can always use endless amounts of cannon fodder. And volunteers are mostly better motivated than draftees."

"That sounds like something a former general would say," I replied with a smile. I wanted to find out whether he had actually been one.

The disclaimer came immediately. "Oh no, I only made it up to Sergeant. I wasn't especially ambitious in the Army. But over the years, you start to figure out how things really work."

At the Nebraska border the old man got off, and a pretty, slender girl with long blonde hair took the seat next to mine. With a dazzling smile, she actually introduced herself as "Blondie," then asked me how my day had been going so far, how I was doing, where I came from, and where I was heading.

Damn! In Germany, I thought to myself, it would be absolutely inconceivable for a cute girl to sit next to me and strike up a conversation.

Blondie, as it turned out, was sixteen, quite a bit younger than I was. She was a junkie who had run away from her mother and didn't have a penny to her name. For a brief moment, I sensed something like solidarity.

"What are you going to do now?" I asked her.

"I'm heading to Vegas to try my luck there."

"Gambling? Roulette? Poker? What are you good at?"

Blondie rolled her eyes.

"I can play with men. Give them blowjobs, maybe more…"

I couldn't hide my shock, and that obviously amused her greatly.

"Want to come along with me?" she asked, throwing me a suggestive look.

I hesitated a moment and thought it over, sighing in order to gain a little thinking time. Drifting through Vegas with an underaged, heroin-addicted prostitute… well, that sounded like the adventure I was after, all right. But also a ton of problems that I didn't feel I was any match for.

"Well," I finally answered, lying through my teeth, "I've got a friend waiting for me in L.A. I can't leave him in the lurch."

Blondie nodded sympathetically. I tried changing the subject to Uncle Sam, but that didn't interest her in the least.

Eventually, I fell asleep. When I woke up, Blondie was gone, and the driver announced that we would be reaching Los Angeles in an hour.

Downtown L.A., Hollywood, Beverly Hills—after exactly three days and nights, my savings were exhausted, but I had finally arrived in paradise: Venice Beach! The most beautiful beach in the greater Los Angeles area was a colorful pedestrian stretch, where rich and poor, blacks, whites, Asians, bodybuilders, palm readers, hippies, tourists, bankers, musicians, Sannyasas, Jews, Christians, Muslims, and youthful Hare Krishna adherents all peacefully co-existed. Hundreds of small arts and crafts stalls, cafes, food stands, restaurants, and clothing stores lined the promenade along the beach.

As chance would have it, here I bumped into Gustl, a dyed-in-the-wool Bavarian with a big bushy beard, a headband, and Stars-and-Stripes pants. Gustl Harry Lechner was one of a kind, a guy with a colorful past, to put it mildly. Sometime earlier, he had sold out his share in a successful Munich tax law practice to the other partners for a song, after someone he'd met at Oktoberfest had offered him a slot in his Beverly Hills international law practice. There must have been a hell of a lot of beer flowing at that Oktoberfest, because when Gustl finally arrived in Beverly Hills and knocked on the door, the famous hotshot lawyer didn't seem to know him anymore.

So now Gustl was using the garage of a German woman, a friend from his school days, to create sand paintings that he sold on Venice Beach. I was allowed to help him in the manufacturing process a little: two glass panes were fitted parallel, perhaps three millimeters apart, into a frame and then sealed all around with silicon, except for a small crack. Then the great master would pour an emulsion consisting of water, oil, and paint into the crack, adding just a dash of sand. The artworks were available in various sizes and colors, and depending on how the buyer rotated them, kept generating new images from the sand.

Gustl was the "President of the Garage," as he dubbed it, and he appointed me "Vice President." I was allowed to spend my nights in the garage, and as soon as his host—who was a strict vegan—was out of the house, Gustl promptly fried us up a substantial portion of scrambled eggs with ham.

If I was willing to sell the sand paintings together with him on Venice Beach, Gustl was ready to offer me a generous commission: 30% for each painting that was sold whenever we were both standing in the booth, but 50% for every painting I sold while working alone. That made running the business more fun, and we could take turns enjoying the colorful goings-on along the promenade, or perhaps going for a swim in the ocean. It was a wonderful time. We had a lot of fun together, but also with the lively people on the beach, the musicians, and the California girls the Beach Boys sang about—quite accurately, as it turned out.

It could have continued this way indefinitely if I hadn't—perhaps this was a mistake on my part—taken stock of things after a couple of weeks. Where did I stand? What did I want to achieve?

Gustl's commission was generous, no doubt about it. But still, how much is 50% of nothing? The fact was, at the moment I had $12.00 in my pocket and was hunting for a challenge that held out some prospects of success.

Gustl fancied that California didn't have any decent bread, pretzels, or weisswurst, and allegedly, according to him, gummy bears weren't to be found in any American supermarket. Maybe we could become millionaires by setting up the country's first gummy bear factory. But we simply lacked the start-up capital.

So we bear-hugged each other goodbye, and I boarded the legendary *Interamericana*, a tramp ship that plied the route from Alaska to Tierra del Fuego. When I headed south, though, it was just a short stretch further, to San Diego, near the Mexican border.

In San Diego, the economic role relegated in New York to blacks was filled by Mexicans, who were a mercilessly underpaid labor force always at someone's beck and call *en masse*. It was only thanks to a fisherman who took pity on me that I didn't completely go to rack and ruin. He offered me $1.50 per hour to sort his daily catch by type and size, at 5:30 each morning. Two cups of coffee were included, and generally I was done with work in two or three hours. I had indeed worked my way up in the world—from sorting hangers to tires and now fish—for a significantly reduced daily wage, in any event.

The money was basically enough for a hamburger during the day and a beer in the evenings, at one of the seedy places at the harbor. Sometimes I got an order of French fries or a second beer. I slept, in relative comfort, in a hammock behind the little houses where the fishermen lived. That guaranteed I wouldn't oversleep.

One day, as the sun had reached its zenith and I was rocking, in a leisurely way, in my hammock, I was approached by two tall, black U.S. Army soldiers, their sharp dress uniforms adorned with ribbons and decorations. After politely introducing themselves as Larry Brown and Washington Theophile Smith, they asked me how my day had been going so far, how I was doing, where I came from, and where I was heading. Finally, they said, "We need you!"

I almost swallowed the gum I was chewing.

"Yes, we need you! The Army needs you!"

"Uncle Sam wants me? Me, Michael Müller from Germany?" I asked in disbelief.

"Yes, Uncle Sam wants *you*!" the two men replied in unison.

"But I'm a German. What does Uncle Sam want with a German?"

"No problem at all," they said. Larry Brown and Washington Theophile Smith invited me, at no obligation, to a Big Mac, an order of fries, and a large Coke at a nearby McDonald's. Just the thought of being able to eat until I was full spurred me to go along. Perhaps it was also smarter not to immediately start belittling the U.S. Army and the Vietnam War. A couple of months earlier, on Leopoldstrasse in Munich, I had been loudly protesting against all that. Along with thousands of other like-minded people, I was chanting "Ho-Ho-Ho-Chi-Minh." After all, perhaps dessert or even another meal from Uncle Sam might be in the offing.

The burger place was right next to the U.S. Army Recruiting Center at the main entrance to the Diego Mall, an enormous shopping center.

Larry Brown, the somewhat slenderer of the two soldiers, suggested getting four Big Mac meals to go, so we could take them with us to the recruiting center, where another soldier named Enrique Castellanos had been manning the fort, so to speak, during their absence.

26

"We have a lot to thank the Army for," Larry said with a serious expression on his face. Enrique, munching his burger, added, "The Army is our home—our family!"

Then the two of them told me a few moving stories from their own lives.

Enrique, as it turned out, came from a Mexican family that had arrived in the United States eight years earlier, without any documentation. His mother worked as a housekeeper for a German businesswoman, while his father held a job as a janitor at a restaurant. Enrique had hung out on the streets without the slightest idea what to do with his life. At eighteen, he said, he was still illiterate, having never attended school. Then came the offer from the Army. He obtained American citizenship, learned to read, write, and cook—in addition to getting his driver's license and receiving weapons training. Then he was sent to Vietnam for a year, where he served as a field cook and was given responsibility for food supplies. Now he was a corporal and eminently satisfied with his life; with the steady income provided by the Army, he was even able to help out his parents.

Larry came from New York City, more specifically, from the Bronx, and had grown up in an environment populated by junkies and drug dealers. His elder brother had been killed in Vietnam, so his mother cried a lot after Larry joined the Army voluntarily. But he no longer wanted to be beaten up by drug dealers for refusing to be a pusher; nor did he want to end up at the wrong end of a needle himself. He wanted to be strong—a real man. After undergoing hand-to-hand combat training at Fort Campbell, on the Kentucky-Tennessee border, he could have thrashed every dealer in the Bronx. But that wasn't necessary anymore because now he was in the United States Army and had found meaning in life.

"Uh, speaking of Vietnam," I said, a bit tentatively, "is it possible that you're mainly looking for cannon fodder for the war over there?"

"Don't worry about Vietnam," Larry replied. "Nixon's under a lot of pressure. The Vietnam War's going to be over soon. If you join the Army today, by the time you've completed Basic Training you'll never set foot over there. But you've got to be clear about something: the Army will make a real man out of you. You'll have to be ready to fight for the United States of America. Maybe they'll deploy you somewhere in Asia, or Cuba, or even in Europe. And another thing—the problem isn't the risk of having to die in Vietnam. It's more that people right here in this country are going to spit on you and try to humiliate you. Our president hates blacks and hippies and says so very openly. So it isn't always easy to serve this president honorably and unconditionally. But in the Army, you learn to be strong mentally as well as physically. Like a real man!"

The three recruiters made me a nearly irresistible offer: for the next three days, I could drop by in the afternoons anytime, eat my fill at Uncle Sam's expense, and ask them as many questions about the Army as I wanted.

Over the next few nights, I didn't sleep well; I kept waking up at about four in the morning. I'd go wandering along the beach and sit on a rock overhang, struck nonstop by the waves. As I thought things over, I stared into the sea, hoping it would furnish me with an answer to the questions burning in my mind.

If I were to join the Army, would I end up fighting in a senseless war and be forced to kill innocent people? And should it ever come to that, would I be able to get away with deliberately missing the target? Would the Army truly make me physically and mentally strong? Into a real man, as Larry Brown had promised?

Ever since childhood, I had dreamed of becoming a parachute jumper. Would this be the opportunity to do that? Would they even accept me into an elite unit like the paratroopers? Could I then finally prove—to my mother and to myself—that I was neither a wimp—a weakling and coward—nor a failure?

On the third day, when Washington Theophile Smith examined my passport, he smacked both hands on his thighs and shook with laughter.

"No way!" he shouted, flashing his snow-white teeth. "Born on the Fourth of July! Did you forge your passport? Or is that really your birthdate?"

"That's my real birthdate. What's so special about it?" I asked.

"The Fourth of July is America's birthday! Independence Day. It's the country's national holiday."

"What happened then?"

"I don't know a hell of a lot about history, but every kid in this country knows that July 4, 1776 is the date when the thirteen colonies declared their independence from Britain. That was the beginning of the nation we've got today," Washington explained knowingly.

"Uncle Sam's birthday?"

"You got it. And you've got to know that for the citizenship test. Washington said, pressing two documents into my hand. One was entitled, "Application for Naturalization." The other was a recommendation letter from his office.

One afternoon I sat in the McDonald's and quickly boned up on the U.S. Constitution, the first verse of *The Star-Spangled Banner* (the American national anthem), and a few facts about American history. I also learned the names and achievements of the most significant U.S. presidents.

The next day at the immigration office, I passed my citizenship test. I had to answer a few additional questions posed by a U.S. government bureaucrat, a rather corpulent and equally friendly African-American woman. Then I was to become an American citizen and receive an American passport. According to the official, there remained only one small problem, however.

"We don't have umlauts in English. This thing has got to go," she said, pointing at the German ü with the tip of her pen. You can choose among *Mueller, Muller,* or *Miller.*"

I settled on *Miller,* and from that moment, I was known as Michael Miller.

After completing Basic Training, I applied to join the Screaming Eagles—the Army's 101st Airborne Division, based in Fort Campbell, Kentucky. After a three-day qualifying examination, I was accepted. I had to swear to God that I would unconditionally obey God, the President of the United States of America, and my superiors. For a brief moment, I was haunted by the thought of what such an oath would actually mean to an atheist.

Larry had been right. The subsequent training as a paratrooper and in hand-to-hand combat made me a "a real man," no doubt about it. Now I had learned how to drive, how to skydive—at least with an automatic parachute release—as well as how to use hand grenades, to handle weapons, and to kill one or several opponents, even using my bare hands if necessary. It was no problem for me to crawl commando-style through mud and under barbed-wire fences, or to climb over roofs, fences, and other obstacles.

After my drill instructor told me one day, "Miller, you've got what it takes to become a sniper," my hit ratio suddenly and abruptly fell off. The thought of snuffing the life out of some unsuspecting human being—someone I had never looked at face to face and didn't even know—with a precision shot, targeted between the eyes … it was a nightmare, one that I held onto the way Fort Knox guards its gold.

Another curiosity proved revealing about my psychological makeup: before making a jump from our C-7 Caribou aircraft, almost all my fellow soldiers were visibly afraid. They trembled, and cold sweat trickled down their foreheads. The worry lines in their faces belied thoughts such as, "What if the parachute doesn't open? Am I going to die? Will I get my legs broken?" All this anxiety resulted in their developing tremendous flatulence, which they began discharging with abandon while the aft ramp was opened.

For me, it was different. I looked forward to every jump. I enjoyed leaping into the void and relished the brief freefall before the static line yanked the parachute out of the backpack. The opening jolt always felt like a little orgasm, courtesy of Uncle Sam. Every minute needed to lazily float back down to earth was sheer ecstasy. I was intently aware of my surroundings—the airspace all around me, as well as the ground target—and

I was very keen about aiming for it as precisely as possible. Even after my very first parachute jump, I longed to savor the sheer, boundless freedom of the freefall, whether in a civilian capacity or as a HALO jumper for the military. Much later, a professor of psychology explained to me that I probably possessed a "jumper gene" that would switch off any fear of jumping, of the great distance, or of heights.

I wanted to get promoted from Private First Class to the rank of Specialist—to Medical Specialist, if at all possible. Medicine interested me. Helping wounded comrades would be the best way to reconcile everything with my conscience. And there was a practical side benefit: medics—the Army's paramedics—always stay relatively far back in the rear, in order to be able to take care of the seriously wounded from the front lines. So I applied to the 326th Medical Battalion, a subdivision of the 101st Airborne Division. I was accepted and assigned to attend the Army Medical School.

Five months later

Da Nang, Vietnam, early December 1971. Larry Brown had been wrong. Together with my buddies Bill McPherson, from Hershey, Pennsylvania, and Isamu Takahashi, who came from San Francisco—both of whom were only around twenty—I found myself back in the Army Evacuation Hospital. The Army Medical School had taught us a great deal about anatomy, vital functions, treating shock, and resuscitation, in addition to having us practice applying bandages and splints. Another key subject was triage—sorting casualties based on whether their wounds were slight, moderate, or serious, or fatal without any hope of survival. But no real blood ever flowed; we were missing real-life, practical experience. So they sent us here. We were to spend four to six weeks, every day, doing rotations in the operating theater and treatment room. Then we would be assigned to our platoons and sent into the field.

The Army Evacuation Hospital was a self-sustaining, 400-bed tent facility equipped with its own electricity and water supply, laundry, and canteen, which we called the mess hall. Eight surgeons, two anesthesiologists, ten nurses, ten orderlies—and trainees like us—worked around the clock in twelve-hour shifts. That meant twelve hours on duty, twelve hours off. Once a week, the surgeons, nurses, and orderlies received a full day off, after which they usually switched from the day shift to the night shift, or vice versa. Bill, Isamu, and I worked only the day shift, and we also got one day off per week. We disinfected wounds, changed bandages, inserted drips, and ventilated patients after they had been intubated. And frequently, we were even allowed to suture patients once the surgeons had finished operating.

One day, as I was hurrying through the patients' tent carrying a couple of IV bags under my arm, a voice behind me hissed in flawless German, "*Hey, Kraut, get over here!*"

How could anybody know that I understood German? 'Kraut' was what Americans had disparagingly called the Germans during World War II, presumably because back then the German diet had consisted primarily of sauerkraut and potatoes. I slowly turned around, glanced at the man's field jacket hanging at the front of the bed, and stared in the patient's face. Finally I said, "Don't *ever* call me 'Kraut' again, Captain Meeker."

The patient, an exceptionally tall man with thick hair, long sideburns, and a handsome dimple in his chin, grinned disarmingly and replied, "Then tell me your name, soldier! We're not in the shit here. No combat's going on in post-op. I don't have any authority over you. Besides, I don't want any. You can just call me Barry. But you do come from Germany, right?"

I nodded and introduced myself as Michael. Since I was wearing a lab coat over my uniform jacket, the captain had been unable to see my name. He let me know that he was a helicopter pilot and had already been shot down twice. His left leg had been shot through and undergone surgery the day before. At the moment, he wasn't allowed to leave his bed, but he wanted to be back in the saddle flying again as quickly as possible, maybe in two weeks, or so he hoped. Then he waved me over to him and whispered something in my ear—an offer that definitely sounded tempting.

The hospital staff spent their free time in various ways: some played cards, others read books, while others stared at the television set in the mess hall, which stayed on twenty-four hours a day. More than a few of them got plastered on beer and whiskey immediately after their shifts were over and slept until shortly before the next one, which always required an ice-cold shower and a cup of black coffee.

Wednesday was mail call, which always meant a flurry of excitement. Most of my comrades read the letters from home aloud to one another, commented about them, and then immediately sat down to write back. I was the only one who never received a single letter and never had one to dispatch. Who was supposed to get letters from me? Or send me anything? My mother? Old friends from school? Nobody even knew I was here. But it didn't bother me that I wasn't receiving any letters. That was something I could easily live with. Sometimes, on mail call day, I went to the post-op ward, resolving to help cheer up a few of the depressed patients a little bit.

Granted, not all of my jokes were funny—some fell totally flat—but I always got on well in the patients' company. For instance, I went to three wounded men in the back of the ward and challenged them: "Hey guys, seize your opportunity now! Get ready! I'm going to count to three. Whoever makes it to the latrine fastest will get sent home today!"

Although all three guys had lost their legs, my announcement did at least coax a tired smile out of them. One man even said, "I won. My latrine is right here—I've just pissed in the bed. Now you can take me home!"

By the time I had completed this duty rotation, I wanted out of there. I didn't want to witness any more suffering or pain. And I wanted to enjoy the sea air and experience the foreign culture here, sample the local food, and have real conversations with people. Then I recalled the offer that the downed helicopter pilot had made me earlier. I waited until Nancy Goodman, the head nurse, had disappeared into her tent. I then fetched a pair of crutches from the supply room and went to Barry, who—keeping one leg up—softly tiptoed out of the ward. The crutches were the straight kind that nestle under the user's armpits. And these were the longest ones we had available. Even then, the pilot, who was six feet, five inches tall, still had to bend over to hobble around on them.

A bicycle rickshaw brought us to the Suzie Wong, a kind of combination bar, restaurant, and nightclub frequented by all sorts of people—GIs, reporters from around the world, NGO workers, local traders and wheeler-dealers, bargirls, housewives, dancers, and hookers alike—all hunting for work and information. Barry had promised to pay me twenty dollars to sneak him out of the hospital for at least four hours in order to go out on the town, then get him back to the ward without drawing anyone's attention, if at all possible. Twenty dollars was a lot of money—considering that the rickshaw ride cost fifty cents, a "33" Export beer cost a dollar, and even that price was already grossly inflated to fleece the GIs. A bowl of Pho Bo (beef soup with rice noodles) or Pho Ga (chicken soup with rice noodles) also cost just a dollar. Even a full hour of nookie with a lovely young local in one of the rooms behind the bar could be had for just ten bucks.

Barry Winslow Meeker turned out to be an ideal drinking buddy and an eloquent conversationalist. He hoisted his leg, freshly operated upon just the day before, onto a table and ordered a bowl of Pho Ga and five beers, along with two packs of cigarettes. He quickly had half the place hanging on his every word—well, at least three packed tables. Barry drank like a fish and smoked like a chimney, chugging down one beer after another while constantly lighting a new cigarette with the stub of the old one. When talking to his Army buddies, he did so in English, obviously. But with the French journalists, he suddenly switched to fluent French. And he spoke to me in perfect, unaccented German. What I found most astounding was that even after ten beers, he seemed cold sober and—exclusively for my benefit—recited the famous German poem "The Immortals" from Herman Hesse's 1927 novel *Steppenwolf*. I had read this masterpiece of German literature a year earlier, while preparing for my final round of high school exams. And now Barry, this American guy, knew more about the book and Henry Haller, its protagonist, than I ever had.

Sometime around midnight, on the way to the urinal, I collided with a tall, powerfully built white man and suddenly heard the German for "Sorry, 'scuse me!" I thought I was hearing things, but I nonetheless replied "No problem" in German.

Not only was the man's skin white, but so was his entire outfit. We got to talking and drank a couple of beers together. The white giant, who came from Hamburg, was a fellow named Ulf Peterson who was working as a male nurse aboard a German hospital ship, the *Helgoland*, which was anchored in the Bay of Da Nang. The stories he could tell were even more thrilling than anything I had heard about combat. Today was Ulf's day off, and mine was the following day. So after our third beer, he suggested, "If you want, I can show you around the *Helgoland* tomorrow. From the inside, I mean."

My eyes grew wide with enthusiasm.

"Man, that would be great! When, where, how?"

"Well, in any case, I've got two conditions," Ulf continued, dimming my enthusiasm a little.

"And those would be?" I asked.

"First off: everything has to be kept absolutely discreet. No talking about it with *anyone*. Second thing: you can't wear your uniform, and while you're on board you have to pretend to be a journalist from a Hamburg newspaper," Ulf explained. He then asked me how old I really was.

"Twenty," I lied.

"Then you couldn't be a fully credentialed journalist. Tell the captain you're twenty-two and working as a trainee, and that you absolutely wanted to go to Vietnam and write a feature piece about our ship. Just in case he asks."

"I don't have any civilian clothing here, not even a pair of jeans. Couldn't you get me a lab coat and some white pants?" I implored him.

We agreed to meet the next day at 1600, at a street food place a couple hundred meters north of where the *Helgoland* was anchored. I could change my clothes there.

Even though it was December, the night air was still pleasantly warm. A gentle sea breeze was wafting through the coconut palms in front of the Suzie Wong. Peddlers, street food vendors, and pretty women who hadn't had any luck inside were all wooing customers. Life here could have been really nice if it hadn't been for this goddamned war. I had heard a great deal about its horrors, but I still hadn't experienced them much.

A gorgeous, exotic young beauty addressed me in broken English: "You handsome man. I love you. Come on! Let's make bum-bum!"

"'Make bum-bum?' What does she want to do, come along with me to target practice?"

Barry, who had already grabbed hold of his crutches for the trip back, explained that "making bum-bum" meant fucking. His expression and the way he was shaking his head indicated what he thought of the whole business. At least, what he thought of it at the moment.

When I turned down the pretty young thing's offer and fobbed her off, saying I'd come back tomorrow, she called after me, "Maybe tomorrow I no can make you happy! Maybe tomorrow we all dead!"

I still hadn't the faintest idea of how accurate at least parts of her premonition were.

A rickshaw drove Ulf back to the *Helgoland*, and another one took Barry and me back to the Evacuation Hospital.

"Did you actually know that someone tossed a hand grenade into the Suzie Wong last week?" Barry asked me.

Horrified, I shook my head and replied, "No! What happened?"

"Two dead and eight wounded. Except for one reporter, all the casualties were GIs. Hardly any girls in the joint," Barry said knowingly.

"Thanks a lot for telling me that now!" I said.

"As I said, there were hardly any girls in the joint. Does that tell you something?"

"Should it?"

"Our intelligence specialists assume that most of the hot-looking girls around here are actually high-ranking Viet Cong officers. They don't just fuck our guys, they want to pump them for information. So if a lot of girls are hanging around the place, like tonight, then you're relatively safe because they're not going to blow away their best people," explained Barry.

"Damn, you sure know a lot of stuff," I said admiringly.

He beckoned me to come closer and whispered in my ear: "But the ladies don't know that their best regulars are from *our* intelligence. Uncle Sam's paying big fat bonuses every day to let them fuck like rabbits and spread disinformation."

We arrived back at the hospital. Barry pressed a finger to his lips and made me swear on my grave to keep my mouth shut about all the secrets he had revealed. We found a nearby palm tree to empty our bladders, which at this point were nearly bursting. Then I helped the cheerful patient into his bed, stowed the crutches in the equipment room, and slipped back to my quarters.

CHAPTER 3

The Longest Day

How long does a single day last? Twenty-four hours? From the time you wake up until the time you go to sleep? Usually, you're up for only sixteen or seventeen hours, but it can also be seventy, eighty, or even more. The higher the adrenalin level, the longer you can keep going. The treacherous part of it is, according to what the wounded soldiers at the hospital told me, is that at some point your adrenalin level plummets and fatigue ultimately wins out. And that's the precise moment—sometime in the middle of the night—when Charlie attacked, firing all his guns at once and burning down half the installation even before our troops could grab their weapons. 'Charlie,' actually 'Victor Charlie,' was of course the universal code name for the Viet Cong—our resolutely tough and implacable enemy.

When I woke up the morning after my excursion with Barry, fate had already determined that this day would become the longest of my life.

My plan was to use my day off as optimally and sensibly as possible. In the morning, I swam around a while in the sea at Red Beach. The section of the beach at Nguyen Tat Thanh Street was very well secured by our boys.

In the afternoon, wearing nothing but shorts and a T-shirt, I made my way to the meeting place Ulf and I had agreed on, 200 meters north of where the *Helgoland* was anchored in the Bay of Da Nang.

Ulf was as punctual as a Swiss watch. He gave me an orderly's white uniform smock and accompanied me aboard the white ship, which had three enormous red crosses painted on both sides. The *Helgoland*, which was just about 100 meters long and 15 meters wide, contained several operating theaters as well as 150 sickbeds. The hospital ship, which had been financed by the West German Federal Government, was operated by the German Red Cross. It had more than 100 crew-members, including eight surgeons, twenty German nurses, orderlies, and medical technical assistants, in addition to a support staff consisting of about seventy Vietnamese laundresses, cooks, interpreters, and local nurses.

I followed Ulf through the large ward on the middle deck. A gruesome tableau accompanied us: a young man, whose body was studded with burns and gashes and whose toenails and fingernails had been pulled off, a severely burned pregnant Vietnamese woman, and an elderly man who had lost his left leg, arm, and eye. Between the beds, children, some injured, some not, ran around playing, and orderlies thronged the crowded room. A door led to the deck outside.

Ulf lit up a cigarette.

"Generally, we don't have any uniformed personnel coming on board," Ulf explained. "Actually we treat only civilians, but if combatants—without any weapons—are brought aboard the ship, we certainly don't refuse to treat them simply because they're wearing black pants and presumably belong to the Viet Cong."

"Like the badly burned pregnant woman?" I asked.

Ulf nodded, saying, "I'm sure that we've got patients lying in bed right next to their enemy. But we've never had any fighting aboard our ship. Nobody's even exchanged a hostile word."

"What happened to the old man who lost his left eye, leg, and arm?" I asked.

"His water buffalo accidentally stepped on a mine out in a rice paddy and got blown to pieces. The water buffalo was the last surviving member of the old guy's family, he told us. He's going to pull through."

"And then what?" I pressed him.

Ulf shrugged, took a drag on his cigarette, and then wanted to know something about me.

"Say, how did you end up in Vietnam, anyway?"

"My mother," I blurted out spontaneously, surprising myself with my own answer.

"Your mother?" Ulf asked in disbelief, adding, "No mother would ever send her son into this goddamned war!"

"Well, indirectly my mother," I said, trying to qualify my previous remark. "She doesn't know that I'm in Vietnam. She made my life hell. She was always pressuring me. In her mind I could never do anything right. So I saved up the money for the flight to the States. Living the dream, you know, going from rags to riches."

"Well, that didn't really work out, I guess," Ulf said good-naturedly.

"At some point, Uncle Sam then—" I began to explain, when suddenly the sounds of battle rang out from the nearby waterfront promenade. Before I could even grasp what was going on, a rocket slammed into the water, close to the *Helgoland's* port side. Ulf, thinking quickly, dragged me inside the ship, where seconds later we heard a second rocket's impact, very close to us. Over the loudspeaker, a male voice made an announcement in German, English, and French, followed by a female Vietnamese voice, presumably that of an interpreter:

"Red Alert. Execute Plan C. Red Alert. Execute Plan C!"

"We're heading out to sea immediately! Help me secure the patients to their beds. And hang on tight once the ship gets underway!" Ulf instructed me.

Personnel were running and stumbling around like crazy, scurrying around like the population of an ant farm. I tried to buckle up as many patients as I could, using the leather belts stowed under the beds.

Suddenly there was a heavy shudder. Intravenous drip bottles and urine bottles went flying around, shattering glass everywhere. Immediately after the crew had taken in the mooring lines, the captain had ordered full steam ahead. Now the proud ship was cruising through the South China Sea at nineteen knots—about thirty-five kilometers or twenty-one miles per hour—its maximum speed. After a few minutes, the captain gave the order to stop engines and drop anchor. The attack, most likely, had come from shoulder-fired Russian RPG-7 rockets, which have an effective range of well under 3,000 feet.

The captain announced over the public-address system that he would be thoroughly inspecting the ship while the rest of the personnel were to restore order in the hospital wards. He set the obligatory review for all hands on the upper deck at 1700 sharp. Ulf Peterson used this opportunity to introduce me to Captain Paul von Hagen and the rest of the staff as journalist Michael Müller, a correspondent from the largest Hamburg newspaper. The skipper, an imposing man with a calm, commanding presence and a classic, snow-white sailor's beard, nodded to me briefly. With a friendly twinkle in his eyes, he then declared, "People, the *Helgoland* has come through in one piece yet again! As far as I know, nobody was wounded. Does anyone know more?"

Everyone shook their heads.

"We'll remain anchored out here a little while longer," Captain von Hagen continued. "This spot is relatively safe from attack. But it's got swells that are bigger than the ones in the bay, so that's going to make our work aboard more difficult, particularly for the surgeons. We'll be running one of the longboats back and forth from the anchorage in the bay every three hours, between 0600 and 1800. That way we can pick up the wounded or bring them ashore. Spread the word. Any questions?"

"Has the *Helgoland* already been attacked more often? Who's behind it?" I asked, trying to sound like a professional journalist.

"Good question, young man," the skipper said. "We invited all the warring sides to come aboard and inspect the ship. They all provided us with written assurances that the ship wouldn't be attacked. But three times over the past couple of months, we've had hostilities and rocket strikes happening very close by. One time, a soldier from the South Vietnamese Army, one of those ARVN kids, accidentally fired off an anti-tank rocket in our direction. On the other two occasions, the parties accused each other of starting skirmishes around the ship. Any further questions?"

Ulf raised his hand and said, "The first time we were scrambled to battle stations—a couple of months ago— most of our glass urine bottles got smashed, as well as some of our drip bottles. Afterwards I immediately submitted an urgent order from supply headquarters back in Germany to get plastic urine bottles and bag drips. We really needed that delivery. It came on yesterday's supply ship, all right. And guess what was sitting in the crates?"

Awkward silence. A very long thirty seconds or so passed, until one of the surgeons finally raised his hand. In a voice hinting at a kind of premonition, he asked, "Glass?"

"You got it. And now the main ward on the middle deck is covered in glass shards and soaked in blood, drip meds, and piss. Not to mention all the extra work involved since now we've got to give every patient a bedpan, even if they just need to take a leak," Ulf declared.

Chief Surgeon Martin Pawlik and Captain von Hagen assured us that they would take a firm stance and dispatch a personal message to supply headquarters and get them to send us plastic urine bottles and drip bags as quickly as possible.

Ulf, cupping his hand over his mouth, whispered to me, "We've already gone through *that* whole song and dance. But even the skipper's personal effort didn't make any difference. In my opinion, all they're sending us from Germany is whatever they don't need for themselves. They haven't got the foggiest idea what's going on over here."

The atmosphere was tense but professional: nobody threw a hissy fit, nobody had a nervous breakdown. Nobody screamed or cursed. Everyone did what had to be done, even attempting a smile along the way. I decided to go one better and whistled *I was Kaiser Bill's Batman*, by Whistling Jack Smith. The others took a shine to that, and several tried to whistle along. The Vietnamese nurses had difficulty whistling, prompting a great deal of laugh-

46

ter and lightening the mood considerably. I tried to teach some of them how to purse their lips properly. At exactly 1800, I was allowed into the ship's mess for dinner—sauerkraut and roasted bratwurst with rice, all served on reusable plastic plates. The rice was added simply because for many Vietnamese, any meal without rice or noodles simply wouldn't have been a proper meal.

Afterwards, we continued cleaning up the chaos resulting from the red alert, as well as attending to patient care. It wasn't until around midnight when a modicum of order was finally restored. Everything had settled down. Ulf grabbed us a couple of beers and some cigarettes. We went on deck and found a quiet corner. It was pleasantly warm outside, a clear, starry night. A gentle breeze was wafting around the anchored ship, which swayed lightly in the swells.

"I've got a problem," I began.

"I know," Ulf replied. "You've got to be getting back."

"What kind of guy is the captain?" I asked.

"Oh, he's terrific. Absolutely, a real stand-up kind of guy. You can talk to him about anything, and he knows how to find a solution to any kind of problem."

At that very moment, the door opened, and Captain Paul von Hagen set foot on deck.

"Speak of the Devil and he shall appear," Ulf laughed.

"I'd like to thank both of you for your dedication," von Hagen said. "The ship is already squared away. And only because everyone has done such a terrific job of pitching in," he added.

"Captain, may I speak to you in confidence?" I asked.

Von Hagen nodded and gestured to Ulf to leave.

"No, please, Ulf can stay. I'd prefer to have a confidential discussion with both of you."

Both Ulf Peterson and Captain von Hagen looked at me expectantly. I took a deep breath, a swig of beer, and a drag on my cigarette. Then I closed my eyes and briefly collected myself. Was the step I now had in mind really the right one? If so, was this the right time and place?

"I am a soldier in the United States Army. Rank, Private First Class. I'm currently in training as a Medical Specialist and stationed at the Army Evacuation Hospital in Da Nang. And I'd like to desert. Can you take me aboard?"

Both men were visibly shocked. At first, Ulf didn't say anything. Even the captain needed to pause and think for a moment. I was glad to give it to him. Finally, Captain von Hagen likewise lit a cigarette and helped himself to more beer. Then he carefully explained his position:

"I'd certainly like to help you out, young man. But let's stick to some hard facts. The West German government is financing this ship at the behest of our American friends because the Federal Republic of Germany has already refused to get involved in the Vietnam War. Keeping your presence on board a secret—that would be practically impossible. If the German government ever found out that I'd granted you asylum, or anything like that, I would catch serious hell from my superiors. What's more, the Americans would demand that I surrender you to them. If I refused, it's entirely possible that the MPs—the military police—would raid this ship. And if they didn't, within a very short time we'd wind up taking on more deserters than sick and wounded."

I immediately grasped that the skipper was completely right.

"OK," I said. "I understand. I hereby withdraw my request. Can I count on your absolute discretion on this,

Captain? You too, Ulf? This conversation never happened!"

Both men nodded, visibly relieved.

"Unfortunately," I continued, "I've still got a problem. Hardly anyone back at the American hospital would notice if I got back at 0100, 0300, or even 0430. But starting at 0500, my fellow Americans, as it were, have reveille. So I already need a good excuse. Starting at 0600, stuff starts getting official. If I don't show up at morning roll call, the best outcome would be two weeks of scrubbing the latrine, and the worst would be the stockade."

Captain von Hagen looked me with almost a bit of sadness. Finally he said, "You'll have to tough it out, boy. At night, this area is Viet Cong territory, both on land and at sea. The VCs shoot anything that moves or that they can't plainly identify as their own. And our launch doesn't even remotely resemble a Viet Cong junk."

"What if I just swam ashore?" I asked insistently.

"Don't get any dumb ideas. The water here is full of sharks. We'll set off in the launch tomorrow morning at 0600 and take you back to the beach."

The captain clapped me on the shoulder in a fatherly way, then excused himself. Over a pack of cigarettes and a couple of beers, Ulf and I talked all night, about everything under the sun—life and death, the futility and absurdity of the war, and the immense suffering it had inflicted on so many people and their families. We also talked about how prayer, regardless of which religion it came from, had ever won a war—or lessened its horrors. It was a wonderful, very heartfelt and moving talk.

* * *

At 0630 I was back at the Army Evacuation Hospital. Ready to greet me at the entrance was Sergeant Wilcox, my immediate superior.

I stood at attention and said crisply, "Private Miller reporting for duty, sir!"

"Where the hell were you all night, Miller?" barked the sergeant. "At the Suzie Wong, getting drunk and laid?"

"No, Sergeant Wilcox!"

"Well, then where were you? I'm waiting!"

"At the Suzie Wong, getting drunk, getting laid, and getting out disinformation!" I replied.

"What kind of disinformation?" the sergeant demanded to know. By now, he was visibly confused.

"Top secret," I shot back.

"And who gave you the order to do that?"

"Military Intelligence," I lied shamelessly.

"Can you prove that?"

"Of course!" I said, piling one lie on top of the next.

"You know something, Miller? Forget last night. Today is your lucky day. I'm promoting you to Medical Specialist!"

The sergeant thrust something into my hand. It was a pair of epaulettes bearing my new rank and the caduceus worn by medical personnel.

"Sew these on your uniform! Right now, Medical Specialist Miller."

I promptly drew myself to attention again. "Yes, Sergeant! May I ask—what have I done to deserve the honor of this speedy promotion? I've completed only five days of clinic duty."

"Our unit, the 101st Airborne Division, urgently needs medics. That's why I've promoted you and Bill McPherson. The doc said you're both ready. You're getting transferred at 0900. Pack your gear and be ready to get into the shit. That means full combat gear, pack, weapon, and medical kit. I expect to see your ass standing tall right here at 0850!"

As though in a trance, I carried out the sergeant's orders. My guts felt queasy. Would I soon be heading to the front? Would I have to shoot people?

At 0900 sharp, six Hueys were hovering over the hospital grounds. They seemed like a swarm of attacking hornets. Only one of them landed. The sergeant next to the starboard-side gunner ordered us to leave behind our seabags, which were stuffed with all our personal belongings, and helped us into the helicopter.

"Welcome aboard, boys!" the sergeant shouted over the din of the rotors. "We'll pick up your seabags later. B Detachment has gotten into a heavy combat situation, and they've requested support. Less than ten minutes away!"

Now I was really getting queasy.

The UH-1 Iroquois, which everyone called a Huey, slowly pulled away from the ground. These helicopters were powered by Lycoming turbine engines that boasted a hefty 1400 horsepower. All told, this machine was an incredible powerhouse, a marvel of modern military and aeronautical technology. It flew like a bat out of hell while imparting a feeling of being invincible, thanks to its majestic command of the skies, the port and starboard gunners crouching with their M60 machine guns, plus backup from the other five choppers in our formation.

We flew so low over the palm groves, tiny villages, and rice paddies that you could actually make out the whites in the eyes of the water buffaloes. I pondered why the water buffaloes reacted so calmly to the choppers' racket. The beasts seemed almost bored. Had they gotten used to it all by now?

Suddenly the sergeant, whose helmet was equipped with a radio link to the pilots and gunners, shouted at us, "The landing zone is hot! The Hueys can't touch down. You've got to jump out of the chopper while it's hovering. Expect immediate enemy fire and run like hell! The gunners will cover you."

Some of the guys crossed themselves. Others slammed the magazines of their M16A1 assault rifles against their metal helmets twice: once to prevent jamming, and once for good luck.

I froze in terror. I had never experienced so much fear in my entire life, or at any time since. I didn't want to die. Nor did I want to kill anyone. I had no idea whether or how it was possible to reconcile both these desires. During Basic Training, they had drilled us with a very simple axiom: if *you* don't kill the enemy, he's going to kill *you*.

My moment of truth had come. The gunners opened fire, giving it everything they had, and we jumped out of the Huey as it hovered just a few feet above the ground. Hunched over, we followed our sergeant through young bamboo grass to a long, extended earthen rampart. In front of it the men from Detachment B had dug themselves in. Lurking beyond were the Viet Cong, who were sporadically firing rockets over the rampart. Whenever anything cast a silhouette against the wall, Charlie immediately began taking potshots at it. The officers from Detachment B and our support unit exchanged a few words. One of them shouted for a medic. I scouted around for Bill McPherson or another medic, but then was forced to realize something—I was the one they'd been yelling for.

A sergeant I had never seen before took me to a severely wounded black soldier, who was very young.

"This is Private Coolidge," the sergeant said. "Took a hit about half an hour ago. He's in a lot of pain."

"Why haven't you given him anything for it?" I asked. A split second later, I realized what a stupid question that was.

"Because one of our medics over there is now treating five other wounded. And the other medic is dead," the sergeant replied curtly, turning around and striding off.

Thick beads of sweat were now bathing Private Coolidge's face; the man was trembling.

"I don't want to die," he cried. "I'm so cold. It hurts like hell," he gasped. Whatever strength he had left was visibly dwindling, and fast.

Now it was up to me. I had to function. Put all emotions aside.

The first thing I did was jab a shot of morphine into his butt. Then I tried to get an idea of how bad his wounds were, but suddenly a rocket slammed into the ground not ten meters away. I hit the deck—threw myself to the ground—shoving my face into the dirt. The detonation was massive, but the mortar fragments had missed me. Private Coolidge, who had been pressing a blood-soaked field jacket against his guts, now lay there, his arms outstretched. Where the jacket had been, his shredded guts were now pouring out, along with a lot of blood and the contents of his intestines still in various stages of digestion. Nobody, during our training, had prepared me for a situation like this. Oh sure, they had shown us films and photos of belly wounds. But the reality was far, far more gruesome than even the most horrific photos could ever convey. Nor had anyone ever mentioned the revolting stench that wafts from shredded guts and the shit bursting out everywhere.

Private Coolidge stared at me, his eyes wide open. But he was dead. No doubt about it. Nevertheless, I spoke to him, squeezed his left upper arm hard, and tried to find a pulse on his carotid artery. Unsuccessfully, of course.

"Medic! Medic!" screamed two soldiers at the other end of the rampart, about 300 meters away, where it gradually leveled off and sank to ground level. I double-timed, as the Army liked to call a sprint. It certainly would have been preferable if the distance had been shorter, but I promptly covered it, despite lugging my combat pack, medical gear, and of course my own Sweet Sixteen, my M16 assault rifle.

One of the squads had been ordered to reconnoiter the Viet Cong positions by amply circumnavigating the field of fire. Once more, it was a young black soldier who had been hardest hit. Once more, a belly wound. His buddies had done the right thing—pressing a field jacket against the wounded man's torso. But the job of assessing the extent of the damage fell to me. I slowly removed the jacket. Once again, blood, guts, and shit began gushing out. But this time, it was even worse—or perhaps, from the wounded man's perspective, better: this guy had a hole torn in his aorta. With every heartbeat, massive jets of blood were spurting out, sixty times a minute. I immediately shoved the field jacket back onto the man's belly to pack the arterial wound. But I knew that the man's life could now be saved only by a competent vascular surgeon, assuming that was even possible—and only under good hospital conditions. I wasn't able to provide any of that. The poor bastard would give up the ghost. Moments later, he was no longer responsive, and just stared at me with wide-open eyes. His entire body trembled und shuddered, making a final, defiant last stand before expiring. He went fast, very fast.

The soldier next him, also an athletic young African-American, held his dead comrade's hand. Tears were pouring out of his eyes.

"I'm Jim. The dude was my best friend," said the man in a tear-choked voice. He barely noticed as I dressed the deep wound he'd received on his upper left arm. The bullet seemed to have gone straight through without hitting the bone. Both Jim and the dead man were from Harlem, the famous African-American district of New York City. They had gone to school together, then joined up together. Both were eighteen, even younger than I was.

And now here I was, all of twenty minutes on the battlefield, where I had already seen two badly wounded men die. I asked myself whether it was a coincidence that both were black—or whether, despite the new anti-racism doctrine, blacks were still being sent to the front in disproportionate numbers? Of course, there were also black officers. And my time in the field was far too brief for me to render any kind of clear judgment. All the same, I would have been glad to prescribe Jim a furlough, ship him home, or at least have him put on the sick list for a few days. But I lacked that kind of authority.

Meanwhile, the other soldiers had positioned themselves three to six meters apart along the entire rampart. My newly minted fellow medic, Medical Specialist Bill McPherson, waved me over and ordered me to fill the gap between him on my left and another soldier to my right. Bill exercised no command authority over me. But in fact it would have somehow looked ridiculous if my entire squad were to assume an attack formation while I remained behind, sitting alone and taking cover with my medical kit, just waiting for some guy to get hit and roll down into my lap. That would have definitely become quickly conspicuous to any officer who actually did possess command authority.

McPherson brought me up to speed on the most recent set of orders, which I had obviously missed. We were to have our M16 assault rifles ready for action locked and loaded. Nobody was to look over the top of the rampart. A lieutenant and a reconnaissance patrol, heavily camouflaged at the far end of the rampart, were to observe the enemy. Once the lieutenant gave the order "Fire at will!" we were to shoot anything that moved on the other side of the rampart.

The waiting was grueling. Thousands of thoughts kept racing through my head.

Thou shalt not kill. If you don't kill the enemy, he's going to kill you. God is on America's side. Did this God even exist? And if he did, then why did he allow this terrible war? Religious instruction—generally Lutheran or Catholic—is required in the German school curriculum. My religion teacher had always answered these sorts of questions by saying that God wanted to test us. But this interpretation never gave me any solace. *What about the enemy's God? What kind of human being is the enemy? What's happening with his wife, his children, his family, who will mourn him when I shoot him?* "We have to defend our country and the world against Communism!" *I don't have to do a goddamned thing! The Communists didn't attack our country, or the world, for that matter.*

We're the ones who came over here. The Vietnamese never did anything to us!

I resolved to deliberately shoot to miss, once the shitshow got going. Ideally, right in front of their legs. That way, I could throw a scare into them and maybe even halt their advance. At worst, I might hit a guy in the leg, but he wouldn't have to die right away.

And the shitshow had already begun: though I didn't actually hear the order to fire at will, everyone was leaving their covered positions, putting their M16s on the rampart and firing away. So I had to do the same. The Viet Cong fighters had all kinds of wild plants and bushes draped over their heads. It looked like an entire tree nursery slowly moving towards us. There were hundreds of them—we were totally outnumbered! But at least for the time being, we still had better cover, ensconced as we were behind the rampart. Or so I thought, until another rocket landed and detonated behind the rampart, roughly in the middle of our position. Agonized screams meant that they'd scored a direct hit in our ranks.

The enemy was still a good 400 meters away, but closing faster and faster. Some of the Viet Cong had stood up and begun charging towards us. Both our M16s as well as their AK47 rifles become only somewhat accurate starting at distances of 300 to 400 meters. I fired a couple of rounds at their feet, and after I'd gotten off thirty rounds, I swapped the magazine for a fresh one.

"You've got to aim higher!" McPherson yelled at me.

What the hell does Bill care how high or where I'm shooting? I thought to myself.

Bill, busily reloading, glanced at me as though he wanted to check whether I was holding my rifle properly. Suddenly a hole appeared in his head, and he collapsed.

I was shocked—and torn with indecision about what to do first. Take care of Bill? Or was he beyond saving? Or was I supposed to halt the Viet Cong advance first? Or should I simply run like hell in the other direction, far from the enemy and this accursed battlefield?

The Viet Cong had already closed within 100 meters of our position. A lot of soldiers were lying on the battlefield, dead. I watched some of them tumble to the ground, as though in slow motion, after taking fatal hits or serious wounds. I fired half my freshly loaded magazine at the enemy's feet. Then I suddenly heard orders being issued in Vietnamese. Of course I didn't understand a word, but it must have been to retreat, because the human tree nursery was suddenly departing faster than it had appeared. Now they were simply melting away into nothingness.

I dashed over to Bill. The enemy round had penetrated his skull, just over his left eyebrow.

"Bill! Bill!" I yelled.

And Bill answered me.

"Michael! I can't really see you!"

"But you're alive, Bill! Are you in pain?"

"My head is killing me. Everything has gotten blurry. I'm dizzy," Bill gasped.

Blood and cerebrospinal fluid were flowing out of the hole, which was a little under one centimeter in diameter. I bandaged Bill's head and determined that there was no exit wound, meaning that the bullet had to be lodged somewhere in his head. Then I had him raise his arms and legs—which he actually managed to do, though only by exerting tremendous effort. I checked his vision by covering first his left then his right eye with my hand. Bill had been blinded in his right eye, and his vision out of the left had become blurry. That was consistent with the wound; the left part of the brain processes images from the right eye, and vice versa.

After the enemy had withdrawn, at least for the moment, the sergeant in charge of Detachment B and his radioman conducted "inventory control," counting the dead and wounded.

"Bill needs to get to the hospital immediately, otherwise he isn't going to make it!" I insisted, even though I didn't know how bad, medically, his case actually was. In both World Wars, some soldiers had taken head shots yet lived to a ripe old age, running around in good shape for decades despite having bullets still lodged in their heads. Other head-wound victims—most notably, President John F. Kennedy—had perished almost on the spot.

The sergeant ordered a medevac chopper and ordered me to take care of the wounded from the rocket strike.

Three soldiers had mainly large shrapnel fragments in their thighs, buttocks, and backs. A fourth man had lost his left eye. After the rocket had come down, he had briefly turned around and glanced over his left shoulder. Where his eye had been was now a huge, gaping, bloody hollow. And then I saw Jim, the black guy from Harlem who had already lost his best friend to a belly wound and had gotten shot through his upper arm. Jim was just sitting there wretchedly, his arms wrapped around his knees and head bowed, bawling like a baby. On top of that, he had both pissed and shit himself.

"He's also got to go back," I said to the sergeant of Detachment B.

"I decide who's going back," the sergeant snapped at me. "And anyone who can still hold a weapon can still fight!"

"But look," I pressed on, "you can see for yourself that the man is completely finished. He's not going to hit anything. He doesn't have any fight left in him."

Only now did the sergeant look at Jim more closely, and saw the bloodshot eyes, the face smeared with snot, and the shit flowing, quite literally, right out of his pants.

"What kind of goddamned chickenshit wimps are those pencil-pushers in Washington sending us? That guy's not worth shit except as cannon fodder!" the sergeant said, further humiliating the badly traumatized soldier. I had the distinct feeling that the sergeant would have preferred to finish Jim off personally.

But all the sarge said was, "The seriously wounded get evacuated first. If there's still room, stick him in the Huey. Otherwise, he stays right here!"

Even before I had properly bandaged up the wounded, the dustoff Huey with the large red cross on the white background on its nose, descended and hovered over us. The sergeant had Bill carried into the chopper while I accompanied the other wounded soldiers aboard. The man who had lost an eye, along with the other men who had taken mortar fragments, sat on the bench between the gunners. The litter holding Bill was locked into place behind the pilot's seat. I told Jim to lie on his belly between Bill's legs, on the lower half of the litter, and to grip it firmly with both hands. That way he could come along, while keeping the rather, well, unappealing seat of his pants facing upward. The Huey was about to lift off when the sergeant reached for me and shouted above the din of the rotors, "Hey, Medic! *You* stay here!"

But I was faster. I let him grab my medical kit, and I let my "Sweet Sixteen" assault rifle fall to the ground as I dived headlong into the ascending Huey. The sarge could do whatever the hell he wanted with my gear. I was certain that the pilot wouldn't turn around just to bring me back. And I was also positive that I could dream up a good excuse, in case they did bring me up on charges for disobeying orders.

I checked Bill's pulse. It was running around a hundred, meaning that he was in danger of going into shock. Using the helmet equipped with a radio unit, I contacted the pilot and said, "The patient with the head wound needs a neurosurgeon. Badly."

"We're heading to the Army Evacuation Hospital in Da Nang. About twelve minutes," answered the pilot.

"They haven't got any neurosurgeon there! And their x-ray equipment is a piece of shit! I know. I was working there until early this morning," I shot back.

"There's a war on, soldier," the pilot replied. "You've got to take whatever you get."

I pressed my case. "Captain, I don't know what kind of alternatives there are. But if we don't get this man to a hospital with an x-ray machine and a neurosurgeon, he's not going to make it."

Pilots enjoyed a certain fool's license in the Army. They were considered particularly clever, adroit, and brave, but also big-hearted and always ready to lend a hand. I couldn't help but think of Barry Meeker, the congenial, multi-talented language genius, in whose company I had spent that unforgettable evening at the Suzie Wong just two days earlier. How many hours ago had that been? It seemed like another world.

Bill's pulse was rapid and getting thready.

"Hey Bill! How're you doing?" I shouted at him.

He gurgled something incomprehensible, but he was still responsive, at any rate.

At that moment, something completely unexpected and inconceivable happened: Jim suddenly pushed himself up from his prone position on the litter and plunged himself out of the helicopter, back first into the abyss below. The whole thing happened so unbelievably fast that I had no chance to intervene. The gunner, concentrating on monitoring the terrain speeding past below, had spotted Jim's body out of the corner of his eye as the traumatized man went tumbling out of the Huey. The gunner immediately radioed the pilot, and the centrifugal force of an abrupt 180-degree course reversal squeezed us against the seats. Only now were some of the wounded soldiers beginning to realize that Jim was missing. Below us stretched expanses of thick jungle that afforded us no opportunity to land. Jim would have almost certainly never survived the hundred-meter fall. He would be listed as KIA, killed in action, and probably receive a posthumous citation for bravery.

The Huey continued on course. After a few minutes, the captain reported, "The commander at Da Nang Air Base wants to know the nature and extent of our guys' wounds. I'm putting you on the radio. First state your name and rank. Then explain the wounds. Talk!"

Static crackled on the line.

"Medical Specialist Keller reporting. Can you hear me?" I asked, a bit uncertainly. I didn't know myself why I had used a fake name. Phonetically, *Keller* sounded a little bit like *Miller.* I had a gut feeling that it just might be beneficial to me to conceal my identity a little.

"Loud and clear! This is Commander Delisio. What've you got on board?" replied the commander in a calm, firm voice.

I relayed details of the wounds. Not a word about Jim, who had plunged out of the helicopter right before my eyes. It simply wasn't relevant here.

"Captain! We're scrambling a Nightingale right away. Set down at Position Golf. The doc will look at the patients," radioed the commander back to the pilot, as I listened in.

"Roger that, Position Golf in five minutes, over," the pilot confirmed.

A short time later, we landed directly next to the tail ramp of a white, twin-engine McDonnell DC-9 bearing the military designation C-9A Nightingale. The plane bore the insignia of the United States Air Force, and its tail fin had an enormous red cross.

A black doctor, visibly exhausted and overworked, his stethoscope dangling from his neck, dispensed with the ritual greetings and examined the wounded in the Huey.

"The head wound can come along," he decided tersely, adding, "but only if the medic flies along to keep an eye on him."

"Where are you headed? When are you taking off?" I asked.

"Osan Air Base in Korea," the doctor replied. "Four and a half hours' flight time. We're taking off in a few minutes."

"How am I going to get back?"

"No problem. We fly several aircraft there and back every day, to relieve the Army hospitals in Vietnam. Come on, get in the damned plane!"

Two airmen—Air Force enlisted guys—loaded Bill McPherson into the Nightingale and secured the litter in the far aft row. We removed Bill's jacket and put it under his head to elevate it a little. The doctor examined him briefly and gave me some instructions.

"Start a drip with saline, and take his blood pressure every twenty minutes. Do not give him any medication. And no morphine—that increases intercranial pressure. Try to talk to him a lot and keep him awake. We can't do any more for him here." Then he disappeared, heading to the forward section of the aircraft while it taxied for takeoff.

The enormous air ambulance could accommodate forty patients. But not all of the beds were occupied, only about thirty or thirty-five of them. The accursed flying tin can reeked of blood, urine, excrement, and death. I was certain that Bill wasn't the only wounded soldier to have come directly from the battlefield. To judge by the stench, the plane was also transporting a couple of belly wounds. The medics had merely wrapped the men in bandages and started an intravenous drip—*load and go*, as it was called in the war. Load them up and get them to the hospital; that's what we had been taught. In the midst of all this, you accepted the fact that many of the wounded would not make it to the destination alive. It was war, after all.

Since waking up to take a couple of laps at Red Beach in Da Nang, over thirty hours had elapsed. But the longest day of my life was still not destined to be over.

CHAPTER 4

An Unwilling Agent

How do I become an agent? Apply in writing or over the phone to the CIA or to West Germany's equivalent, the *Bundesnachrichtendienst*? Or better still, just drop by in person? In any event, that would attract the intelligence service's attention, and be certain to trigger a thorough background check. Communications channels are monitored for weeks, months, or perhaps even years on end. If you're considered "clean," then you've got a realistic chance of getting hired as a secretary, doorman, or as part of a cleaning crew—but never as an agent.

Agents don't apply. They're recruited! Most of them come from military units, where their particular suitability has distinguished them. Civilians have mainly two opportunities—if they possess rare or unusual abilities or occupy interesting positions in the enemy camp.

Strictly speaking, my career as an agent began at the very moment when Bill McPherson drew his last breath. Aboard the C-9A Nightingale, close to the cockpit, the doc and a nurse were busy resuscitating a patient. I was left all alone with Bill in the aft part of the plane. He resembled me a little bit. But only a little. We were about the same height and had roughly similar hair and eye color. He appeared somewhat older than I did—and he was dead. I took off my jacket, which had my name tag sewn on it, and gently switched it with Bill's, which was lying under his head. After glancing around the aircraft, I also switched our dog tags, as our identification was called. These tags listed a soldier's name, service number, blood group, and religion. Michael Miller, blood group type A-negative, Catholic, had just died. I was now Bill McPherson, blood group B, Rh-positive, Protestant. And I intended to desert.

The decision to change my identity came spontaneously. The opportunity to do it probably existed only for this brief moment. Was it the right thing to do? Would it ever benefit me? I didn't know. A deserting Bill McPherson would be hunted down no less than a deserting Michael Miller. Maybe I could just gain some time this way—critical time. I envisioned the wildest scenarios. For instance, if I were caught as a deserting McPherson, I could sow actual doubt about my identity. Then, while the authorities were trying to find out who I really was, maybe I would have a second chance to escape. Maybe I could rescue myself, stark naked right down to my underwear, by running to the German embassy. Once there, I would trot out a story about a crazy girlfriend, stolen papers, and language problems. Then, outfitted with fresh clothing from the embassy and a German passport issued to Michael Müller, I would be repatriated to Germany. It was definitely no mistake to run through various plans in my mind. But things probably turn out differently than we think.

My goal was as clear as the water that freshly rises from a mountain stream: no more war, never again! To achieve this goal, I was ready to lie, cheat, steal, and fight—just not kill!

Our flight still had another hour to go. Nobody was paying any attention to me or to the dead man. Everyone was preoccupied with himself. My first problem would be getting out of Osan Air Base. It was undoubtedly surrounded by fencing and kept under strict surveillance. Casually slipping in and out, the way I had recently been doing at the Army Evacuation Hospital in Da Nang—pulling that off wouldn't be possible here. Or would it?

I rummaged around in the dead man's pants and found a few items:

A photo of a very pretty woman with gorgeous dark eyes and long, blonde, curly hair. It could have been Bill's mother in her younger years, or even his older sister or girlfriend. The only word written on the back was "Mary."

$23 in small bills.

Bill McPherson's military ID card, indicating his date of birth.

What would happen to the deceased Michael Miller? After the plane landed and his death was confirmed, he would be shoved into a gray-black plastic body bag and flown back to the United States in one of the next transport flights. He'd be marked as KIA, killed in action. One of his two dog tags—everybody in the military wore two, for exactly this reason—would be attached to the big toe of his right foot. The other would be sent with his ID card back to Washington, where it would be determined that Private Miller had not specified any next of kin, and that he had been promoted to Medical Specialist shortly before his death.

And what would happen to McPherson? If anyone spoke to me within the confines of the Air Base, it would be necessary for me—depending on the situation—to dream up a good story very quickly. If they captured me outside the military area, I would be, as Bill McPherson, deemed a deserter and have to expect a long prison sentence. In every other possible scenario, McPherson would presumably be listed as MIA, missing in action, and Mary still would not have to mourn so soon.

An announcement from the cockpit interrupted the eerie silence.

"Captain speaking. The runway at Osan Air Base is temporarily closed, so we're going to land twenty miles north, at Suwon International Airport. Ambulances are going to bring all the wounded to the base hospital. We'll be landing in twenty minutes."

In all likelihood, an emergency landing or some other incident at the air base had made the diversion necessary. What did that mean for me? I was wide awake, and I resolved to use every escape opportunity that might come my way. And I defined my next objective: getting as far away as possible, as quickly as possible! Every other need—sleeping, eating, a cold beer, or a cigarette—had to take a back seat. I would need only water. Nothing else.

When we landed at Suwon, several military ambulances were awaiting us, some large, some smaller. First, the copilot opened the enormous cargo door in front of the port-side airfoil. Then he ran towards the rear, where he expertly lowered the aft ramp, a stairway with ten steps, down to the ground. Since the copilot was totally focused on this task, he didn't even glance at the patients on board. I climbed down the aft ramp, snappily greeting a couple of soldiers who were coming towards me to unload our air ambulance. I walked the short distance to the terminal without looking around once, careful not to proceed too slowly or too fast. I crossed the terminal and briskly saluted the watchstander at the exit, a small, older man in uniform. He was not a soldier; that much was certain. He could have been a policeman, a customs official, or simply just a guard. In any event, he gave me a friendly return salute.

Three taxis were standing in front of the airport building. I wanted to head for the train station; from there, I would take the first possible train to Seoul, the capital city. The first taxi driver shrugged. The man didn't speak one word of English. The second driver waved me over to him and kept talking at me nonstop. No matter what I asked or said in English to him, he just kept on talking—in Korean, obviously. Based on his facial expression and gestures, I inferred that he didn't like Americans. Perhaps he just didn't like soldiers, or maybe it was just me. The third taxi driver gave me a friendly greeting. Whether it was honest or phony remains an open question. But he didn't speak a word of English either.

I didn't know where I was—fifty kilometers from the capital? 500? Nobody here understand me, I didn't understand any of them, and I was unable to read the street signs or anything else. I vowed to myself that in the future I would visit only countries where I had already acquired at least a rudimentary grasp of the language. "Please, thank you, good day, goodbye"—you really did have to be able to manage at least that much, along with counting up to twenty, getting directions, ordering food and drink, and understanding the replies! But how was I supposed to have prepared myself for this country and its language and writing? A few hours ago, I had not even known that today, I would be landing in Korea as Bill McPherson.

I was starting to get hungry and thirsty, and I sensed a whiff of depression and despair descending over me like a gray veil. If I got caught here, my absence would already be deemed as AWOL, Absent Without Leave, and I would draw a severe punishment. I had to get away from this place, far, far away. As fast as possible, as far away as possible, and as invisibly as possible. I crossed the street and resolved to avoid the main boulevard, opting instead to take the side streets and byways into the village. That way at least, it seemed to me, there would be a low probability of encountering any of my fellow soldiers or the military police. But if the villagers held the same opinion of Americans as the second taxi driver, I would have to expect to be pelted with stones or to be struck by a flowerpot hurled out of a window. I commanded myself to stay awake. Wide awake—even though my last, brief nap was already thirty-seven hours behind me.

Suddenly I noticed that I had company: a small, wizened old man with long, straw-white hair was slowly following me. He was on a bike, maintaining a respectful distance of five to ten meters.

I stood still, turned around and looked him in the face. He also remained standing. I eyed him suspiciously. Despite his age, he looked athletic, sitting there on his bike, and I wasn't sure whether I could have caught up with him.

"Hello, Mister!" the old man called out, smiling and waving.

I scanned my surroundings and moved slowly towards the old man. In hand-to-hand combat, I would have definitely outclassed him, even if he had been carrying a knife.

When I had gotten within a meter of the old man, I rendered him a military salute, putting the palm of my right hand to my temple.

"How are you?" the old man asked, in perfect English. "How has your day been so far? Can I help you?"

How my day had been going— well, I preferred not to tell him that. But now, the sight of a native who spoke English was more than welcome. Unless he turned me in or wanted to lure me into a trap.

"Thank you, I'm fine," I said. "And how are you? Where did you learn such good English?" I asked him by way of reply.

"I'm very well. I studied English at the university in Seoul, but that was a long time ago. Afterwards I taught English and geography around here for thirty-three years," the old man replied. It sounded believable.

"That's quite an accomplishment," I said appreciatively, hoping to make the praise sound heartfelt.

"Where do you want to go?" the old man asked.

"To the train station."

"And then?"

"To Seoul, into the capital."

"I understand! To visit your uncle. Just a couple of weeks ago, I obtained a train ticket for one of your comrades. He also wanted to visit his uncle in Seoul and spoke no Korean."

Huh? Which uncle? Maybe he meant Uncle Sam, I thought to myself, puzzled.

Wordlessly, we looked at one another in the eye for half a minute or so, and suddenly it became clear to me. The old man knew what I was intending to do—and he wanted to assist me.

* * *

The man showed me to a spot on his bicycle rack. After a period of silence—we had traveled all of one kilometer—I offered to change places, because the teacher, despite being quite athletic, was quite visibly struggling to take us both. So now I was the one doing the pedaling on this bike, which was much too small for me, with the old man giving me directions from the rack. I pedaled a good hour, mostly on level stretches, sometimes up gentle hills, until, shortly before sunset, we reached the eagerly anticipated train station. The old man bought me the ticket and a large bottle of water, accompanied me to the platform, waited with me for the train, showed me to the car I had to board, and wished me lots of luck.

As the train moved away, I waved goodbye to him. I was deeply moved. Without the old teacher's assistance, I would have been utterly lost in this foreign country. In retrospect, I regretted not having hugged him tightly. He had certainly earned it! But perhaps in this culture, which was so alien to me, that would have also been an enormous faux pas.

I cautiously wended my way through the entire train, from the first car to the last, in order to determine whether there were any other white people, soldiers, or American military police on board. In the event I encountered the latter, I was mentally prepared either to flee to the roof or to jump off the train, depending on how fast it was traveling. I realized that certainly by now, if not earlier, I was considered a deserter. If I were caught, or if someone betrayed me to the U.S. Army, I would have to reckon with a long sentence in a military prison once my identity was ascertained. In a pinch, by furnishing false information about my identity, I could still cause some confusion and gain time.

The train was fairly full; I was the only soldier and the only white person on board. I wasn't sure whether the

Korean population regarded American soldiers as welcome protectors and friends, or as despised warmongers. I took off my olive-drab Army jacket, turned the sleeves inside out, and donned it again. That way, nobody could see my name tag, the U.S. Army patch, or my rank insignia.

Most of the passengers smiled at me in a friendly way, but it was impossible for me to get a true glimpse into their hearts and minds. On one of the narrow wooden benches, I sat next to a girl who might have been thirteen or twenty-three, for all I knew. Across from us was an older, haggard woman who had a baby pig with her in a woven basket. After a while, she took the young sow out of the basket, stroking and cuddling it a way that I had previously seen people do only with domesticated house pets.

The girl next to me, whose age I was unable to gauge, nestled her head against my shoulder and—fell asleep. It was a deep, sound slumber. Her mouth was half open, and her breathing audible; to describe it as snoring would have been a slight exaggeration. I sensed and enjoyed, quite consciously, her warmth and human closeness. It was a wonderful feeling, one that I had not experienced for a long, long time; after the events of the past forty hours, it did me a world of good.

After four or five hours of travel, and making several stops along the way, the train stopped, and everyone got off. Underneath the Korean lettering on the platform sign, it read *Namyeong-dong.* This had to be the final destination in Seoul.

According to the station clock, it was already late in the evening, just after 11:30 p.m. I was hungry and thirsty, and urgently needed a change of clothing. I vowed that I would pinch at least a T-shirt and a pair of pants from the first clothesline I could find.

The passengers had quickly scattered in every direction. And there were no signs of clotheslines anywhere. Nor were there any street stands, stores, or even taxis or rickshaws like those I had seen in Vietnam. Maybe I was just on the wrong side of the train station, which suddenly seemed completely dead.

I walked into the dark, strange city, slightly downhill, until I reached a large river. Then I went downstream to the first bridge, under which I made camp for the night. It was uncomfortable, rocky, and cold. The temperature was far colder here than in Vietnam. I crouched in a corner where the least amount of wind was blowing, lay my head on my knees, and tried to sleep a little. But I couldn't. Too many thoughts kept racing through my head.

Would Bill still be alive, had he not glanced sideways and told me to aim higher? Would Jim's suicidal plunge from the Huey and the wretched series of events beforehand ever become known? Did anyone even really know how many GIs had been shot in the head or in the belly? Or how many suicides there had already been in Vietnam?

I suddenly experienced a feeling of joy—joy that it was my fellow soldiers who had gotten it instead of me. I regarded this feeling as profoundly immoral and tried to suppress it. But it kept coming back until dawn finally came. Interspersed with this feeling were images of Barry, Ulf, Captain Paul von Hagen, Sergeant Wilcox, Private Coolidge, Jim, and finally Bill McPherson, whose identity I had commandeered, and in whose head a hole had suddenly appeared.

In the early dawn light, I washed my face in the icy river. I would have all too gladly taken a gulp. But in Basic Training we had always been warned about drinking water of unknown origin without boiling it first. I was so hungry that my stomach hurt; it was growling audibly. I climbed up the embankment to the bridge and discovered a plaque with Korean and Chinese lettering on it, as well as an inscription I *could* read—*Han River.*

At some point I stumbled onto a street with several food stands. None of the things sizzling and steaming there in the early morning hours even vaguely recalled anything like a Western breakfast. All the dishes looked instead like hearty lunch items. I ordered a soup they called *pollock*, a hot broth with dried fish, bits of tofu, scallions, and egg whites. I also bought a large bottle of water. My five-dollar bill occupied an entire armada of friendly Korean men and women with calculating the exchange rate and making change in Korean won. The warm soup did me a world of good. Now I only had to get rid of the damned Army uniform. Surely I would be able to scare up a simple T-shirt, a regular collared shirt, and a pair of jeans. Far from it! I frittered away half a day in an unsuccessful search for clothing. There simply wasn't anything in my size.

I had to keep going. Far, far away. To the airport, to observe how it operated and the people there, to sound out my chances. But where was the airport? Nobody I talked to spoke English. I didn't understand Korean, nor could I read the writing, all of which drove me to the brink of despair.

Salvation approached in the form of a house sign: *Mrs. Kim's English-Korean Language School.* The neatly dressed school head, a middle-aged lady, received me on the first floor. She seemed like an angel to me. Unshaven, unwashed, and in a filthy olive-drab uniform, a bit shamefacedly—but with a friendly smile—I poured out my woes. Mrs. Kim's perfect Oxford English reminded me of my school days. In this situation, it sounded as buoyant as the first movement of Mozart's Night Music. The teacher didn't ask where I came from. She appeared to ignore my outfit, and even went to the trouble of drawing a small map of the town for me. Going down to the Han River, over the first bridge to the other side and then farther downstream, I would reach Gimpo International, the country's largest airport. On foot, the trek would take a good four hours, maybe even five. Then Mrs. Kim took another slip of paper and wrote down a couple of words, in case I had to ask for directions along the way or wanted to take a taxi. The Korean money I still had as change from breakfast ought to be enough. She also wrote that down on the note.

Two worlds were battling in my heart as I tried to reconcile my feelings of exuberant gratitude with discreet Asian reticence. At last, I simply bowed, very slowly, deeply, and submissively, whispering: "Thank you so much! You have just saved my life!"

The teacher nodded only a brief farewell, with a barely perceptible smile that I more or less interpreted to mean, "Don't exaggerate so much! That was simply Asian politeness. Perhaps you've learned a life lesson."

I hailed a taxi on the *Saechang-ro* and handed the driver Mrs. Kim's note.

During the taxi ride, I tried to forge together a plan. The most adventurous thoughts whirled through my head. Could I, perhaps, sneak into the freight processing area, empty out a large suitcase, climb into it, and fly somewhere? Did the hold of a freight plane even contain enough air pressure and oxygen?

I just had to get away from here as fast as possible—to Australia, Europe, North or South America, whatever the cost! Anything was justifiable, except murder. But no matter how I looked at the matter, any practicable plan required three things I lacked: a passport, credit card, and an airplane ticket. The passport would have to be one issued to a white male between the ages of eighteen and twenty-eight. Everything else was secondary. I figured that Koreans would have just as much difficulty distinguishing one white face from the next as white people do with Asian ones. So I could expect some degree of leeway there. It would also be very nice, if not absolutely necessary, to get a cold Coke to keep me awake and to sharpen me up, as well as some cash, a shower, and civilian clothing.

At Gimpo International Airport, I handed the taxi driver the remainder of my Korean won. With a friendly look, he nodded, and remained just as silent has he had throughout the entire trip, even as I exited the cab.

I decided to spend a great deal of time observing and analyzing everything going on at the airport—the flight schedules and destinations. Which service counters were most heavily frequented? Where did the baggage end up after check-in? Where do they check passports? What kind of routine and schedule did the guards have, and what routes did they take? Where did the cleaning crews work? Were there waiting areas?

Even before I could obtain a proper overview of the place, I discovered a long bamboo wall just to the right of the entrance. Behind the wall, there was a restroom that I headed for immediately. Being able to empty my bladder made my reconnaissance of the whole airport a lot more relaxing. Right next to the restroom, I was surprised to notice a sign reading *Shower*. I had expected any number of things, but certainly not an airport shower. Exactly what I needed now! The stench of my own sweat had been revolting even to me for quite some time. A cool jet of water blasting down, maybe a bar of soap—now that would be paradise on earth!

In the shower facility, which apparently could be used at no charge, there were three cabins next to one other along the wall, and a long row of clothing hooks along the opposite side. One of the cabins was in use, but the other two were available. Each shower cabin was furnished with a small washcloth and soap bar. I tore the clothes off my body, all set to jump into the empty shower. But just then, my eyes locked on the beige suit coat hanging on the hook next to mine, together with a white hat, beige pants, and a brown satchel. In one of the suit's inside coat pockets, I quickly discovered, was a ticket indicating merely a flight via SFO that terminated at IAD, whatever that meant. The passport had been issued in the name of a Mike Love. The suit also contained a wallet stuffed with baggage claim stubs, cash, credit cards, and business cards. The man in the photograph was a good ten years older than I was, and heavier. He also had a mustache.

Some opportunities come along only once in this life; they've got to be seized immediately. I forgot all about the shower, and as fast as possible I slipped into Mike Love's shirt, pants, and suit jacket. Then I grabbed the satchel, rolled up my Army uniform, and jammed it under my arm. All that I left on the hook was Mike's underwear. I'm not a monster, after all.

While Mike continued whistling away, enjoying his shower, I got the hell out the room. I was pouring sweat. I stuffed my Army gear into the large trash can in the adjacent restroom. Mike's clothing, which was somewhat too big for me, hung loosely, and the belt buckle pin seemed to be longing to get a new hole punched into the leather.

Suddenly, a flash of insight made me shudder. I had made a mistake—a really big one! Maybe the biggest mistake since joining the Army. A mistake that might decide everything!

I dashed back to the shower room, where I heard Mike shutting off the water. Just as the shower cabin door was opening, I grabbed his underwear—the sole item of clothing remaining—right off the hook. For a fraction of a second, our gazes met. I will never forget the combination of sheer outrage, anger, and helplessness in Mike Love's eyes as he saw me in his beige suit, with his brown satchel, and his white hat perched upon my head. Would he dare—stark naked—to chase me through the airport concourse? Would he be able to catch up with me? Whose side would people—and the police—take if I were attacked by a naked man?

After sprinting a hundred meters without even bothering to look around, I slowed down to a brisk run and made it to the men's room in the part of the airport diagonally opposite, where I tossed Mike's underwear in the trash. Then I locked myself in one of the toilet stalls so I could take inventory in peace and acquaint myself with my new identity.

I was now Mike Love, twenty-nine years old, hailing from Lexington, Kentucky, the United States of America. According to my business card, I was a journalist with the *Washington Post*, the same newspaper which, in cooperation with *The New York Times*, had published the Pentagon Papers ten months earlier. These documents were a study proving that preparations for the Vietnam War had been made long in advance, and that the American people had been deliberately lied to by their government about both the cause of the war and the reasons behind it. I had a Master Card and an American Express Card, and I was a member of the Pan American Airlines WorldPass club. In my pocket, I found a copy of the *Washington Post* dated a few days earlier, some cookies and chocolate bars, and a paperback novel entitled *The Good Earth*, by Pearl S. Buck. My flight was departing from Gate 3, heading to IAD via SFO, wherever these destinations might be; I was yet to find out. My baggage had already been checked through, and the Pan Am flight would be ready for boarding in twenty minutes.

The gate was easy enough to find. A uniformed Korean man glanced at my ticket and my dark blue passport, embossed in gold with the American eagle and the lettering reading *United States of America*. Without looking any further, he waved me through.

Waiting to board the aircraft, I settled down in one of the rows of seats in front of Gate 3, unfolded the *Washington Post*, and pretended to read it. In reality, my thoughts kept dwelling on the naked man standing in the shower. Mike Love! A hell of a name! If you mumbled or slurred the name a little, it sounded like "make love," which reminded me of the hippies at Venice Beach, with their slogan, "Make love—not war!" How right they had been, indeed!

The real Mike Love, stark naked, would undoubtedly have a hard time of it, at least for the next few hours, probably even days, or perhaps weeks. The Korean police would wrap him in a towel, then want to take him into custody and interrogate him, in Korean, of course. At some point, they would consult an interpreter and perhaps even a consular officer from the American embassy. But all that could easily drag on for days. Verifying his identity without any kind of papers, in light of the tenuous channels of communication between Asia and the United States, would require a lot of time. The only way to dispatch a photo of Mike Love from the United States to Korea was via air mail. The journalist would survive the whole affair and perhaps even fashion a good story out of it someday. For me, it was a matter of sheer survival. Each additional day spent in this senseless war could have forced me to shoot or even kill someone. And on top of that, I could have easily ended up like Private Coolidge or Bill McPherson.

The *Washington Post* had booked Mike Love in First Class. Very pleasant, indeed. The first thing I did after takeoff was make my way to the airplane lavatory. It was my body's first contact with soap in sixty hours. The soap bar was small, with the airline's logo on it, but at this moment felt as valuable as a chunk of gold. The water tap ran only ten seconds at a time. It didn't matter. Passengers in First Class also received a little toilet kit containing, among other things, a disposable razor, a disposable toothbrush, and some toothpaste. Personal hygiene—at long last—was a real treat! The final glimpse in the mirror was astounding: I looked old. *War and sleep depriva-*

tion make you old, I had heard somewhere along the line. It's probably true. I wondered…was the process reversible?

SFO, I had already pretty much guessed, stood for San Francisco. At the immigration window, the officer, a black woman, said I looked different without the mustache and ought to have my passport photo updated. Otherwise, she remarked, I might run into trouble at some later date.

"Or I could grow a moustache again," I smiled, taking back the passport and waltzing through the checkpoint.

Now, I still didn't know what IAD stood for; it was the airport where my baggage had been checked through. Dallas? Denver? I let myself be surprised, and a few hours later I landed at Dulles International Airport, in Washington, D.C.

At the exit, a man was holding up a sign reading *Washington Post – Mike Love*. My head lowered, I scurried past him. Washington, D.C. would have actually been the ideal place to give Richard M. Nixon a good dressing-down. But the President wouldn't grant access even to a Mike Love together with his press pass. I decided to take the next Greyhound bus and travel to Nashville, Tennessee. Once there, I would rent a room in a cheap motel, have a couple of beers in one of the numerous saloons, bars, or clubs there, and ponder what to do next. Maybe Elvis Presley, Dolly Parton, or Johnny Cash were singing there at the moment. And besides, I already knew my way around Nashville a little, thanks to a few weekend excursions during my training at Fort Campbell, Kentucky, which is only an hour's drive away.

I found a room at the Nashville Legends Motel on Second Avenue, near Broadway. I shut the door, put down my suitcase without even knowing what it contained, and threw myself on the king-sized bed—fully dressed, face down, and legs spread out—and slept for a full twenty-six hours. After all, I hadn't had a decent night's sleep for the past eighty-eight hours, except for a couple of brief, half-assed naps with my eyes half-open.

Still wearing Mike's baggy clothes, on Nashville's Broadway I indulged myself in an American breakfast par excellence: pancakes with maple syrup, hash browns, eggs sunny side up, and fried bacon. To flush it all down, I had some orange juice, a glass of ice-cold water, and a steaming hot cup of bottomless coffee. I loved poking the fried eggs and watching the yolks flow slowly over the hash browns.

The next thing I did was buy myself a pair of jeans, a blue shirt and a white one, a couple of T-shirts, some underwear, a dressy sports jacket, and a pair of shoes. I was finally human again!

Except for a copy of the previous month's issue of *Penthouse*, the contents of Mike's suitcase were useless: dirty laundry, socks, a roll of toilet paper, a collection of Asian hotel soaps, various toilet articles, and a Kodak camera loaded with color film. Without dwelling much on the matter, I shoved the camera into the pocket of my new sports jacket.

A walk along the nearby Cumberland River ought to clear my head, I thought. Had Elvis ever strolled around here to find inspiration for a worldwide hit?

With each step, it became clearer to me that I did not want to be on the run forever. And I did owe something to Mike Love and Bill McPherson, or at least to their families. At the riverbank, as the sun went down, I put my plan together.

The next morning, I went to the same restaurant, on Broadway in downtown Nashville, and ordered exactly the same breakfast I'd eaten the day before. It was simply too good to resist! I relished every bite, for I realized that it might well be my final breakfast as a free man.

Then I took a taxi to Fort Campbell, right up to the barriers at the enormous Army post's front gate. I flashed my press ID and claimed that I had an appointment to interview the commanding officer, Brigadier General Thomas McKee Tarpley.

One of the two watchstanders made several phone calls while holding my press ID and turning it over and over in his hand. After what felt like an eternity, a young soldier in a jeep picked me up and brought me to a room in one of the barracks. The place didn't exactly look like a commandant's office. It was a spartanly furnished room containing a desk with a typewriter and telephone on it, three chairs, and a bookcase with a few newspapers and some Army literature.

"My name is Collins," said the soldier. "I'm the press officer in charge here. Go ahead and ask your questions, Mr. Love, and I'll see how I can help you."

"Please understand," I replied, "that I have to conduct the interview with the post commandant personally," I replied, opting to first attempt the obliging tack.

"Unfortunately, that's impossible without an appointment," Collins replied.

"But I've got an appointment. Today, at 11:30!" I insisted.

"For one thing, the general is in a meeting at the moment. And we haven't found any appointment with you in his calendar. So you'll just have to make do with me," the press officer said.

I fumbled for the camera in the pocket of my sports jacket and decided to up the ante:

"The *Washington Post* is one of this country's most important newspapers. My assignment is to conduct an exclusive interview with Brigadier General Thomas McKee Tarpley. It's supposed to be printed on the front page of the paper the day after tomorrow, along with his portrait. My secretary made the appointment and had it confirmed a good two weeks ago. I don't think the general is going to like the story I'll have to write if his office screws up the appointment—and if you, Press Officer Collins, send me all the way back to Washington without letting me do my job."

The press officer mulled it over for a moment, then said, "Please wait a moment, Mr. Love."

The moment lasted until one in the afternoon, presumably the exact amount of time until the general had finished lunch. PAO Collins then escorted me into the general's office, which was thoroughly representative of the breed and appropriate to the man's position. Any visitor would have been immediately impressed by the enormous Stars and Stripes hanging in the window, and the awards, honors, and photos of the general's various impressive duty stations hanging on one wall. On the other side was a well-stocked bookcase, and the far wall boasted a map of Vietnam studded with numerous flags and colored pushpins.

The brigadier general, sporting a tan, greeted me with the customary handshake reserved for civilians. His thick, bushy eyebrows concealed dark, penetrating eyes. His most congenial feature was a pronounced cleft chin.

"You're from the *Washington Post?*" the West Point graduate asked, frowning critically.

"Yes," I replied briefly.

"By publishing the Pentagon Papers, your newspaper did tremendous harm to our country at a difficult time. Why did you do that?" the general asked me.

"American citizens have the right to know how their government made preparations for the Vietnam War," I replied. "The study was commissioned by the Defense Department itself. And the Supreme Court approved its publication. May I ask you a few questions?"

The general nodded.

"How long have you been commanding officer at Fort Campbell?" I began.

"Since February of this year."

"How many young men have you sent to this senseless war since then?"

"I don't know, Mr. Love. And if I did, it would be classified information that I would not be permitted to disclose to you. Moreover, this war is *not* senseless. We have to defend our country and the world against Communism. You've surely heard of the domino effect. If we lose South Vietnam to the Communists, then we'll lose South Korea next, then Taiwan, then Thailand and so forth. We cannot allow that to happen."

"But you are subordinate to the Defense Department, aren't you?" I asked.

"Correct!" replied the general.

"But countries have to defend themselves only when they're under attack. Was the United States attacked by North Vietnam?" I asked.

"We also have the duty to support our friends and allies if they are attacked," the general retorted. "You've got no idea what's going on in Vietnam! The Viet Cong are attacking the peaceful South Vietnamese, burning down their villages, raping their women, and killing their children. We can't just stand by and do nothing!"

"May I tell you a story?" I asked.

"Well, my time is limited, but go ahead," said the general.

"My real name is Michael Miller. I am a medical specialist in a unit under your command. Six months ago, you swore me in at the big barracks yard, along with 200 other new recruits," I began. Then I proceeded to tell him everything, starting with my recruitment in San Diego, right up to this very moment when, as Mike Love, I had been escorted into the general's office. I tried to be certain not to omit any detail that struck me as important, even the part about how the heavily traumatized 18-year-old Jim from Harlem, his pants full of his own shit, had plunged out of the Huey to his death. Making the full confession afforded me an unbelievable inner relief. With each episode that I related, I felt as though I was jettisoning one enormous emotional burden after another.

The general stared at me contemplatively for a long time. Then, finally, he said, "Mr. Love, Mr. McPherson, Mr. Miller, or whoever you are—you're either completely crazy or just stupid! And you know what I think?"

I shrugged.

"That story of yours is nothing but one gigantic pack of lies! Military intelligence will review your statement. Should it prove to be true—what I consider almost impossible—you'll end up doing a couple of years in the stockade, for desertion. But if you've made the whole thing up, you're going to be spending some time in the loony bin. The question is, which is better for you? We shall see."

The general, shaking his head, ordered me taken away.

I had to be fingerprinted and photographed. Although I claimed to be Michael Miller, the photos were captioned Miller/McPherson/Love. A mug shot with three names under it had to be a rarity.

My one-man cell was around six square meters, furnished with nothing save a cot, a blanket, and a bucket. The walls were dripping with filth. The few clean spots were decorated with trite graffiti like *Kilroy was here* or *Fuck the Army.*

Worst of all, it was December, and this winter the Kentucky nights were cold. I really froze my ass off. If there was anything I hated, it was the cold! Half the night I longed to be permitted to shovel snow in the barracks yard simply because the exertion warmed me up. Sometimes it was possible to briefly chat with my fellow prisoners, and an additional portion fries at lunchtime beckoned, to help me keep up my strength. Delightful!

Every day, I was interrogated for several hours, and I had to repeat my story again and again, first to the military police, then to military intelligence, then to the CIA, to the FBI, and yet again to agents and specialists from the State Department and the Defense Department. The good part about the interrogations—they did provide unlimited coffee and cigarettes.

Christmas was depressing. We prisoners, together with the guards, were allowed to sing *Silent Night*, to attend Mass, and to read aloud a passage from the Bible. I was not particularly enamored of the Church or the fairy tale of Mary's immaculate conception resulting in the Virgin Birth. If a God really did exist, then he wouldn't always look the other way whenever you really needed him. But the fact that he always had to test people—that was something I simply couldn't believe.

Between Christmas 1971 and New Year's 1972 I was interrogated twice more. The long-promised lawyer I had been fervently awaiting never arrived.

A flood of thoughts coursed through my head. When would I be transferred to a larger cell? How long would I have to remain in custody? Would it have been better to tough out yet another ridiculous school year living with my mother so I could finally graduate? No, definitely not! I'd sooner spend a couple of years in a military prison than let myself be tormented and humiliated one more day by that dictatorial biddy of a teacher! Had it been a mistake to join the Army? Yes and no. Yes, because I so naively fell into the recruiters' trap. No, because I hadn't killed anyone, and in a very short time I'd gained a tremendous amount of life experience. Would I be able to escape from military prison and—without hurting anyone—obtain a new civilian identity for myself on the outside? Maybe from someone who had died in an accident? Or perhaps even better, someone who had been killed in Vietnam. After all, I already had some experience performing that kind of switch. Time will tell…

At 0900 on January 4, 1972, a Tuesday, my cell door opened, and General Thomas McKee Tarpley entered, as large as life, accompanied by two MPs. It was a rather inopportune moment because the room was cramped—and I happened to be sitting on my bucket. The general looked away discreetly while I finished my business and pulled up my pants. Why hadn't the bastard let me know ahead of time? I resolved to offer him neither a handshake—he probably would have refused—nor a salute.

Was I actually still a soldier, or dishonorably discharged as a deserter? I seized the moment and asked, "General, when is my lawyer coming? And am I still actually a soldier until my court martial?"

The general ignored my questions, replying instead, "You've surprised me, Miller. A lot, in fact! Your story appears to be true. And now I'm going to surprise *you*. You've got a visitor."

"My lawyer?"

"Perhaps you won't even be needing one anymore. Listen to what the man has to say to you. But don't fuck it up. It might be your only chance."

The general and the MPs escorted me to an interrogation room. Sitting there was the unlikeable, pockmarked CIA prig with the enormous, bulbous nose, the one who had already wanted to hear my story twice. Great surprise. What was I supposed to do now? Tell him the whole thing for a third time?

The general departed, but not without first informing me, with a smug smile planted on his face, "The 101st Airborne Division and the 326th Medical Battalion— your unit—were completely withdrawn from Vietnam on 23 December. They've since returned to Fort Campbell."

By letting me know that, General Tarpley probably wanted to say that I could have spared myself the trouble of deserting, given that the unit had been shipped home two weeks later in any event. But even in a war's final days, how many soldiers are killed or in turn have to kill more of the enemy? The fact that I had deserted—it was a good thing, except for one small detail: I had to get out of here!

As always, the interrogation room table had been decked out with a large coffee pot, two tin cups, an ashtray, and a pack of Marlboros. But this time, a few things were different: there was also a carafe of water, a couple of glasses, and a plate with five chocolate donuts. A couple of other things had changed as well: gone were the interrogation microphone and tape recorder. For the first time, the guards left me alone with James Colby, the CIA agent. And Colby, too looked different than he had at the previous interrogation session. For the first time, he was wearing a pistol—and no sunglasses.

"Agent Colby," I asked him, "what do you want me to do, celebrate your birthday with you? Or bump me off? Or do you want to hear my story again? I've already told it to you twice, so you'd better hope that I still feel like bothering."

"Let's have a smoke first," Colby suggested, holding out a pack of Marlboros with a couple of cigarettes shaken out. I nodded wordlessly and grabbed one. Colby gave me a light with his Zippo, which was engraved with the logo of the 82nd Airborne Division. Then he lit up his own cigarette, inhaled deeply, and let the smoke waft slowly from his bulbous, misshapen nose.

"Miller," he began, "do you know that at the Agency, we've never been able to find a single agent who changed his identity twice within forty-eight hours and traveled halfway around the world practically broke?"

I shrugged.

"Obviously, you've managed to pull that off. And even without any intelligence training or official support. So we would like you to come work for us," Colby continued.

After a long, emphatic pause, I asked, "What are the terms?"

"You will receive six months' training at the CIA, and for the next ten years, you will be obligated to carry out at least ten missions per year as an escape agent," Colby said. "The job involves helping people escape to the West—people from the Eastern Bloc, also sometimes through third countries, who are in danger or who want to defect to us. But unlike your recent solo escapade, this time the CIA will equip you with papers and sufficient money for expenses. And you'll receive a handsome bonus for every successful mission," he promised.

"And what if something goes wrong?" I asked.

"Now you're disappointing me, Miller. Nothing can be allowed to go wrong! If it does, you won't be able to expect any help from us. We won't know you. If you do something stupid, you can waste away sitting in prison in Moscow, Prague, or Sofia for twenty years. Or just get a bullet in your head. But you aren't stupid, Miller, are you? This is your chance. If you confirm this agreement with your fingerprints, tomorrow I'll drive you over to Langley, and you'll be a free man. Well, almost a free man."

Colby held a sheet of paper in front of me.

"Why 'almost'? And why does it say 'Martin Cooper' here?" I asked.

"Because during your training, the only way you can leave the CIA compound alone is with special permission," Colby explained. "'Martin Cooper' will be your pseudonym among your new colleagues. You'll also receive a new CV. Your actual history must remain an absolute secret. The only person who will learn your real name is your agent controller once your training is completed."

After yet another long, emphatic pause, I then said, "I'll need to think it over."

Colby was now getting really angry.

"What's to think over, Miller?" he shouted. "Five years in prison for desertion? Or your freedom—and training to become a top-notch agent with the world's most powerful intelligence service? And prospects for a great career, adventure, and travel, not to mention one hell of a lot of money? Which do you like more? I can also take this contract with me, march right through that door, and let you rot in here!"

"Come back again tomorrow," I replied, grabbing myself a chocolate donut.

Agent Colby slammed his fist, twice, against the door, and once the guard opened the door for him, he disappeared without saying goodbye.

Nobody came to visit the next day. Had it been a mistake to send Colby away empty-handed? Would I really get five years in prison for desertion? How would working as an agent for the CIA limit my future life plans? What plans, anyway? Colby would probably just want to let me stew in my own juice, then come back after a couple of days. Mentally I drew up two lists, one with the goals I wanted to achieve in the next few years, and the other with a couple of conditions of my own that I would insist upon—assuming that Agent Colby ever did come back again.

And return he did, the following day, no less. I requested a few extra freedoms, such as paid training as a freefall parachutist, as well as the right to decline assignments if I wanted to finish high school, attend university, or embark upon some kind of occupational training. I also bargained for a higher starting salary from the CIA during my training. Agent Colby had to first consult with his superiors and redraft our agreement. But we settled everything soon enough.

The CIA training surpassed anything I had imagined, far and wide. It was altogether more demanding, more multifaceted, more exciting, and more adventuresome than I had expected, even when measured against my previous military and medical training. Instruction took place on "the Farm," located at Camp Peary, Virginia, not far from Williamsburg and 155 miles south of CIA Headquarters. For some exercises, we also traveled to Arizona or various large cities.

At the CIA, attributes and activities proscribed by civilian life were elevated to a true art form—primarily lying, cheating, stealing, corrupting, dissimulating, diverting others, breaking into cars and dwellings, and forging documents. Another integral part of the curriculum, naturally, included the art of killing—quickly and silently.

Camp Peary had its own auto racing course, where we were allowed to test reinforced cars to their limits, including burning rubber, wildly accelerating, and flipping over. In groups of four, we traveled to Chicago, Los Angeles, and Miami, just for a day at a time, where we rented vehicles and took turns playing hunter and prey smack in the middle of town. The CIA handled all the police citations we received for speeding or other traffic violations. The same went for all the damage we caused. It was only the personnel who weren't allowed to suffer harm. Sometimes it was quite simple: you ducked into a side street or a backyard as soon as your pursuer was out of visual range for just a second, and the game was already won. At other times, there were car chases and pursuits worthy of Hollywood, swerving across three lanes of freeway traffic in order to reach the exit at the last second. Motorcycle and foot chases were also part of the training program, along with the art of professional concealment. In the role of a pursuer, you also had to develop a feel for when you had gotten burned—that is, when your cover was blown, when you were made or fingered as an agent and immediately had to suffer the respective consequences. Depending on the situation, it mostly boiled down to making yourself invisible or getting the hell out of there, and what's more, in such a way and in a direction that your opponent least expected.

Based on my experience at Gimpo International Airport in Seoul, I proposed that we fan out to international airports for a couple of days and steal passengers' passports and tickets, then replace them as inconspicuously as possible, just in time for departure—all purely for training purposes, of course. But unfortunately, the suggestion was turned down.

The CIA engaged professional magicians and actors to instruct us. The magicians taught us how to divert other people's attention. Every agent had to master at least three amazing magic tricks. My favorite was to hold two passports in my right hand and briefly wave my left hand over them. Then there was only one passport—with the other one in an astonished onlooker's jeans pocket.

Our actor instructors showed us how to analyze various behavior patterns and to slip into the roles of other people. Tensed-up neck muscles, flaring nostrils, and twitching eyelids had to be noted and correctly interpreted. For the first time, I became aware of how differently Russians, French, Mexicans, Germans, British, and Americans differ just by their everyday behavior, their body language, and the manner in which they sit, walk, and stand. I had to play out all these roles before a critical audience. On top of that, we learned how to change our appearance using glued-on beards and wigs, as well as hats, baseball caps, and different outerwear—under extreme time pressure, too, while walking or running. Within just thirty seconds, I metamorphosed from a businessman in a suit, white shirt, and necktie into a hippie wearing a dirty T-shirt, complete with a beard and a long-haired wig. We also learned how to be as motionless as department store mannequins and play dead. Both these skills could save your life. The acting lessons placed great demands on our cognitive abilities. We had to memorize multiple-page texts and recite them in a Spanish, Russian, British, French, or German accent. Another course component involved memorizing long series of numbers and alphanumeric combinations, a skill necessary primarily for another specialization, namely, coding and decoding secret messages. A special telephone number made it possible to reach CIA Head-quarters at no charge from any telephone booth around the world, except from the Eastern Bloc and other Communist countries. A secret area code prefix enabled us to call around the world at no charge.

Maintaining secrecy was a key topic throughout. You had to play your role to perfection, but never reveal more than was absolutely necessary. Case studies illustrated to us how quickly you could land in a trap, and how, with just one careless word, our colleagues had often paid for their lives. For that reason, we would never learn about the overall background of an assignment, but only the part relevant to our task.

The instructor's favorite saying was, "Trust nobody, not even your own mother!" In my case, he was preaching to the choir. Nobody had ever abused my trust as often and as shamelessly as my mother had done. Once, she even ratted me out to my math teacher after I told her that I'd copied off a classmate. Each of us received a failing grade instead of the "B" we had previously gotten. And at home, my mother beat me for the bad grade. So her nonstop abuse of my trust had been the best schooling for my upcoming life as an agent.

Two enormous banners adorned our training classrooms. In enormous letters, they contained two sentences we were supposed to internalize like a mantra:

Never get caught!

We don't know you!

The art of inconspicuously transferring objects, microfilms, and documents was just as intensively practiced as the exchange of identical-looking briefcases, bags, and backpacks, as well as how to use large and small dead drops.

We were trained in the use of various weapons, among them models from manufacturers such as Smith & Wesson, Colt, Browning, Beretta, Walther, Heckler & Koch, Makarov, and Kalashnikov. We had to strip and reassemble them, recognize at a glance which ammunition was correct for which model, and of course to fire them. The program also included the use of silencers and secret weapons specially produced for the CIA, such as one-cartridge ballpoint pens and umbrellas, ammunition with above-average penetrating power, and rifles with extremely high precision and range. Mobile weapons training was completed in the Arizona desert. In the searing midday heat, we fired from moving cars or motorcycles at mouse-gray rubber puppets, taking turns shooting from the driver or passenger seat.

At Lake Pleasant we spent an entire day from dawn to dusk in training to operate speedboats, after which we passed the night in the desert next to a campfire. The next day, we chased each other around the lake with jet skis. At Coolidge Airport, situated about sixty miles south-southeast of Phoenix, Arizona, we received our so-called pinch-hitter flight training in a decrepit old Cessna 180. In just five days, we learned how to safely operate an aircraft—lifting off, cruising, and landing—as well as everything we needed to know about instrumentation, navigation, aeronautical radio protocol, and flying under the radar.

Back at Camp Peary, they trained us how to climb into houses and to open various types of locks using a skeleton key, a couple of hairpins, or a credit card. We also learned how to quickly break into cars and hotwire them.

Particularly enjoyable was the classroom instruction given by "Chemical Charlie," a somewhat older chemistry professor who always had a boozy joke at the ready. You were never certain whether he was really drunk or just putting on an act. We also never knew for sure whether what he was relating was true or merely a joke. This uncertainty tremendously enhanced our attentiveness throughout his entire lectures. Chemical Charlie taught us how utensils available in any supermarket could be used to manufacture both knockout drops as well as highly effective explosives, and how psychotropic drugs from the MK-Ultra project were used for interrogations.

Things got really wild during the demolition lessons, which taught us how to handle dynamite, plastic explosives, homemade explosives, how to blast doors off their hinges and to blow cars and even entire houses to kingdom come. That was truly spectacular!

Every morning began with physical training and Krav Maga. That also included defending yourself from knife attacks and the alluded to, constantly practiced silent killing, preferably by prying the target's skull from his Atlas vertebra.

Role-playing exercises were also very popular, ranging from soft to hard. For example, you sat at a table and told your counterpart—who kept rotating out—spontaneously concocted life stories. The counterparts were allowed to ask three questions; afterwards, they assessed the narrator's believability and body language.

The hard exercises involved mutual interrogations, for which psychological—and sometimes even physical—pressure was exerted, with the goal of either bringing your partner to his knees or learning to skillfully resist *his* pressure. We also tested each other with a lie detector over hours of interrogation until we could lie so perfectly that the sensitive device no longer budged, even from the most outrageous lies.

Forged passports and documents were generally provided by a special division of the CIA. Still, we learned a couple of fundamental principles of passport forgery, and we were at least supposed to be able, if necessary, to swap out a passport photo.

What I found interesting, and especially important for my future deployment area, were the "corruption lessons." The CIA was convinced that every person was fundamentally corruptible; it would depend only upon the amount involved, or upon a "favor" of great importance to the adversary one hoped to win over. One of the basic rules was to pay bribes as early as possible, and in the correct amount, to a lone decision-maker. The CIA maintained lists of the salaries earned by police and customs officers in Europe and in all the Eastern Bloc countries. Depending on the type of service desired, the amount of a bribe was supposed to range between a month's and a year's salary.

At the end of our training, we took a three-day exam at CIA Headquarters in Langley, Virginia. We never found out how well we had acquitted ourselves in the individual subjects; nor did we receive any certificate or diploma.

Yet I had passed the exam, and with it, I obtained the official license to lie, cheat, steal, and kill. Only one thing, under any circumstances, was strictly forbidden: *getting caught!* If that happened, the license I had labored so mightily to earn would be forfeited immediately, and every agency would disavow any knowledge of my mission—or of me.

CIA Director Richard Helms made a brief farewell speech to everyone graduating. Right around this time, the *Washington Post* was publishing the first news stories about the break-in at the Watergate Hotel. Helms, visibly enraged, quizzed our group, albeit purely in a rhetorical way: "What did the burglars do wrong here?!" Without waiting for a reply, he answered his own question: "They let themselves get caught! What a bunch of *incompetent failures!*" It really sounded as though the burglars had been CIA agents whom our boss no longer wanted to know or hire—after they had been caught.

My contractually arranged freefall course had been forgotten. Instead, I was offered a sizeable amount of money that I could independently use to finance an equivalent training program, including meals and accommodation, at a civilian drop zone of my choice. After completing the training at Camp Peary, I went to Lake Elsinore, California—the birthplace of formation skydiving—where I spent six full weeks earning my USPA B, C, and D licenses, along with credentials as a rigger, jump master, and instructor. I had been bitten by the skydiving bug! By the end, I had completed 143 jumps, flown in a 16-way formation several times, and possessed my first personal parachute, a B-12 TU, together with a reserve one.

CHAPTER 5

A Cry for Help—from Tehran

I was back in Munich.

Boris, my old school friend with the shoulder-length, curly blond hair, was always in good spirits. He was spending most of his time listening to loud music and smoking tons of weed. He had made it through high school and was now waiting to get accepted to a university to study philosophy. Boris's parents, both of whom were Czechoslovakian refugees, were letting him stay on in a small room in their apartment. His father Josip, a genteel man with a thin mustache, worked as an editor and news announcer for Radio Free Europe/Radio Liberty, an anti-communist, CIA-financed propaganda station located in the English Garden, Munich's most famous park. Whenever Josip was reading out the news, Russian jamming stations always kept trying to render his broadcasts impossible to hear by superimposing noise over the airwaves. And whenever the broadcasts became inaudible, Radio Free Europe/Radio Liberty, in turn, amplified its own signals until listeners could hear the broadcasts again. That's simply the way things were in those days, during the Cold War.

Boris's father liked me. His mother, Maria, not so much—especially when she discovered that after my mother had kicked me out, I had climbed over the balcony on the first upper floor of the apartment building on Gebelestrasse and moved in with Boris.

Now it was like that again. Boris had granted me asylum after my return from the United States. I shimmied a bit farther up the gutter drainpipe, and with one pull-up swung myself over the first upper-floor balcony. The room behind the balcony door, which was always kept open, was divided by a large wardrobe. One side housed Boris and his beloved turntable, his collection of what looked like a thousand records, and a shoebox containing his pipe, bong, rolling papers, and weed.

My mattress was on the other side.

After the unedifying visit to my mother and the abjectly failed attempt at reconciliation, I now sat with Boris, smoking a fat doobie to the sounds of Amon Düül II. I opened the three letters from the *Kreiswehrersatzamt*, the Bundeswehr's district recruiting office. The letters included my draft notice as well as two reminders setting new appointment dates. In other words, I was supposed to be drafted into the Bundeswehr and serve my eighteen months of mandatory military service. But first, of course, they wanted to ascertain my physical suitability or fitness to serve. Reporting for the military physical was required by law in the Federal Republic of Germany for every male citizen over eighteen years of age. Anyone who failed to appear for his physical had a warrant put out for his arrest, and if found would be forcibly hauled before the *Feldjäger*, the military police of the German Army. The last possible date, I was informed, was the following Thursday. That was in two days' time.

Totally high, Boris enjoyed himself hugely when he saw the notice for my physical. He threw himself on his bed, practically busting a gut laughing, and drove me nuts by insisting that I immediately read him aloud the letter from Tehran. The hell I would. As stoned as we both were, I could put off reading it until Boris passed out. Unfortunately, I also fell asleep, so the letter had to wait.

* * *

Drifting off to sleep, I was gently accompanied by fond memories of the letter's author: Fatemeh Farahani, whom everyone in our circle called "Fae Fatima," had been the great love of my youth. We'd met at a party and hit it off immediately. We stayed up half the night in long philosophical discussions about anything and everything—religion, teachers, and our parents. Fae's relationship with her father was strained in a similar way that mine was with my mother.

But there was a fundamental difference: while Fae did feel misunderstood by her father, she nevertheless also had the feeling that he loved her above all else. I, on the other hand, had long since felt absolutely no love whatsoever emanating from my mother, just hatred and bullying. Fae remarked, "A child with a mother like yours will either crack—or become incredibly strong and learn how to master life with complete autonomy. I admire your self-confidence and your inner strength! You definitely have your mother to thank for that."

I had never looked at it that way. But perhaps Fae Fatima was right.

One day—the domestic situation had become unbearable once again—we resolved to take off for the weekend and take a trip somewhere really nice. At a party one time, I had heard about the town of Heidelberg. It was supposed to be especially splendid. So on Friday after school, I told my mother that I'd been invited to a birthday party. I shoved my pocketknife into my jeans pocket, along with my entire life savings, which amounted to a grand total of 12.70 Deutschmarks. Then I picked up Fae Fatima, and we hitchhiked across the entire city to the autobahn entrance heading towards Stuttgart.

At the time, I was sixteen and Fae was fifteen. Two centimeters shorter than I was, she was simply stunning—slender but not too thin, with a cute ass and splendid breasts. Fae's cleavage always remained hidden away from interested glances because she always wore, or had to wear, turtleneck sweaters. Her bronze complexion, her long, silky, pitch-black hair, her large, dark eyes, her fine, well-proportioned facial features, and, last but not least, her genuine, unforced laughter all combined to make her the loveliest girl on the planet!

We soon noticed that drivers pulled over for us more quickly if Fae stuck out her thumb than if we both stood on the side of the road. So Fae stopped the cars, and only after she had gotten the driver to agree to take her along did she then ask whether I could come along too. At that point, I would jump out of the bushes. It almost invariably worked. Just in time for the sunset, we stood in the courtyard of the magnificent Heidelberg castle, with its captivating view of the Neckar River, the old bridge, and the medieval city. I gently put my arm around Fae's shoulders, and we silently enjoyed passing the time until the sun disappeared behind a dark cloudbank. Storm clouds were already gathering when we descended from the castle's hill. When we arrived in the medieval town, which looked completely dead, the rain was coming down in buckets. Completely drenched, we made our way to the train station, and I blew half of my travel budget for two portions of bratwurst with sauerkraut, whole-grain farmer's bread, and a can of Coke that we split between the two of us. A hippie couple we met at the train station knew about a half-finished abandoned house where we could spend the night. The floor was hard and the night drafty and cold. But we had no alternative.

Never before had I felt so close to Fae. We cuddled together, quite intimately, keeping each other warm. I gently kissed her on the forehead, and we fell asleep.

Early the next day, we set off on the return journey, again by hitchhiking. On the second stretch, between Karlsruhe and Stuttgart, we had an eerie experience: a seemingly reputable gentlemen, about forty, waved us over to his brand-new white BMW 2002. Fae took the front passenger seat and I sat in the middle of the back seat. The man said he was a teacher and that he always had to keep up on current events. For that reason, he liked to read the newspaper a lot. Nothing at all objectionable there. But as the BMW was whizzing along the autobahn in the middle lane, doing a good 160 kilometers per hour, this teacher reached into the console, pulled out some newspaper's thick weekend edition, laid it on the steering wheel, and then calmly began to read. After what felt like an eternity, he finally glanced up at the road briefly and jerked the steering wheel to get the car back into the middle of lane. Then continued with his reading, totally unperturbed. We implored the man to keep his eyes on the road, but he ignored us. In fact, quite the opposite: he seemed to be getting a kick out of terrifying us. At some point, he did finally look up from the newspaper—but only when the cars to both our right and left began honking at us for drifting out of our lane. The guy also refused to stop and let us out. This nightmare driver told us we didn't need to be afraid since he knew the route anyway.

Back home, both Fae and I came in for beatings because we hadn't been at home all night. But the adventure we called *life* had been worth it—Fae and I were completely on the same page about that.

* * *

While Boris was still asleep, I carefully and quietly opened up the airmail letter from Persia. Fae Fatima's father had closed his carpet business on Munich's prestigious Maximilian Street. He and his daughter had moved to Tehran, where he had good contacts to the Shah's family and better prospects. His wife had stayed behind in Munich. Fae had been torn away from her friends and high school just one year before graduation. At the German school, located in Tehran's Gholhak neighborhood, Fae had to learn to read and write Farsi, a language that she had previously known only phonetically. One kept hearing that the Shah of Iran had a strong Western orientation, but nonetheless the abrupt move to Tehran must have been a massive culture shock for Fae. She was in complete despair, and her letter was a bit confusing. She wrote that she wanted to take her own life, and that her last wish was for a couple of German books that I was to send her. But a few sentences later, she asked me to rescue her from the dire straits she was in and bring her back to her mother. The letter ended with three dried-out tears with little hearts drawn around them, along with another girl's Tehran telephone number. It belonged to a school friend who would help me contact Fae, should I ever come to Tehran.

I folded up the letter—I had to let the contents sink in a little first—and put it in the left hip pocket of my jeans. I thought it all over. What should I do now? Earn my high school diploma and attend university? The money left over from my CIA training would not be enough. Maybe later. Perhaps scout around for a traineeship? Definitely! But which? Sit tight and wait for the first CIA assignment? Waiting will turn you into a depressive mental case. And besides, the CIA wouldn't even be able to reach me if I didn't have a proper address and residence. I had to do *something*, so I set the following priorities: apartment, army physical, car.

Boris let me use his telephone for a couple of days to call nearby apartment listings that had been advertised in the local Munich papers. But there was nothing suitable to be had. Only one single landlord told me to call again, two days later, in the event that another interested tenant decided not to take the apartment.

Promptly at 0800 on Thursday morning, two passport photos in hand, I stood at the *Kreiswehrersatzamt*, the district recruiting office at Dachauer Street 128, to be physically examined from head to toe. After two hours, I received my military ID—and was completely flabbergasted. Next the ink stamp reading "fit for duty," they had actually added a handwritten notation: "Not suitable for paratroop duty."

Unbelievable! I had just successfully completed training with the world's toughest airborne division and logged 143 civilian parachute jumps, but now the German Bundeswehr was classifying me as "unfit for paratrooper duty."

Of course, I certainly didn't want to go from the frying pan into the fire and join the Bundeswehr after having served in the U.S. Army, but out of sheer curiosity, I had to ask why I had been deemed "unfit" to be a paratrooper. And for good measure, I provokingly added, "If I can't become a paratrooper, then I refuse to serve in the military."

After an hour's wait, I was introduced to the Chief Medical Officer, an older, fatherly sort who was obviously close to retirement. The Bundeswehr doctor frowned and looked me right in the eye.

"Do you really want to be a paratrooper, Mr. Müller?" he asked.

I had nothing to lose, so I replied, "Actually, I wanted to refuse to serve, but if that's not possible, then it should be the real thing, not fooling around in a sandbox."

"You've got *pes traversoplanus*, what's commonly known as flat or splayed feet," the doctor said. "As a paratrooper, you have to be able to withstand forced marches for days at a stretch while wearing jump boots. But if that's really what you want, be my guest," the doc said, changing the notation on my ID to "At own request also fit for paratrooper duty." Then he stamped and signed the entry.

Even during my schooldays, which had been marked by a pacifist outlook, I had thought long and hard about the issues of being a conscientious objector, of comprehensive refusal to perform any kind of service, and of alternative civilian service. I knew which option was best for me. The same day as the physical, I located the small building, located at Schreberweg 1, that housed the Maltese Aid Service. I obligated myself as a conscientious objector to work sporadically as a paramedic once or twice a month for ten years. Of course, first I had to complete a first-aid course, an internship at a hospital, and a paramedic course. I would have been all too glad to add that I had already been a medical specialist in the U.S. Army and had treated severely wounded soldiers in the Vietnam War. But that would have been unwise, and in any event, it wouldn't have truncated the training period any. With a bit of a smirk on my face, I promptly booked all the requisite courses, in order to put the whole business behind me as quickly as possible.

When I called a second time to inquire about the apartment that hadn't yet been leased, I felt like I had won the lottery: the place was still available! It was furnished, and situated in the rear courtyard of a building located in Munich's Schwabing neighborhood. I immediately went to Belgradstrasse, made a cursory check of the place, and signed the rental agreement. The place consisted of a bathroom, eat-in kitchen, and a bedroom with a double bed. It was small, but the whole thing was ideal for me, and still quite a bargain.

I walked around a bit and explored my new neighborhood. On Viktoriastrasse I spotted a basement bar called *C'est la vie!* and decided to have a beer there a little while later. The joint had retained all its wood decor and imparted a cozy atmosphere, also because it was illuminated by nothing except warm candlelight.

On my very first evening there, I met Manfred, a medical student with a full beard and large, glittering eyes. He enthusiastically described his dissection course earlier that afternoon, at the Anatomical Institute on Pettenkoferstrasse. He had stripped the skin off a deceased organ donor's hand to expose all the muscles, sinews, and veins. When he tugged on a certain sinew with the forceps, he said, the fingers on the dead hand curled up. Manfred treated me to a beer merely because I had listened to him with such patient interest. His girlfriend, he explained, always wanted to throw up whenever he launched into these topics, particularly when he went into detail. Finally Manfred asked me, "So, what do you do?"

I fell silent for a time. My experiences over the past fifteen months could have filled a book, but I wasn't permitted to tell anyone about them. That was something I would have to get used to.

I finally replied, "I rented an apartment today, right near here, on Belgradstrasse. A real stroke of luck. Now all I still need is a car."

"Do you have any ideas about where to get one?" Manfred asked.

"Any kind of old crate will do, as long as it runs. It can't be too expensive, and if at all possible, it should be able to make it to Tehran and back," I replied spontaneously. Fae's letter had clearly worked its way into my unconscious mind and—although I still didn't have any specific plan—I was probably already contemplating a trip to Tehran. Manfred's eyes lit up.

"Then I absolutely have to introduce you to my brother Diogenes! He's a chemistry student in his eighth semester, and he's got a truck driver's license. He's been spending the semester breaks for the last couple of years driving big rigs for Hirsch, the freight forwarder, between Munich and Tehran. Last year he took some time off and drove his old VW Beetle all the way to India. I think he wants to sell the car now. My brother's also coming over here tomorrow evening."

"You've simply got to introduce me to him! How about earlier, at around lunchtime?"

It was now five minutes to one o'clock in the morning. As the staff went around snuffing the candles and the electric light filled the room, music wafted through the bar. It was crooner Reinhard Mey's popular song:

Gute Nacht, Freunde
es wird Zeit für mich zu geh'n
was ich noch zu sagen hätte
dauert eine Zigarette
und ein letztes Glas im Steh'n
(Good night, friends
It's time for me to go
What I'd still have to say
will take one smoke
and one last glass on end.)

The next day in the early afternoon, I found myself sitting at the wheel of a totally awesome fourteen-year-old dirt-covered VW Beetle. I drove the bucket of bolts up and down Leopoldstrasse twice between Munich's Victory Gate and Freedom Square. The old crate would probably have crumbled into a heap of dust if somebody washed it. I had never driven a car with a manual transmission and a clutch, so inevitably the engine stalled several times. Diogenes, whose real name was Fritz Bartelt, measured about 190 centimeters tall and must have weighed around 120 kilos, and he shared both the bushy beard and approach to life espoused by the actual Diogenes of Sinope. It was something of a miracle that this latter-day Diogenes could even fit into the Beetle's passenger seat; I couldn't imagine that he had ever been able to squeeze behind the wheel. Diogenes smiled only a little at my poor mastery of the manual transmission, occasionally glancing out the window with a bored expression on his face. Manfred sat in the back while explaining how the Beetle's four-on-the-floor stick shift works, occasionally intervening helpfully.

Diogenes swore to Zeus that the old beater—which had already racked up 97,000 kilometers—would easily make it to Tehran and back. He wanted seventy Deutschmarks for the car. I offered him fifty "because it keeps stalling."

Diogenes burst out laughing.

"'Because it keeps stalling!' Manfred, did you hear that?"

Manfred also laughed, and I joined in.

When we all finally stopped laughing, Diogenes stuck out his hand.

"Fifty Deutschmarks, it's a deal. Treat the old girl well. She'll find the way to Tehran on her own."

So I now had a car. I filled up the tank and spent the whole afternoon practicing with the stick shift transmission on Schwabing's main boulevards—to the great joy of other urban drivers, undoubtedly. Munich's traffic was already in near-gridlock due to the 1972 Summer Olympics, which were in full swing at the time.

At the *C'est la vie!* that evening, Diogenes regaled me with some of his exciting travel experiences. He had a ton of valuable tips—for instance, that the General German Automobile Club, the ADAC, offered excellent maps as well as a completely laid-out itinerary from Munich to Tehran. Also, it was necessary to obtain a document known as a *carnet de passage* in order to bring the car into and out of various countries without having to pay customs duties. And in Istanbul, Diogenes said, I should check out the Pudding Shop, a café of sorts where travelers from all over the world touched base with one another and swapped ride shares for gas money. Diogenes even knew of an inexpensive Tehran hotel, the Amir Kabir on Naser Khosrow Street. For just $3.00 the hotel offered fan-equipped rooms, though the shower, which always ran lukewarm, cost an extra ten cents for each use.

That very night, I resolved to drive to Tehran and liberate Fatemeh Farahani, my Fae, from her father's clutches. I issued my first major rescue escape assignment to myself, as it were. The undertaking would first necessitate thorough planning. But conversely, time was also of the essence—I had to act quickly, before Fae hurt herself, was forced into marriage, or dispatched by her father into the desert.

Every morning, I showed up at my internship for alternative civilian service at the clinic, which was situated on the right bank of Munich's Isar River. In the afternoons, I worked on my VW Beetle. And late in the evenings, I picked up tips from Manfred and Diogenes at the *C'est la vie!*

Fluffing up pillows, serving breakfast, and emptying urine bottles and bedpans—all that was certainly a slight underutilization of skills for a U.S. Army Medical Specialist who was even capable of performing an emergency appendectomy. But in this life, you have to take what comes your way, and try to derive some benefit from everything you do. I was glad to treat the seriously ill patients in my ward with the same attention I would bestow upon guests at the Presidential Suite at Munich's Hotel Bayerischer Hof. With a cloth napkin draped over my lower arm, I served patients their chamomile tea, bowing deeply. On top of that, I tried to glean these patients' final wishes, quite literally from their eyes, asking them frequently whether there was still anything I might do for them. Many of them thrived on that, and a few even became a bit cocky.

"You can give me a hand job," breathed an elderly patient who was riddled with terminal cancer. These words were his last before he closed his eyes forever. At any rate, he died with a grin on his face.

Customizing the old Beetle was very intensive work, especially considering that I had very little experience using tools. But it was fun. The first order of business was thoroughly cleaning the interior before carefully washing the entire car by hand. The car's actual colors finally became visible: the Beetle had red doors and a red roof, while the front end and the rear hatch were blue, as were the fenders. Now that was something!

On Landesbergerstrasse there was a do-it-yourself garage catering to hobbyist mechanics. For just a small fee, you could rent every kind of equipment, including a hydraulic lift, tools, a polishing machine, and even a welding unit. Since everyone working on their vehicles at the place shared a similar fate, we engaged in a lively exchange of experiences. The owner, a master auto mechanic, gladly dispensed advice but never laid a hand on anything. Just for the sake of practice, I changed all the tires, removed and replaced the spark plugs, tightened the fan belt, and even removed and reinstalled the generator. I wanted to get a feel for the Beetle, which was to become my closest traveling companion for around 10,000 kilometers.

My idea to hollow out the back seat—so that, if necessary, I would be able to hide Fae Fatima during one or more of the border crossings—drove me to the brink of despair. The car's battery, located underneath the back seat, could be shifted around, but doing that wouldn't be enough. Raising the coil suspension springs by replacing them with a plywood board would also be useless. It just wouldn't work, mainly because the transmission tunnel, which ran the length of the entire car, could not be lowered by even one centimeter without blocking the shifting gears. It simply wasn't possible! Trying to devise an alternative, I squeezed myself into the small empty space between the rear seat's backrest and the engine compartment and tried to stick it out there for an hour. It was uncomfortable and painful, but if I could manage it, so would Fae. She was slender—and smaller than I was. Underneath the driver's seat, I mounted two bolted-on aluminum plates between which I stashed $1,000 as "emergency money." On the bottom of the plates, I attached several strips of Velcro. It would be possible to keep flashlights and wrenches handy there, but also pistols, ammo magazines, combat knives, wire saws, and other kinds of useful gear. Finally, I stretched some thin nylon fishing line around the interior door handles and secured an alarm siren, about the size of a pack of cigarettes, to the driver-side door. If someone should open one of the doors by more than a hand's width, the nylon fishing line would pull a pin out of the alarm unit, causing a shrill siren to go off. My handmade alarm system worked perfectly!

After a week, it was time. The Beetle, jammed with canned food, camping utensils, a gas cookstove, sleeping bag, and clothing, was ready for departure. So was I. The internship at the clinic could be put on hold without any problem. Dr. Schäfer, the friendly young doctor in charge of my ward, assembled a first-aid kit, handing me a plastic bag stuffed with medication, bandages, wound dressings, salves, and disinfectant to take along. Dr. Schäfer said he was envious of my trip. All I had told him was that I wanted to go to Tehran to visit an old girlfriend from my school days.

Uschi, an attractive medical student with freckles and a lustrous mane of thick red hair, had rescued a twenty-liter shampoo canister from disposal in the hospital trash, rinsed it out thoroughly with hot water, and handed it to me as a spare gasoline canister. I was really moved! Then Uschi yanked me into a gravely ill patient's room, bolted the door, and surprised me with a moist, hot, deep-throated farewell kiss that was bound to leave me flashing hot and cold, and to stand all my hair on end. It was terrific! Pure insanity! But did that have to be *now*? It made parting a bit harder because I sensed that Uschi could have taught me something when it came to sex, which had been somewhat lacking in my life thus far. Or had she kissed me so passionately just now because she knew that we wouldn't see each other for a long time, perhaps ever?

In the evening, I had a rendezvous with Manfred and Diogenes at the *C'est la vie!* and paid for a couple of rounds.

At precisely five minutes before one o'clock in the morning, we all joined together and hummed:
Gute Nacht, Freunde
es wird Zeit für mich zu geh'n
was ich noch zu sagen hätte
dauert eine Zigarette
und ein letztes Glas im Steh'n
(Good night, friends
It's time for me to go

What I'd still have to say
will take one smoke
and one last glass on end.)

And we did exactly what Reinhard May exhorted his listeners to do.

At around six the next morning, I got underway. On the autobahns through Germany and Austria, my Beetle ran in peak form, almost managing its rated speed of 115 kilometers an hour. The *autoput*, Yugoslavia's national highway, proved a challenge. Trucks and self-appointed stock-car racing drivers passed me left and right, honking loudly. The road was lined with wrecked vehicles.

When I parked at Belgrade's main train station and climbed out of the car, people were smiling at me and calling out "Buba, buba!"

I cheerfully returned the greeting, saying "Buba, buba!" back.

An hour later I had wolfed down an enormous portion of ćevapi, a Balkan minced meat dish, along with some djuvec rice. I'd also purchased a ten-year-old Makarov pistol with two magazines, each of which held eight rounds. I would never have thought it would be so easy.

Unfortunately, I couldn't try the piece out. Sure, with cocaine you can sample a little, putting it on the tip of your tongue to taste whether it's genuine. But you can't very well take a newly acquired pistol and shoot a lamp from the ceiling to see whether the thing works.

I resolved to immediately continue traveling. My objective for today's leg of the journey was the little Serbian town of Niš, in southern Yugoslavia. I pulled in just as it was getting dark, and made camp on the edge of town between a small forest and the Nišava river.

The next morning, after the sun had relentlessly driven me out of my sleeping bag, I ventured a couple of laps in the ice-cold river. After that, I was wide awake, all right. I scouted the immediate environs, pulled back the slide of the heavy Makarov, chambered a round in the barrel, switched off the safety, and placed the pistol on the passenger seat.

Driving off, I fired left-handed out the open car window at a Coke can that I had previously placed on a woodpile, and—bull's eye! OK, the target had been only a measly couple of meters away, but hitting it left-handed—and from a moving car—certainly made everything more difficult. All I wanted to do was test the thing to see whether it even fired at all.

In town, I greeted the locals with a friendly "Buba, buba!" and ordered myself a strong coffee. The men laughed, answered "Buba!" and nodded understandingly. A lively debate ensued, from which all I could discern was the repeated phrase "Buba." The rest of it was unintelligible.

At some point, I figured out that 'Buba' wasn't a form of greeting, but rather the nickname for my car; it meant nothing more than 'Beetle.' I liked that! From now on, my beat-up old car had a name.

As I departed, Buba honked loud and clear—even though I hadn't pressed the horn button at all. I guess the car had to demonstrate a will of its own, just because it now had a name.

After about two hours I reached Dimitrovgrad, right before the Bulgarian border. The Serbian border guard waved me right through. The Bulgarian one glanced briefly at my passport and the interior of the car, and then he also waved me through. It was almost too quick for my taste, so I requested an entry stamp in my passport. To get one, I had to stop and visit the customhouse. Doing that furnished me the opportunity to carefully observe how the opposing traffic was running. They were inspecting the incoming vehicles' undercarriages with mirrors, and having dogs sniff around in every car! So it became clear to me that attempting to smuggle drugs or people to the West from this border crossing would be a bad idea.

In Edirne, at the Bulgarian-Turkish frontier, Turkish border officials ordered me to empty everything—really and truly everything, right down to the last can of food and pair of underwear out of the car and to spread it all out on a large table for inspection. Customs officials opened up the trunk and engine compartment, folded back the rear seat's backrests, and even removed the hub caps. But they didn't discover the pistol I had hidden underneath the driver's seat.

Smuggling Fae Fatima in Buba over these borders would have been a foolhardy thing to do. I simply had to think of something else. And fast!

In Istanbul, the traffic was dreadful and Buba an embarrassment. The car honked nonstop and for no reason. In all likelihood, every jerk of the steering wheel was triggering a short-circuit in the horn's wiring. Since it was impossible to circumnavigate the traffic circle around Taksim Square in the heart of the city without turning the steering wheel, Buba kept on honking until a friendly police officer granted us an extra right of way with his whistle. Buba's uncontrollable honking forced me to make a difficult decision: let the car simply continue honking—in any event, Istanbul was a unique cacophony of rattling and honking cars—or disconnect the horn, thus silencing it for the rest of the trip. I chose the latter option.

For three days, I walked back and forth between the Marmaray Sirkeci train station restaurant in the city's European section, the infamous Pudding Shop, located diagonally across from the Sultan Ahmet Mosque, and the bazaar. I spent time observing the people and the discreet exchange of money and goods; I also established contact with fences and petty crooks. In Istanbul, you could get everything: hashish from Afghanistan, marijuana from India, opium from Anatolia, revolvers, automatic pistols, machine guns, hand grenades, belly dancers, and prostitutes. But the item I wanted was the only thing that always prompted my contacts to shake their heads and bid a quick farewell.

On the third day, I observed two thieves in the bazaar. One of them distracted a tourist while the other filched the man's wallet from his jacket, lightning quick, and bolted. I immediately sprinted after him, but maintained a certain distance in order to avoid detection. The thief slowed down; so did I. At some point, the youth disappeared into a store that sold meerschaum pipes. Walking past, I saw out of the corner of my eye how the thief handed over his ill-gotten gains to a bearded old man. I immediately knew that this old man was who I needed. The elderly have life experience, wisdom, and street smarts, and in the East, they are more highly valued and respected than in the West. After the thief had left the store and the old man had resumed hawking customers, I slowly ambled over to him.

"Young man, come on in!" he said in German, trying to tempt me. "Just have a look around."

"Nice pipes," I said, nodding appreciatively.

"All hand-carved, best quality from Eskisehir, make a good price!"

"How is it that you speak German so well?" I wanted to know.

"Was twenty-two years in Düsseldorf. Worked as street cleaner. But now back in home city. With whole family. You like some Cay?"

I nodded, and the old man, clearly delighted, poured me a glass of Turkish tea. Black tea, sweetened with a lot of sugar, lubricates the gears of negotiating, and everything is already a done deal—or so he probably thought.

"I don't want to buy a meerschaum pipe. I'm looking for something else," I explained to the man.

"Something else? Something made of leather or silver? Or clothing? How can I help you, my friend?" the old fellow asked, visibly eager to make a sale.

I beckoned him over to me, quite close, and whispered in his ear to be certain that not a soul around could have heard: "I need a passport, Effendi!"

I needn't have bothered whispering.

"A passport?" the old man called out loudly with an expression of astonishment. Pausing briefly, he then said, "Did someone steal your passport?"

"No," I whispered, "I need a passport of a young Turkish woman, around twenty, with a residency visa for Germany."

The old man sipped his tea silently and thought it over.

In light of my experiences over the past few days, I had a glimmer of hope that kept growing the longer the old man kept pondering. And he was taking his time about it!

"What you pay?" he finally asked.

Fully conscious that we were at a bazaar here, I offered 150 Turkish liras the equivalent of about thirty-five Deutschmarks.

"A thousand liras!" the old man demanded laughingly, sipping his Cay.

"Three hundred!" I countered.

"Impossible for original with visa. Eight hundred—my best offer!" the old man said.

I offered 450, and we settled on 600 Turkish liras—but only if the passport was perfect.

"Is really perfect! So perfect, you will never believe," the old man laughed mischievously.

"Okay. When can I pick it up?" I asked.

"In two hours. A hundred liras down payment!"

I didn't have any other option, so I gave the old man the 100 liras. But the whole thing still seemed a bit fishy to me. It wasn't humanly possible, in just two hours, to forge a perfect passport according to my exact specifications, complete with a visa thrown in for good measure. Not even CIA specialists would have been able to pull off a stunt like that. What *was* still possible, though, was a carefully targeted theft of a similar-looking passport. But the time to execute that was extremely short. I decided to get something to eat, walk around at the Bosporus a little, and let myself be surprised. Worst-case scenario, the man would abscond with my 100 liras and be impossible to track down. It wouldn't really wipe me out.

But after two hours, the old man proudly handed me a Turkish passport containing an attractive woman's photo. And inside the passport was a visa valid for Germany. I examined the document as thoroughly as I could. Then I noticed that the bearer was a lady already thirty-two years old. Citing this small blemish, I was able to pull off some last-minute haggling—resulting in a final payment of only 400 liras instead of 500. I would be able to wangle altering the date of birth on my own. We sealed the deal with a glass of Cay. Finally, I could not resist asking the old man where he had obtained the passport and visa so rapidly.

"My daughter," the old man smiled. "The passport is my daughter's. Four weeks you can do whatever you like with it. Then she will report it as lost."

The next morning, thoroughly satisfied at having taken a major step towards rescuing my Fae, I set off on a small car ferry—besides Buba, just three additional vehicles had been able to squeeze onto the floating death trap—heading from the city's European section across to Asia. Farther to the south in the city, two segments of an uncompleted bridge jutted into the Bosporus. This masterpiece of engineering was slated to open the following year, on October 29, 1973, to commemorate the fiftieth anniversary of modern Türkiye's founding.

I made good time on the stretch heading to Ankara. Every corner was graced with homages to Kemal Ataturk, the father of modern Türkiye, to whom this country owed such an enormous debt of gratitude. It was Ataturk who had replaced Arabic writing with roman letters and whose confident, open-minded statesmanship had earned the tremendous esteem of the entire world. Under Ataturk's presidency, democracy, human rights, and the strict separation of church and state had been equally as important to him as safeguarding the rights of religious minorities and condemning racism. A truly great man!

The road to Kirikkale was mountainous and full of curves. It was hard to imagine how buses and large trucks could handle it, considering that steering my Beetle, a more maneuverable vehicle, already demanded quite some doing. A couple of times, I was just barely able to dodge the "kings of the road." Burned-out wrecks in the valleys below offered a cautionary tale that this didn't always end well. Passing through Yozgat and Sorgun, I made it to Yildizeli by sundown. Sitting next to the car, I heated up a can of ravioli and warmed myself up a little over the flame of the Esbit solid fuel cube. There was still enough water left to drink and for rinsing off the utensils, but not enough for me to wash myself. The next morning, unwashed, without breakfast and without coffee, I drove the fifty kilometers or so to Sivas and resolved to give my body what it was needing most urgently now—a bath!

Fortunately, every Turkish city and village had someone who spoke German—or someone who at least knew another person who spoke it and could fetch them. Most of my interpreters had been in Germany as guest workers and were overwhelmingly helpful, friendly, and hospitable. It made me feel ashamed because I knew that in Germany, these people often had not been received with the same cordiality.

In Sivas, I was referred to the local Hamam, a strictly sex-segregated Turkish bath.

After stripping off my clothes and wrapping a large bath towel around my middle, I stood—somewhat at a loss—in the large, round, tiled temple, adorned with Middle Eastern ornamentation. In the center, several blocks of heated marble were arranged in a circle, and next to them, a bunch of brawny, good-looking men who had also wrapped bath towels round their loins. Had I accidentally ended up in a club for gay men?

"Bath? Shower?" I somewhat awkwardly asked the men in the room, in both German and English.

The men laughed. None of them spoke a word of either language and—unlike what so often happened on the road—not one of them set about to locate a brother, nephew, or uncle to serve as interpreter. Instead, they signaled, in a friendly way, that I should find one for myself.

Oho, this is going to be fun! God help me if one of these guys hits on me! All I want to do is take a bath! I thought to myself, and shrugged my shoulders hesitantly.

Then the biggest, strongest guy among them seized the initiative. He was a bear of a man, with an enormous mustache and a broad grin on his face. Tarzan-like, he beat his hairy chest with his right hand, then simply said, "Mustafa!"

In obeisance to the precepts of politeness, I beat my chest with my right hand and said, "Michael!"

Those words were the only two that we would exchange during the next two hours. Everything else was accomplished via gesticulating. Mustafa led me into a large room containing several washbasins and bade me to clean my body thoroughly with clear water. Then he ushered me to one of the well-heated marble blocks, soaped up my entire body, and rinsed off the soap with clear, lukewarm water. After a brief relaxation phase, Mustafa administered a massage at once so brutal and so splendid that I will never forget it as long as I live. I would have never imagined that my ribcage would be able to withstand the weight of a man as heavy as a sumo wrestler kneeling on it while he wrenched my head left and right. I could hear my vertebrae cracking no less than the popping of every knuckle on both my fingers and toes, as Mustafa adroitly pulled on them after he finished the massage. Before he could leave, first my arms, thighs, and calves had to be kneaded like pizza dough. The back massage enabled me to feel every one of my ribs for the first time, and I could sense the knuckle of Mustafa's thumb in each and every vertebra. A firework of sensations for every masochist! A tendency which—until now—had remained completely latent with me.

After the massage, Mustafa lathered me up once again, this time with a hemp bundle drenched in soap. My entire body was engulfed in sweet, aromatical soap foam, my pores opened up on the warm marble, and my skin soaked up the soap as gratefully as a wet sponge. Yet the languorous relaxation was short-lived. Mustafa, already standing over me like the executioner over his victim, grinned diabolically and, with relish, pulled on a pair of rough leather gloves. He used them to vigorously rub every centimeter of my smooth, hairless skin so intensively that I harbored doubts that the human body's largest organ has only three layers.

Several rounds of water poured over me concluded the ceremony, and when I left the Hamam, I felt not only reborn, but so thoroughly cleaned, right down to my pores, it was as though I had never before properly washed myself in my life.

* * *

Between the ages of twelve and fifteen, I had well-nigh devoured the adventure novels of Karl May, the biggest braggart since Munchhausen and the world's most-read

German author. Besides May's bestselling Winnetou series, his novels set in the Middle East, featuring Kara Ben Nemsi and Hadschi Halef Omar, were naturally also required reading. One of these novels is entitled *Through Wild Kurdistan*. And that's exactly where I now was, in Kurdistan. I wondered—how had Karl May been able to describe the steppes and mountains of the eastern Anatolian high plain in such detail—long before traveling through the region himself?

Ascending, Buba struggled harder and harder with every meter gained, snorting like an old tractor on its last legs. I decided to tinker with the carburetor a little to enable the engine to get more air at the higher elevation. After all, Erzurum lies 1,950 meters above sea level. It was cold there, very cold indeed. I resolved to drive a bit farther towards the Iranian border. But it didn't get any warmer—just colder! As dusk fell, I forced Buba to perform the day's final duty, whereupon I reached a small rise then turned around 180 degrees. What a splendid view of this endless valley expanse! Once again, a single Esbit solid-fuel cube would have to suffice for warming both me and a can of ravioli. Then I snuggled up on the Beetle's back seat, deep in my sleeping bag, and covered myself with everything I could find by way of clothing and blankets.

In the middle of the night—I had already been sleeping for a while—a loud bang woke me up. I thought it was thunder, and looked at my watch. It was exactly one in the morning. I debated closing the small crack I had left open in the window of the passenger-side door. A second, louder bang followed, and a third. Then an entire salvo. Was I having bad dreams—or was someone shooting here?

Suddenly I saw a rifle barrel banging on my passenger-side door, and I could make out a soldier's silhouette: "Wake up! Open up!"

Another four or five shots rang out. Then everything went quiet again. This was no dream. A young soldier was actually trying to open Buba's passenger-side door.

"Just a second!" I yelled, jamming my upper body forward between the front seats and rolling down the passenger-side window.

"Please! Drive off!" a pale young soldier told me.

"Drive off? Why? And how come you're speaking German?" I asked.

"I grew up in Germany, but I had to return home to perform two years of military service. Every Turkish guy does. Our outposts get fired at by the Kurds almost every night, and we shoot back. You've parked right in the line of fire," the soldier informed me.

"What am I supposed to do?" I asked

"Just drive down into the valley find a rest stop there. Up here it's going to keep up like this until dawn. But so far nobody's been killed or wounded here."

"That's reassuring," I let the nice soldier know, "but up to now there also haven't been any rattling old VW Beetles rolling through the line of fire, right?"

"If you want, I'll give you cover fire," offered the soldier.

"It's settled down again just now," I observed, "so only if the others start shooting at me—then let them have it with both barrels, okay?"

"Wait a second. I'll talk about it with my buddy and tell you when you can drive off," the soldier replied.

Wearing nothing but my underwear and T-shirt, I squeezed myself between the front seats and got into the driver's seat. I checked to see whether my Makarov pistol was still underneath the seat, within easy reach. I wondered whether it would be helpful to get a little involved in the skirmish. Then I took an old sock, cleaned the fogged windows, and rolled down the driver's side window to prevent them from clouding up again. It was cold as hell outside, but I was still pretty much roasting. During the seemingly interminable wait, I lay my upper body down onto the front passenger seat to make it harder for any stray round to accidentally hit me at full impact in case the shooting suddenly started up again.

The young soldier scared the hell out of me with two powerful blows on the car's roof: "You can drive off! Good luck!"

I started Buba's engine, turned on the headlights, and let the car roll in neutral down into the valley. When I had covered a good half of the way there, a shot from the Kurdish side broke the stillness of the night. Three shots responded from the opposing side. That was supposed to be my cover fire? Somehow, I couldn't ward off the feeling that both parties were happy if ammunition had been saved and no blood had been spilled. The fratricidal war between Turks and Kurds seemed completely senseless to me, in any event, especially since both peoples had more in common with each other than do almost any other ethnic groups.

In the valley I parked under a large pine tree, but sleep now eluded me no matter how much I twisted and turned—until sunlight flooded the valley. Then I got really tired and fell asleep in my sleeping bag, on the back seat.

* * *

When it got warm and stifling in the car, I pulled myself together, aired out both Buba and my sleeping bag, and got behind the wheel. In the first village I came to, there was strong Turkish coffee with a lot of sugar and a piece of day-old baklava. I studied my maps. I wanted to reach Agri by midday and to make it to Iran before sundown.

Three days of living on ravioli heated on an Esbit cookstove meant that a decent restaurant meal was on the top of today's agenda. I parked Buba in front of the *Murat Lokantasi*, a simple eatery in Agri on the eponymous river. I threaded my fishing line through the door handles and activated my alarm system. Due to a lack of sufficient language skills, I went into the kitchen, at the owner's invitation, and showed him what appealed to my palate: three lamb cutlets, rice pilaf, and mixed vegetables. The meat was seasoned and roasted right before my very eyes, so that my mouth was watering even as everything was being prepared. It tasted even better than it looked! And afterwards there was a big glass of Cay. The best meal since Istanbul! I had totally forgotten to ask about the price—but otherwise, you'd never treat yourself to anything! When asked for the bill, the owner scrawled the number 3.5 on a piece of paper. I did a moment's calculation and asked, in disbelief, "Turkish liras?"

The owner nodded. I generously rounded it up to four liras and the man thanked me effusively. Four Turkish liras equaled 88 German pennies. Why the hell had I stashed twenty cans of ravioli and been living off these over the past several days in a country where for the same price you could have a feast, including a hot beverage and tip?

During the entire stretch to Dogubeyazit, jutting into the sky in my direction of travel was a majestic snow-capped mountain—Mount Ararat! Here is where Noah's ark was said to have been stranded after the Flood.

At the border station on the Turkish side, an elegant imprint reading *Gürbulak Hudut Kapisi* (Gürbulak Border Gate) was stamped in my passport, and I carefully observed how the passport controls operated—on the opposite side, too. Both Turkish customs officials seemed to be going about their business quite casually.

The border town on the Iranian side was called Bazargan. It took a while until the Iranian border guard, a slender, middle-aged, almost emaciated man with a hook nose and an inscrutable poker face, headed towards me and signaled for me to get out.

"Salaam! Passport!" he said.

I returned the greeting with a reciprocal "Salaam" and handed him my passport. He held it upside down for a while, leafing through it backwards. Only when he discovered the photo did he turn the passport right side up.

I quickly noticed that he spoke nothing but Farsi, so we had to communicate by means of gesticulating. He pointed at Buba, a gesture that was very unspecific. I pointed to the trunk, which, of course, on a VW Beetle is located at the front. The customs officer shook his head. Then I pointed to the engine compartment. More head-shaking. The car's interior? Even more headshaking. What the hell did the man want to see? Nothing at all? Then he ought to just stamp my passport and let me through.

Then, with the swiftness and purposefulness of a dowser detecting a vein of water, the wiry border guard bent under the driver's seat and quickly snatched out my Makarov, switched off the safety, and fired the pistol once in the air.

I was flabbergasted! All right, after the skirmish between the Kurds and Turks I had no longer been careful about pulling the blanket over the aluminum plates to which the pistol had been attached with Velcro. But how was it that he had searched exactly there, and nowhere else? The shot he fired into the air must have alerted all his associates. Had the moment arrived for some proper baksheesh? I estimated that an Iranian border guard earned a salary of $100 a month, maximum.

The man tapped my passport with the barrel of the loaded Makarov, which still had the safety off. With a furrowed brow, he ordered me to follow him.

While following behind him, I employed some sleight-of-hand to sneak a $100 bill out of my jacket, fold it lengthwise, and shove it underneath my watch strap on the inside of my left wrist. If the border guard or one of his associates suddenly wanted to see my raised hands, I could pull the bill out of the strap with my middle and index finger, then wave it around to deescalate the situation.

Inside the little customs shack, to my astonishment, nobody was around but the two of us. The shack's sole contents consisted of a chair, a desk, a red telephone whose wires weren't connected to anything, and a couple of handstamps along with their ink pads. The border guard sat down, laid my Makarov on the desk, leafed through my passport to find an empty page, and began writing.

For a brief moment, sudden inspirations from my CIA training flashed through my head: *Grab the weapon—blast his head off—get the hell out!*

But the man hadn't done anything except surprise me by discovering my pistol. Why should I kill him?

After the border guard had filled up an entire page of my passport with handwriting, he stamped it *Entry – Bazargan*, complete with the date according to the reckoning of the Iranian calendar. Then he grabbed the Makarov—with the safety still off—and gesticulated with the barrel at what he had written. Finally, he returned the passport and pistol, dismissing me with the same poker face with which he had initially greeted me.

Apparently, the border guard was interested only in having the weapon properly declared and noted in my passport. He had simply ignored the fact that *he* was the one who had found the weapon in my car. Language problems? Generosity? Bureaucratic laziness? Iranian mentality? Different laws? Whatever! Relieved, I started off to Tehran, and just after crossing the border, I was simply astonished. The previous 1500 kilometers of rocky, dusty roadbed, studded with potholes, abruptly morphed into a well-maintained four-lane highway heading straight for the horizon. Not only had the United States groomed Shah Mohammed Reza Pahlavi as the country's authoritarian ruler and established numerous military bases in Iran, but the Americans had also invested a tidy sum in the country's infrastructure. To the right and left of the impeccable concrete roadbed, the desert stretched out, endlessly wide. It was 300 kilometers to Tabriz, then another 700 kilometers to Tehran. Plenty of time to think things over.

How was my Fae doing? How would our reunion turn out? Would she be prepared to go on the lam with me? Would her mother in Munich take her back? Would we get closer to one another than we had in Heidelberg back then? How would it feel when we kissed each other with the same abandon that the medical student Uschi had kissed me farewell? Would we sleep together on the journey back? Would she want to do it on Buba's back seat with me, or only out of gratitude? I resolved not to sleep with Fae Fatima during the drive back, come what may. Maybe later. I had made my way to Tehran because I liked Fae, because I had the feeling I could do a good thing, and, last but not least, simply out of a desire for adventure. And matters ought to be left at that.

* * *

In the Amir Kabir Hotel on Tehran's Naser Khosrow Street, the fan-equipped room cost U.S. $3, exactly as Diogenes had said. The foyer was graced with a rectangular fountain, lovingly decorated with flowers. Both the fountain and the elegant marble floor suggested a much better class of hotel. In the sparse, yellow-whitewashed room there stood a clean, made-up bed with a clean linen cloth for a cover and a small pillow. Plaster was peeling off the walls. From the ceiling, a lightbulb was hanging on two wires, with the fan next to it. There was no wardrobe and no nightstand, just a nail in one of the walls, and on the other one a large sliver of a broken mirror. The nicest thing about the room was undoubtedly the window, with a view of the inner courtyard with the soothing, splashing fountain. For the shower—which my sweat-soaked body craved more than anything else—I actually had to pay U.S. $0.10 in advance. For that, when I opened up the tap all the way, all I got was a little lukewarm water. It took what seemed like half an hour until I covered my entire body with water this way. In this country and at this time of year, water was precious.

It was late in the afternoon. Freshly showered and dressed, I went down to the reception and called Fae's friend, the one whose telephone number Fae had included in the letter. Jasmin spoke fluent German and was very friendly. She promised to let Fae know where I could be found.

Right after exchanging a few Deutschmarks for Iranian rials at the reception, I received a call: "Michael! You're really in Tehran? What a surprise!" said Fae.

"Yes, I took off right after getting your letter. Sending a reply would have taken longer than the drive from Munich to Tehran. How are you doing? Can we meet?"

"Did you fly? Or did you take the bus?"

"I got here by car, an old VW Beetle," I replied.

"Can you be at the main entrance to the German School in Gholhak tomorrow afternoon at two? It's in the north part of town. Everyone around there knows the school. Then I'll come out and look around for a VW Beetle with Munich license plates."

"Great, let's do it. I'm already really looking forward to it," I said.

"So am I," whispered Fae. Then she hung up.

Now I was in a terrific mood. I looked around the neighborhood in the hotel's immediate vicinity for a good restaurant, and treated myself to a tasty shish kebab with saffron rice, roasted tomatoes, and onions for sixty rials, which came to about 2.50 Deutschmarks.

On the way back to the hotel, I noticed the extremely wide channels running between the sidewalks and the streets. These rain gutters were almost as wide as the sidewalks themselves. Whenever it does rain here, it probably comes down in buckets, so they have to provide sufficient drainage. Due to the scanty, sometimes nonexistent streetlighting, pedestrians had to be careful not to stumble into one of these enormous channels.

That night I slept well—really well!

I used the next morning to explore the city on foot a little. The Amir Kabir was centrally located, relatively speaking. The main city park was 300 meters to the west, and twenty minutes' walk along the magnificent Ferdowsi Avenue led me to the famous National Jewelry Museum, housed in the Iranian Central Bank building located diagonally opposite from the German Embassy. At the museum, I marveled at the sumptuous Pahlavi Crown, the priceless, 182-carat Daria-i-Noor diamond, and finally, the legendary Peacock Throne. All the while, I was being followed by inconspicuous, gray-suited men wearing dark sunglasses. My shadows bore a name: SAVAK, the Shah of Iran's dreaded, notorious Intelligence and Security Organization.

My heart beat faster upon looking in my rearview mirror and seeing Fae head toward me. She was wearing brown jeans and a light-yellow T-shirt. Her pitch-black hair was wafting in the wind, and her beaming smile was already discernible at a distance. I climbed out of the car and went to her. I would have gladly clasped her in my arms and held her very tightly. But there were passersby on the street, and I wasn't sure how this kind of greeting would go over around here. Fae stuck out her hand to me. No kiss like in Munich. This restraint was probably due to the customs of the country.

"Lovely to see you, Michael! You look great!" said Fae.

"You too!" I replied.

"We're having a school festival today. There's really a lot going on! Want to come along?"

"Is it that easy?" I asked, somewhat startled.

"The German School in Tehran is the largest German school outside Germany itself. We've got over 1500 students here, so I'm sure you won't stand out," Fee said, motioning for me to follow her. She crossed the street and went through a gate, behind which stretched an enormous, well-tended lawn.

A festive mood prevailed. Colorful balloons floated in the air, school bands were playing both German and Iranian music, and there were Hamburg-style fish sandwiches, fries, Allgäu egg noodles slathered in cheese, shish kebabs, and lamb chops. Fae introduced me to Jasmin, her best friend, the one who had spoken with me on the phone. Jasmin could have passed for her twin sister. Fae then showed me her classroom and the gym. It definitely seemed as though she would feel comfortable here. But sometimes, appearances can be deceiving.

"I would really like to talk with you in private! Can we do that somewhere?" I asked.

Fae thought a moment.

"We could drive just ten kilometers north of here. That's where the city ends, and the mountains begin."

I nodded.

Buba was struggling because Tehran lies at a high elevation, and in addition to that, has a steep north-south gradient. The city's Gholak neighborhood was already 500 meters higher than the Amir Kabir Hotel, and now the road heading northbound was substantially climbing yet again. I had to take a break to adjust the carburetor again in order for Buba to get enough oxygen.

We stopped on an isolated mountain road at a place wide enough so that two oncoming cars could drive past one another. However, the entire time we stayed there, not a single car came. In either direction.

After we got out of the car, I hugged Fae and pressed her body against mine. It just had to be! Fae silently hugged me back and held me tightly against her wonderful breasts.

Then I came right to the point that was weighing most heavily on my mind.

"Your letter sounded very despondent," I began. "You asked me to rescue you and bring you back to Munich. That's why I'm here."

Fae remained quiet. A long time. So long, in fact, that I cautiously broached the subject again, asking her, "Has something changed since you wrote the letter? Do you really want to go back to Munich?"

Fae didn't say a word. Finally she plucked up her courage and ended the torturously long silence.

"When I wrote you the letter, I was severely depressed. I even wanted to take my own life. Then my dad took such wonderful care of me… He promised me that after graduating high school I could go wherever I wanted. Then I felt better. Believe me, I'd like nothing better than to drive off to Munich with you right away. But that would break my father's heart. On top of that, he's hidden my passport."

"No problem! I've got a passport for you," I said, playing my trump card.

"*Whaaat*? Lemme see!" Fae Fatima shouted. I couldn't tell whether her shout was one of horror or joy. I showed her the passport that I'd bought off the old man in Istanbul.

"But that isn't me," Fae exclaimed.

"All I need is a passport photo from you. Then I'll swap the pictures so perfectly that we can safely make it back to Germany. Trust me! We can also get your passport photo taken along the way, in Tabriz. If you want, all you need to do is to hop in the car, and we'll drive straight to Munich immediately," I offered.

Once again, Fae lapsed into a long silence; tears were streaming out of her eyes. I embraced her and held her tight for a while, until she slowly pulled away from me, saying, "I'm scared. I don't think I can do that. Not now!"

"I want to help you. But no way do I want to force you into doing something you don't want. Do you need some time to think it over?" I asked.

Fae Fatima nodded.

"How long?"

"Maybe…a week?" Fae said inquiringly.

I thought it over briefly. I had now driven such a great distance that everything shouldn't have to hinge on a single week. Surely I would find a way to somehow pass the time.

"Okay, Fae. Maybe I'll travel through the country a little, and in about a week I'll get in touch with Jasmin again. My offer still stands. I can hardly wait to find out how you decide."

Before we got back into the Beetle, Fae paused a moment and said, "Look at what a terrific view we've got from here! To the south, all of Tehran is spread out at our feet, and to the north, behind this mountain, there are even taller mountains. You can even go skiing there in the winter. And right behind that lies the Caspian Sea."

* * *

The Amir Kabir hotel also maintained two hostel-style dormitory rooms, each of which contained eight beds.

Here, globetrotting travelers could bunk down for U.S. $1 per night. In these dorms, travelers from all over the world were busily engaged in lively exchanges about their experiences. I simply joined in and keenly listened to the stories being told. One Dutch hippie couple was totally enthusiastic about Kabul, the capital of Afghanistan, and I recalled that Diogenes had also waxed lyrical about it.

"How far is it to Kabul?" I asked.

"Two thousand kilometers—but it's really worth it!"

"What's the best way to get there?"

"There's the option of going either by car or by bus. But the roads are really bad, at least after you cross the Afghan border, so if you take your own car you can't drive at night. The bus drives straight through, and the entire trip takes about thirty-three hours, including a couple of piss breaks. The bus departs from the station here every day at six in the morning and costs six bucks U.S. each way."

For a little baksheesh, I was able to store Buba in a garage that belonged to one of the hotel owner's brothers. In order to prevent the helpful brother from getting any dumb ideas, I showed him—without letting him look into the car's interior—my alarm system and made him believe that I was the only one able to deactivate it with the key to my Munich apartment. In the event anybody broke into the car, I said, the system would keep blaring loudly until the battery was finally drained.

The next morning, I was sitting in the bus to Kabul. Thirty-three hours there, five days' stay, another thirty-three hours for the return leg. In eight days I would be back in Tehran and find out what Fae had decided.

It was distinctly more relaxing to be relieved from worrying about road and traffic conditions. Instead, I was able to comfortably cruise through the region on the well-upholstered seat of an Afghan bus while sometimes gazing out the window. The ride across the Iranian plateau offered breathtaking views of the Elbrus mountains in the north and the Great Salt Desert in the South. Heading through Shahrud, Sabzevar, and Mashad, we crossed the border at Taybad, down into the Valley of Herat, and then about 2300 meters up the mountain again to Chaghcharan, in Afghanistan. Despite the high elevation, the road was lined with a wide variety of mountain vegetation. One of the two bus drivers, who took alternating shifts, explained to me during a break that some of these herbs had terrific healing properties and grew nowhere else in the world. On the downhill side, shimmering blue, red, and violet fields of opium poppies delighted the eye, like the Dutch tulip fields, which I knew only from brochures. The Kingdom of Afghanistan had been ruled by Mohammed Zahir Shah for almost forty years. The Pashto king opened his country up to the outside world, allowed girls to attend school, and governed his country through a *loya jirga*, a large council in which the numerous Afghani tribal chieftains could exchange their views and unify.

Sometime in the afternoon of the second day, we reached Kabul. I found an affordable hotel in the city's Shahr-e Kohna quarter. The rooftop terrace afforded an expansive view of the alleys and byways of the Old City, and from it I could observe the population's lives and activities. The women wore black veils or burkas, and the men had on brightly colored long pants with knee-length collarless shirts over them, and Pashtun caps on their heads. One was driving three goats before him, while another was leading a donkey laden with sacks. The scene reminded me of stories from the Bible. I imagined that life in the time of Jesus of Nazareth must have resembled something like this.

I took a tour of the city on a German-made bus—manufactured by the company MAN—*Maschinenfabrik Augsburg-Nürnberg*—then visited the magnificent Pul-e Khishti mosque, the country's largest. Next I saw the Palace of the King, who governed his country so wisely and peaceably, and finally the marketplace. On the Koch-e Murgha, a busy Old Town commercial thoroughfare known as Chicken Street, I thought my eyes were deceiving me: walking right alongside an Afghani policeman was a man wearing the uniform of a Munich foot patrolman. I couldn't resist speaking to him: "Hello, Officer! What on earth are you doing here?"

In a friendly voice with a Bavarian-accented timbre, the policeman replied, "We've been invited by the King to train the Afghan police on behalf of the Free State of Bavaria. So sometimes we go on foot patrol with our colleagues." We exchanged some small talk for a few minutes, and both of us got a kick out of such an unusual encounter, so far from home.

* * *

Once back in Tehran, I rang up Jasmin and asked her to let Fae know I was back in the city, and that she could reach me at the Amir Kabir.

Fae called me the next day and informed me without any fuss that she had decided to remain in Tehran with her father. But she did say that she had enjoyed my visit very much. I sympathized and wished her all the best, although—I have to admit—I was a little disappointed.

When I hung up, for a moment I thought I felt a tear welling up in my right eye. But I had been deluding myself. I couldn't cry. Why should I, anyway?

What I did feel like was having a good meal and some alcohol! A couple of streets away from the hotel, I spotted a restaurant run by Armenians—and hence Christians, so I could get a drink. I ordered myself Armenian tomato soup seasoned with onions, garlic, and herbs, Armenian kofta (a kind of meatball), Armenian beer, and, last but least, Armenian Ararat brandy.

The next day I fetched Buba from the garage, filled up the tank for 100 rials, and set out for home. In Erzurum, I decided that this time, I would take the route along the Black Sea through Trabzon and Samsun, just because I hoped that the nights there would be somewhat warmer than in the high country.

During a stop for gas in Türkiye, just beyond Trabzon, a young Turkish guy was bent on buying my U.S. Army sheath knife off me. I had been wearing the knife on my belt throughout the entire trip. Naturally, I did not sell it! The man claimed that it was illegal in Türkiye to openly carry a fixed-blade knife of this size on your belt, and that such an offense could result in fines and prison time. If I didn't sell him the knife, he said, he would tell his friends at the police about it. What a bunch of crap! It was a ridiculous threat, and I ignored it.

Unfortunately, that carelessness actually did get me three days' detention in a Turkish village jail. The one-man cell was considerably filthier than the one at Fort Campbell had been, but at least it was warmer. The very first thing my jailors did was to attach an ankle shackle with a chain about a meter long. And the chain actually had a heavy steel ball at the other end. Unbelievable! Until then, this was something I had seen only in cartoons. The food looked so unappetizing that I just made do with a few bites of rice. On the third day, I was suddenly released—without any charges or proceedings—for a baksheesh payment of 500 Turkish liras, and to my great amazement, I even got my U.S. Army sheath knife back.

North of Samsun, a flat beach with fine sand beckoned invitingly for a swim. I did a few refreshing laps in the Black Sea, poured the contents of my reserve canister into the tank, and took a leisurely drive further along the coast. After about forty kilometers, at the edge of a village called Cakalli, Buba quit on me. Neither fine coaxing nor tinkering with the carburetor could persuade the car to start. Not even cleaning all the spark plugs helped. As had already occurred so often in Türkiye, this time around I also had good luck—one of the villagers spoke German and immediately mobilized a colorful squad of muscular countrymen. Ten Turks pooled their strength to lift Buba onto the bed of a truck. I was simultaneously moved and impressed, and wanted to express my gratitude with some baksheesh. But the men unanimously and categorically refused. True men of honor, these Turks! Most of them, anyway.

The truck brought Buba to a repair shop in Kavak, the next largest town. The master mechanic there, who had trained at Daimler in Stuttgart, spoke a little Swabian. He immediately suspected the carburetor, from which there was now dripping some sort of undefinable gunk. He disassembled the part completely, then cleaned and reassembled it, and soon Buba was purring along as usual.

I really got worried when the problem kept recurring every forty or fifty kilometers. It was still a good 2500 kilometers to Munich! And it wasn't always in a town when Buba's engine quit. Once I had to march ten kilometers in blazing midday heat back into the previous village to get help. The towing operations were quite the adventure. They ranged from lashing Buba to a Toyota with a meter-long hemp rope to transporting the Beetle on a donkey cart. The donkey struggled hard and needed an exhausting five hours to haul its owner, Buba, and me around twenty kilometers over hill and dale. I generously gave the helpful man far, far more than he had charged, and I requested that he prepare a feast for his donkey.

After the fourth breakdown like this, I observed not merely greasy gunk pouring out of the carburetor, but also outright foam. Then, suddenly, the scales fell from my eyes: in Samsung, I had used—for the second time—the reserve canister that had been rescued for me as a farewell present from the hospital trash by Uschi, the woman medical student. The canister had previously contained shampoo! Although Uschi had promised she had thoroughly rinsed out the canister with hot water, the gasoline had probably nevertheless dissolved traces of the shampoo, causing the mixture of shampoo and gasoline to clog the carburetor. After yet another round of cleaning the carburetor, draining the contents of the gas tank, and refilling it, Buba made it all the way—with just a few lapses—to my apartment on Belgradstrasse in Munich. Once there, Buba finally gave up the ghost forever; the engine no longer turned over. It just didn't want to keep going. Not even the road service guy from the ADAC, the General German Automobile Club, could get Buba to start. He declared my loyal traveling companion an irreparable pile of junk.

With a heavy heart, I had to have Buba towed and scrapped. Getting that done cost me 50 Deutschmarks— exactly the same amount I had paid for the Beetle.

CHAPTER 6

Shots Fired in Istanbul

Wednesday, October 25, 1972

I had been back from Tehran for about three weeks, and over the last fortnight I had successfully completed my internship at the clinic, and in tandem with that, the paramedic course.

At three in the morning, in the middle of the night, the telephone jangled. Groggy with sleep, I grabbed the receiver and answered, "Müller."

"We're going away for a couple of days, darling. Pack a couple of things. We'll meet at eleven in the morning under the column at the Angel of Peace," a friendly female voice told me in a personable American accent.

"Okay," I confirmed, and hung up.

The conversation hadn't lasted ten seconds, and I knew what to do. Although there would have been several hours remaining for me to sleep, there was no more thought of that. Four months ago, after my final examination at CIA Headquarters in Langley, I had been placed under the command of two liaison officers: one at the Frankfurt Rhine-Main Air Base, who was in charge of Middle East assignments, and another in Salzburg, who handled jobs in the Eastern Bloc. I packed my toilet articles, some underwear, and two shirts in a small travel bag, and at 0535 I took the first train out of Munich Central Station heading to Frankfurt am Main.

'Column at the Angel of Peace' was the code for a meeting with my CIA handler on the Rhine-Main Air Base, at the south end of the Frankfurt airport. The tall, athletic officer with the crewcut and aviator sunglasses identified himself as Joe Smith. After a quick briefing, he handed me two passports, three tickets, and an envelope full of money. Then he bade me farewell with the edifying line: "If anything goes wrong, this meeting never took place. The United States Government does not know you and has nothing to do with the affair."

I nodded without a word, took a taxi to the civilian section of the airport, memorized my new identity, then checked in for the Istanbul flight at the window of Hava Yollari, or Turkish Airlines. Departure was set for 1355, arriving at 1710.

Since this was my first assignment, they probably didn't want to overwhelm me. It was supposed to be an easy job: hand over the passports and be done with it. And for that, I would get to spend a short vacation in Istanbul—and receive a nice chunk of money.

Istanbul again! What a city! After arriving at Yeşilköy Airport, at the duty-free shop I was greatly excited to find the LP "Machine Head," the latest masterpiece by the hard rock band Deep Purple. I also bought a bottle of a Turkish cologne with a heavy, sultry fragrance, as well as a bottle of Jim Beam. Then I took a taxi into the city and had the driver drop me off at the Hotel Ordu, on the Ordu Caddesi. The room was simple, but good enough for two nights. The passports and tickets were supposed to be handed over on the following day, at 10:15 in the morning in the airport men's room. As a deception tactic, my flight to Munich would depart a day later, via Cairo.

But first of all, I now had fifteen hours at my disposal in this history-steeped city—Constantinople, Byzantium, or whatever this pearl of the Middle East happened to be called. I set out to explore a couple of new sections of the pulsating metropolis, areas that had remained uninvestigated during my previous visit here a few weeks before. I wandered north, over the Galata Bridge, a floating pontoon structure, and enjoyed the view of the Golden Horn. Hobby anglers were casting their lines from the bridge into the water, and barbecuing some of their fresh catch right on the spot over buckets of glowing charcoal. Restaurants and shops selling carpets, bric-a-brac, and sweets lined the streets between the Galata Bridge and Taksim Square; exhilarating Middle Eastern music could be heard everywhere. People seemed to be enjoying life! Right after I began scouting around for a good restaurant, my curiosity was piqued an especially full one, blaring especially loud music. I ventured a couple of steps into the room, in which every table was occupied by well-dressed people cheerfully feasting. Then a young man came up to me. Surely, I thought, he intended to request that I leave the place, due to my inappropriate clothing—I was wearing nothing but jeans and a plain blue shirt. To my astonishment, he inquired of me in good German: "Would you tell me which city you come from?"

"Munich," I replied tersely.

The young man's facial expression brightened: "Ah, Bavaria, Oktoberfest, lederhosen, King Ludwig! I went there once. Beautiful city. I grew up in Duisburg. My parents worked there. My brother is getting married today. I would be delighted—and I'm sure he would be too—if you could be our guest."

So, unexpectedly, I spent a wonderful, spontaneous evening at an illustrious wedding party, where I was wined and dined with the country's best delicacies at the table they showed me. Everybody went to great lengths to help me understand and appreciate the Turkish culture and way of life. After several glasses of Raki, a clear anise liquor that's made cloudy by adding a little water, I danced exuberantly to Turkish music with the newly-weds and guests. Never in my life, not even during my last trip across Türkiye, had I ever experienced so much unadulterated hospitality!

The trip was already worth it just for this evening alone; during the party, I had almost forgotten my original purpose for being there. But the job would be an easy one: hand over the passport and ticket inconspicuously and be done with it.

The night was brief, mainly because a muezzin from the minaret just ten meters away from my hotel window persistently kept trying to convert me to Islam.

Around ten the next morning, I arrived at Istanbul's Yeşilköy Airport. The men's room that had been described as a rendezvous point, near the main entrance, was closed due to construction. Signs directed the public to a make-shift, temporary restroom a few feet off the main entrance. I observed the surroundings and reported to the men's room promptly at 10:15. Several men were standing at the urinals. There were four lockable stalls, one of which was occupied. None of the men at the urinals even remotely resembled my subject, Paul Keppler, whose American passport I had with me. I locked myself in the stall next to the occupied one and waited a moment. Then I whispered, "Let the sunshine in, Paul."

Not a stir. I spoke up louder: "Let the sunshine in, Paul!"

Still no reaction whatsoever to the stipulated code.

I decided to climb onto the toilet bowl and peek into the neighboring stall. Sitting there was a man, his pants pulled down, staring straight ahead.

"Pssst! Paul! I've got something for you!"

Startled, the man glanced up and pulled up his pants. No doubt about it—he was the man in the passport photo: round face, a slight exophthalmos, around sixty, gray hair.

"Everything all right?" I asked. The man nodded wordlessly. I handed him the passport and ticket, whereupon my task—as spelled out in my assignment—was completed. But I had a funny feeling.

As I was leaving the makeshift restrooms, there was a bang, and the numerous pigeons that had settled on the plaza in front of the airport building scattered, flapping into the sky. I was unable to make out the bang. Was someone around here shooting pigeons with an air rifle? No, the noise had been louder than an air rifle—but not as loud as a .45 magnum. Maybe a small-caliber rifle? A second bang followed, then a third, and I sensed a stabbing pain in my left calf.

Twisted ankle? Pinched nerve? These were my first thoughts. Suddenly I saw the hole in my jeans and felt the blood oozing into my left shoe. All of a sudden, Paul Keppler was close behind me; he seemed visibly confused. I grabbed him by the hand and yanked him, lightning quick, into the first taxi waiting in line in front of the airport. The car was only a few meters away.

"To the bazaar! Quickly—*vite, vite, rapido, schnell, schnell, yallah, yallah!*" I shouted in every language I could think of, flashing a $100 bill in the driver's face.

Had the shot been meant for me? Or for Paul Keppler? Or maybe it really was just for one of these pigeons?

My leg hardly hurt, but wouldn't stop bleeding. Probably a flesh wound, or a bullet lodged in my calf. I summarily relieved Paul of his necktie and put an improvised tourniquet over my jeans and against the wound. The taxi driver had a distinctly unconventional driving style, dashing through multiple red lights, then abruptly stopping for green ones. At times he drove too slowly; at others, too fast. It was a good thing, too—anyone pursuing us who attempted to match this driving style measure for measure would have been quickly busted. But I was unable to spot anyone in pursuit, and I recalled what I had learned at Langley: *Never lull yourself into a false sense of security! Put yourself into your adversary's position! Make things as tough as possible for him!* So the thing for it was to get out of the taxi, simply bolt through the bazaar's crowds and serpentine byways, then grab another taxi on the other side—that ought to make life hell for anyone giving chase! If you've already been wearing a tail for a while, where will your pursuer waylay you? In your hotel? At the airport? At the train station? At the border? You've got to be faster than he is—and choose a direction he won't suspect.

An hour later, Paul Keppler and I were sitting in a bus bound for Ankara. I abandoned the bottle of Turkish cologne, with its heavy, sultry fragrance, as well as the bottle of Jim Beam, leaving them as a treat for the receptionists at the Hotel Ordu. But it was a shame about the brand-new Deep Purple LP. It was simply too far removed from Turkish tastes in music and would likely end up in the trash.

Paul Keppler wasn't particularly talkative. After about an hour's ride, he confessed to me that he was afraid. I tried to reassure him, whispering, "Fear is a poor advisor. Tell me who or what you're afraid of, and I'll help you. In Ankara I'll get us tickets for wherever the next flight is heading. But there will be situations that you will have to handle alone. For instance, check-in, passport control, and customs. It could get dangerous if we show up there together."

"You've given me an American passport," Keppler said, almost reproachfully. "Whatever English I taught myself back in Saxony is really terrible. At school they teach you only Russian in the German Democratic Republic. I'm afraid the guards will notice I'm not American and that my name isn't Paul Keppler."

I spent the remaining four hours of the ride bolstering Paul Keppler's self-confidence and drilling him on getting through every conceivable situation at check-in as well as at passport control and customs, all in good English. And we thought up a plausible biography for him, containing true components that he liked and was able to remember.

It worked! Shortly before midnight on the very same day, we landed at Frankfurt Airport. Using the secret, toll-free CIA number in Langley, I sent for Joe Smith to come to a café at the airport, and I briefly summarized what had occurred. He took charge of Paul Keppler. Somehow, I couldn't resist the impression that Joe already knew everything I was telling him. This damned poker face didn't seem a bit surprised. But he surprised me—with a nicely filled envelope.

It was far more than I had expected. But I already knew what to do with it. The outcome of my first "hot" assignment put me in a happy, satisfied frame of mind just as much as my principal's financial recognition did.

I never did learn who Paul Keppler really was and why they wanted to bring this timid creature to the United States. To this day, a deep scar on my left calf serves as a memento of my first assignment.

CHAPTER 7

Death in the Sleeping Car

A few days after returning from Istanbul—by now it was November—I used some of the fee money from my first assignment to buy myself a new car, and I put aside something for a road trip and the next few months. Buba's successor became a four-year-old, bright yellow Ford Capri with a black roof. And it wanted to be driven. Now while I had already traveled around half the globe, I knew my own country hardly at all. That was due for a change. Germany and a couple of neighboring countries' cities that sounded interesting ought to be manageable in a month. My trip first took me to Hamburg, at the other end of the Republic, then through Bremen, Osnabrück, Amsterdam, Dusseldorf, Cologne, Frankfurt, Stuttgart, Zurich, Vienna, Graz, Venice, and Milan, then back to Munich. But I hadn't reckoned with the sudden onset of winter weather right at the beginning of my journey. In wet snow and slush, Hamburg's Reeperbahn isn't even half as enjoyable as on a pleasantly warm summer evening. The same goes for Amsterdam's canals and for Lake Zurich, as well as the Prater, Vienna's famous amusement park. Even the Piazza San Marco in Venice didn't have much real charm, although there it wasn't snowing—just cold and uncomfortable, with the rain coming down in buckets. I had learned my lesson: between mid-October and Easter, to hell with Europe and its cities, for all I cared!

It was 11:00 p.m. Suffering from a slight head cold, I was back in my apartment slurping a cup of peppermint tea when the phone rang.

"Hello, Michael, do you know who this is?" asked a friendly female voice in a slight American accent.

"But of course! Michelle!" I lied, "How're you doing?"

For a brief moment, there was silence at the other end of the line. Then giggling.

"Good guess! Do you feel like going with me to a concert tomorrow? A Mozart piano concert, the afternoon performance at three o'clock. I've got two complimentary tickets."

Now my doorbell buzzed three times.

"All right, darling. We'll meet at the entrance," I replied and hung up.

The conversation had lasted under thirty seconds and contained three code words familiar to me:

'Concert' stood for a longer mission briefing. 'Mozart' meant a meeting place at the counter of the American Express Bank at the Residenzplatz in Salzburg. And finally, 'complimentary ticket' meant that both out-of-pocket expenses and a travel allowance were covered.

At long last, I was getting the opportunity to make the acquaintance of the second of my two CIA agent handlers, and Salzburg, even in a snowstorm, was easier to reach than the Rhine-Main Air Base.

I arrived a bit early, so I ambled through Grain Street in Salzburg's Old Town, passed by Mozart's birthplace, and treated myself at the Café Tomaselli to a tasty Sacher torte and a "Tomaselli Melange" topped with whipped cream. At precisely 3:00 in the afternoon, I entered the American Express Bank and asked for the branch manager.

"Whom shall I say is calling?" asked the older lady at the counter.

"Mr. Cooper. I have an appointment," I replied.

After a few minutes, a tall, slender man in his fifties with thin hair and nickel-framed eyeglasses appeared. He was wearing an immaculately pressed brown suit with a crisp white shirt and an understated beige necktie.

"Mr. Cooper, I've been expecting you," he said. "My name is Frank Steiner." The branch manager extended his hand, escorted me into his office, and shut the door. He immediately noticed my glance briefly lingering on the thick padding covering the office door.

"This room is absolutely bugproof," Steiner said, gesturing, not without a measure of pride, to a small box squatting on his desk. The device, he explained, would immediately recognize and disrupt any radio signal emitted by a hidden bug. Then Steiner leafed through a file, compared me against the photo it obviously contained, and told me, in perfect German with a charming Austrian timbre, "There's a little bit of info about your training here, and it says that you're supposed to be one of our best escape agents. But I can't find anything about how you came to the CIA. That's unusual. Were you in the Army?"

"I am not permitted to tell you that, sir," I replied.

"Very good! That's what I wanted to hear," Steiner said. Speaking to his secretary over the intercom, he ordered two mélanges, each of which she served with a glass of water. Then he offered me a cigarette and began pacing back and forth in the room uneasily.

Finally he sat down again and said, "I want to be open with you. We lost a good man. He was smuggling people who were important for us out of the Eastern Bloc into the West, through Bulgaria."

"What do you mean by 'lost'? Was he murdered or captured?" I asked.

"We don't know. His last activity obviously went awry four weeks ago. He hasn't reported back since then. Moreover, neither the Russians nor the Bulgarians have offered to make any exchange. But also, it would still be too soon for that—assuming he's still alive," Steiner replied.

"How did he previously operate? What route did he use to bring his subjects into the West?" I wanted to know.

"He rode on the sleeping car to Sofia, where he stowed the respective subject all the way to Germany in a secret hollow space on the railroad car."

"Who knew or knows about this secret hollow space?"

"SDECE, the French intelligence service. And the CIA," Steiner replied.

"How come the French know about it?"

"Every sleeping car used in the European railroad system is operated by the international sleeping car company, CIWLT, which stands for *Compagnie International des Wagons-Lits et due Tourisme*. It's a French outfit. Don't ask me who installed the secret compartment, but in Compartment 13 of every car belonging to CIWLT, there's one of these stowaway spaces located under the floor. And it's large enough to conceal an adult."

"If the secret of the hiding place has now leaked out, they're going to be tightening the checks at every border crossing," I said. "You don't by any chance want to use me as cannon fodder and lose another good man, do you?" I asked, a bit insolently.

"It wasn't the hiding place that got exposed. The most recent subject arrived in the West safe and sound. It's only our man who has disappeared without a trace. Presumably it occurred to the Bulgarians that he was frequently spending time in Sofia, always for just a day or a couple of hours."

"And what if—in the event that he's still even alive at all—he talks and reveals the hiding place? Perhaps he's even being tortured?" I asked apprehensively.

"He won't talk. He was in Vietnam, and the Viet Cong tortured him for four months before we were able to free him. He didn't betray a single name or a single one of our positions," Steiner replied.

"And if I take the job and remain in Sofia every time for an entire week, don't you think that would draw attention?" I asked in disbelief.

"We've thought up something better," Steiner continued, countering my question with another one: "Who can hang around at the train station without drawing attention to himself? And who has absolute authority over the entire sleeping car?"

"The sleeping car conductor!" I replied, without having to ponder the matter for long.

"Correct! We want to propose to you that you get yourself trained as a sleeping car conductor and use this job to smuggle the subject out. That's the perfect cover, and you can earn yourself a tidy sum in the process!"

After a brief pause to think it over, I asked, "What does a sleeping car conductor earn? And how long is the apprenticeship?"

"It's more like on-the-job training than a proper apprenticeship. They're looking for people right now! Most of them are allowed to travel along every route after three months. The salary is hardly enough for you to live on, but anyone who gets the hang of the routine earns good tips. A lot of them also smuggle slivovitz and gin into the West, and into the East they smuggle ball-point pens, brand-name fountain pens, compact radios, and nylons. But you should concentrate on your task. Even during your training phase you should keenly observe what's going on, and where the opportunities and risks lie. For doing that, you'll be paid an extra $1,000 U.S. by us, over and above your salary, either in cash or American Express traveler's checks. As soon as you're allowed to go on every route alone, report back to me, and you'll receive your first assignment. Are you game?"

"How much is the bounty if I get people to the West?"

"$3,000 U.S."

"$5,000!" I demanded in a firm voice. "After all, I am risking something, maybe even my life."

Steiner hesitated for a moment. Then he gave me his hand and said, "Okay, $5,000! But only for successful missions—when the subject arrives in the West alive. The *Wagons-Lits* representative in Munich is called ISTG, the International Sleeping Car and Tourism Company. The address is Bayerstrasse 16, at the Holzkirchner station, the southern annex of Munich Central Station."

"I know the place. I'll apply there tomorrow, right away!"

"Wait a moment, Mr. Cooper! Your name at the ISTG will be Hans Gruber, and you come from Passau. Here's your passport, as well as your curriculum vitae, today's expenses, and an advance for the training period."

Steiner shoved a thick envelope in my hand and escorted me to the exit.

"How did you actually know that I would agree to do it?" I asked him as we were saying our goodbyes. But all Steiner did was laugh and leave me awaiting a reply.

* * *

The ISTG office in Munich was staffed by two individuals, Mr. and Mrs. Dombrowski. Mr. Dombrowski was the boss. Nobody knew what he actually did, aside from being the boss. Mrs. Dombrowski, a voluptuous blonde of around fifty with pinned-up hair and trendy, black-rimmed glasses, served as his secretary. She did the hiring and was in charge of the staff rosters, bookkeeping, and pay packets. She offered me her hand and said, "You can start tomorrow. Come here to the office at seven in the morning. You'll then ride with the cleaning crew to the Pasing switching yard."

"How come the cleaning crew?" I asked.

"First off, you've got to become thoroughly acquainted with our coaches—and that involves cleaning and vacuuming them, as well as making up the beds. That has to be learned above all else. Later on, when you go on your own trips, you will have to be able to do that on your own. Our cleaning crew does it on a siding in Pasing, but only after the longer trips."

"And how long does this bedmaking and cleaning training period continue?" I wanted to know.

"As long as it takes until you can do it in your sleep and I've found someone who will take you along to break you in," replied Mrs. Dombrowski.

So every day, for two long weeks, I cleaned the royal blue sleeping cars with their stately gold *wagons-lits* emblem on each side, and made up bunk beds: a snow-white sheet over the mattress and another one underneath the burgundy wool blanket, which was tucked into it with nary a crease. Naturally, in an unguarded moment I also inspected Compartment 13. In the floor underneath the carpeting, there was actually a lid that could not be opened except with a triangular socket key. This lid was obviously the well-camouflaged access to the secret compartment, which could have just as easily been a maintenance hatch leading to the pipe conduits and cable ducts.

Every Monday, Mrs. Dombrowski handed me the pay packet, an envelope with a handwritten wage statement and cash, including coins. The earnings for six workdays at six hours each were just enough for a full tank of gas and a couple of evening beers at the *C'est la vie!* It was inconceivable how someone who made beds and did this cleaning could live on that.

After I passed my exceptionally demanding bed-making examination under the stern eyes of a Yugoslavian cleaning lady, things were to get underway. Mrs. Dombrowski handed me a brown uniform, the kind worn by the sleeping car conductors. It fit well enough and came complete with the requisite cap. She declared that starting the following day, I was to be assigned to Mr. Strauss, her most senior employee, to learn on the job. My first run was a trip from Munich to Genoa, then back two days later. She said she would let Mr. Strauss know.

Promptly at 1900, a good half hour prior to the train's departure, I, Hans Gruber, was standing on Platform 12 of Munich Central Station in my sleeping car conductor's uniform. I boarded the *Wagon-Lits* sleeping car, which easily stood out due to its color and emblems, and looked around for Mr. Strauss. He was kneeling on the floor at the front end of the car, trying to kindle the coal oven mounted there. It was designed to heat the entire car via circulating hot water. Naturally, Mr. Strauss had not been informed, and instead of greeting me, cursed like a sailor about old Dombrowski. He said he had told her a thousand times that he wanted to make all of his trips alone and didn't need any greenhorns watching him or asking stupid questions. Strauss was a ham-fisted, unrefined sort with an angular, pockmarked face and a powerful build, roughly the same age as Mrs. Dombrowski. He always had something to do, but during the entire twelve-hour train ride, he ignored me as though I weren't even there. I was first able to score some points with him at the siding in Genoa, where I made up fourteen beds spotlessly while he, in the same amount of time, managed to finish only four. Now, for the first time, he spoke with me and acknowledged that working alone, he needed a good four hours to handle all the beds. He offered to have a meal with me. I coolly declined, and we arranged when and where we would reconnoiter for the return trip two days later.

For the next thirty-two hours, I was now free to roam around Genoa: the harbor, the bay, and the tiny medieval houses built all over the hills. On this day, the city of Christopher Columbus's birth had but one small flaw—it was presenting itself in the wintertime. And as I already knew from my road trip, in winter, the most beautiful city in Europe is only half or a quarter as beautiful as it is in the summer. I would even say, a tenth as beautiful— perhaps, actually not even at all!

First I found—at a certain time interval from Strauss— the somewhat shabby hotel where Wagon-Lits rented rooms for their conductors. It was situated at the west end of the Via Balbi, only a few hundred meters from the Genova Piazza Principe, the main train station. I checked in, dropped off my travel bag in the room, and went to the closest pizzeria.

They brought the chianti quickly, but the salami pizza took an unusually long time. After having ravenously inhaled about half of it, I unexpectedly bit into something rock-hard, nearly breaking off a tooth in the process. There was a nail in the pizza—a great big bent, rusty nail! I called over the waiter and showed it to him, actually expecting an apology, perhaps even an espresso or a glass of grappa on the house. Far from it! All the waiter did was happily thank me for the found nail, which had broken off his pizza shovel. He had sorely missed it, because otherwise his tool would have completely fallen apart. I decided to let the matter go. After all, we were in Italy.

The Via Balbi was a true feast for the eyes, not just due to the imposing facades and balconies of the houses. During the day, the street, more of an alleyway, was lined with businesses, bars, and restaurants. Nights, the Via belonged to the red-light district. Hundreds of gorgeous girls in miniskirts plied their trade here after nightfall. I made an astonishing discovery: almost every one of the ladies had with her an iron tub, one-third full of glowing charcoal, and stood straddling over it. Wispy clouds of smoke rose out of the buckets. As soon it got too hot for one of the ladies between her legs, she would walk around the iron tub before straddling it again. I grinned to myself, shaking my head. Smoked pussy! They had to be the first to have come up with that! I'd never seen anything like that even in Amsterdam's red-light district or on Hamburg's Reeperbahn, although it had been considerably colder there!

"I'm Franz," said the man who was standing before our sleeping car half an hour before departure. Grinning from ear to ear, he stuck his hand out to me, adding, "Sorry that I was in such a bad mood yesterday. Today I'll explain to you everything you want to know, as well as what you don't want to know!"

It always makes me somewhat wary when someone does a 180 overnight. But an apology also evinces a human dimension. I accepted and said, "I'm Hans. Looking forward to working together!"

During this journey Franz Strauss actually explained a great deal to me, for example, how to check tickets and how we could issue new ones for passengers who hadn't booked any. He also showed me which doors, hatches, and hiding places could be opened with the ISTG four-way spider wrench, which consisted of two interior square sockets of differing sizes, in addition to a triangular interior socket and a four-way exterior square socket. He didn't mention the compartment hidden in the floor. Did he know about it?

"What trade did you actually learn?" I asked

"I was a butcher," he replied. "First an apprentice, then a fully certified one, a master. In Landshut, where I grew up. But at some point I wanted to get out of there and see the world. Then I saw an ad in the local paper and applied at ISTG. I've been with them ever since. It's been twenty-two years now."

And then Franz gave me a veritable secret tip: "You've got to check out people's shoes."

"Why their shoes?" I asked, astonished.

"Hand-sewn shoes made from the best leather, perfectly spit-shined—that's what reeks of good tips! Then you've got to hustle. If they're wearing worn-out, neglected shoes, they won't tip. And then you'll barely have to lift a finger at all," he said knowingly.

Over the next two and a half months, we crisscrossed Europe, traveling from Stuttgart to Budapest, from Paris and Prague to Munich, from Munich to Belgrade, and from Belgrade to Istanbul or Athens. Every stretch lasted between eight and fifteen hours, depending on the amount of waiting time at various borders, plus time spent on preparation and cleanup. Franz enjoyed the fact that thanks to my presence, he could take a nap now and then and be spared many hours of energy-sapping work making up beds. After all, he was no longer the youngest guy around.

Most frequently, we serviced the route between Munich and Belgrade, and the most-read book on this stretch was Agatha Christie's worldwide bestseller, *Murder on the Orient Express*. Once, someone left a copy in one of the compartments after finishing it. I confiscated it and devoured it on the return trip while an intense snowstorm was raging outside. The murder took place in a car of the same construction as our sleeping car, as it had to stop, due to large snowdrifts just before the city of Brod—which we ourselves were about to pass through. Brilliantly plotted and with an unusual conclusion!

As he always did when visiting the Yugoslavian capital, Franz had purchased thirty bottles of Maraska slivovitz and five cartons of Morava cigarettes for just a handful of dinars. Then he stashed the goods under the six cover plates around the ceiling lights in the aisle of the railroad car. No customs officer had ever looked here, he explained to me, and if one should hit upon the idea, then he would say he didn't know a thing—after all, the aisle was accessible to all the passengers in the entire train. Franz could sell the liquor and tobacco in Germany for ten times the price, and that way he could supplement his salary a little. The people with spotless, spit-shined shoes were becoming farther and fewer between. All the same, on each leg of the trip, Franz had to shell out two bottles of slivovitz: one went to the Yugoslavian cleaning lady, who had graded my bed-making examination. She picked up the bottles at the siding in Pasing. The other went to Mrs. Dombrowski.

"If you get in good with Mrs. Dombrowski and bring her a little something from each trip, then at some point you can mention your preferences for the work schedule," Franz advised me.

He bent down and pulled a metal bar out of the carpet.

"These T-bars are designed to keep the aisle carpets stretched apart at certain intervals. Actually, it's enough just to kick the carpets hard against the floor. But sometimes they come up and become a tripping hazard. Then you've got to tamp them tight against the floor again. Your best bet is to use your heel. And you know what else these rods are good for?"

I shook my head, and Franz continued: "For self-defense! You can use them to bash someone's head in! But mostly it's just enough to take the iron bar in both hands and threaten people with it. And something else—you can use these T-bars to lock people in—and a lot more securely than by using the four-sided key, because anyone can get hold of one of those. The compartment doors open outward. This bar is exactly as wide as the aisle, maybe just a couple of millimeters shorter. So, if you use some kind of suitable object, like a knife, fork, or screwdriver, to pry the bar up on one side, pull it out, then jam it between the compartment door and the wall of the aisle—nobody's ever going to escape!"

"Have you already tried that out?" I asked.

"Yeah, one time," Franz said. "It was in Vienna, on the run back from Belgrade. Two delightful gentlemen, both in suits, helped themselves to an empty compartment and refused either to pay or leave. You ought to have heard them rant and rave when I locked them in with the T-bar! It's still like music to my ears. Then, when we got to Salzburg, I handed them over to the Austrian border police. That took the turpentine out of their bark, all right!" Franz explained.

After completing my apprenticeship, or, better said, on-the-job training, for another four weeks—I traveled as the sleeping car conductor in charge—alone through Europe, to garner experience, to apprehend things unfiltered, from my own perspective, and to obtain a sense for what just might become important for me. For some time now, I had noticed that Compartment 13 stood empty practically all the time because people refused to book it, presumably out of pure superstition. And in addition to that, I noticed that the Bulgarian border officials always had dogs with them, were already on board in Sofia, and conducted their passport checks and sporadic luggage searches by slowly working their way aft, from the first to the last car. On this run, the sleeping car was the last one after the dining car. The customs officials had to get off in Dimitrovgrad, the first station on Yugoslavian territory, and ride back to Sofia on the next train. If they made slow progress with their checks, then by the time they reached my car, there would be time enough only for a cursory glance at the passports. On the other hand, if they worked their way through the other cars quickly, then in the sleeping car they would order every suitcase opened and stand around in the aisles for a long time. Then they even asked me about the "German Frauleins," wanting to know whether I could procure them a couple of porno magazines. That's a question they would never have asked in Franz's presence. And a good idea, in the event that perhaps a diversionary maneuver should be necessary.

* * *

Steiner was exceptionally enamored of my accomplishments. He wanted me to take charge in the following week of a subject in Sofia—a Bulgarian nuclear physicist who had long sought to defect to the West and could usefully serve the American government. However, the scientist spoke only Bulgarian and Russian. Steiner showed me a picture of him. In Sofia, a reliable man would accompany the physicist to the train and place him directly in Compartment 13 of the sleeping car. All I would then have to do is drop the man into the floor hatch at an opportune moment. Quite simple.

On the other hand, it was difficult to convince Steiner that in this instance, I was the one who had to specify the date. The trips ran either from Munich to Belgrade, from Belgrade to Istanbul, or from Belgrade to Athens. Usually, personnel were swapped out in Belgrade. It would be hard enough to obtain a double run straight through Istanbul and back on the following day. But that was the only way I would be able to ride on the sleeping car continuously from the stop in Sofia all the way to

Munich. As quickly as possible, I would try to get assigned to this run, then report again.

Two thoughts preoccupied me over the following days, before we set off on another short run to Genoa. First, how I could get Mrs. Dombrowski to assign me a double round trip—which, according to union rules, wasn't allowed—and secondly, what could minimize the risk of the Bulgarian customs dogs sniffing out someone hidden under the flooring? Then I remembered Chemical Charlie, our professor at the Farm.

"All of you, mark my words: coal absorbs toxins and odors! That can save your lives someday!" he had declared in one of his lectures, scrawling on the board, in great big letters, the sentence "*Coal sucks it all!*"

For some time now, I had noticed the small tailor shop just a few meters away from my apartment, located at the corner of Belgradestrasse and Destouchestrasse. I brought the proprietor, a friendly Greek lady, an old quilt cover that I had shortened a bit on the open side. I asked her to use the sewing machine to close it up all around once again and to stitch in small squares measuring between ten and twelve centimeters across. Then, going to ten separate pharmacies in Munich, at each one I bought five boxes containing carbon tablets—medicinal carbon that can be taken in the event of diarrhea or poisoning.

The quilt was ready after my return from Genoa. I pulverized the carbon tablets with a soup spoon and filled the quilt with the coal dust through small incisions in the individual pockets. This little bit of tinkering took me all night. Naturally, all the incisions had to be cleanly sewed back up again, but once the work was done, I was good and proud of the stench-eradication quilt I had devised for myself, and was able to relax and catch a couple hours of sleep. The next day, I brought Mrs. Dombrowski a "little souvenir" from Italy consisting of an enormous basket packed with various delicacies and fine wines—chianti, ramazotti, cinzano bianco, Parma ham, and Italian salami.

Mrs. Dombrowski was delighted and gave the green light to my request for a run from Munich to Istanbul and back, albeit no sooner than fourteen days. I let Steiner know by telephone when the subject would have to board in Sofia, and three days later my agent controller confirmed the date to me.

On the two-day journey from Munich to Istanbul, the sleeping car was only half full. There was nothing noteworthy—except, perhaps, the couple in Compartment 17. He was a businessman, in his mid-fifties, in an expensive suit, with perfectly polished shoes, while the woman was a nice-looking brunette around twenty years his junior. The man was very talkative, and every half-hour he kept ordering two piccolos, until my small on-board bar was empty. Then he continued with hard liquor. He always paid up immediately, and each time, he gave me a sizeable tip. The trim brunette was his secretary; it was quite obvious that the two of them were in a relationship. What was really interesting, however, was the device that the businessman had invented. He claimed to have developed a ship that could reabsorb oil slicks in the sea. He said he was on the way to Istanbul, where he wanted to wrap up a large sale to a Turkish shipowner. He proudly showed me his sales brochures and photos. The oil absorption device rather resembled an oversized, very wide, motorized catamaran with a large collection tank positioned between the two hulls.

"How long does it take until a vessel like yours has absorbed all the oil leaked into the ocean from tanker that's sprung a leak?" I wanted to know.

"Good question," grunted the inventor, annoyance in his voice. "That depends on the tanker's size and the weather conditions."

"Say, in the case of a mid-sized tanker," I pressed him.

The man grunted again, his brow furrowing as he thought it over for a while. Finally he said, "Well, if ten of my ships are deployed for twelve hours a day, and assuming the anchorage where the oil can be dissolved is no more than ten nautical miles away from the deployment area, then it would take around two months. Longer, in rough seas."

"And what does a ship like that cost?" I asked.

"35,000 Deutschmarks," the inventor-businessman replied, shoving a couple of brochures and his card into my hand and remarking, "You come into contact with lots of people. If you broker a sale for me, you can receive a commission equal to ten percent of the sales price!"

For a brief moment, I actually pondered whether being a sales representative hawking oil-absorption ships would be a job for me.

* * *

At 2255 the Orient Express, as our train used to be called in the style of the days the old luxury train plied this route, left Marmaray Sirkeci, Istanbul's main railroad station. According to the schedule, it was due to arrive at the main station in Sofia at 0710 the next morning and depart for Belgrade ten minutes later, with a brief stop-over in Dimitrovgrad, where the Bulgarian border police had to get off. The closer we came to Sofia, the greater my tension became. Would the subject be punctually "delivered"? What would I do if the subject or the person transporting him to me had already been under surveillance for days? In the event of a conflict in the railroad car, how would I be able to intervene? How many years would I get in a Bulgarian prison if I were sentenced for aiding and abetting an escape?

Too many ifs, ands, or buts! I would simply have to react to any situations as they arose, but for now, I just had to keep cool.

We arrived in Sofia on time. At the head of the train, I saw four Bulgarian border police officers boarding with a dog. Two Germans and a Frenchman had reserved places in the sleeping car. As prescribed by regulations, I directed them to their compartments and checked their tickets as well as their passports' expiration dates.

But where was my subject? It was three minutes to departure! I looked around in Compartment 13. The man actually sitting there was an older sort, intimidated- and pallid-looking, who resembled the man in the photo shown to me. Now everything had to proceed very quickly. I briefly checked the aisle in both directions, locked myself with the subject in Compartment 13, shoved back the carpeting, opened up the hiding place in the floor, and motioned the man to crawl inside. By folding up his legs and lying on his side, he fit in it nicely. I laid the odor-eliminating blanket I had prepared over him, sniffed it by way of demonstration, and indicated to him with gestures how important it was to keep the blanket over his body. Then I closed the floor plate, pulled the carpeting over it, pulled it tight with the end plate, went out and locked up the compartment. As a rule, empty compartments remained locked and were opened only when customs officials so instructed me in order to prevent stowaways from sneaking aboard. That's how I wanted to keep things during this trip. Everything was supposed to proceed quite normally, as always.

After a while—the Bulgarian border guards were due to arrive in my car in around ten to twenty minutes—I was overcome with the urge to see whether everything was all right in Compartment 13. Opening the hiding place and peeking in to see whether the man had also dutifully pulled my odor-eliminating blanket over him would have been too time-consuming and too dangerous. But I at least wanted to check whether he was calm and not going to panic or even scream for help if someone entered the compartment.

I opened Compartment 13 and was horrified: there stood a dark-haired, slender, good-looking man in a silver-gray suit, attaching a silencer to his pistol. Spotting me, he aimed the pistol right at me. I retreated, lightning quick, slammed the door shut, and jammed it with the four-way socket wrench I was still holding in my hand. Then I further barred the door with the nearest T-bar within reach, just as Franz had showed me how to do.

Besides me, there was nobody in the aisle. I stood in front of Compartment 12, holding my breath while listening for anything coming from Compartment 13. Everything was calm. Just the monotonous clattering of the wheels on the tracks. Not a shot went off. What on earth was I supposed to do? The border guards were entering the front end of my car and waving me over to them. I quickly removed the T-bar from the door and kicked it onto the floor, between the carpets, without anyone noticing.

"Everything all right?" a customs officer called over to me.

"Yes, as always," I replied, as calmly as possible.

The border officers checked every compartment, one by one, ordered travelers to produce their passports, and looked into a few suitcases.

My heart was pounding like hell when they ordered me to open up Compartment 13.

It was empty, the window had been shoved down all the way, and the curtains were wafting outwards. The officials' German shepherd dog happily wagged its tail, but didn't detect anything. Or did it? The dog briefly sniffed at the hiding place under the floor, then turned away. The officers looked out the window in every direction, then closed it. They instructed me to keep the windows closed but didn't become suspicious. Who would jump out of a train window while still in Bulgarian territory?

Before leaving my car, one of the customs officials asked me whether I had remembered his porno magazine. I hadn't.

Next time! I promised, and felt very, very glad when the whole pack of them left the train in Dimitrovgrad.

The fact that the dog hadn't detected anything over the hiding place in the floor—and the fact that the man with pistol had disappeared—were an inexpressible relief to me. But never should one lull oneself into a false sense of security! Perhaps the guy had indeed climbed out the window of Compartment 13, only to make it back into the train through the window in Compartment 12 or 14. Scarcely imaginable, given that both compartments were occupied by passengers and had been checked by the customs officials. Had the man perhaps barricaded himself in one of the lavatories? Going through my sleeping car, I inspected all its compartments and lavatories; then I checked the adjacent dining car before treating myself to a cigarette and a cup of coffee in the conductors' compartment. I thought things over. What had the man wanted? Had he been targeting me, or did he have some kind of relation to my subject?

I went back into Compartment 13 again, locked myself inside, and opened the hiding place. Coal dust was spilling out of two holes in my odor-eliminating blanket. I pulled it back—and matters went from bad to worse:

The subject had two bullet holes in his left chest; he was obviously dead. But I had to make absolutely sure. In these cramped conditions, the best idea I could devise was to squeeze one of the man's eyes out of its socket. Quite certainly the man would never have let that be done to him, had any breath of life been remaining in him at all. I laid the blanket over the body and secured the hiding place. In doing so, I also noticed the bullet holes in the floor hatch and the burgundy-colored carpeting. Since the carpet had already received a few black burn marks from stepped-on cigarette butts, neither the customs officials nor I had noticed the holes earlier.

For half a day and half a night, I rode with the corpse on board across all of Yugoslavia and Austria. I kept asking myself: What on earth had I done wrong? Should I have disarmed the man with the pistol, then broken his neck and hurled him out the window, the way I had learned to do? Okay, I had learned how to disarm a man and break his neck, at least, and I'm sure I would have managed to throw him out the window. Then my subject

175

would still be alive and the murderer dead. But it also could have been the case that the intruder had already shot the Bulgarian before I surprised him in the compartment, in which case he wouldn't have been actually attaching the silencer, but instead removing it after having completed his mission.

I would have preferred to disembark at the Salzburg border checkpoint and go to Steiner straightaway. But a sleeping car without its conductor surely would have drawn the attention of Austrian or German customs officials. So I stayed on until Munich, where the car was uncoupled and passengers continuing on their journey had to reboard other trains.

I called Steiner to request an emergency meeting, then jumped into my speedy roadster and drove to Salzburg.

Steiner was, as the saying goes, not amused, but he remained calm and businesslike when I told him my story.

"Where's the body now?" he demanded to know.

"At the shunting yard, in the Pasing district of Munich. Usually, anywhere from three to five of those conspicuous royal blue *wagons-lits* are standing around there. They get a cleaning and then wait to be put into service again. The car containing the body is no. 1214708. It might be departing for another run as early as tomorrow. Then it'll be hard to trace. It may even go all the way to Istanbul or Athens with the body on board," I replied.

Steiner placed several telephone calls, none of which was altogether illuminating to me, especially since they contained a number of codes I was unfamiliar with. Only the corpse's location, along with the number of the sleeping car, were repeatedly mentioned.

Finally, my agent controller said to me, "We'll dispose of the body, Mr. Cooper, don't worry about anything on that account! I would urgently advise you, however, to avoid Bulgarian territory for quite a while. It's possible that the murderer was from Bulgarian intelligence and that you're now on their radar. They don't fool around, those boys."

I nodded.

"Try to obtain a run to Prague," Steiner said, "and contact me as soon as you know when you can be there."

"Yes, sir. And—since I'm already there—what about my fee?" I asked hesitantly.

"Mr. Cooper, we had agreed on 5,000 Deutschmarks as a bounty for every subject that you bring into the West alive. That wasn't the case here," Steiner stated emotionlessly.

He was right.

* * *

Mrs. Dombrowski handed me my measly sleeping car conductor's salary in a pay packet, right down to the last penny.

"Mr. Gruber, I've been having real problems with my boss due to your back-to-back round trips. We can't do anything like that again, not even once!"

"Problems with your husband?" I asked.

"The fact that my boss also happens to be my husband has nothing to do with business. At the end of the day, my husband has to answer to our Paris headquarters, and they don't want our staff remaining on duty more than twenty-four hours at a time. You've now got a few days off. Next Wednesday, you'll be taking the night train to Paris. It departs Prague at 1912 and arrives in Paris at 0945 the next morning. Arrival to Prague and return from Paris by train. I'm still in the process of getting the tickets ready for you."

Obviously, the *Wagon-Lits* headquarters in Paris was having personnel problems again. The French enjoyed going on strike, and they did so a lot. At the moment, this suited me just fine. I rang up Steiner and passed along the dates to him. Three days later, I was ordered to report "to the concert" in Salzburg.

Sitting in his bugproof office, Steiner described the factual situation: "We're proceeding from the assumption that your Bulgarian subject was murdered either by Bulgarian intelligence or by the KGB. We don't know the extent to which both of these intelligence services exchange information with the StB, Czechoslovakian intelligence. So for security reasons we've decided that the hiding place in Compartment 13 will now be off-limits for a longer time period, perhaps even permanently."

"It's unlikely that Bulgarian customs officials have become aware of your name *and* that Bulgarian intelligence is sharing the information with the KGB and the StB. But it's a possibility that can't be ruled out, so we've taken the precaution of issuing you a fresh passport. It's been issued under the name of Hans Schulz. That way, you won't have any problems if one of your coworkers from the railroad or the cleaning crew addresses you on a first-name basis."

Steiner handed me the passport and slurped his mélange.

"Now, Mr. Cooper, let's talk about your next assignment. It involves a female KGB officer who speaks fluent

English, Czech, German, and French, besides her native language, of course. She works as a decryption specialist at the KGB's Prague office and wants to defect to us."

Steiner handed me a photo of an attractive blonde with wavy hair and a beaming smile. He remarked, "This is how she normally looks."

Then he handed me a French passport issued in the name of 'Marie Mercier.' The passport photo depicted a woman with a serious gaze and short, black hair, wearing dark-rimmed eyeglasses.

"And that's how the lady's going to look when you make her acquaintance. She will ask you for the third-class sleeping car. That's the code word: third class! The sleeping cars don't have any, so normally nobody would ask for that. Once the lady establishes contact with you, give her the passport, the train ticket to Paris, and a ticket for the sleeping car. The train stops within German territory only once—in Nuremberg at 2318. Ensure that the subject gets off the train there. We'll handle everything else."

Happy about not having to fashion a new odor-elimination blanket, I rode back to Munich.

* * *

The only express train scheduled for my arrival day pulled into Prague's main station by noontime. So I had the entire afternoon free, and used it to amble over to Wenceslas Square, just a few minutes away. Wenceslas Square was more of a boulevard than a square. Not even five years earlier, Soviet tanks had overrun peaceful demonstrators and crushed the Prague Spring. Television images from those days remained indelibly etched in my memory. The Soviets feared a domino effect, the same way the Americans did in Vietnam.

As had been the case on earlier trips with Franz, a restaurant on the Vltava served food at an unbeatable price, and everything was exceptionally delicious: Ossetra caviar as an appetizer, Crimean sparkling wine, beef roulades, and for dessert, palaccinka—a kind of thin crepe—all for just ten Deutschmarks. Since in my job you never knew which meal was going to be your last, or whether you might be living on nothing but bread soup for a few years, I let every morsel delectably melt over my tongue.

At 1830, the train heading to Paris was already arriving on Platform 2. I settled into the conductors' compartment, processed the oncoming passengers, and anxiously awaited my subject. Darkness had already fallen. A strange, eerie mood prevailed on the platform. Smoke was billowing out of a manhole cover, and the sparse illumination covered only isolated segments of the platform, so that it was impossible to precisely make out how many people were around. Three? Five? Perhaps even more?

1905. All the passengers in sleeping cars were processed. The train was supposed to depart in seven minutes. My subject had not yet reported.

1912. Departure time. Nothing was stirring.

I looked out the window. Suddenly, an announcement over the loudspeaker, in Eastern European-accented German, broke the ghostly quiet: "Mr. Hans Gruber, please report to Counter 3! Mr. Hans Gruber, please report to Counter 3!"

The announcement was extremely loud. A man standing on the platform, directly next to the pressure-box loudspeaker, flinched in fright. I saw two men rush at him and drag him out of the weak lighting into the darkness.

A number of thoughts flashed through my mind. Had I just witnessed my own arrest? Were they now searching for Hans Gruber throughout the entire Eastern Bloc? How much protection would be afforded me by Steiner's new passport, issued in the name of Hans Schulz? Where was my subject? Should I take off my uniform and conceal myself somewhere in the train? Maybe in Compartment 13? Or should I simply go ahead and do my job as though nothing had happened? I resolved upon the latter, though I didn't know whether that was the best option.

1916. Four minutes after the scheduled departure time, the train began rolling. I felt a little relieved. But the battle still hadn't been won. We would still be traveling on Czech territory for a good two hours. Customs officials could always still arrest me and pull me off the train at the station at the border, in Rozvadov. Where had the subject gotten to? Had she hidden herself aboard the train and entered the sleeping car only later? Had the operation been betrayed? Or had the subject herself committed the betrayal?

After about half an hour, four customs officials entered the sleeping car, this time with a dog, which was not always the case on this stretch. They checked the passengers' passports. Finally, while standing in the aisle, one of them asked for mine. He examined the document with exceptional thoroughness, slowly leafing back and forth through it, and then, in a friendly tone—in perfect German—he asked me: "May we search your uniform, Mr. Schulz?"

The question was purely rhetorical, for the request wasn't one I couldn't have exactly refused.

"Of course!" I replied.

It was possible that they were looking for the subject's papers and didn't have the faintest idea how close they were. I had taped Madame Marie Mercier's passport and tickets in the panel accessing the ceiling lighting, directly over their heads—exactly where Franz always stashed his slivovitz bottles on our Belgrade runs. The customs officials prolonged their search of my luggage and the entire conductor's compartment. They found nothing and bid me a polite farewell.

When the German customs officials boarded the train in Waidhaus, I felt a sense of enormous relief! The subject didn't report. In Nuremberg, only four male passengers disembarked.

Immediately after my return from Paris, I drove to Steiner and briefed him.

"You've really had a run of good luck there, Mr. Cooper! But as an agent, you've been burned, at least for Eastern Europe. And on top of that, I would strongly advise you to keep away from any sleeping car, if you want to stay alive!" Steiner informed me.

"That's how I see the matter too," I concurred, "but what about my fee this time? None of this was my fault."

"Results need no excuses! The question of fault is completely irrelevant here. The agreement was that the money would be paid only if the subject arrives—alive—in the West," Steiner stated soberly. As we parted, he added, "Be glad that you aren't rotting away in a Czechoslovakian prison now—instead, you're a free man. You can come and go wherever you want and do whatever you want. That's worth a hell of a lot more than a few thousand dollars, isn't it?"

I nodded, and silently left the American Express Bank on Salzburg's Residenzplatz.

On the drive home to Munich, I mentally sized up my work as a sleeping car conductor on behalf of the CIA. Twice, I had risked my life, working five months for starvation wages; the bottom line was that I didn't have two pennies to rub together. Perhaps I really would have been better off trying my luck as a sales representative hawking oil-absorption ships...

CHAPTER 8
Code Peking Duck

I swore to myself that I would never work on a contingency fee basis again. There would have to be a fixed salary—or better still, a fixed salary plus a contingency fee.

It also became clear to me that I couldn't remain an agent forever; nor did I wish to do so. Some decent occupational training was sorely needed! Preferably, several kinds, and right away! If a solid three-year occupational training program meant that I could neither accept long-term assignments nor travel around the world for extended periods of time, then for that reason alone it definitely ought to be worthwhile.

I applied for three positions that interested me—bridging the gap in my curriculum vitae resulting from the time spent in the U.S. Army and at the CIA Farm with imaginatively contrived travel accounts—and was accepted for all three. The training programs to become a certified male nurse, a certified parachuting instructor, and a paramedic—a profession in the process of being newly created—could easily be completed in parallel. I could attend nursing school during the day, while attending paramedic courses in the evenings, and undergoing training on the weekends to become a German parachuting instructor. And besides, the entire business didn't really constitute work anyway. As Confucius had once so wisely proclaimed: if you do what you truly enjoy doing, you'll never need to work a single solitary day again in your life!

I was also mulling over the idea of going back to finish my high school diploma after completing the various occupational training courses, and—assuming I could obtain one of the coveted slots—attend medical school. But these were dreams for the future.

Given the specialized knowledge I had obtained as a Medical Specialist, I found it difficult to hold back in class at the nursing school in Munich-Grosshadern. The nurses doing the teaching didn't like it at all whenever one of their charges knew more than they did. With the parachutists, things were totally different—they eagerly soaked up all the know-how I was able to contribute from my instructor training at the United States Parachute Association. Even the Southern Bavarian Aviation Agency, the responsible subdivision of the Upper Bavarian government, was receptive to my suggestions for improving training for parachutists and parachuting instructors.

In case the CIA contacted me, I would avail myself of the right I had negotiated to decline an assignment during any occupational training. But the CIA didn't contact me. And I didn't contact them. For weeks. Months. Until one night—it was the middle of September 1974—the telephone jangled, and a friendly lady with an American accent said: "Peking Duck, tomorrow at 1300!"

Groggy with sleep, I confirmed, "Peking Duck, tomorrow at 1300!" and hung up.

What on earth had I done? What did 'Peking Duck' mean? Had that been merely a dream? No, the telephone was lying in my bed, and I wasn't normally in the habit of sleeping with my telephone in the bed.

I switched on the light, scribbled "8 S/13 Peking Duck" on a slip of paper, and laid it on top of my alarm clock. With the lack of sleep I was now suffering, I could have completely forgotten about the nighttime phone call.

My alarm clock rang at six. I saw the slip of paper, reset the clock to eight, and was glad to be able to grab a couple extra hours' sleep. Then the 'S' on the slip of paper reminded me to call in sick at the nursing school—the first time I had done so since beginning my training there. I made some coffee for myself and pondered what 'Peking Duck' meant. It was a code word for a meeting spot from a list of code words that I had seen and memorized once, a considerably long time ago. Damn! What the hell did 'Peking Duck' mean? I looked in the Munich telephone book, then in the yellow pages. There actually did exist, on Barerstrasse, a restaurant called Peking Duck. But that would have been too simple, and anyway, not a code. A Chinese restaurant? China? Chinese tower? Yes, that was it! The Chinese Tower, in the English Garden!

At 1245, I was inconspicuously strolling—at a respectful distance—around the wooden pagoda, the center of one of the city's most popular beer gardens. Then I saw him! Sitting there was a man I recognized, and one whom I would have never, ever associated with this location. He was drinking a beer, smoking a cigarette, and relaxing with the *Süddeutsche Zeitung*, Munich's main newspaper. The man was tall and slender, with thick, dark-blond hair, a pleasant cleft chin, and a distinctive Fu Manchu beard. It was none other than Barry Winslow Meeker, the helicopter pilot I knew from Da Nang. I approached him slowly from behind and said, "Don't ever call me 'Kraut' again, Captain Meeker!"

Barry turned around, laughed, and greeted me effusively.

"Barry! Awesome to see you! What have you been doing for the last couple of years?" I asked.

"Two weeks after our excursion to the Suzie Wong, I was just about feeling ready to fly again, but my unit was pulled out of Vietnam and disbanded," Barry replied. "For my last year in the Army I had my choice of duty station, so I got myself transferred to Germany. Coleman Army Airfield. I love Germans and their culture! After getting my discharge, I worked here and there as a freelancer. Then I heard from a friend that they wanted to build an air rescue station at Traunstein Hospital. It's only the third station of its kind anywhere in Germany, after the ones in Munich and Nuremberg. So I've been flying a Bell 206 for half a year now."

Barry finished his beer, suggested that we take a walk around nearby Lake Kleinhesseloher, then asked about my plans for the future. I skipped over part of my life, mentioning only the paramedics, parachute jumping, and the nursing training that I had just begun.

"You're nuts!" Barry said. "I sure as hell wouldn't voluntarily jump out of a perfectly good airplane! Not in my lifetime!"

We rented a rowboat. Barry rowed out to the middle of the small lake, laid down the oars, and got down to cases: "We're working for the same outfit. From this point out, it's strictly confidential. Not a peep to anyone, okay?"

"Okay," I replied, nodding.

"Last month I completed a job working for a lawyer here in Munich," Barry continued. "Departing from Germany, I extracted his family by helicopter from

Czechoslovakia. They're all East German citizens. I made it over the border by flying at low altitude. Nobody noticed anything—neither German nor Austrian air traffic control. Same for the Czechs and the Russians. Piece of cake! Only the CIA caught wind of it somehow."

"How come?" I asked.

"In my opinion," Barry replied, "there are three possibilities: one, the NSA tracked my low-altitude flight from Bad Aibling using special radar; two, the CIA was tapping my telephone; or three, they were tapping the lawyer's phone."

"And now?"

"The CIA wants me to fly people along this route across the Iron Curtain for them too. And they want you and me to work together. You were at the Farm, you're an escape agent, and you completed pinch-hitter flight training, right?"

"You know that I'm not allowed to talk about that," I answered, nodding.

"There's a reason I picked this spot for us to talk. Are you on board?" Barry asked.

"What kind of people are these, the ones we're supposed to extract? Are we talking about one run, or several? What are the terms and conditions?" I wanted to know.

"We aren't informed of the identities of the people we're picking up. Maybe they're KGB or Stasi officers who want to defect, perhaps Poles, Czechs, Hungarians, or Rumanians who can be useful to the CIA. Each time, we will receive three-person deliveries at the stipulated landing site from our people on the other side of the 'curtain,' as it were."

Pausing briefly, Barry elaborated further: "Your task is to ensure that they're sitting in the helicopter within ten seconds. There are supposed to be multiple runs at irregular intervals. The CIA will pay us ten flight hours for our preparation time, then of course for the flight hours accrued and $3,000 U.S. as a bonus for every head rescued. I thought we can divide that amount into $2,000 for me—since as the pilot I bear more responsibility—and $1,000 for you. So just for getting three passengers loaded into the chopper quickly, that's $3,000 U.S. for you, or around 8,000 Deutschmarks!"

"What happens if something goes wrong? What if the people aren't at the stipulated site? If we're betrayed, and someone starts firing at us? Then we're risking our lives and getting—nothing! I actually didn't want to work for bounty payments anymore!" I exclaimed.

"Nothing will go wrong. Believe me, we'll be able to pull it all off easily. But if you're afraid of the residual risk, then you aren't the right man for the job," Barry stated.

"Give me a day to sleep on it," I requested.

"You've got one minute!" Barry replied. He added, "And that's actually too much already. As a pilot I've got to make the right decision within a second when an emergency strikes. That applies to you too, if we want to be a team."

Even while he was still speaking, I gave Barry my hand and said, "I'm in!"

We agreed to complete as many of the CIA-financed flight hours as possible over the next few weekends. We would also practice rapid passenger boarding, as well as joint navigation and cooperation. And I also already had an idea with regard to the passengers, at least.

* * *

At 1400 on the following Saturday, September 14, 1974, I met Barry at the Jesenwang airfield, located a few kilometers west of Fürstenfeldbruck. He had already pulled the Jet Ranger out of the hangar and was checking the airframe for visible cracks, as well the main rotor along with its rotor head and linkage, the air intake for the turbine, the gear chamber, and the tail rotor. Barry then swung himself into the pilot's seat and explained the functioning of the steering controls to me as he operated them. I stood next to the chopper and could see what happened when Barry moved the stick, how the angle of inclination of the main rotor blade changed when he pulled on the pitch control, and how the rear rotor responded when the pedals were actuated. There followed a crash course in aerodynamics and helicopter mechanics. Next, Barry handed me a copy of the helicopter's manual and gave me exactly one day to memorize the ten front panel instruments he had marked, including their names, functions, and default values.

I tossed the highly detailed manual onto the passenger seat of my Ford Capri. Then we knocked back another espresso. For every mission, correct timing was decisive. At 1445 precisely, we climbed into the helicopter, and Barry, slowly and adeptly, revved up the turbine, constantly monitoring the turbine outlet temperature, the rotor speed, and a few of the other instruments. For the first time, I became truly aware of the fact that it isn't possible to simply hop into an aircraft and start it up like a car. Instead, you have to run through a procedure, like a ceremony, until all instruments and components are in alignment with one another. At 1450 the chopper was airborne. We flew over the Amperauen nature reserve, over Germering, Gräfelfing, and Martinsried, and after ten minutes we landed on a large meadow at the southern end of Sauerbruchstrasse, around fifteen meters from a freestanding tree, where three people were waiting. As the helicopter's skids touched ground, Barry clicked a stopwatch he had attached with Velcro next to the fuel gauge. I jumped out, sprinted to the passengers, signaled them to follow me, and jockeyed them onto the bench seat in the passenger space before jumping back into the co-pilot's seat and nodding to Barry.

"Twenty-six seconds—way, way too slow," Barry noted, as the meadow, at the edge of which my entire nursing school class stood waiting, became smaller and smaller below us. Not one of the thirty nursing students—twenty-seven women and three men—wanted to miss out on my offer to go on a free helicopter ride. I had announced it in the hospital cafeteria during the noon break the previous day. Their willingness was also fostered by the fact that most of the women nursing students lived above the school's classrooms, on Marchioninistrasse, so they could get to the airfield in a few minutes. We flew over the clinic in the Grosshadern section of Munich, over Würmtalstrasse, over the Waldfriedhof—the forest cemetery—and the autobahn interchange known as Munich-Kreuzhof. After five minutes, we landed back at the starting point. Three faces beaming with joy climbed out of the helicopter, as I had drilled them to do, on the pilot's side and ran ahead to the meadow's edge, while I led the next group of three to board the machine. Barry, dissatisfied, shook his head: "Twenty-four seconds—you've got to make it in under ten!"

The problem was that God—assuming there is one—had given me only two hands, but there were three passengers I had to position. I ran through simulations using various techniques. One time I called out loudly to everyone, saying they should grab one another's hands, then pulled the first person to the helicopter, with the other two in tow. Another time, I grabbed hold of one person with my left hand and another with my right while shoving the third one in front of us. It was more difficult than expected, and there was no surefire formula. Each group behaved differently.

After around two and a half hours of round-trip flying, Barry and I had indeed made my entire nursing school class very happy, but the two of us were deeply dissatisfied. The brief return flight to Jesenwang passed in silence. After stowing the Jet Ranger in the hangar, we found a quiet spot at the Fliegerstüberl, the airfield restaurant, where we could talk without being disturbed.

"Why are you so fixated on doing everything within ten seconds?" I asked Barry.

"CIA guidelines," he replied. "Old values based on experience performing evacuations from war zones. This boarding time also applied to hot landing zones in Vietnam. And if we want to err on the side of caution, we've got to classify all areas behind the Iron Curtain as war zones."

I said, "In Vietnam, the Hueys' doors were usually left hanging open. Can't you have at least one door to the passenger space hanging open on the Jet Ranger as well?"

"That could be done, but would produce unfavorable aerodynamic effects. We would no longer be as fast or maneuverable. And besides, we would gain a maximum of two seconds," Barry informed me.

"I did my best. What else could I still do differently?" I asked, an undertone of despair creeping into my voice.

"Then it just wasn't good enough! You can always improve," Barry said. He continued, "We've gotten under fifteen seconds only twice: once during the ninth flight—we made it under fourteen seconds—and once during the tenth flight, when we came in at twelve seconds. Both times, you were waving to the passengers even before landing. So the people must already be running towards the helicopter before it lands. All you'll need to do then is help them get aboard, and you may have to shove the last one in. That's the only way it can work! We have to make that a condition for the agents who deliver the people to us. And they've got to herd the subjects along so that nobody is running behind the chopper. Otherwise, the rear rotor is going to make mincemeat out of them, and we won't be able to lift off."

"Razor-sharp analysis! Excellent idea," I said effusively. "So how can we practice that again?"

"Tomorrow we'll go on a longer navigational flight. Then we'll see how many flight hours we have left, and you can think about where you can scare up a couple more round-trip candidates."

I stayed up half the night plowing through the Ranger's manual, particularly the instruments that Barry had marked. At 0700 Sunday morning, we met in Jesenwang for a briefing. Barry explained to me that he wanted to fly to Marburg to visit an old friend. The special circumstances involved were that while flying en route—total flying time was around two and a half hours—he intended to maintain an altitude below 100 feet or thirty-five meters. That way, we could practice flying all the way through under the radar, without air traffic control. The Jesenwanger tower was unmanned prior to 0800, so our departure would not draw any attention there. Navigation at this extremely low altitude was significantly more difficult than at higher ones. If you're flying between 500 and 1000 meters over the ground, it's still possible to make out—when they're still several kilometers ahead—distinct reference points such as television towers or billowing smokestacks. When your altitude is only thirty-five meters, visibility doesn't extend all that far.

We settled on the following division of labor: Barry flew a course bearing exactly 329°, which, in purely absolute terms, should take us to Marburg, but could also deviate by a few kilometers due to crosswinds.

On my lap I had a Jeppsen flight chart, marked with a straight pencil line running from Jesenwang to Marburg, with horizontal lines intersecting it at intervals of five minutes' flying time. If a church or an autobahn was marked on a horizontal line to our left, but actually turned out to be on the right when glancing out the cockpit, I alerted Barry to it. He then ascended sharply, reoriented himself, corrected the course, then dropped back down to 100 feet. This procedure was fun at first, but the longer the flight continued, the more and more arduous it became. After the last horizontal line on my chart, Barry climbed a bit, and I searched for the landing spot using the precision binoculars I had acquired especially for our upcoming missions. It was a meadow west of the Dammühle country inn, which itself was located around three kilometers west of Marburg. I quickly espied the meadow, nestled between two small forest groves, and saw a beer garden's umbrellas. From a bird's eye view, they looked like mushrooms sprouting into the sky.

Barry made a precision landing right next to the beer garden—without knocking over its umbrellas—then shut down the turbine, let the engine cool off, and set the rotor brake. In the beer garden, he introduced me to Teddy, a friend of his from the old days and an enthusiastic helicopter buff. We ate some Hessian stuffed cabbage rolls, drank beer and coffee, and enjoyed the splendid autumn day.

Barry took Teddy in the helicopter for a tour over Marburg, and then, with the engine still running, picked me up to start on the return flight. This time, we flew at an altitude of 2,000 feet, making it significantly easier to get our bearings, and we officially notified air traffic control that we were planning a refueling stop at the Egelsbach airport, around twenty kilometers south of Frankfurt am Main.

On the flight from Egelsbach to Jesenwang, Barry actually quizzed me about a few of the instruments, their functions and default values, and asked me to look on with him. There was a reason for that, because on almost every instrument, the ideal values had been made recognizable by green shading. But I had done my homework, so I was familiar with the reason and purpose behind correct values for torque, gas producer, and TOT, the turbine outlet temperature. I knew how fast we could fly at maximum speed, and a few things more.

"How come there isn't actually any pinch-hitter flight training for helicopters?" I asked.

Barry had read my thoughts, and replied with a question: "No idea. Want to fly?"

Of course I did! Nodding vigorously, I replied, "Yes, sir!"

"Then go ahead and grab the center stick with your right hand, the pitch with your left, and get to work on the pedals!" Barry challenged me, letting go of the controls and lighting up a cigarette.

After I had managed—somewhat stiffly—to successfully maintain course and altitude, I got the urge to do a really hard-core 360° turn.

"To the right or left?" Barry asked.

"To the left!" I shouted back—that was the side I was sitting on and could see better while looking out the window.

"Then check the airspace on your side and give a loud 'Clear left!' once the coast is clear. After that, pull the center stick gently to the left, tighten up on the pitch slightly, and apply some left pedal."

I did as Barry instructed, and it worked! After recovering from the turn, though, I was 150 feet lower than before and no longer exactly on course.

"And now the same thing to the right. Clear right!" Barry shouted.

This time around I hazarded a somewhat steeper turn and tightened the pitch somewhat too hard, so at the end of the maneuver I was around 200 feet higher than at the beginning.

"Not all too hard at all," I decided.

"You're right about that—once the chopper has gotten airborne," Barry confirmed. "Taking off, landing, and hovering in the machine are considerably more difficult. But perhaps we'll leave practicing all those for some other time."

We had barely an hour and a half of flight time left on the CIA-financed credit balance. During the process of taking on passengers, the helicopter's skids were never allowed to touch the ground longer than ten seconds. I devoted some thought to where I could find people with whom we could practice the boarding again, this time with a new strategy. With my friends from the *C'est la vie!* perhaps? There weren't enough of them. At best, two or three groups would assemble. With my fellow parachutists from the Munich parachuting club? They would hardly be enthusiastic about making five-minute round-trip flights. They would want to climb to 4,000 meters and do nothing but jump, jump, jump! Finally, I thought of my paramedic colleagues, all of whom were highly responsible, reliable buddies who had certainly earned a helicopter ride! I managed to convene twenty-one strapping rescuers to the Jesenwang airfield for the coming Saturday. I issued everyone three guidelines: they had to form groups of three at a prescribed place, dash off to the helicopter as soon as it set down to land, and it was extremely important that they avoid the tail rotor.

It went off like clockwork! Boarding time ran between five and ten seconds! Granted, the rescue paramedics, due to their profession, were probably already faster than John Q. Public, but now we knew it was feasible to keep within the time constraint, provided the passengers ran to the chopper.

Satisfied, Barry and I went for a walk—the safest way to prevent anyone from eavesdropping on us—and discussed means of communication, code words, and procedures for an assignment. I sensed that we had enjoyed the same training. Barry would inform the CIA that we were ready. The assignment was supposed to be issued exclusively to him, and he would then inform me. The times and dates Barry gave over the phone were actually one day earlier, minus two hours. Thus, in the event our telephone calls were being tapped, the mission would have already been completed if they were expecting us. We agreed upon original code words for various rendez-vous points such as the Jesenwang airfield, the Riem airport in Munich, and the corrugated-metal hangar at the Traustein Hospital. All that remained was the "Peking Duck"!

The first assignment wasn't long in coming, and made it necessary for us to meet again. Barry had gotten several large-scale flight charts. One of them showed the area between the Kvilda and Horní Planá, two villages in the southwest of the People's Republic of Czechoslovakia. Inscribed on this chart were target areas Alpha, Bravo, Charlie, Delta, and Echo, and for each of these, we had detailed individual maps. We thoroughly discussed all the maps. Barry was to find out the precise target area only on the morning of the day we went into action. At least one of the three subjects would wear red or orange outer clothing.

"During the entire mission, we'll be inside Czecho-slovakian territory only four minutes. And out of that we'll be spending one minute in the hot zone, maxi-mum, including ten seconds' boarding time," Barry reckoned.

* * *

Wednesday, 1430, Jesenwang Airfield. Barry had already hauled the chopper out of the hanger. He waved me over to him. We strolled back and forth on the meadow next to the hanger.

"There's been a change of plans," Barry whispered, a little tense.

"What is the plan, anyway?" I asked. "Where are we flying to?"

"Okay, you don't know that yet. At exactly 1700 we're going to be operating in target area Bravo. Here's what's new: we won't be flying low the entire time. First, we'll be making a completely normal excursion to Deggendorf, a special airfield that's unmanned during the week. Flight time there is fifty-five minutes. Then you and I will go through the charts again and fly under the radar to the target area," Barry explained.

Twenty minutes later we were airborne. When we reached an altitude of 1,000 feet, Barry handed me the controls and lit up a cigarette. I struggled a little to maintain course, altitude, and speed, mainly because the chopper was somewhat sluggishly responding to my commands. But I quickly got the hang of it, giving Barry, who was a chain smoker, the opportunity to inhale a couple more cigarettes before taking back the controls for the descent and approach to Deggendorf.

We were early, much too early. Presumably we'd had a decent tailwind. Barry let the turbines cool down and set the rotor brake.

In an hour and fifteen minutes, the operation would be over, and we would be landing exactly at this spot again. CIA colleagues would take charge of the subjects. A tanker truck from the U.S. Army was supposed to top off the fuel.

We reviewed the plan yet one final time and smoked one final cigarette.

"Is there a Plan B for emergencies in case something doesn't go right?" I asked Barry.

"In the event of an emergency, we're going to have to improvise. But don't even think about overshooting the ten seconds' boarding time!" Barry said.

"You'd leave me behind?" I asked, appalled.

"That's something you've got to assume. But I'll treat you to a beer if you make it out of Czechoslovakian prison after twenty years!" Barry joked, adding, "Don't worry about it. Nothing will go wrong. We'll pull it off. And what's more, with the greatest of ease."

He revved up the turbine and climbed on an east-bound course. The next hour would be life or death, both for ourselves and for the three refugees whose fates were unknown to us.

We flew at 120 knots, around 220 kilometers per hour; the entire way, we remained only a few meters above fields and meadows, and we darted right under high-tension wires. Shortly before a small forest grove, Barry pulled the Jet Ranger up steeply, in order to maneuver it barely above the treetops. We avoided flying directly over villages, bypassing Schaufling, Lalling, Grafenau, and Neuschönau to the north until we spotted the tiny village of Mauth. Before entering the airspace over the village, Barry executed a sharp 90° curve. The centrifugal force in the curve was so powerful that I wasn't able to raise the binoculars to my eyes until after we were flying straight ahead again.

The border ran through the middle of the Mauther Forest in the north of the village, and just at the end of the grove was our target area Bravo. According to our information, this section of the border was secured by nothing except barbed wire, which was checked by patrols only sporadically. After we had flown at low altitude over about a third of the forested area, Barry sharply pulled the helicopter up to about 1,500 feet—in order to keep us out of range of small arms fire, and to furnish me good visibility. I quickly discovered what we were searching for: south of the Czechoslovakian village of Kvilda ran a road and a river—the Vltava—heading out of town. Precisely at the point where the road and the river ran most closely together, three people were standing. One of them was wearing a red shirt. I was unable to make out any additional people, vehicles, or suspicious elements in the immediate vicinity.

The time was 1658. I pointed out the landing spot and Barry shot towards it, and in a daring maneuver, flared out the Jet Ranger and hovered in reverse another two meters, while I already had my door open and was standing on the skid. The subjects came running to us from four meters away. All I had left to do was open the rear cabin doors, jockey the people inside, and we were already airborne again. The whole evolution hadn't consumed ten seconds, perhaps not even five.

I turned around and looked into the faces of three older gentlemen, whose terror was now yielding to sheer relief. One of them had a few tears rolling down his cheeks. I envied him. With a friendly smile, I shouted into the back, *"A warm welcome! Herzlich willkommen! Dabro paschlovit!"*

The latter phrase was supposed to be Russian, understood throughout the entire Eastern Bloc. At some point, I had written it down phonetically and learned it by heart.

During the descent and approach to the special airfield in Deggendorf, we spotted an olive-drab U.S. Army tanker truck and an inconspicuous gray car. Both were still moving, but stopped when they heard us. Perfect timing!

While one of the soldiers set about refueling the Jet Ranger, we handed the subjects over to our colleagues. All three of the men we had evacuated bid farewell to Barry and me with a handshake. Only one of them—it was the one who still had tears rolling down his cheeks—insisted on getting out of the CIA's Hertz rental car yet one more time. The agents seemed tense. They didn't know what would now come; they were already reaching for their concealed Smith & Wesson-made Colt pistols. Then the small, portly man, who had forced his way out of the car yet again, threw himself on Barry—who towered over him by at least two heads—hugged him and squeezed him tight so warmly that Barry too began welling up with emotion and tears of joy. Eventually it was my turn. I enjoyed the embrace and hugged the man back. A warm, glowing feeling coursed through my body, from head to toe. Unfortunately, I was unable to weep.

Shortly after takeoff, Barry handed the pitch, stick, and pedals over to me, lit up a cigarette and instructed me, "Keep climbing until you reach 1,000 feet, then level off!"

In other words, at an altitude of exactly 1,000 feet, I had to reduce the pitch, so that the chopper stopped climbing and maintained this altitude. Then he told me what course and speed to take. It was an edifying feeling to be allowed to pilot this 317-horsepower thunderbird through the air. But as awesome as flying it was, it was also clear to me that I was far from being capable of flying a helicopter. Had I attempted—without an experienced pilot at my side—taking off, landing, or executing a swift, steep curve, an autorotation, or a hovering maneuver, I would have mercilessly plunged to earth.

"The guy who hugged us like that at the end gave us the feeling that we've really done some good!" Barry told me.

"You've got that right!" I replied. "I would be all too glad to know where the three men came from, what their previous fate had been, what their professions were, and why the CIA had organized their escape. Do you think we'll ever find out?" I asked.

"No, probably not," Barry replied, a bit wistfully.

* * *

We flew additional operations at irregular intervals, at different times of day, and into various target areas. As it became routine, the tension disappeared. Nevertheless, we prepared for every operation thoroughly, as though it were a matter of life and death. Above, all, the timing had to be kept, down to the exact minute, and during the boarding process, even down to the split second. Our subjects and fellow agents on the other side of the border were able to rely on us—and we could rely on them.

Everything ran smoothly until one day, during his usual pre-flight check, Barry opened the transmission housing under the main rotor hub assembly, shook his head, closed the housing again and climbed down to the ground. Then he announced, "No way am I flying this bird!"

"Why not?" I asked in dismay.

"It's got a centimeter of oil standing on the metal trough underneath the transmission. The oil is really close to the turbine, which heats up to 900° Celsius. And besides that, we'll go down like a stone if the transmission ever stops receiving lubrication."

I understood.

"What do we do now? Any alternatives?" I asked.

"We haven't got a chance—but we'll try it anyway!" Barry shouted, running to the airfield restaurant. I followed on his heels.

Barry grabbed the telephone and dialed a number. He spoke calmly and slowly, in his congenial, sonorous voice, as though we had all the time in the world. I listened tensely, trying to conjecture what the person at the other end of the line was saying whenever Barry paused.

"Haiko, it's Barry here. Can I charter a Jet Ranger from you?" – "Now. Immediately!" – "I'm in Jesenwang and I've got an assignment, but the machine's leaking transmission oil." – "If you tank up the machine and run through the preflight check right away, I'll definitely owe you a beer! There's no point unless I can take off from Munich right away. Otherwise, I won't make it back by sunset." – "Okay, talk to you soon."

Barry hung up and asked me, "Can we take your car? It's faster than mine."

I nodded, but didn't miss out on the opportunity to drive my Ford Capri myself—finally putting to the test everything I'd learned during the CIA's special driver training, both on the Farm and in Arizona. Disregarding the entire German vehicle code and every speed limit, I raced to Munich's Riem Airport. Meanwhile, Barry pored over the flight charts and fiddled with the E6-B navigation calculator, a kind of slide rule that can be used to calculate flight times in the event of variously strong headwinds, tailwinds, side winds, and drift.

"In absolute terms, we can't be at target area Echo on time. And you know what the shittiest part is?" Barry asked.

I shook my head, while devoting my entire concentration to the traffic and overtaking everything possible.

"The shittiest part is that two hours ago, the CIA confirmed the target and exact time. I returned the confirmation, so there's no chance of correcting it. They're relying on us. Understand?"

I nodded. Reaching the Munich airport in a rally-worthy record time of thirty-three minutes, I parked at the end of the row of waiting taxis, simply because that was the parking space closest to the main entrance. We raced through Security—Barry flashed his pilot's ID and identified me as his passenger. A few minutes later, we were in the air.

The pilot relayed his flight plan—while we were already airborne—to the Munich air traffic control, stating our destination as Vilshofen on the Danube, and squeezed every last bit of power from the helicopter. Like every motorized aircraft, the Jet Ranger has a normal cruising speed, indicated by a green band in the middle of the air velocity indicator, as well as a "velocity never exceed" range—the maximum speed that must not be exceeded. Should the pilot do so, the aircraft will usually first begin to vibrate severely, and at some point it will break up, leaving nothing but a heap of parts.

Barry pushed the performance capability of the Jet Ranger, its turbine, and its airframe to their limits, and at times beyond. Whenever the helicopter began to vibrate, he pulled back on the stick a little and reduced the pitch one or two centimeters, only to then bump up to the limit immediately again.

"Shit! We're not even close to making it on time," cursed Barry.

"How late are we going to be?" I asked worriedly.

"I estimate between fifteen and twenty minutes. That's goddamned long. Conversely, I wouldn't wait so long for the subjects. But we should put ourselves in the refugees' shoes. Imagine—you've been waiting for this moment for years. Your life is in danger. Then you were promised a rescue operation. And the helicopter doesn't arrive. Five, ten, fifteen, maybe twenty long minutes. What would you do?"

I scanned the detailed chart. Target area Echo was in a meadow one kilometer south of the village of Nová Pec, exactly where the dense forestation ended, and the Bohemian forest petered out into small groves and meadows. Standing in the middle of the target area were a large tree, and a small one could be made out twelve meters south of it. We were supposed to land eastwards of the line between these two trees, as close to them as possible.

"I would simply wait under one of those two trees and run from the cover as soon as I heard the noise of the rotors. Even if it takes half an hour or an hour. There's no reasonable alternative. What are they supposed to do, just throw in the towel and head back to wherever they had come from? Or look for a place to sleep in the village? Or get themselves mauled by wolves in the Bohemian forest?" I said, summing up the situation.

"Okay. I'll land at the exact stipulated position. As we're making our descent and approach, have your binoculars out and try to spot the subjects, as well as any other people or anything suspicious. If the coast is clear,

I'll make an exception and stay in the target area for two minutes, max. If nothing is moving by then, we'll fly back," Barry decided, dropping back to low altitude after we had flown over the Danube, south of Vilshofen.

After a breathtaking twenty-five-minute, nap-of-the-earth flight, we reached the target area seventeen minutes late. As Barry was setting the skids onto the ground, three men, one wearing a red jacket, ran towards our helicopter. I helped them aboard, shut the door to the passenger space, and heaved myself onto the co-pilot's seat. Barely ten seconds later we were flying home.

A few days after the recently completed operation, which, happily, had gone off without a hitch, Barry and I were summoned to the "concert"—i.e., a longer meeting—at the CIA's quarters at Rhine-Main Airbase. We drove to Frankfurt together in my Ford Capri. During the ride, Barry regaled me with a few exciting stories from his adventurous life, which had started out quite prosaically. Originally, he had aspired to become a teacher; only in the Army had he discovered his passion for flying.

Present at the emergency meeting with Barry and me were my agent controller Joe Smith and a specialist whose specialization was not elaborated upon. The issue, of course, was the degree of risk posed by failure to comply with the stipulated time frames. We jointly worked out contingency plans for ways in which such situations could be handled in the future, from both the side of the "escape agents" and the "feeder."

In the event that we, the "escape agents," were ever again delayed for unforeseeable and unavoidable reasons, we would have to arrange to arrive exactly thirty or sixty minutes after the stipulated time. That would enable the subjects to seek secure cover for so long. In the augmented emergency plan, two alternative options were considered: a three-hour period after the stipulated rendezvous time for evacuation flights scheduled in the morning, and a twenty-four-hour one for operations planned for the afternoon.

Inasmuch as anything should ever go awry with the "feeders" after we could no longer be contacted, the agents and the subjects would be instructed to display something white at or near the collection point—a shirt, towel, sheet, or the like.

My objection—that we would then abort the mission even if a Czechoslovakian housewife chanced to have a piece of white laundry fluttering on the clothesline—fell on deaf ears. The feeders and the subjects, we were promised, would be drilled to keep any white material off the landing site if aborting the mission wasn't necessary.

At the conclusion of the meeting, Barry and I each got an envelope. That was always a little bit like Christmas, because each individual envelope that I had received for my flight missions so far contained more money than I had received as salary in the entire year during my training as a male nurse. And I already had a few envelopes lying under my mattress!

* * *

We had to wait an unusually long time for the next assignments, but they all went off smoothly.

That is, until the beginning of 1975, when we had an operation in target area Delta, located on a meadow between two forests at the southwestern edge of Strážný, only three kilometers as the crow flies from the German-Czechoslovakian border. Shortly before descent and approach, we had to fly over a thickly forested mountain chain. Afterwards, the view of the target area was unobstructed, and I could hardly believe what I was seeing through my binoculars: four men standing there. One of them was wearing a red shirt.

"They've got *four* people standing there, Barry!" I shouted over the intercom.

"Why four?"

"Hell if I know! One's wearing a red shirt. All four are relatively tall and muscular. I wonder, could it be a trap?"

Barry broke off the descent and approach. Held the helicopter at an altitude of about 200 meters and a distance of 300 meters from the landing site, he asked, "Can you see whether one of the men is carrying a weapon?"

"No!" I replied.

"What's that supposed to mean, 'No'? You can't see it? Or none of them is carrying a weapon?"

"I can't get a peek into their socks, obviously, but it doesn't look like they're armed," I answered.

While Barry, hovering over the spot, rotated 360 degrees, he scanned the terrain himself and asked me, "Do you see a vehicle, people, or anything suspicious somewhere?"

"No," I replied.

"Good, then I'll land now. I'm giving you fifteen seconds! No arguments in the hot zones, no fighting. If necessary, shove all four of them into the passenger space!" Barry shouted.

He was right. It was simply too dangerous to argue, while still in the landing zone, about who was excess baggage. And besides, the CIA wanted us to create as little fuss as possible, without leaving behind any traces.

Even before landing, I stood on the skid, jumped off the moment we touched down, opened the doors to the passenger space, and helped the men, now charging towards us, into the helicopter. I had to give the last guy a real shove in the ass to get him inside. He was lying across the other passengers, and I noticed he was wearing rubber boots and had rather strong body odor.

After takeoff, I shouted out my obligatory salutation into the back, *"A warm welcome! Herzlich willkommen! Dabro paschlovit!"* Adding, in both German and English, that we had expected only three people, I asked what had happened. Nobody replied.

Suddenly I sensed we weren't gaining altitude, and that we weren't flying in the same direction we'd come from.

"What's up, Barry?"

"We're too heavy! I won't make it over the mountain. I've got to follow the valley, heading south!"

I anxiously monitored the needles on the instruments. Almost every one of them was entering the red zone— except for the velocity indicator. Never before had we flown this slowly during an evacuation.

"We're at the performance limits! We're flying like a lame duck right before it crashes. Somebody has to get out!" Barry shouted, preparing to land in a meadow.

I already had someone in mind for precisely this scenario. It was the man with the rubber boots. Somehow, he was out of place among the others. I briefly paused and thought it over: what would happen to the man if we dumped him now? What kind of an earful would we catch from the CIA if he was in fact one of the subjects?

And what would he tell the authorities, assuming he wasn't one of the subjects?

"You decide who gets kicked out, Mr. Escape Agent. Now! And make it quick!" Barry said, in a voice at once commanding and despairing. I'd never seen him like this.

"I'll get out! But please, not here! It's less than a kilometer to the border. I've already spotted Philippsreut from the air. Even a lame duck should be able to make it that far in a minute or two," I begged.

Without a word, Barry revved up the turbine back from idle. After struggling to gain some altitude, we saw before us a road with a border crossing, which Barry immediately flew around in a large arc and at a low altitude. We landed on the first meadow immediately behind the border fence, which cut a deep swath in the forest and could be readily made out from the air.

I climbed out, placed the man with the rubber boots in the co-pilot's seat, and shut the doors.

Even as it took off, I could tell that the lame duck had once again become a real helicopter.

It was about a half-hour's walk to Philippsreut, and once there, I held out my thumb on the road to hitch a ride to Munich. After two frustrating hours, I was eventually both glad and grateful when a jolly Lower Bavarian guy drove me as far as Passau. From there, I took the train to Munich.

Late at night, Barry called me and said merely: "Peking Duck, as usual!"

That was the kind of telephone call I loved. Brief, to the point, and without any risk!

The next day we met in the beer garden at the Chinese Tower, exactly where we had had our first reunion eleven months before. Barry related that the refueling and the transfer at Deggendorf had proceeded rapidly and without any snags, as always. One of our people, who spoke fluent Russian and Czech, had been able to clarify that the fourth man was a farmhand from the region who had always wanted to go to the West. He had simply tagged along spontaneously, and now wanted to relocate to the United States and apply for asylum. The agents had taken him along and handed Barry two envelopes, one of which was for me.

* * *

Drama in Aiding Escape: Helicopter Pilot Fired Upon. These were the headlines, with minor variations, appearing in the tabloid press on Monday, August 18, 1975— first in Germany, and soon worldwide. Underneath were photos of a Jet Ranger and of Barry Meeker. The spectacular mission was covered by the *Passauer Neue Presse*, the *Trausteiner Wochenblatt*, the *tageszeitung*, the Munich evening paper, the *Abendzeitung* (*AZ*), the *Sueddeutsche Zeitung*, Munich's premier newspaper, the *Frankfurter Allgemeine Zeitung*, as well as the *New York Times*, *Pravda*, the *Bayerischer Rundfunk* (Bavarian Radio), and *Zweites Deutsches Fernsehen* (ZDF), one of Germany's publicly financed television stations.

According to the reports, Barry, commissioned by the attorney for whom he had carried out his first evacuation flight a year earlier, had flown together with his friend Teddy on Sunday, August 17, to a stipulated rendezvous point at Černá v Pošumaví, south of Horní Planá. Once there, he was supposed to pick up a sixty-year-old East Berlin truck driver, his fifty-four-year-old wife, their fourteen-year-old daughter, and a nineteen-year-old student, then fly them all to the West. Teddy was probably supposed to take charge of the role that had been mine during our CIA-financed flights. It was astonishing to me that in the wake of our last experience, Barry would have planned a flight with an assistant and four subjects. But the student, whose weight was stated by the press as forty-eight kilos, and the young girl together probably weighed less than our uninvited friend with the rubber boots had all by himself.

The subjects had not assembled at the stipulated target at the designated time, and still had to cover a greater stretch to reach the chopper. After it had been on the ground for two minutes, shots suddenly rang out and the drama began to unfold. The student and the sixty-year-old East Berliner were already sitting in the helicopter when the fourteen-year-old girl took a bullet in the leg and fell. She was dragged by Teddy to the helicopter and heaved into the cabin by her father. Finally, a bullet tore through Barry's left elbow, and the Jet Ranger took even more hits. Barry signaled that he could no longer wait. Teddy and the woman couldn't make it into the helicopter. Despite his injury, the fuel loss, and limited maneuverability, Barry still managed to fly the helicopter to Traunstein and land there, right in front of the hospital where he had worked as a rescue helicopter pilot. Since the surgeon on duty couldn't be dissuaded from reporting the gunshot wounds to the police, the matter became public.

Barry Winslow Meeker lost his German pilot's license and went back to the United States. The rescued East Berliner's wife had to spend three years in Czechoslovakian prisons, while Teddy got six. In addition, due to the enormous worldwide attention aroused by the fateful flight of August 17, the CIA abandoned this escape route.

CHAPTER 9

The Oil Minister

After I had completed my training as a rescue paramedic and parachute-jumping instructor and had my nurse's exam under my belt, I resolved to work for a half a year where I had most enjoyed it during my training. These were the places where you could peer most deeply into people, into both their bodies and minds.

So I spent six months working at the university's psychiatric clinic, at the department for involuntary commitments, located on Nussbaumstrasse. I listened to people's life stories and tried to cheer up depressed patients, while making the prescribed sleep deprivation more tolerable for them. I also calmed down manic patients and tried to immerse myself in the world of schizophrenics, whose tremendous creativity often fascinated me. Following that, I spent six months working in the operating theater of the university's surgical clinic, directly across the street. I was allowed to pass instruments to the doctors and obtain a close, upfront look at open bellies, pulsating hearts, or amputated leg stumps. I would have been all too glad to lend a hand, even if it just meant performing a small appendectomy or at least suturing a belly after the operation. But this work was reserved to the junior doctors.

The work at both stations was tremendous fun, but I wouldn't have wanted to be employed there over the long term. By the time I'd experienced all the different varieties of cases, it was starting to get boring. For me, at least. And when it came to the nurses and caregivers who had been working in psychiatry for a long time, I could not escape the impression that their patients' behavior had rubbed off on them a little.

Shortly before I switched yet again, this time to emergency surgery at the Munich-Schwabing Hospital, I fell in love with Birgit, an OR nurse.

Birgit bestowed upon me the loveliest smile I'd ever seen on a woman! It made her doe-brown eyes beam, and two dimples adorned her cheeks whenever she smiled. Birgit had a well-proportioned oval face and medium-length brown hair. She was a genuinely natural beauty! One of these rare specimens who looks equally good with or without makeup. I'll never forget our first kiss—during a walk in the Isar River bottomland. The kiss was so intense that I got goose pimples—not only on my arms, but also on my entire body, from head to toe. And Birgit even took an interest in parachute jumping; on the weekends she became one of my quickest students. During the week, we often cooked together, or sometimes we went to the movies or the theater, and had loads of fun with each other.

Until the telephone jangled one day at three in the morning.

"We're going away for a few days, darling. Pack a couple of things. We'll meet at eleven in the morning under the column at the Angel of Peace," a friendly female voice with a slight American accent instructed me.

For a moment, it took my breath away. I'd received the exact same call for my first assignment a few years ago.

Birgit was awake. What should I say? Refuse the meeting? On the other hand, the envelopes under my mattress, the contents of which I had been using to beef up my paltry salary over the past three years, were nearly empty now, hankering in despair to be refilled.

"Hello, darling—are you still there?" the voice asked.

"Yes!"

"Can I rely on you?"

"Okay," I confirmed, then hung up.

"Who on earth was that, calling on the phone at three in the morning?" Birgit asked.

I took a deep breath and tried telling the truth, or at least part of it.

"I've got to take the first train to Frankfurt in a couple of hours and meet an old acquaintance."

"But that was a woman's voice on the line just now, wasn't it?" Birgit insisted.

"Yes. She always calls whenever I'm supposed to meet my acquaintance in Frankfurt," I replied, which was literally the truth.

"Hey, just how stupid do you think I am?" Birgit demanded to know.

"Please don't make a scene now! I'll explain it to you later when I've got more time," I said, trying to mollify her.

Birgit stared at me, more appalled than she had ever been since we'd met, and shook her head furiously.

"And another thing," I added, "please call in sick for me. I was supposed to have the late shift today."

"You're crazy!" Birgit replied, turning away from me, insulted, and drawing the covers over her head. Surely, she would have deserved an explanation now. And a farewell kiss. But it wasn't the right moment to talk with Birgit about my CIA missions, nor was there any time for that. And besides, it wasn't at all clear whether I was supposed to talk with her about it at all. So far, the question hadn't come up. I quickly tossed a few things into my travel bag and left the apartment building. I could wait just as easily at the main train station.

* * *

Monday, March 12, 1979, 11 a.m.

Joe Smith, my CIA agent controller at Rhine-Main Airbase, had aged greatly since the last time I had seen him, together with Barry, at our emergency meeting barely four years ago. Almost euphorically, he greeted me by announcing, "Cooper, we've got something for you! Now you're really going to be able to show us what you've got!"

"I can't wait!" I replied.

"Since Ayatollah Ruhollah Khomeini landed in Tehran a couple of weeks ago, things over there have been getting pretty intense. The Revolutionary Guards have started executing former ministers and civil servants without much in the way of due process. Now we're somewhat concerned about Ali Reza Khan, the Shah's former oil minister. Specifically, we think that he knows more than we do about Iran's oil resources—he's the former head of the National Iranian Oil Company. That's why the CIA's offering a $50,000 bounty payment to get him out alive and has made preparations to evacuate him."

"Ever since that disaster with your colleague in Salzburg," I replied, "I'm no longer working for bounty payments. I'll do it for a fixed fee of $25,000 U.S., plus $25,000 more if I'm successful. Otherwise, count me out. I'm not risking my neck again for nothing!" I said.

"Which Salzburg colleague are you talking about?" Smith asked.

My heart felt like it was dropping into my guts. Could it be that Steiner wasn't working for the CIA at all? Maybe even for the other side? Was that the reason the assignments kept going south, and for his refusal to pay? I frantically tried to recollect my first meeting with Steiner and, simultaneously, to gain some time: "I'm not mentioning any names. You already know who I'm talking about," I said portentously.

Joe Smith looked at me seriously and staged an overly long pregnant pause. Then he burst out laughing.

"Yeah, good old Steiner! He coordinates operations in Eastern Europe, mainly. But you're done with those! – Let's make it a $20,000 U.S. fixed fee and $30,000 more if you successfully deliver the subject here in Frankfurt or in Langley!"

"Fine," I said, "but I've still got a couple of things in Munich to take care of. And I've got a vacation coming up and so forth. This business is now coming as a major surprise. I haven't done anything further for the CIA for almost four years now."

"That's no doubt a poor joke, Mr. Cooper! The Iranian Revolution won't wait for you to take your vacation! And besides, you yourself asked for some time off to be able to complete your nursing training, right? You're flying to London-Heathrow today at 1720 on British Airways, and from there you'll be taking another BA flight to Tehran's Mehrabad Airport. Your name is Thomas Freeman, and you're a reporter for Reuters news agency. After your operational briefing, you'll receive your tickets, your British passport, your press credentials, and your curriculum vitae. As well as a

British passport for the oil minister. He'd better shave his beard."

I nodded thoughtfully. Did I have any choice? Also, $50,000 U.S. was quite a tidy sum, one for which a person could make some effort and take some risks.

Joe Smith explained to me which middleman I would be able to use at Tehran's Great Bazaar in order to get in touch with Ali Reza Khan. The latter, it was believed, had already gone underground. Smith showed me a photo showing the minister next to the Shah, and then gave me a phone number that I could use to summon a reliable, English-speaking taxi driver. This driver would then get us over the Turkish border at Urmia—altogether legally—using our British passports. In the event any problems should arise, I would have to bribe a Kurdish leader to assist us further. The local Kurds, it was believed, had a pro-Western attitude and were eager to help, especially a certain Sheik Akar Ahmad—a name I was supposed to keep in mind. Once in Türkiye, the minister and I would then have to slog our way to Ankara, by bus, taxi, or any other means, and finally grab the first possible flight to Europe or the United States. Once again, the whole thing sounded like child's play—but it wasn't! I could virtually smell that!

"How come I can't just book two flights from Tehran to London, using our British passports?" I wanted to know.

"Because there's a manhunt underway for the minister and nineteen other people at the bus station and at the airport, and there's a strong risk of someone recognizing him, even without the beard and with a British passport," Smith replied.

"So you think they would recognize us at the airport and at the bus station, but not at the Turkish border crossing. How does that jibe?"

"Based on a couple of factors, we're assuming the manhunt isn't being extended to the border crossings. For one thing, the infrastructure is lacking—people to issue instructions, to copy the wanted lists and photos, and to distribute them at all the country's border checkpoints. Secondly, the overwhelming majority of the border guards are illiterate. Of course, you're free to circumvent the border. Improvise! Figure something out based on your own on-scene assessment. Results are the only thing that counts! If something goes awry, we've got nothing to do with the matter. Nor do we know any Reuters reporter named Thomas Freeman."

On a map, Smith showed me the escape route.

"A few years ago, I drove from Munich to Tehran and back in an old VW Beetle, so I do know part of the route. Wouldn't it be simpler to use the border crossing at Bazargan?" I asked.

"No," Smith replied. "On the stretch from Tehran to Bazargan, you'd be an extra 100 kilometers in Iranian territory, and it's got three checkpoints. Going via Urmia means you'll have only one checkpoint. Each of these is a potential risk," Smith added, surprising me with his detailed knowledge. Then he gave me $10,000 in American money, primarily in large bills, which I was supposed to stash in my pants and jacket pockets, as well as inside a money belt. And finally he gave me a worn black knapsack containing an additional $10,000 sewn into ten compartments, each of which had an additional $1,000 in bills of various denominations. According to Smith, the mission's success essentially depended on my adroit application of the politics of baksheesh. Bribes, he asserted, always had to be available in sufficient amounts, and in U.S. dollars. None of the people offering assistance would accept traveler's checks, credit cards, or Deutschmarks. Nor would I get very far with Iranian rial banknotes, which bore the Shah's likeness and had now become almost worthless. Usually, however, payments of even $10 or $20 U.S. would suffice to buy silence and gain support. Sometimes it had to be $100 or even $1,000. For the taxi ride into Türkiye, Smith said, one of our agents on the ground had promised the driver $2,000—ten times the usual rate.

Naturally, a good reporter also has to be equipped with a professional camera, so the CIA had procured me a brand-new Nikon F-2 and a handful of slide film. In addition, Smith presented me with yet another special gadget: three small diversionary bombs, built into cigarette packs and equipped with time fuses. When set off, these things were supposed to spew fire and smoke for a few minutes while making a huge racket. They could be used to divert a mob, for example, in order to escape, or to get into or out of a building, vehicle, or hiding place. I had to smile. I fancied myself a little like James Bond after having been introduced to his latest toy by Mr. Q.

Last but not least, Smith—not without a measure of pride—drew a pistol out of the knapsack.

"A 9-millimeter Italian Beretta 92," he said, "the latest model, with a double-stack magazine. You can get off fifteen shots without reloading. If necessary, you can use it to wipe out an entire checkpoint's garrison at a single go!"

The gun was a beauty, but I wasn't convinced. "I am *not* packing a weapon! Besides, I would hardly make it through customs carrying that thing," I commented.

Joe Smith replied, "You've got documents in your passport permitting you to carry the weapon. That'll take care of the security check in Frankfurt and customs in London. As for Mehrabad Airport in Tehran, nobody's running any checks at present. According to our most recent information, they've got twenty to thirty Revolutionary Guards sitting there, but only two or three of them can read and write. In the mornings they adjust the stamp for the others, so the illiterates don't have to do anything except give incoming travelers a critical look and stamp their passports without really checking. We're in close contact with our embassy, and know a bit more than you hear in the news. Ayatollah Khomeini discharged all civil servants, effective immediately— administrative officials, teachers, police, customs officials, and soldiers. Prison guards have fled, leaving the gates wide open. Tomorrow you'll experience the chaos for yourself, and you might even be able to exploit it for your mission. The Revolutionary Guards are mostly between twenty and forty, and during the Shah's time, the majority of them were unemployed, underprivileged, uneducated men, frequently criminals, even. They've got the power on the street now. Only the mullahs exercise any authority over them. Think about that, even if a Revolutionary Guard can't read your passport or your press credential and doesn't understand a word of English. Act as inconspicuously as possible. And dye your hair black!" Smith handed me a package of hair dye and the heavy pistol.

I accepted the hair dye but firmly refused the pistol: "I am definitely not taking that thing along!"

Next to the conference room there was a restroom, where I dyed my hair and eyebrows black. While waiting for the dye to be fully absorbed, I packed the contents of my travel bag into the knapsack, checked its numerous secret compartments as well as the papers, and memorized my new CV. So I was now called Thomas Freeman. In the passport photo, I actually had black hair. If necessary, would I be able to pass as a native, at least visually? Perhaps. In any event I would have to work on my bearing and body language, the way I had learned to do at the Farm. Also among the papers was a telex confirmation to Reuters from the Sheraton Hotel in Tehran about a room for me, rented for a week. It was the city's best hotel and the meeting place for news media reporters from all over the world. I was already excited to find out how my 'colleagues' were sizing up the situation there and whether, despite the Islamic Revolution, a glass of Scotch could be had at the hotel bar for anyone offering hard currency. After all, quite a few journalists were potential alcoholics.

The waiting time at Frankfurt Airport was just barely enough for two phone calls of importance to me.

The first call was to Dr. Fritz Liebl, a good friend and parachuting buddy, who had completed his first parachute jump with me at the age of sixty. He was still very keen about jumping. Fritz was good people—a generous, kindhearted guy. He was a physician who maintained a general practice in Munich-Fürstenried. He always had lots of patients, perhaps because he also took plenty of time for each of them, and sometimes he even allowed people to smoke with him in the treatment room. His patients could also talk to him about whatever was weighing on their minds. Once, Fritz offered to help me out, saying, "Whenever you need a doctor's sick note to stay home from work, just tell me. Everyone gets them anyway, provided they use the right magic words or manage to fake it. We can cut out the bullshit between friends!"

And now I did need a sick note, for fourteen days, as a precaution. I called Fritz, and without any ifs, ands, or buts, he promised me to send my employer the note before the day was out.

That's what real friends are for, I thought to myself gratefully.

The second call, by far the more difficult one, was to Birgit. But there too, I had a stroke of luck—only her answering machine picked up.

"I love you, darling!" I said. "But I've got to go away on urgent business for a week or two. I'll explain everything to you when I get back. Anyone who asks after me— please just tell them I'm sick. Flu, fever, and so on. Love you! Ciao!"

* * *

Tuesday, March 13, 1979, 8:25 a.m.

The plane landed right on time at Tehran's Mehrabad airport. I was tense to find out whether the customs checks really were as lax as Mr. Smith had predicted. But—there weren't any checks at all! Passengers like me, who were toting only carry-on luggage, simply went right onto the street and hailed themselves a taxi. Most of the people were still waiting for their suitcases at the baggage claim carousel. And then I saw yet another line of people at one window. I asked the person standing at the end of the line what he was waiting for.

"We want to get an entry stamp for our passports because we're afraid that without it, we could have problems when departing. You never know..."

I spared myself the annoyance of standing in line and decided to head directly to the hotel. But there were no more taxis. Suddenly, a khaki-colored Datsun pickup truck rolled up to the taxi stand, and the driver waved to me.

"Taxi?" I asked.

"Yes, get in!" replied the driver in English, smiling. He was an older, somewhat raffish-looking man with a mustache.

I seriously doubted this taxi was an officially licensed one, but I liked the guy because he spoke English, for one thing, and for another, because he had such a mischievous smile on his face. And besides, given the chaos the country was currently experiencing, it was probably totally irrelevant whether taxi passengers were ripped off officially or unofficially. Regardless of what happened, I had no intention of going to the police—who, according to the information provided by my agent controller, were nonexistent. The only exception was the Islamic police force now being established, which most certainly wasn't interested in taxi licenses and fare rates.

"Sheraton Hotel," I gave as my destination.

"Where are you from?" the driver wanted to know.

"England," I answered monosyllabically.

"Well, that's better than being an American, in any event!"

"Why is that better?"

"Because the Americans are Iran's worst archenemies. That's what our new leader, Ayatollah Khomeini, is saying on television and radio all day long. And people believe him!" my taxi driver told me.

"And you? What do you think?" I asked.

The man paused a long while, scrutinizing me with a serious mien before his mischievous smile at some point returned: "I love the Americans," he said. "And the English, and the French, and the Italians. But if I were to say that out loud here, they would lynch me right on the spot!"

"Why is that?" I asked.

"It's just the mood, ever since they drove the Shah out. There was a lot of poverty under the Shah. And Khomeini promised all these poor people prosperity and power if only they praised Allah and followed him. I'm a Muslim too. But it's not that simple. My name is Ali. What's yours?"

"Thomas."

After we drove a few kilometers, the streets were packed with people shouting loudly. We couldn't go any further.

"I'd better go there on foot. How much farther is the Sheraton?" I asked Ali.

"Don't do that! It's too dangerous. It's still a good five kilometers," Ali told me.

"What else can I do then?"

"You can spend the night with my family and me. You'll be safe there!"

Now that was suddenly too much closeness and familial intimacy for my taste. I explained to Ali that I wanted to get out of the cab and go on foot, and I inquired what I owed him for the taxi ride.

"Give me whatever you want. And I'll write down my telephone number, in case you need help. And I'll wait here at the corner for another fifteen minutes unless it gets too dangerous for me too."

I gave the taxi driver five dollars, stuck the slip of paper with his telephone number in my pants pocket, shouldered my knapsack, and bid the man a friendly farewell.

The mood was, in fact, explosive. I had never before seen such throngs of people on the street, not even in Munich during the large demonstrations against the Vietnam War. Thousands of Iranians were chanting fanatic slogans I did not understand, and a few hundred women, shrouded in black, screaming their nerve-racking tongue trill, seemed to be concurring with them. As inconspicuously as possible, I crept along the walls of buildings. Right there in the middle of the street, clamoring demonstrators were burning an American flag and pouring gasoline over an outsized effigy of incumbent U.S. President Jimmy Carter, which they then torched. Over and over, the word 'America' sounded from the clamor. They were probably hollering "Down with America," or something along such lines.

A blond man about my age was photographing the scene. Next to him was a slender young woman in jeans and a loosely thrown-on veil. They could have been a journalist and her photographer. Suddenly, stones were flying. The young man was struck on the back of the head. Blood was running through his hair and his white shirt. He looked around, terrified. Then another stone, violently flung from the crowd, hit him on the forehead. Blood spurted from his gaping wound. Stumbling, he pitched forward. The delicate young woman helped him up, and the two of them ran for their lives, as fast as their legs could carry them. Now the rage of Allah and his

227

disciples was being directed at a television crew from NBC, the American television network, who had been filming the scene. They were three burly men, presumably the cameraman, the sound engineer, and the reporter. But they too were just barely able to escape the mob while taking a severe beating. Everything had played out within a few minutes. It was a good thing that I had listened to Joe Smith and dyed my hair black. But my gut feeling was telling me that the CIA had erred if they fancied that a fake identity as a reporter could protect me. I slowly crept my way along the wall of the building, against the throng of people, and resolved to toss my expensive camera equipment into the next garbage bin, then burn my press credentials. And I decided to avoid the Sheraton. As I reached the intersection where I had gotten out of Ali's taxi, and saw Ali still waiting in it, I had a better idea.

"Can you drive me into Naser Khasrow Street and drop me off right where it starts? If you do, I'll give you a brand-new Nikon F-camera and a couple rolls of unexposed film."

Ali said nothing. I noticed that he wasn't too crazy about the whole business. Who, after all, would swap an expensive camera like that for a simple city taxi ride? Still, he eventually nodded, and we set off. He didn't believe that my offer had been meant in all seriousness until after I got out, when I laid the camera together with the films on the passenger seat. Then he also got out, thanked me, and bowed deeply.

I strolled a few meters down the street and checked into the same hotel in which I had stayed seven years ago. The receptionist at the Amir Kabir didn't recognize me, and it was a good thing, too. The room still cost $3

U.S., the plaster was still peeling from the walls, and the view of the inner courtyard, with the fountain, still soothingly splashing away, put my mind at ease.

It was 1140 in the morning. I didn't want to lose any time. I shoved my knapsack under the bed, burned my press credentials in the room's ashtray, and thoroughly aired the place out. Then I went down to the reception area, where I called the taxi driver whose number Joe Smith had given me.

"Ali!" a male voice answered. Is every Tehran taxi driver named Ali, or was that only a coincidence? Intuitively, I reached into my pants pocket and compared the memorized number I had just dialed against the one my taxi driver had written down earlier. The numbers were indeed different, so I now mentally designated as 'Ali 2' the man whom the CIA had selected as my driver. We arranged to meet at 1400 at the northern entrance of the Great Bazaar, only a few hundred meters away from the hotel. As a symbol of recognition, he was to be holding both a Koran and a bottle of Coca-Cola in one hand. I made my way there right away, especially because first, I wanted to meet our middleman, a custom tailor on Mousavi Alley in the bazaar, directly next to a kebob restaurant.

But, contrary to the usual practice in such cases, no code word had been stipulated with the custom tailor, a thin, distinguished older gentleman. He claimed to be unacquainted with any Ali Reza Khan. It took a solid hour and two full pots of strong black tea seasoned with Middle Eastern spices before we trusted one another.

"Please ask the minister if he can be ready to depart tomorrow morning at 0530, and where I can pick him up. Tell him he should shave off his beard and wear old, shabby clothing. I'll come back at 1600 and expect your answer," I instructed the custom tailor.

At 1400, I kept a lookout for Ali 2 at the northern entrance of the bazaar. A man was holding a bottle of Coke in one hand and a Koran in the other—not quite what we had agreed upon—but he was by far the only person holding these items. He had to be the one, and he was, too.

I proposed conducting part of our discussion in his car, which would also give me the opportunity to give it a once-over, after which we could take a brief walk. The vehicle, a twelve-year-old Toyota Corolla, was pretty beat-up. It had clocked 186,753 kilometers; the tires were worn, and it had no spare. With a bit of luck, we could make it into Türkiye, but to execute my Plan B—circumnavigating the border crossing, off the paved road—this vehicle would be altogether unsuitable.

As we strolled towards Panzdah-e Khordad Street, I asked Ali 2 how quickly he could be ready for action.

"As soon as I've got the money. $20,000 U.S. in cash!"

"We agreed on $2,000 U.S.," I replied, recalling that this amount was already ten times the usual price.

"I've been thinking it over. The risk has gone up. I now demand $20,000!" said Ali 2.

"I haven't got that much. $5,000 is my final offer," I replied, in the hope he would refuse. I had a bad gut feeling about this guy.

"I know you can get the money. You can get it from your embassy if you have to. It's still $20,000!"

I thought about it for a moment and concluded it would be better not to tell Ali 2 what I was thinking. Otherwise, he could betray me and jeopardize the mission. As long as he thought he was still in the running, he would keep his mouth shut.

"Okay," I said, "I'll need some time to come up with that amount. I'll contact you as soon as I have the money."

I double-timed it to the Amir Kabir, requested the telephone at the reception desk, and called Ali 1—from now on, simply Ali.

"Aren't you in luck, Thomas! I've just had a quick bite at home, and right now I'm driving back through the city again," Ali said.

"How fast can you be at the spot where you dropped me off three hours ago?"

"At the beginning of Naser Khosrow Street? In fifteen minutes. You want your camera back, right? That's what I thought right away," mused Ali.

"No, the camera belongs to you! All I need is a taxi. See you soon!"

After exactly fourteen minutes, Ali was at the stipulated meeting spot. One big fat bonus point for him! I sat down in the passenger seat.

"Where to, my friend? You're in good hands with me. I'll drive you wherever you want, even for the entire week," Ali offered.

"A gift is a gift, and it stays that way! I'll pay for wherever you drive me. But I'd like to ask a couple of questions."

"What kind of questions?"

"Are you really a taxi driver? Or did you train for another profession?"

"I was a teacher. English and history. But I was fired four weeks ago. I've somehow got to earn money for myself, my family, and my brother's family."

"How come for your brother's family?"

"My brother Ahmad was murdered six weeks ago."

Tears welled up in Ali's eyes as he continued, "It was during a demonstration. He just happened to be standing on the same side as the Shah's followers, and the Shah's opponents beat him to death! He was simply pummeled to death! Even though he hadn't done a thing! Can you imagine that?"

"My most heartfelt condolences," I said, lowering my head. I gave Ali a while to block out the pain, then I asked, "Does the pickup belong to you?"

"It belonged to my brother. He used to supply fruit and vegetable dealers. But that business is now defunct. So I'm now using the pickup as a taxi, even though it's actually too big for that. I'm afraid the Revolutionary Guards are going to take it away from me, the way they've already confiscated my neighbor's car."

"May I take a closer look at the pickup?" I asked.

"How come? Do you want to buy it, maybe?" Ali asked as we were both climbing out.

"No, just looking. Do you have a spare tire?"

"No, why? Nobody in Tehran has a spare tire."

The tire tread was still somewhat acceptable. I looked around a little, climbed back in, and determined that the vehicle's interior was safe for a confidential talk.

"Can I rely on you not to tell anybody a thing about what I'm now discussing with you?"

Ali nodded silently.

"Tomorrow morning, can you drive me, and an acquaintance of mine, into Türkiye by way of Urmia? And what would that cost?" I asked.

Ali's brow furrowed, and he looked at me with the sad expression of a father who cannot fulfill his child's most heartfelt wish.

"I'm afraid I can't do it."

"Why not?" I asked.

"It's hardly even possible for Iranians to leave the country. In order to do that, we need very, very serious reasons and special dispensation, which nobody is issuing right now," Ali replied. "On top of that, I don't have a passport," he added.

"Then could you drive us as far as Urmia?" I asked.

"Yes, I could do that," Ali replied, but with so little enthusiasm in his voice that I pressed him further: "Can you? Or can't you? I'll pay, no matter what! So what would that ride cost?"

"Normally, $200 U.S. But for you..."

"I'll pay you $300 U.S. if you can be right at this spot tomorrow morning at five on the dot, with a full tank of gas and ready to drive me with my acquaintance to Urmia!" I offered, extending my hand to Ali.

"It's a deal!" said my trusty taxi driver, accepting.

Satisfied, I marched back to the Bazar-e Bozorg, the grand bazaar of Tehran, assured myself that nobody had followed me, and entered the custom tailor's shop. Not a soul was around.

The middleman handed me a small slip of paper containing two names separated by a slash.

"The man you're looking for will be standing at this intersection tomorrow morning at 5:30, ready to travel. Please be punctual!"

"Where is that? Can't you give me the exact address of where he's staying?" I asked.

"The man is staying with his former cleaning lady, on the edge of one of the poorer quarters in the city's southeast, not especially far from here. He just didn't want to give me the exact address."

That sounded plausible, though it could also be a trap. I thanked him, and as I was taking my leave of the custom tailor, I gazed deep into his eyes to detect flickering or twitching eyelids. Something revealing uncertainty or lying. But nothing was there.

I was slowly starting to get hungry. No wonder—after all, ever since arriving in Tehran, I hadn't eaten a thing. I wanted to see whether the Armenian restaurant near my hotel was still in business, and whether they were still allowed to serve beer.

The restaurant was still open for business. The food was good, the price reasonable. Upon inquiring, I even got a beer, though it wasn't listed on the menu and cost considerably more than the meal itself. The mood was gloomy. Everywhere, in the hotel, in the bazaar, on the street, or in the restaurant, you could tell that people were afraid—most especially those who had prospered somewhat under the Shah. They now feared those who hadn't prospered so much.

* * *

Ali showed up right on the dot. I showed him the slip of paper with the street name, and asked him, "How long do we need to get there?"

"Ten minutes," he replied.

"If we wait there, it could draw attention. Drive slowly around the block and see to it that we're at the intersection by exactly five-thirty."

"Nothing in Tehran is more conspicuous than a car driving slowly when it could go fast!" Ali laughed.

"Okay, just drive fast, then!" I replied.

The few cars cruising along the street at this hour seemed to be actually engaged in drag racing. Ali raced his old truck up and down Ferdowski Avenue as fast as he could, without regarding any traffic signals.

"We've got more than enough time. Why aren't you stopping for red lights?" I asked.

"In Iran," Ali lectured me, "right-of-way doesn't belong to the guy who's got the green light, but rather the guy driving the bigger car!"

The timing was perfect: as we drove up to the rendez-vous spot at exactly five-thirty, a figure moved out of the night darkness towards the intersection, which was illuminated only hazily by a weak, ancient streetlight. I climbed out of the pickup truck, went toward the man, and knew immediately—it was the subject! Ali Reza Khan, a tall, corpulent man with oily, slicked-back hair, a full beard, and wearing a dark blue suit, appeared exactly as he did on the photo that Joe Smith had shown me, the one depicting the minister standing next to the Shah.

"We've got an appointment. Please come with me!"

I told the minister—who, strictly speaking, was only an ex-minister—to get into the pickup and sit down on the bench seat between Ali and me. Right off the bat, the minister struck me as being as unlikeable as my driver had been likeable from the first second we had met at Tehran Airport. I always paid heed to my gut feeling, for it had already saved my life a number of times. On the other hand, I had a job to do, and had to somehow reach a modus vivendi with the man.

"You got my passport?" That was the first thing the ex-minister wanted to know.

I nodded, countering with another question: "Didn't they tell you to shave off your beard and show up in old, worn clothing?"

"Yeah, they did. But nobody's going to tell me when I'm supposed to shave and what I'm going to wear!" Ali Rezi Khan replied furiously.

I instructed Ali to drive to the Amir Kabir Hotel and wait there a couple of minutes, because I wanted to speak with the gentleman about something in private. I kept a lookout along the way, but never got the feeling that someone was following us.

The receptionist was sleeping when I grabbed the key to my room, which, in any event, was paid up until noon, and went up to the first floor with the ex-minister.

"From now on," I told him, "your name is Hassan Asghari. You're a British subject with Iranian roots, born in London. You work in London as a bus driver. You drive one of these nice red double-deckers. Can you remember that?"

"Yeah. Now gimme my passport!" Hassan demanded.

"Only once you look the same as on the passport photo. The beard has to go!" I insisted, handing Hassan a pair of scissors and some shaving gear from my knapsack. I told him to hurry up.

"That's extortion! You will pay for that!" snorted Hassan. The hotel guests were still asleep, and the bathroom next to my room was empty. That would abruptly change in fifteen minutes or half an hour.

While Hassan set about shaving, I had yet another idea. Maybe it was a little mean, but it was imperative.

"Gimme my passport now!" Hassan demanded, as he stepped back into my hotel room, now freshly shaven.

"Not yet! I've got to ask you to do something else first. Take off your pants and suit jacket, and use your suit to thoroughly wipe the floor, especially under the bed, where most of the dust has gathered!" I requested of the ex-minister in a friendly tone.

The man—who was a head taller than I—exploded in sheer rage and grabbed me by my shirt collar, but before he could say a word, I vigorously bent his thumbs backwards and slammed him against the wall. He screamed loudly in pain.

"Listen up, Hassan," I said sharply, resolving to immediately dispense with formalities with the London bus driver. That meant dropping any polite forms of address. No more 'Sirs' or 'Misters' for this guy. "Next time," I continued, "it's *really* going to hurt. If we want to survive everything here, we've got to cooperate with each other, and we can't keep working at cross purposes. Now look. A man wearing a snazzy, custom-tailored suit who lets himself be chauffeured around here in an old pickup truck is going to arouse immediate suspicion. If you don't have anything else to put on, then at least you've got to make whatever you're wearing look old and shabby. The more wrinkles and dust, the better. So hurry up now, and get cracking. We don't have much time, and it's *your* life on the line!"

Falling silent, Hassan used his suit jacket and pants as a dust rag to wipe the floor of my hotel room, even under the bed and in the particular corners I pointed out to him. I sensed how he was inwardly seething and brooding. He wasn't the type of man who followed instructions, but rather one who had been issuing orders, probably his entire life. I also feared that he was unaware of the seriousness of his situation, or was suppressing any thoughts of it.

237

After the work was finished, I handed Hassan his passport. He had earned it!

At dawn we left the city, heading west. After a good hour's drive, I broke the silence: "We haven't been properly introduced. I'm Thomas. Our driver's name is Ali. My acquaintance, who wants to drive to Türkiye with me, is named Hassan."

Ali's mischievous smile, which I got such a kick out of, spread over his face. He told me, "With the beard and suit—when it was still clean, anyway—your friend Hassan looked exactly like a man I've often seen on television and read about in the papers."

"Surely Iran has a lot of men who look like Hassan. He's a bus driver in London," I lied, and Ali knew it.

"Bus driver in London," he murmured softly.

"Can we maybe listen to a little music? Do you folks here have a good radio station?" I asked.

"There are only two radio stations left. One with Islamic music, mostly Koranic Suras in song form. The other broadcasts Khomeini's speeches over and over, all day long. Which do you want to hear?" Ali asked.

"Unfortunately I don't speak Farsi, so I can't understand what Ayatollah Khomeini has to say to your people. But I'd enjoy hearing a couple of Koranic Suras—that sounds Eastern and mystical, somehow," I said, although country music would been more suited to the barren desert landscape, as far as my taste was concerned.

"But only if you both want to!" I added.

Neither of the two Muslim men wanted to.

"Can you estimate when we're going to reach Urmia? And won't we have to fill up the tank in the meantime?" I asked Ali, after we'd been driving for three hours.

"We'll be in Zanjan in about an hour. We can stop and take a break there. We'll get some gas and something to eat, drink some tea, and buy fresh water. Then we'll still need approximately six hours to reach Urmia. We should be able to make it there before sundown."

At the gas station, a great deal of lively activity was going on. Besides food stands, there were a number of market stalls selling clothing, hookah pipes, pictures of Ayatollah Khomeini, and Koran editions in every size and price range. I would have been all too glad to outfit Hassan in some Kurdish duds with bloomers, a vest, a belly sash, and a turban. But he categorically refused; in his opinion, the problem wasn't with him, but rather the people who recognized him. Finally, I bought each of us black-and-white checkered fringed shawls. The head-scarves could be worn loosely around the head, resembling a Kurdish turban. Over some tea and shish kebabs, I convinced Ali and Hassan that we should all put on these traditional head coverings before arriving in Urmia. Then I wanted to pay Ali for the gas to fill the tank, but he refused, saying that it was included in the stipulated price for the journey.

"Absolutely out of the question. I'm covering expenses like gasoline and food, in any event!" I insisted. "So how much did the gas cost?"

"One dollar," Ali replied.

"What cost one dollar? A liter? A gallon? I mean, how much was it to fill the entire tank?"

"One dollar. A complete fill-up cost a dollar!"

I glanced at the gas pump and converted the Iranian rials into dollars. Ali was right! I did recall that gasoline in Iran was cheap, but *that* cheap? It was still surprising. It probably had something to do with the revolution. The subsidized rial price had remained in place, while the exchange rate in relation to the dollar had dramatically plummeted. Traders, restaurateurs, and hoteliers wanted to see dollars; otherwise, they were adjusting their rial prices to the galloping inflation rate. Only the now leaderless National Iranian Oil Company, whose former boss I had just invited to lunch, had left its prices in rials at levels remaining from the Shah's time.

Before we resumed our travels, Hassan asked me to speak with him privately. I signaled Ali to wait in the pickup, and marched with the ex-oil minister behind the restaurant stand and down along the street some distance.

"He's recognized me! That's going to put both our lives at risk. You've got to shoot Ali!" Hassan implored me. By Allah, I hadn't reckoned with this demand!

"I don't have any kind of weapon," I replied.

"What kind of morons do they have working at the CIA? They send you on a dangerous mission like this without even giving you a weapon to pack along," Hassan griped. "Then I'll just have to shoot him myself!"

"So you've got a weapon?" I asked, astonished.

"Yes, a Beretta!"

"An Italian Beretta 92, with a double-stack magazine?" I asked, recalling the weapon that Joe Smith had insisted on foisting upon me back in Frankfurt.

"No, a Beretta 950. For the past fifteen years, I haven't gone anywhere without carrying it on me."

"This peashooter with eight cartridges in the magazine and one in the fold-up barrel? I'm very familiar with this pistol. I can strip it down and reassemble it blind, and I'm a good shot. Give me the pistol and let me handle it," I offered.

"So you'll bump off Ali? You're really going to kill him?" asked Hassan. He wasn't buying it.

"Yes! I'm a professional, after all! Have you ever actually killed a human being?" I asked Hassan.

"I don't want to talk about that right now. But if you kill him, that'll be fine by me. How do you want to get it done?"

"Well, when we get to a point that seems suitable to me, I would instruct Ali to turn off the street," I said, "then drive two or three kilometers into the desert where nobody else can see or hear us. Then I'll ask him to crank down the window. You bend over forward and hold your ears. Then I'll shoot him in the head. The bullet will exit the other side of his skull and through the open window. It'll go fast and painlessly, and there won't be any mess. We'll dispose of the body at the scene. Then I'll keep driving," I said, explaining my plan.

Hassan seemed satisfied. Nodding, he said, "Okay. That's how we'll do it!"

"Then give me the pistol now!" I demanded.

"It's in the car, in my jacket pocket. You're not getting it until we reach the spot where we're knocking him off."

Ali was in a great mood, and he told me that he would enjoy driving even more after having a small meal and a glass of strong black tea. On top of that, he said, we were truly pleasant traveling companions. He said he had also ridden with people who bickered during the entire trip and had even gotten into fistfights. Especially on such a long trip, he commented, it is very pleasant when everything proceeds harmoniously.

From time to time, small, barely discernible roads branched off from the main highway. They presumably led to the local farmers' saffron fields, ending up in the middle of nowhere. For what I was planning to do, using one of these roads seemed safer. After all, I didn't want to get stuck now offroad in the craggy steppe country. I instructed Ali to turn right on the next one of these roads coming up.

"How come?" he asked

"I'd just like to know where these small roads lead. To saffron or poppy fields? There aren't any villages or people anywhere near here. Please drive two or three kilometers down one of these roads. Then we'll turn around and head back," I said. At the very next opportunity, Ali complied with my wish.

"Okay, you can turn around again here."

Ali turned the car around.

"Stop the car and crank down the window."

Ali did what I wanted, and I also rolled down my window.

"You guys hear this silence?" I asked.

Neither man replied. Hassan was slowly reaching into his jacket.

"Give me the weapon!" I demanded. I was prepared for everything. While Hassan slowly handed me his Beretta 950, I tried to read his expression. It was radiating fear and distrust. It wasn't Ali who was frozen with fear, but rather Hassan. He didn't bend forward the way we'd discussed; nor did he hold both ears.

"Hold your ears and bend forward!" I shouted.

Now both of them, Ali and Hassan, were holding their ears and bending forward.

The Beretta 950 has an interesting design. Because it's so small, it's especially popular with agents. I'd trained on the Farm with one. There's always one cartridge chambered in the barrel that can be flipped up. I removed the cartridge and threw it out the window. Then I yanked out the magazine and flung the weapon—without its magazine—far into the desert steppe.

"You can close your window again and drive back, maybe a bit faster than we came here," I told Ali. Dangling my arm out the window, every ten or twenty meters I popped another cartridge out of the magazine until it was empty, finally tossing it behind us.

"But you *did* want to shoot him!" shouted Hassan.

Saying that was a mistake. Perhaps just as big a mistake as the one Ali had made when he had said he thought he had frequently seen Hassan on television. How much simpler life on this planet would be if people didn't immediately say whatever they were thinking at the moment! How much blood had already been spilled because people—without any necessity for doing so at all—had simply said the wrong thing at the wrong time, unbidden and uncoerced?

"I never wanted to shoot Ali," I said to Hassan. "But would you have voluntarily given me your weapon? Of course I could have disarmed you—you can bet on it. But a single-action pistol with a cartridge in the chamber can still always get off one shot. So this way, it was simpler," I continued, adding, "Ali won't betray us. Guaranteed. I'd bet my life on it."

"You two wanted to shoot me?" Ali asked, confused.

"No, Ali, nobody wanted to shoot you. I just had to use a trick in order to get hold of Hassan's pistol, which is now lying out there in the desert. That's all there was to it," I said, trying to calm him down.

Hassan was boiling mad, but pulled himself together and kept his mouth shut.

"What are you actually going do once we're in Urmia?"

I asked Ali. "Surely you aren't going to drive back to Tehran at night?"

"No, that would be too dangerous. I'll sleep in the car and start heading back tomorrow at sunup."

"Then I've got a better idea: we'll take a hotel room this evening, all three of us, and have dinner together. You can drive back tomorrow. Or the day after that. I have to ask you to stay long enough until I know whether I may still need you. I'll pay you $50 U.S. for every day you spend waiting, as well as for your food and accommodations," I proposed.

"I can do that. But tomorrow I'll have to call my wife and tell her I'll be coming later. Otherwise she'll start worrying," Ali replied.

"Of course you can call home. Just as long as you tell nobody, absolutely nobody—not even your wife—that we've got ourselves a passenger you might have seen on television. And not a word about what we've discussed. That's vital for both Hassan as well as for me. Can I one hundred percent rely on you?" I asked Ali, giving him an urgent look.

"Yes, I swear by..." Ali said in a firm voice.

"You don't have to swear. I am totally relying on you! You know what's at stake! Think of your brother!"

Ali nodded.

"And how am *I* going to get anywhere tomorrow?" Hassan wanted to know.

"You'll get in a taxi and ride into Türkiye. At the border, show them your passport and tell them you're a London bus driver, and that you've been making a brief trip to visit family."

His brow furrowed, Hassan thought it over and ran his hands over his face in silence. He was becoming increasingly afraid. Ali grinned almost imperceptibly. After a while, I said, "Don't be afraid, Hassan. I'll be accompanying you until you're safe, and a bit further. I don't know yet whether we'll be able to use our passports to go through the regular checkpoint, or whether we'll have to circumnavigate it. That's something I want to discuss with the Kurdish leader, Sheik Akar Ahmad. He's a man we can trust."

As we drove along the southern tip of a gigantic salt lake, Ali said we would soon be reaching our destination. I had him stop, and I insisted that we all tie our black-and-white checkered fringed shawls around our heads, turban-like. First and foremost, it was a matter of concealing Hassan's identity. The ex-oil minister resisted vehemently. When it became clear to him that we wouldn't drive any farther without the turbans, he finally yielded to peer pressure.

Shortly after dusk, we reached Urmia and checked into the first hotel we saw. The Morvarid, on the shore of the Shahar River, was simple, clean, and inexpensive. I took a room with three beds for $5 U.S. per night. This was the only way I could keep an eye on my traveling companions.

We asked for the largest, best-known restaurant in town and headed over there. While Ali and Hassan were noticeably reticent, I asked the owner, as well as the guests at the larger tables, whether they knew where I could find Sheik Akar Ahmad. They responded with shrugs, whereupon I emphasized that I wanted to speak to him about an important matter and was staying at the Morvarid. I would have gladly treated everyone to a round of Raki, but in light of the new political situation, I wasn't sure whether that would have been a good idea.

My gut feeling told me that a lot of the men in the restaurant knew the Kurdish leader, and that someone would convey him my wish to get in touch.

* * *

Thursday, March 15, 1979, 9:15 a.m.

We had just finished breakfast in front of the hotel when two disguised men in black Kurdish dress drove up on an off-road motorcycle. The man on the passenger seat had a Kalashnikov slung over his shoulder. They inquired after the man who wanted to speak to Sheik Akar Ahmad, and I answered, but resolved that all three of us would ride to the Kurdish leader, mainly because I didn't want to let my traveling companions out of my sight.

"Have you got a car?" the Kurds asked.

I pointed to the Datsun. The pickup truck had a front bench seat for three people, as well as the cargo bed. I didn't have to worry about who would sit where. The Kurds peremptorily decided that one of them would drive while the passenger with the Kalashnikov would ride in the bed with us. However, there was still a minor matter that they could not dispense with: we all had to wear black blindfolds, so that we would be unable to take note of the route to the tribal chieftain.

Ali and Hassan began panicking. Both the Shah as well as Ayatollah Khomeini had led their opponents to their deaths wearing black blindfolds. I asked for a moment of quiet and did some thinking. A trap could not be ruled out, but was rather improbable. What worried me more than the blindfolding was the notion of leaving Ali and Hassan alone, because I was afraid that upon my return, Ali would be on his way home and Hassan would be walking around the market, undisguised. Then I suddenly thought of the "naked man trick," which had stood me in good stead right at the outset of my career. I had Ali give me the car key, asked the Kurds to wait a moment, and went up to our room with Ali and Hassan.

"If you refuse to wear blindfolds—something I can certainly understand—then I'll ride to the sheik alone. I'll be back in a couple of hours. But under no circumstances do I want either of you to leave the room. Do you both understand that?" Both men nodded in relief.

"If you're quite definitely not leaving the room, then you won't be needing any clothing. Kindly strip down to your underwear and stuff everything in your pillowcase!" I told both men.

"Why? We'll stay in the room anyway, just as we are," Hassan said, outraged, while Ali concurred with him.

"Because I'm not taking any chances! And because our lives are at stake! There isn't any more time for debate. Either you two do what I say right now, and make it snappy, or I'll drive off in the pickup truck and never see either of you again," I threatened sharply.

As the two of them stood before me in their underwear and handed me the filled-up pillowcases, I ordered them to crawl under the bedsheets and hand me their underwear as well. I tied up the pillowcases and took them along with me. After closing and locking the hotel room door, I shoved a wooden match between the door and its frame, a few centimeters from the upper right-hand corner. That way, upon returning I could tell whether the door had been opened during my absence.

The bags of clothing landed on the pickup truck's bed, and the seating arrangement was clear: one of the Kurds drove the pickup, I sat blindfolded in the middle, and the Kurd with the Kalashnikov sat on the other side, next to me.

Sheik Akar Ahmad somewhat resembled a prince from one of the fables in *A Thousand and One Nights*. He was wearing a white turban, white bloomers, a crimson belly sash and a crimson vest trimmed with gold brocade. His reception room could have competed with a number of museums specializing in oriental art: heavy Persian rugs on the floor and on the walls, delicately carved furniture, a samovar, tea tables, tea glasses, silver spoons, a large bowl full of dates, and tiny porcelain equestrian figurines.

The man, whom I estimated to be in his mid-forties, asked me, in perfect English: "Who are you and what can I do for you?" Meanwhile, one of his servants set about pouring me a glass of tea.

"My name is Thomas Freeman. Are you Sheik Akar Ahmad?" I wanted to affirm.

The sheik nodded.

"Then I'd like to talk with you frankly. I am supposed to accompany an acquaintance over the border into Türkiye, and I am requesting your assistance. It goes without saying that if you can and wish to help me, I shall reciprocate."

"Is the man we're talking about here Ali Reza Khan?" inquired the sheik.

Startled, I attempted to conceal my surprise, replying, "Please understand that I cannot mention any names."

"Oh, you've already done that! I read it in your eyes," the sheik replied. He continued, "Last week, an American embassy employee—presumably a CIA agent—recruited a taxi driver, who was supposed to drive the former head of the National Iranian Oil Company into Türkiye, along with an escort. The taxi driver is a traitor and wanted to squeeze money from both the CIA as well as Khomeini's people. They're already expecting you both at the checkpoint!"

"How do you know this?" I asked, as emotionlessly as I could.

"Two of my men are working undercover as Revolutionary Guards, one of them at the checkpoint."

"What do you propose?" I asked.

"First off, you've got to get rid of the taxi driver. Either execute him or put him safely out of commission for the next thirty-six hours!" the sheik replied.

"I didn't hire the taxi driver you're talking about. I told him I would still need more time to procure the money he was demanding, and that I would get back to him. We've arrived with another driver, one who enjoys my confidence."

"That sounds very good. Still, you shouldn't trust anyone except yourself," the sheik lectured me. Those were the exact words they had constantly drilled into us during the training at the CIA camp.

"Where are Ali Reza Khan and your driver now?" asked the sheik.

"Esteemed Sheik. You have just now given me good advice, advice that I shall gladly heed. Please tell me first how you can assist me. Then I will tell you where the two men are to be found."

Sheik Akar Ahmad smiled appreciatively and explained: "There are two options for safely circumventing the checkpoint. One is to use horses. That takes around ten hours, and all of you would have to be experienced riders. One of my men will accompany you. He'll spend the night in Türkiye and come back with the horses the following day. The second option is to take three off-road motorcycles. My men will drive. You'll sit on the pillion seat of one motorcycle, and Hassan will take the pillion seat of the second one. The third motorcycle will carry drinking water, gasoline for the return trip, reserve ammo, and emergency repair and first aid kits. The journey will take five to six hours for the two of you, and my men will come back the same day."

"I like the motorcycle option better. How quickly can you organize that, and how much will it cost me?" I asked.

"My men can depart tomorrow morning at dawn. What can you pay? What is this man's life worth to you?" the sheik asked.

"$10,000 U.S. in cash," I replied.

"$10,000? That isn't much for a human life. And it isn't much when you're familiar with the CIA's budget. But if we Kurds help, we're not doing it for the money, but rather for ideological reasons. Something much more preferable than money, though, would be a gift you can make to me," the Sheik said.

"Tell me your wish, and I shall attempt to fulfill it, insofar as it is within my power to do so," I offered him.

"We had a sand-colored Datsun pickup truck exactly like the one you rode in. Until the Revolutionary Guards stole it from us. We really miss this vehicle," said the sheik.

"The truck belongs to my driver," I replied. "Perhaps I can persuade him to sell it. Ali Reza Khan and my driver, by the way, are currently lying naked in our hotel room, covered with nothing but a sheet. That way, they can't run off. Their clothing is packed in pillowcases, sitting in the bed of the pickup truck."

The sheik liked the story so much, he had to laugh out loud. It's probably a rare occasion that anyone has heard a sheik laugh so loudly. It was an opportune moment for me to sum up the situation.

"Your men will come to the hotel with three motorcycles at 5:00 am tomorrow morning," I said. "Your people ought to prepare a document for the sale of the Datsun. If my driver is willing to sell, I'll pay him, one of your men can sign the contract, and he'll get the keys. If my driver doesn't sell, we'll have to respect that, and I'll give one of your men $10,000 U.S. in cash. Then we'll get going. Where in Türkiye will your men drop us off?"

"In Gever. The Turks call the place Yüksekova. It'll be easy for you to continue along from there."

The sheik sealed our negotiation with a powerful handshake, instructed his people to drive me back, then called out, "Once you get to the edge of town, you can take off his blindfold!"

When we reached Urmia, I asked both Kurds to go to a restaurant of their choice and get three roast chickens, a substantial portion of saffron rice, three large bottles of water and a large Coke.

In front of our hotel, both Kurds switched to their motorcycles, while I took the provisions and lifted both pillowcases, which were full to bursting, from the truck's bed and marched up to the room.

The match was still wedged against the upper right corner of the door—a good sign. My two pals were lying there obediently, covered only with a sheet, and snoring—one of them louder than the other. The only reason to wake both of them would have been the freshly roasted chickens, but even those could wait. I decided to go to bed as well. Staring at the ceiling, I pondered what could still go awry, what I had overlooked or insufficiently thought through. Nothing occurred to me. Except for one prank—namely, I had no idea what Iranian humor was like, and it was time to find out.

I locked both pillowcases filled with clothing into the room's only wardrobe, and yelled, "Wake up, people, food!"

Ali and Hassan were sleeping so deeply that I had to repeat my announcement, a lot more loudly, and shake both men by the shoulder.

"Where are my clothes?" asked Hassan, groggy with sleep. Ali was also looking at me inquisitively.

"People," I said with a serious face, "your clothes were incredibly filthy and reeking of sweat. So I took them to the laundry first. They'll be ready tomorrow."

Hassan's face grew red with fury.

"Whaaat the hell? I want my clothes—now!"

Ali, a bit depressed, added, "That wasn't a good idea at all, Thomas. So how am I supposed to go to the reception desk to call my wife?"

"Aren't you guys hungry at all?" I asked.

"Without my clothes, I'm not eating a thing!" Hassan protested. Ali was likewise shaking his head.

I allowed myself a little time before announcing, "I've got one piece of bad news and two pieces of good news for both of you. Which do you want to hear first?"

"The bad news!" Ali asked.

"The bad news is, none of us will be leaving this room until tomorrow morning. At most to take a leak or for a quick phone call. It's too dangerous, and it's putting too much at risk."

Once again, I made a kind of pregnant pause and waited until Hassan asked, "So what's the good news, then?"

I opened up the wardrobe, gave each man his pillow-case stuffed with clothes, and said, "The first piece of good news is, you can put on your clothes again, but they're just as unwashed and full of sweat as when you handed them over to me."

Ali immediately shot me his mischievous grin, the one that had endeared me to him from the moment we had first met. Even Hassan managed to crack a smile. Both men were so happy that they didn't even demand to hear my second bit of good news, namely, the successful negotiations with the sheik.

Swearing Ali and Hassan to the utmost confidentiality, I reported to them how my visit to the Kurdish leader had unfolded, and I made it clear to both men that they would be jeopardizing mainly their own lives, should they repeat anything we were discussing here.

After thoroughly thinking it over, Ali was prepared to sell me his pickup for $10,000 U.S., so that I could make a present of the vehicle to the sheik. He had the necessary paperwork on hand.

In order to ensure that Ali didn't open his big mouth and jeopardize our mission at the last second, for safety's sake Hassan and I stood next to him while he telephoned his wife.

"Don't worry about anything. I won't be home until tomorrow evening," was all he was allowed to say.

* * *

Friday, March 16, 1979, 5 a.m.

The Kurds arrived punctually and sealed the deal with Ali to sell the vehicle. With everyone present as a witness, I paid our trusty driver $10,000 U.S. in cash on his bed, and laid an extra $300 for the trip on top of that, plus $50 for the extra day. I bid him farewell with a heartfelt embrace.

Hassan and I each got onto a motorcycle, swinging ourselves onto the pillion seat behind the Kurdish driver. The support motorcycle alternated between riding ahead and behind us. After forty kilometers along the country road, we headed south, toward the mountains, where things became uncomfortable: steep downhill stretches, sharp curves, then steep uphill grades, all of which pushed the performance capacity of man and machine to their utmost. The Yamaha XT 500's suspension struts were groaning under Hassan's weight, and at one point, during an abrupt acceleration, he slid off the pillion seat and made a hard, ass-first landing on the terrain. The Kurds decided that Hassan and I had to switch motorcycles from time to time, so that no single machine would be overly burdened with Hassan's weight. For just about four hours, we suffered through the strenuous endurance trip. Then we reached a paved road again—and were in Türkiye!

My ass was sore, and Hassan was definitely no better off. I consulted him briefly about whether we ought to continue on foot from this point, especially since we were safe now.

"How much farther is it to Yüksekova?" I asked one of the Kurds. He indicated that it was another thirty kilometers.

"Is there a taxi or a bus anywhere around here?" I wanted to know. The Kurd shrugged. We requested a short break to think things over. Then we resolved to cover the final stretch to our destination on the motorcycles.

At the Yüksekova city limits, in parting I pressed $100 U.S. into each Kurd's hand. The three men had amply proven their sheer physical and mental dedication! Then I wanted to get rid of my three diversionary minibombs, the ones built into cigarette packs. I didn't need them any longer, and they posed the risk of unnecessary problems at an airport security check. With pantomiming worthy of the professional stage, I explained to the Kurds what the little packs were able to do. I set one of them to go off with a two-minute fuse. Right on time, the thing began to bang, crackle, smoke, and spew flames. A real eye-catcher, which would have surely served its purpose in any emergency. I gave the Kurds the two remaining minibombs as presents.

Within the same day, we found a bus connection to Ankara, with a transfer in Diyarbakir. Altogether, the trip took twenty hours. From Ankara, we flew via Paris to New York. Hassan slept most of the time. When we landed in New York, he insisted on visiting some distant relatives, or at least claimed as much. It took me some time and effort to persuade him to board another flight to Washington, D.C. Indeed, I literally had to force him, since I had taken back his passport.

It was a short taxi ride from the Washington D.C. airport to CIA Headquarters in Langley, Virginia. All the same, I didn't let the ex-oil minister out of my sight for a second. At every red light, I was ready to have to hold him down or to dive after him, in case he wanted to bolt from the vehicle.

* * *

Sunday, March 18, 1979, 8:38 p.m.

I handed Ali Reza Khan over to my taskmasters. All he said in parting was, "I hope we never see each other again!"

"Same here, Mr. Khan. All the best!" I replied.

My colleagues sewed $50,000 U.S. into my knapsack, adding a receipt confirming that I had won the money playing poker in an Atlantic City casino, so that I wouldn't run into any problems at customs.

Two weeks after I had extracted the ex-minister from the country, Ayatollah Ruhollah Khomeini, very statesman-like, allowed his people to vote about their future. On Monday, April 1, 1979—long before all the votes were fully counted—he proclaimed the Islamic Republic of Iran, for which 98.2% of all Iranians eligible for the franchise had voted. In the following days and weeks, hundreds of former civil servants and Shah loyalists were executed. The oil minister, quite certainly, would not have survived that.

* * *

Wednesday, March 21, 1979

Once home, I was finally able to refill the several empty envelopes under my mattress. In the long term, I wanted to consider an alternative, perhaps a safe or an account in U.S. dollars at my savings bank. But things were still going fine this way, and I was enjoying the feeling of

256

being able to live off the fat of the land again for a longer time. I tossed the casino receipt into the wastepaper basket.

Half an hour after I called her, Birgit was standing at my door. Had she missed me so much? Or was she primarily curious to hear my explanation?

She refused me the welcoming kiss I had been so badly yearning for, and shrank back in horror: "What did you do to your hair?"

"Is it black, brown, or dark blond? I had dyed it black, and now I can't get the coloring out. I've washed it twice already. Maybe I'll have to re-dye it blond or simply let it grow out," I replied.

"What kind of bullshit is that? Carnival time is over! Where were you all this time? And who was that bimbo calling in the middle of the night?" Birgit wanted to know, fuming.

"If I'm to explain it to you, you've got to promise me absolute confidentiality. You must not tell anyone about it, not even your best friend. Promise?"

Birgit hesitated a moment before nodding and confirming, "Promise!"

"The woman who called during the night was from CIA Headquarters in Langley, Virginia, in the U.S. I do occasional work for American intelligence. Whenever they need me, they generally call at that hour because it's the best time to reach me."

"And what exactly do you do for American intelligence? Birgit asked derisively.

"I'm not allowed to tell you that. Otherwise, it wouldn't be secret, after all!" I ventured.

Birgit put her chewing gum in the wrapper, aimed for my wastepaper basket, missed, then picked up the gum and put it in. Then came what had to happen. She saw the only thing that was lying in the basket: the thrown-away casino receipt.

"You're not any kind of agent. You're a gambler, and you've won a pile of money! That piece of ass on the phone was probably calling from the casino, inviting you to a poker tournament. That's how the high rollers are treated. Why are you lying to me?" Birgit wanted to know.

I asked myself whether it would be better for Birgit to believe I was an agent or a gambler. Finally I said, "Would you possibly take back the question and not ask about it further if I used part of my ill-gotten gains to invite you to a wonderful vacation? California, Arizona, Nevada?"

CHAPTER 10

German Hostages in Bushehr

Birgit was amazing! Even thinking about her gave me butterflies in my stomach, and I often experienced heartfelt, stirring emotions. As we became more and more intimate, the sex got better and better, making us outright addicted to one another.

We each had the other's house key, and now we were taking turns with the cooking. Tuesdays and Thursdays, we ate over at my place, Wednesdays and Fridays at hers. We made a game of trying to outdo each other with fresh culinary delights. It was a real challenge for me, especially since up to that time my specialty had consisted of heating up cans of ravioli and refining their contents with gobs of butter, parmesan cheese, and Italian herbs.

Birgit had been in charge of training me in the operating room during my time at the university's surgical clinic on Nussbaumstrasse. I had the utmost respect for her professionally. Operating surgeons hardly ever had to demand an instrument from her—all they had to do was reach out their hand and she would already be handing it to them. In difficult cases, she often stood at the table for hours on end without a break, and she knew every step of hundreds of different procedures by heart—simply brilliant! On top of that, she had a sense of humor, whether in the OR, in the sack, or at the jump site, where we spent our free weekends together. Birgit wanted children, just as I did. And she was the first woman with whom I might have imagined myself starting a family.

We were tremendously excited about our upcoming tour of the U.S. West Coast: Los Angeles, San Diego, Lake Elsinore—the birthplace of formation jumping—as well as Phoenix, Flagstaff, and Las Vegas. On a trip like that, things don't always go according to plan. You have to be considerate of the other person, and you become better acquainted in the process. I toyed with the idea of proposing to Birgit in Las Vegas, assuming everything went well. At the jump site there, you could even get married during a freefall, accompanied by a reverend who comes along for the jump and is allowed to legally perform the ceremony in the air.

* * *

Tuesday, July 10, 1979, 9:30 a.m.

I had just gone on duty at the emergency surgery department of the hospital in Schwabing, having set a broken forearm in a cast and drunk a cup of coffee, when the head of personnel called me over and said, "I've just received an unusual call."

I looked at him quizzically, and he continued, "The head of personnel at Kraftwerk Union, a Siemens subsidiary, urgently needs an experienced OR nurse for their company hospital in the Persian Gulf."

"What's so unusual about that?" I asked.

"I thought it might be something for Paul. He's already been working for us for ten years and really enjoys traveling. And besides, the company hospital over there pays double what we can, and Paul is always short of money. But the funny thing about the phone call was—you're the one they absolutely want! And right away, and at any price! They even offered me a transfer fee for releasing you. Good people are what I need, not the money. We're not in the big leagues here," my personnel head informed me.

"Can't I just hear the offer without any obligation?" I asked.

"As if you could do that! They've already left an air ticket for you at the Lufthansa counter at Riem Airport. I'm supposed to inform you that your flight to Frankfurt is leaving today at 1150, and you're supposed to report at the gate of the company tower building promptly at 1400. That's at Kaiserlei, in Offenbach. It's a Frankfurt suburb—allegedly, everybody's familiar with the building. I'm not all that enthusiastic about this business, but the man there was quite friendly. You're entirely free to decide! The best I can offer you would be to move your vacation up. Otherwise, you would just have to quit if you decide to take the job. That'd be a shame!"

My personnel head stood up, stretched out his hand to me, and looked deeply into my eyes. I couldn't read his expression; nor did I want to. When I was already in the hallway, he called out after me, "You need to bring along your passport and proof you passed your nursing test!"

* * *

Tuesday, July 10, 1979, 1:45 p.m.
Kraftwerk Union Towers, Offenbach

I arrived a tad early. The neatly dressed, middle-aged lady at the reception desk offered me coffee and Danish. At 1400 on the nose, she brought me into a conference room on the nineteenth floor. From here, you could glimpse a terrific view of the Main River and the Frankfurt city skyline.

The receptionist introduced me to a man who immediately set about the proceedings: "Mr. Undersecretary of State—Mr. Müller. Mr. Müller—Undersecretary of State Lautenschlager."

I had actually been expecting a personnel head, not an undersecretary of state. Was I playing in the wrong movie here? If yes, then the whole business seemed really exciting indeed! I resolved to simply wait and see what unfolded.

The dark mahogany conference table had ten comfortable leather armchairs around it. Only five people were in the room. The undersecretary of state passed around little cards and felt-tip markers, so that each person could write out a name tag. Then we briefly introduced ourselves, starting with the undersecretary of state.

"My name is Hans Werner Lautenschlager. I'm the direct advisor to Germany's Foreign Minister, Hans-Dietrich Genscher, and I'll be chairing this session," Lautenschlager began.

"My name is Gertrude Schlecht. I'm the keeper of the minutes."

"My name is Karl-Friedrich von Borsch, the chairman of the Kraftwerk Union board."

"Werner Krause, of the German Federal Intelligence Service, specializing in Middle Eastern affairs."

"Horst Schmitt, of the German Federal Intelligence Service, specializing in Middle Eastern affairs."

"My name is Michael Müller, surgical and psychiatric nurse," I stated for the record.

The undersecretary of state ordered me to hand my passport to the men from German Intelligence to submit it to thorough inspection. The gentlemen compared my documents with theirs, cast a distrustful look at me, then curtly confirmed to the undersecretary of state: "He's the correct Müller, all right."

Next, they distributed confidentiality agreements, which everyone present had to sign. Nothing discussed in this room would be allowed to reach the public, and every signatory was put on notice that any violation or noncompliance, would mean having to reckon with a fine of 50,000 Deutschmarks, or imprisonment lasting up to five years.

Mr. von Borsch, the host, now took the floor: "Kraftwerk Union AG—KWU for short—has been overseeing the construction of a nuclear power plant since 1975 on behalf of the Shah's government. The facility is located in Bushehr, on the Persian Gulf. Two pressurized water reactors were planned. At present, Block 1 is 85% complete and Block 2 is 50% complete. Until last year, 5,000 German nationals were still employed at the construction site. Worldwide, it was the largest one ever operated by a German company, complete with an enormous camp compound, a canteen, swimming pool, bank, supermarket, hospital, school, library, and even its own television studio. Unfortunately, after the Islamic Revolution we had to suspend construction and withdraw most of our people—due to the volatile political situation, for one thing. On top of that, the Atomic Energy Organization of Iran stopped making payments on April 1, once the Islamic Republic of Iran was proclaimed. Hence, we officially terminated the contract as of June 1.

"Additionally, under no circumstances do we want the Islamic Republic to get in a position of being able to manufacture nuclear weapons with our support," the undersecretary of state added.

"On that point, I can allay your concerns," the Kraftwerk Union board chairman chimed in. "It isn't so easy to manufacture weapons-grade material from the slightly enriched uranium 235 that would have been necessary to operate our pressurized water reactors. In order to derive weapons-grade material, it would also be necessary for Iran to procure enrichment facilities with high-grade gas centrifuges, along with research reactors, and, above all, know-how that they lack. All that would take decades! We're much more worried about our 141 employees still at the construction site, including the site manager, several technicians, foremen, warehouse operators, secretaries, auto mechanics, firefighters, cooks, and their spouses. As long as talks with the new government continue, Iranian employees are supposed to briefed on the maintenance measures necessary to preserve the construction site. But now, the negotiations in which the German Federal Government was participating have foundered. – Would you care to take it from here, Mr. Undersecretary of State?"

At this point, the undersecretary of state looked less than enthusiastic about taking the floor. After some throat-clearing, he explained, "Our negotiating partners let us know that although Ayatollah Khomeini, on the one hand, does not regard nuclear power as being compatible with Islam, on the other hand, he also thinks that what was started should have to be completed. And at the expense of the builder-owner—who, in Khomeini's mind, has already received enough money since the start of construction, in any event. He therefore decreed that the remaining German nationals would have to train

Iranian workers how to build the nuclear power plant as rapidly as possible. Now every German national who still wants to leave the camp would have to be replaced by a German expert who demonstrably possesses the same qualifications."

"That sounds like government-run extortion coupled with hostage taking!" I exclaimed.

The undersecretary of state paused briefly, took a deep breath, then replied, "And that's exactly what it is—but *never* say so publicly! That goes for everyone here in this room. If the media ever catch on, the situation's going to escalate!"

"Do the people involved even realize that they're being held as hostages?" I asked.

"The only people informed about it are Mr. Wiesenthaler—he's the site manager—as well as the last remaining physician. The others still think that delays are occurring simply due to the large number of people willing to leave the country, as well as to the small number of flights still presently making it out. But our people are already getting uneasy. Every day now, they're pressuring the site manager for information about when their departure documents will be arriving," replied the Kraftwerk Union chairman.

"How are you communicating with your site manager?" I asked.

"With great, great difficulty! We've been trying to call him several times a day, and he's been trying to call us too. If we're lucky, once a week we're able to establish a connection that lasts longer than two or three minutes," Borsch elaborated. He continued, "We've got a man in the camp who urgently has to be replaced!"

"The nurse!" I inferred.

"Oh, he managed to get out early. But our Dr. Zimmermann is married to an Iranian doctor. The two of them have a three-year-old child, and Dr. Zimmerman-Zadeh is seven months pregnant. On top of that, Dr. Zimmermann has been suffering from heart trouble for some time. The Zimmermanns have been struggling for months to obtain air tickets and exit documents. Tickets for departing Iran are extremely difficult to obtain; the waitlists are long. The couple has all their papers together now, but only one thing is missing: Dr. Zimmerman needs a successor! Are you up to it?" the Kraftwerk Union man asked me.

"If I don't have to operate, sure," I replied.

"Dr. Zimmermann would introduce you as his successor and hand the hospital over to you. Purely a formality! There hasn't been a real emergency at the facility for a long time since it's been shut down anyway. You might have to hand out some headache pills or apply sticking plaster," Mr. von Borsch told me.

"Hold on a moment," I said. "So, then you don't want to hire me as a nurse in your company hospital, but rather as a phony doctor. Mainly, you need me as an exchange hostage. Has anyone even thought the whole business through already? Is there a plan for getting the 141 people and me out of there?"

"Including you, there would still be only 141 German nationals in the camp, since Dr. Zimmerman would already be gone then," the undersecretary of state calculated, continuing, "Yes, we've even thought a major step ahead. *You* are the key to solving our problem—we're pinning our hopes on you. You've been recommended to us as an Iran expert and evacuation specialist. Are you our man?"

"Your information is correct, but I still don't know whether I'm your man," I replied, without inquiring whence the recommendation had come. Inquiring about that would have been impertinent, and besides, I could readily imagine the two possible answers: "It's a secret" or "CIA."

Werner Krause, of the BND—West German Intelligence—spoke up: "We've been thinking that an exchange with Dr. Zimmerman would be the ideal opportunity to infiltrate you. You could then convey the escape plan to Mr. Wiesenthaler."

"Which escape plan?" I asked.

Now it was the undersecretary of state who was chiming in again: "The escape plan we want to work up with you jointly. That's why we're having this meeting. I would prefer we not leave this room until we've got the plan whipped into shape!"

Intuitively, I rose from my seat, perhaps to convey particular emphasis to what I now had to phrase in no uncertain terms: "Right now, nothing but sheer chaos is reigning in Iran! If my cover gets blown, it could cost me my life, or—perhaps even worse—prison and the most gruesome torture imaginable. So, we can continue discussing some potential plan only if you guarantee me absolute decision-making authority and complete support! Let me give you an example of what I understand that to mean: if I consider a new passport with a different name to be expedient, then I'll get it. Same goes for a traceable medical license certificate and doctor's ID. Should I require 140 new passports for all the hostages, then I'll receive them. If I want a suitcase with a false bottom and half a million in hundred-dollar bills to cover bribes, then I'll get them. And besides all that, I will—of course—receive a reasonable and proper fee!"

An embarrassed silence hovered over the room for a few moments, until the undersecretary of state arrived at a decision: "Good, consider it done. What kind of fee did you have in mind?"

"A million Deutschmarks," I bluffed, as though I were sitting at a high-stakes poker game.

The undersecretary of state gasped. "I can't pull that off!" he said finally. "We've never paid that much to a single agent before. Besides, if you can do the job, you shouldn't be doing it just for the money, but also for the hostages and out of patriotism. We were thinking of 50,000 Deutschmarks for you, tax-free."

Naturally, I had bluffed too high, so after a brief pause, I made a counteroffer: "How about we settle on a fixed fee of 100,000 Deutschmarks, plus 1,000 Deutschmarks for every German citizen who is returned to German soil unharmed? The German Federal Government quickly took in that much, after all, just from the taxes paid by a rescued hostage. That's my final offer!"

I sat down again.

"Agreed!" the undersecretary of state said, nodding. He instructed Ms. Schlecht to record our agreement in the minutes, then he asked the people from German Intelligence to submit the results of their research, as well as their proposals.

"At present, there are two main escape routes out of Iran," Schmitt began. "One of these is the overland route through Tabriz, into Türkiye; the other is along the coast, to Bandar Abbas, then across the Strait of Hormuz to Kumzar, in Oman," he added.

"Do we perchance have a map of Iran as well as a layout of the nuclear power plant's construction site?" I interrupted.

"No, but we'll obtain the country map," came the embarrassed reply of the man from German Intelligence. The chairman of the Kraftwerk Union's board of directors sent the woman in charge of keeping the minutes off to find a copy of the plant layout.

"For transportation, we believe that the Kraftwerk Union construction site's vehicle fleet has a number of vehicles available, including forty-two VW-made Type 181 jeeps and three 404 Unimogs. In addition to that, our American friends have informed us about an automobile dealer in Shiraz who would sell us several old American school busses. Given the fact that the Iranian people are now venting all their rage at Americans, it would be wise to repaint the busses white or beige. There's enough paint on hand in the camp to coat two busses," Schmitt elaborated.

"And then I'm supposed to lead the caravan into Türkiye?" I asked, in a slightly derisive undertone.

"All the German nationals would probably fit in two school busses and two Unimogs," said Schmitt placatingly.

"That's absolutely out of the question," I said, determined to straighten the man out. "It's far too great a distance, and it's got too many checkpoints! I can't possibly tote the amount of necessary baksheesh. And on top of that, there are always a couple of unbribable fanatics. Almost nobody escapes into Türkiye via Tabriz nowadays."

"It's a significantly shorter distance to Bandar Abbas," Krause, the man from German Intelligence interjected.

He added, "We could dispatch speedboats over there from Oman to pick up all the German nationals."

"So how far is it from Bushehr to Bandar Abbas?" I wanted to know.

"Around 700 kilometers, I think," Krause replied.

"That isn't any kind of alternative as far as I'm concerned!" I exclaimed. "For one thing, this stretch is also too long, and for another, it's logical to expect that the Revolutionary Guards are going to seal off Bandar Abbas soon, maybe by tomorrow, perhaps in a week's time. And besides, we would be dependent on boats and on the weather holding up. Those are too many uncertainty factors! Haven't you even considered an air evacuation? By helicopter or aircraft?" I asked.

"Yes, we did," Krause explained. "The German Federal Government wanted to charter a Lufthansa aircraft. They even had pilots who had voluntarily declared themselves ready for the operation. But when we found out in the meantime that all flights out of Iran have to land in Tehran first, where they are thoroughly checked, we scuttled the idea. They'll never let the Kraftwerk Union employees depart via that route!"

"You just leave worrying about that to me," I said, somewhat arrogantly. Then I asked Krause and Schmitt, "What, if anything, do you know about the mullah of Bushehr?"

Both men looked at one another cluelessly and shrugged. "Nothing!"

I stood up again. Somehow, I had the feeling that by standing, I would make myself better heard: "Mr. Undersecretary of State, Mr. von Borsch, Messrs. Krause and Schmitt—to rescue a group of people this large, I consider air evacuation to be the only possible way! Using air evacuation enables us to benefit from Iran's present lack of a functional bureaucratic infrastructure, and from the fact that communications—both overall and among the authorities themselves—are either bad or nonexistent. I can imagine that air traffic control in Tehran doesn't know what air traffic control in Bushehr is doing, and that the most influential mullah in Bushehr doesn't always know what an ayatollah or an energy minister in Tehran wants. Before we delve into specific planning, I would have to know whether the offer with the Lufthansa aircraft is still good. If at all possible, the pilots should be present at our next meeting so that they can provide details about the aircraft type, its passenger capacity, and range. Perhaps they can contribute a couple of ideas for mechanical emergencies and some deviations from the flight plan.

"On top of that, I'll need all available information about the mullah of Bushehr—where he grew up, what kind of education he has, whether or not he speaks English, whether his congregation is rich or poor, how much he earns in a year, his corruption index, his strengths and weaknesses. If it's absolutely necessary, make some inquiries among your American counterparts. Those people know what's going on! And if you do, please also ask them about the current state of communications among the authorities and both relevant air traffic control zones. You can also prepare an old suitcase containing half a million dollars in a false bottom. And a two-year-old passport, made out to Dr. Dagobert Dussmann, including entry and exit visa stamps from Türkiye, dated June of this year. My 1977 license to practice medicine must be registered with Ludwig-Maximilian University in Munich, and it has to be verifiable. Some

Revolutionary Guards even have an uncle in Germany who's a physician and can do some quick research to find out whether a Dr. Dagobert Dussmann actually passed his state medical exam in Munich. Also, I require a photo ID of myself as a doctor, a map of Iran, the current ICAO air charts, and, in fact, both the smallest-scale charts for instrument flying that the pilots can bring along right away, as well as the largest-scale aeronautical pilotage charts, all of Iran, the neighboring countries, and all the countries bordering the Persian Gulf. How quickly can you deliver all this?"

Krause and Schmitt looked at each other.

"What do you think, Horst?" Krause asked.

"Two to three days," Schmitt said.

At this point Undersecretary of State Lautenschlager interjected, "That's got to happen a lot faster, gentlemen! I'll take care of the suitcase with the money. You two ensure that the pilots are sitting with us at the table tomorrow and that we've got all the maps, charts, and plans there, so we can proceed full steam ahead on this thing. We'll meet back here in this room again tomorrow at 1400. If Mr. Müller's new passport isn't ready until evening, that won't be a tragedy. But really, gentlemen, get on the stick! If absolutely necessary, take a couple of people from your HQ in Pullacher into your confidence. I've got to report to Foreign Minister Hans-Dietrich Genscher tomorrow, and when I do, I do *not* want to have to tell him that German Intelligence is proving to be the weakest link in the chain!"

Schmitt and Krause threw me filthy looks. As we filed out, I asked Mr. von Borsch to find me a good hotel in Frankfurt, and he immediately set about doing so. Before I bid my farewells, Ms. Schlecht returned with the plans for the nuclear power plant. I briefly glanced at the enormous sketch drawings and facility plans and asked her to make manageable copies formatted with A4-sized paper, so I could easily carry them around.

* * *

The view from my room on the nineteenth floor of the Frankfurt Intercontinental Hotel was terrific, the hotel itself luxurious. I let Kraftwerk Union pick up the tab for dinner—duck breast filets in orange sauce with pureed potatoes. Then I made my way to the area around the train station, to imbibe a little liquid courage. Not for the assignment, but rather for the inevitable telephone call that had to be placed this evening.

It was Tuesday. I was actually supposed to do the cooking with Birgit today. I stepped into a phone booth, lifted the receiver and called home.

"Michael! Where are you holed up? I've been worrying about you!"

"In Frankfurt."

"Then our dinner together this evening is probably out. What are you doing in Frankfurt?"

I took a deep breath.

"Birgit," I began, "you know I love you very much. But I've got to go away again, unfortunately."

"Don't give me this agent or poker tournament shit all over again! What it's supposed to be this time? You do know that our vacation flights are set for next week, right?"

"You've just got be strong now! I'm afraid our vacation isn't going to happen."

"I can't believe this," Birgit shouted into the telephone, with a hint of despair in her voice. "I told you what will happen if you bail on me again. But I never thought you would wreck our big vacation, the same one I had been looking forward to so much!"

Then Birgit began to sob loudly, and soon hung up.

I waited a couple of minutes before picking up the receiver again and calling her back.

"Birgit, listen, I really am awfully sorry. The tickets are sitting in the drawer of my night table. They're both yours now. Maybe you can get a girlfriend to travel with you. You can endorse my ticket over to her. Once I'm back, I'll explain everything, and I'm inviting you to come on another terrific vacation. You won't have to pay a penny, and you'll still have a big wish that I'll grant you!"

"Good-bye, Michael," Birgit said, hanging up again.

CHAPTER 11

All Power to the People!

"They're going to flog you!" Krause had said, laughing diabolically. "A hundred lashes on your back. Including a discount. It could even be 150—fifty lashes for each bottle!"

He had packed the three bottles of eighteen-year-old Glenfiddich Single Malt Scotch Whisky exactly the way I had ordered: putting thin bubble wrap between the bottles and cans in which this fine liquid was usually delivered, with each can wrapped individually in metallic-blue Christmas paper. Whisky had never assumed as much importance to me as it did now!

* * *

Friday, July 13, 1979, 12:25 p.m.

In Zurich, gazing out the window of the Swissair flight during take-off, I realized that I was quite consciously exchanging life in a civilisation marked by a legal system as well as police and fire departments that were all functional for a life without any rights or security. Air France and Swissair were the only airlines still flying to Tehran. And in fact, if the Iranian authorities found the whisky bottles upon one's arrival in the country, they could rip the shirt off my back and flog me right on the spot. But I took the fifty-fifty wild card. Yes, I figured that I had an even greater chance that nothing of the kind would happen.

The aircraft landed at Tehran Mehrabad at 2255. The connecting flight to Bushehr on Iran Air took off the next morning at 0735, meaning that I had to be back at the airport at 0530. A room had been booked for me at the Tehran Sheraton. Again! I did the math to determine whether it would even be worth bothering to stay in the hotel after factoring the travel time there and back. But still, five hours in a hotel were always better than six and a half hours on an airport waiting-room bench, especially at night, when my taxi driver wouldn't have to deal with traffic obstructions and street demonstrations. I took my suitcase from the baggage carousel and headed for the exit. The customs window was unoccupied—even Revolutionary Guards have to sleep. On top of that, it was Friday, the Islamic day of rest, comparable to Sundays in the Christian world. The taxi driver ignored the traffic lights and signs, and en route to the hotel as well as on the way back to the airport, he drove as though the devil were chasing him alone through the streets—which was not quite the case. Then the other driver, who also thought he was the only one out and about at this hour, was given a wide berth, with lots of honking and squealing tires. I thrust down the thought about what might happen if a real crackup occurred. Would an ambulance ever come? And where would they take anyone who was injured?

* * *

Saturday, July 14, 1979, 7:45 a.m.

The flight from Tehran to Bushehr was supposed to last an hour and a half. I was the sole Westerner on board. What was going on the Boeing aircraft was like nothing

I had ever experienced on a regular airline. Chunks of flatbread were flying over the seats, like frisbees. Those who had some, shared it; those who didn't, helped themselves. Plenty of social justice! Even I got some. What astonished me most, though, were the live chickens and lambs—right there in the cabin! Of course, it was more pleasant for the animals to spend the flight sitting on the warm lap of an Iranian peasant woman, having their chins tickled, rather than suffering in cold cages in the hold below. A paradigm of low-stress animal husbandry! But how do you toilet-train a chicken? Especially when it's agitated? I sensed we could learn a lot from these people.

After just under an hour, the captain announced, in excellent Farsi and barely comprehensible English, that we were having engine trouble and would have to land at the airport in Shiraz. Panic began spreading among the passengers. Some of them were weeping. Most became completely motionless. Yet the landing proceeded without any problems; it was even an unusually gentle one.

All around the airfield stood an enormous number of helicopters that stretched in every direction to the horizon, as far as the eye could see. Never before in my life had I seen so many helicopters in one place! And now I remembered: Barry had told me that he'd spent half a year as a trainer in Shiraz, and that this airport was the world's largest helicopter base outside the United States.

We fellow sufferers were herded into a waiting space that was far too small. From here, I could observe how one helicopter after another was taking off, circling the compound, and landing again. It rather looked as though a few of the pilots who had defected to the Revolutionary Guards wanted to keep at least a small part of the heli-

copter fleet operational. The remainder would relentlessly fill up with sand and decay to nothing.

After a solid five hours' wait—it was around 1400, and
the sun had turned the room into a sauna—we were
informed that the damage to the engines could not be
repaired before the day was out. We were loaded into
small busses and distributed to various small hotels; we
were supposed to report at the airport the following
morning at 0900. I knew that Boeing and most other
U.S. companies had not been delivering any additional
spare parts to Iran since the beginning of June. I also
knew that qualified aircraft mechanics could hardly be
found in the country anymore. So the repairs could easily drag over several days. But did I have any choice?

Yes, I did! All I had to do was find an English-speaking
taxi driver who was ready to chauffeur me ad hoc over
the high plateaus of Fars Province, then down to Bushehr,
on the Persian Gulf.

Two hours later, with my battered suitcase filled with
half a million U.S. dollars, I was sitting an equally battered, but significantly less valuable Toyota Corolla, letting Ali—that really was his name!—give me a seesawing
ride over the mountains around Dasht-e Arzhan. He
wanted $100 U.S. for the trip and estimated it would take
six hours, which turned out to be seven.

* * *

Saturday, July 14, 1979, 11:30 p.m.

Standing watch at the entrance to the enclosed Kraftwerk Union camp were two Revolutionary Guards who
did not want to let us pass under any circumstances.

Shortly before midnight, a white SUV roared up. A young, athletic man dressed in black, whom the guards had obviously notified, stepped out and shined his enormous, industrial-strength flashlight at us.

"Good evening," said the man with a stony face. He demanded my passport and asked me what I wanted here.

"I'm Dr. Dussmann," I replied. "I'm supposed to relieve your physician, Dr. Zimmermann. Unfortunately, the aircraft I was flying in experienced engine trouble. We had to make an unscheduled landing in Shiraz. That's why I'm coming by taxi," I explained.

"Hey, fella, take a load off! Everyone wants to bail, and like, now someone else's here from Germany! My name's Freddy. I guard the construction site. So I'm in charge of security—you could say, a jack-of-all-trades! Welcome aboard!" said the man, greeting me with a delightfully thick Bavarian argot.

"Dagobert," I said, extending my hand to him.

"'Dagobert,'" laughed Freddy. "I've never heard that except on *The Mickey Mouse Club*. Where did you get a dipshit name like that?"

"I chose it myself," I replied, truthfully.

Freddy loaded my suitcase in his German VW jeep while I paid off the taxi driver, then we drove into the camp. But to what part of it? Everything looked like it had died off.

"The camp is dead at this hour," Freddy said knowingly, "but if you want, you can sleep on the couch in my bungalow until tomorrow morning. I do my rounds every two hours, then I'll introduce you to Dr. Zimmermann at 7:30. He's usually already at the hospital by then."

I gratefully accepted the offer. This Freddy was my kind of guy! He was bald, with steel-blue eyes, and above all he radiated an almost uncannily pleasant sense of calm that I've witnessed among only very few people.

When I was in the process of positioning my suitcase within sight of where I'd be sleeping, Freddy asked, "Hungry?"

"In all honesty, yes," I replied. "I haven't eaten a thing since the in-flight dinner on Swissair, before we landed in Tehran. That was yesterday evening." I forgot to mention the chunk of flatbread on the short domestic flight.

"I can warm up a can of ravioli for you."

I'd reckoned with anything happening today, even a flogging, just not with a dyed-in-the-wool Bavarian heating a can of ravioli for me at midnight!

* * *

Sunday, July 15, 1979, 7:30 a.m.

Dr. Zimmermann, a slender man in his mid-forties with a narrow face and sparsely sprouting blond hair, was delighted to see me.

"I've already been expecting you since yesterday," he said. "But it's a good thing that you've simply made it over here at all. You cannot even imagine how grateful my wife and I are. Without your arriving to relieve me, we'd never make it out of here!"

"Glad to do it!" I replied.

Dr. Zimmermann led me through the clinic's spaces, showing me the emergency room, the OR, the patient rooms, the intensive care ward, and the radiology and lab facilities—indeed, there was even a high-tech dentist's chair.

"Things used to be really hopping around here," he said. "Three doctors, two nurses, three caregivers, and a clinical lab scientist were kept busy round the clock. Since we're the only hospital in Bushehr, we also treated the local population—to the extent we had the capacity to do so. But the aid program was suspended and most of the German construction workers recalled. It's been absolutely dead here for the past two months. The sole emergency I had last week was the wife of the man in charge of our motor pool. She had been stung on the hand by a wasp.

"But one interesting thing is still going on: around midday every Tuesday, a Huey from the Shell Oil Company lands here. Right in front of the hospital. It'll fly you—if you want—out over the sea to one of their off-shore drilling rigs, where you're supposed to hold office hours for the workers. You can get some terrific Chinese food at the rig's canteen, and a fabulous return flight. The tradition got started sometime around six months ago, when they landed here with a real emergency. The mission is unofficial, and none of the rules and regulations provide for it. You're free to continue with these little jaunts if you want. I always found them a highly welcome change of pace."

Solemnly—and visibly relieved—Dr. Zimmerman handed me two keys: one to the hospital and another to the small, locked cabinet containing the hard drugs and narcotics.

"So you're the head of the clinic now! I've still got to introduce you to the construction site manager. Then you'll receive a VW jeep, a walkie-talkie, and your own bungalow. And I will be leaving all of you in the dust, quite literally, in fact," the doctor rejoiced.

"Just a moment," I asked, "do you actually know Mullah Hashemi?"

"Yes. He was my last actual patient. A couple of months ago, I operated on an anal fistula he had."

"Could you be so kind as to introduce me to the mullah? It would be extremely important to me," I said emphatically.

"Hm … Actually, I wanted to go to my wife as quickly as possible and convey the good news to her. But I can hardly refuse you a request. Why don't we drive over to see the construction site manager first? Then we'll go visit the mullah."

I quickly rummaged a host gift for the mullah out of my suitcase, which Freddy had put in the treatment room. Then I followed Dr. Zimmermann.

The construction site manager, Mr. Wiesenthaler, a somewhat stocky fellow in his mid-fifties with slicked-back brown hair and horn-rimmed glasses, greeted me in a friendly, albeit reserved manner. I requested a private meeting in the near future.

"You're now heading off to see the mullah for the first time. I don't have to go along. Afterwards we'll see about getting together, assuming there's time. Otherwise, just come by my office tomorrow morning," Mr. Wiesenthaler told me.

Regarding Dr. Zimmermann, I commented, "He didn't seem particularly overjoyed about my arrival."

"Mr. Wiesenthaler has just been a bit, well, introverted recently," the doctor replied. "The pressure he's under from all the people who want to get out of here once and for all, along with uncertainty about how things are supposed to continue—it's all getting to him. And he isn't the only one!"

The Bushehr mosque, to my surprise, was unguarded. Both the mullah, who was arrogating tremendous power to himself, as well as his followers, appeared to feel very secure. An ancient-looking religious servant, seemingly consisting of nothing but skin, bones, and a white beard, escorted us to the region's top holy man. Dr. Zimmermann introduced us.

In polished English, Mullah Hashemi greeted us: "A warm welcome to Bushehr and the Islamic Republic of Iran!"

This short, rotund man with gold-rimmed eyeglasses and a full, black beard reminded me a tad of the parish priest who had taught religion classes during my childhood. Their initial positions too, were indeed not at all dissimilar, although the mullah had now quite suddenly and abruptly attained a lot more power. The holy man imparted a mild, benevolent impression. It was scarcely conceivable that he was capable of enforcing Sharia law, the Islamic legal code, let alone order a single lash of the whip.

After fifteen minutes of respectful mutual small talk over a glass of tea, I had a good gut feeling. I thought we could do business with one another. Before departing, I handed the mullah my host gift, a present wrapped in metallic blue Christmas paper. I said, "I've brought along some…medicine for you."

I could only hope that the information furnished by the CIA to German Intelligence was correct—to the effect that Mullah Haschemi was an alcoholic who treasured an eighteen-year-old bottle of Glenfiddich Single Malt above all else. If an error or perhaps even some joker had infiltrated the chain of communication, I would soon have to reckon with some considerable difficulties. If the information was correct, I would be in the local strongman's good graces, especially since this holy man's source for the precious liquid had recently been cut off. Two weeks ago, every foreigner supermarket that had previously been quite lawfully allowed to sell spirits had been closed on instruction from the new Tehran government, and all their remaining liquor inventories destroyed. The Bushehr store's proprietor, who had regularly supplied the mullah via backdoor channels, had been—not altogether unjustly—accused of un-Islamic intriguing as well as espionage for the United States. He had been hanged by a crane in front of his former supermarket, and they had let his corpse dangle there until just a week ago.

Back in the camp, I received a freshly overhauled VW Type 181 German jeep with a full tank of gas, my walkie-talkie, and the key for my relatively centrally located bungalow. It was midday, and the heat was like a furnace. I lightened my suitcase by several kilograms' worth of souvenir presents, then availed myself of the opportunity to introduce myself in the canteen, which was pleasantly air-conditioned and still well-frequented.

"My name is Dr. Dagobert Dussmann," I began. "I'm the new doctor here, and I'm always available for any problems you might have! I've brought you a few current magazines from Germany that you can't obtain here, like *Stern*, *Spiegel*, *Bunte*, *ADAC Motorwelt*, and a few others. Help yourself to the stack at the entrance. But please, when you're finished, pass them along or put them in the library."

Then I handed the German cook two kilograms of semi-mature Gouda and three kilograms of top-notch Italian Parma ham, requesting that he slice up the latter ultra-thin and have it served over the next few days as a special treat at breakfast or dinner. Perhaps a little culinary boost could lift the mood somewhat.

The Germans looked at me as though I were some kind of alien; they couldn't fathom why someone was coming here while for weeks they had all been united in a single wish—to get out of the camp and back to Germany!

* * *

Tuesday, July 17, 1979, 11 a.m.

I was about to familiarize myself with the hospital, its spaces, the equipment and instruments on hand, the medications both inside the drugs cabinet and elsewhere, plus the doctor's bag and its contents.

Then Freddy entered the waiting room.

"Doc, we've got an emergency! May I bring her in?"

"Let's go!" I replied cluelessly, looking forward excitedly to my first official act.

A girl of around five had an enormous, gaping wound on her lower jaw. The child was accompanied by two figures in tattered clothing, presumably her parents. The interpreter whom Freddy had brought along, straight from Wiesenthaler's office, was a study in stark contrast: a very pretty young Iranian woman in a tight gray business skirt and white blouse, complete with Nefertiti eyeliner and burgundy lipstick. The obligatory black chador was unostentatiously draped around her head. She interpreted for me:

"The girl climbed up a date palm tree and slipped off. As she fell, one of these sharp pieces of bark on the tree trunk sliced through her lower jaw."

"Can she open her mouth wide, please?" I asked, and the interpreter duly relayed the message.

The child's entire body was trembling. The wound did not look good. The hole was so large that underneath her tongue, it was possible to look straight through her lower jaw.

"Okay," I said, "now I'm going to clean the wound and bandage it. The child must then be brought to the nearest hospital or to a surgeon as quickly as possible to be operated upon."

The interpreter explained in Farsi. The girl's father got into an intense battle of words with her, then fell to his knees. Bowing over and over, he shouted, "Allah uh akbar!" while the wife threw herself to the floor, screaming and howling like a banshee, as though she herself were gravely injured.

"What's going on?" I asked the interpreter?

"The father says that his daughter will die if you don't operate on her. There isn't any doctor for miles around who could do it."

"Well? Is that true?" I asked the interpreter.

"Yes! We don't have any other hospital in Bushehr. The closest one is eighty kilometers away, in Borazjan, and it's closed most of the time. There's no medication, and no doctor."

"Tell the parents ..." I paused briefly and thought things over. Would anything about the situation have changed, let alone improved, if I were to tell the parents that I wasn't a surgeon or even a doctor? No! They had no alternative. Nor did I.

"Tell the parents that I'll operate on their little girl. But all three of you have to remain here—you as the interpreter, and the parents to hold the child tight and reassure her."

I tried to establish a rapport with my small patient and to gain her confidence. Kneeling down to her, I smiled and looked into her eyes. I stroked her hair and asked the interpreter to explain to the little girl that she first there would be a couple of pinpricks, after which she would no longer feel any pain, and afterwards everything would be fine.

In the dentist's office I found lidocaine, a tried-and-tested local anesthetic, and drew off five injections using the thinnest needles on hand. I administered three generous injections at two puncture points each around the wound to be operated on, keeping the other two syringes in reserve, at the ready. The girl behaved bravely and calmly as her parents continued talking to her and holding her arms. After a few minutes, the sensation of pain was supposed to yield to a fuzzy one of numbness. I cleansed the wound with hydrogen peroxide, which simultaneously stanched the bleeding somewhat. While waiting for the local anesthetic to take effect, I looked around for antibiotics, and finally secured a small vial of ampicillin. The white powder was actually intended for the preparation of transfusions. I opened the vial and thrust it into the interpreter's hand. Then we could get going.

The little girl's tongue frenulum—the small fold of mucous membrane extending from the floor of the mouth to the midline of the underside of the tongue—was severed. Somewhere, I had heard that a person's tongue frenulum mustn't be too short or too long; otherwise, articulation difficulties would arise. So for starters, I set about suturing the tongue frenulum back together, doing my utmost to keep it the same length it must have been before, and using the type of stitches that dissolve on their own after a week. Suturing the tongue muscles and the oral mucous membranes just above them proved extremely difficult. In particular, because some saliva glands are located under the tongue, blood and saliva had moistened the incision's edges, and these kept eluding me.

Right at this difficult moment, I heard a noise that made my heart beat faster, something more than inconvenient at this point in time, however. The noise sounded like a rug being beaten ever more loudly. It was the Shell Oil Company's Huey, which landed here every Tuesday afternoon and was supposed to take me to the offshore drilling rig for me to hold office hours!

"Freddy!" I shouted.

Freddy, who had been waiting in the anteroom, burst in.

"Tell the pilot that I'm in the middle of an operation. He should come back in two hours!"

Freddy nodded, and I continued feeling my way around to suture the mucous membranes. Following that, starting at the underside of the lower jaw I reattached the tongue muscle and the fascia, or connective tissue, as well as I could. During the operation, I asked the interpreter to repeatedly introduce just a pinch of ampicillin into the wound, in order to prevent infection. The dermal stitches, which came at the end, were the simplest part of the procedure.

I had done what I could. Perhaps the operation hadn't gone altogether perfectly, but without the surgery the wound would have surely become infected, probably leading to the girl's death. I thanked the interpreter, who had administered the antibiotic into the wound without batting an eyelash, and I praised my brave young patient. Her parents were to bring her back for a follow-up check in a week.

Freddy returned and said, "Sorry, the pilot won't be returning today. He has a tight schedule and can't come back until next week."

"Too bad, really too bad!" I said. I would have been all too glad to check out the life and goings-on aboard an offshore rig like that, as well as to take the opportunity to find out whether they perhaps had a satellite telephone.

I went with Freddy into the canteen for lunch. He told me he was a "black sheriff" who had been delegated by the ZSD, the civilian security service, to monitor the construction site. The ZSD, along with several training facilities for judo, karate, tae kwon do, and aikido, belonged to Carl Wiedmeier, an icon who had made martial arts all the rage in Munich. And Freddy was one of his closest confidantes.

"But what use can judo and karate be to you," Freddy lamented, "when your opponent has a firearm? And what good does weapons training do if you aren't allowed to carry one yourself? Sometimes I feel like a toothless tiger!"

"The two of us already are," I let slip softly.

"What did you say?" Freddy asked.

"Nothing, just thinking out loud," I replied.

The construction site manager, who had given me such a chilly, brief reception the day before, wasn't in the canteen.

"He's always the first to come and the first to leave," Freddy let me know.

It wasn't a simple matter to convince Mr. Martin Wiesenthaler, *Dipl.-Ingenieur*—a graduate professional civil engineer—that we mustn't hold our private conversation in his office. He didn't at all care for the fact that I was now leaving the camp with him sitting in the passenger seat of my car. I drove to the nearest empty beach.

"Let's take a little walk," I suggested, getting out. Mr. Wiesenthaler followed me, having no choice, then remarked sarcastically, "Oh, I do so love this cloak-and-dagger stuff!"

"Likewise," I replied. "It's even part of my job." By now, it ought to have dawned on the construction site manager. But it didn't.

"Your office walls are tissue-paper thin. Your secretary is an Iranian woman. So is your interpreter. And the matter I'd like to discuss with you is top-secret! Give me your word that you will maintain absolute silence about what I'm about to tell you," I demanded, holding out my hand and looking him right in the eye. Reluctantly, he shook on it.

"I haven't come here just as a physician," I continued. "Rather, I've got a plan to get all of you out of here, exactly fourteen days from today, to be precise."

"Well, now I'm really excited!" Mr. Wiesenthaler said, suddenly giving me his undivided attention.

"The plan was crafted in my presence, together by the German Federal Foreign Office, German Intelligence, and Kraftwerk Union. On Tuesday, July 31, at 8:30, a chartered Lufthansa aircraft will be landing in Bushehr. Every German national is going to get on board, and the plane will depart at 9:30. None of the passengers are to be informed until the previous evening, and then they'll have to be ready to travel within twelve hours," I elaborated.

"That's ridiculous! The Iranians are never going to let us out of here!" Mr. Wiesenthaler said, by way of commenting on the plan.

"You just let me worry about that. Under no circumstances may the plan be revealed at an earlier time. And nothing about it can be allowed to leak to the outside. Not to your closest confidantes, and not when you contact the folks back home, either. When was the last time you phoned Germany?"

"A week ago. I try every day, but it works only sporadically, and usually the connection gets cut off pretty fast. But why all this cloak-and-dagger nonsense? People here are pressuring me more and more with every passing day. They would rejoice at your 'glad tidings,' if that's what your news really is," the construction site manager told me.

"The plan could founder if the central government in Tehran gets wind of it—for instance, by tapping a phone call, or from your secretary or interpreter, who tells her parents about it, when they relay it further, and so on," I countered. "The plan *will* work! Trust me! But I'm going to need your support. I'll ensure that processing at the airport goes smoothly so that we can take off. You make sure that everyone, and I mean every single German national, is ready to depart at the Bushehr airport on July 31 at six in the morning."

"How am I supposed to do that?" Mr. Wiesenthaler asked. "This morning, the Revolutionary Guards simply confiscated half our vehicles and made off with them! If

I distribute the 141 German nationals in the camp among the remaining vehicles, then I would have to squeeze seven people into every VW jeep, along with their luggage. Absolutely impossible!"

"It's a good thing you told me this. I'll devise a solution," I said, trying to placate him. "We've got to touch base regularly, and I've got to be kept in the loop about things like any changes in the vehicle fleet, changes to the camp guards, any possible encroachments, as well as any changes in the mood among both German and Iranian employees. But please, not in your office! We'll arrange meetings, sometimes in the camp, sometimes outside, but always at different locations and at a suitable, proper distance from other people. – What is your actual relationship with Mullah Haschemi?"

"There isn't any. I don't know him," Mr. Wiesenthaler said to my astonishment.

"But the mullah is now the court of last resort in the territory where the construction site is located!"

"As far as we're concerned, the Atomic Energy Organization of Iran is in charge, and nobody else," replied Mr. Wiesenthaler.

"When was your last contact with them?" I asked.

"Around a month ago. At that time, they represented that the Iranian people, under our guidance, would complete construction of the power plant. Not a single German expert would be allowed to leave the country unless replaced by someone equally qualified. But I'm telling you, things are so chaotic, it's utterly unimaginable. Two days earlier, Tehran was still adopting the position that the nuclear power plant was incompatible with Islam, and we could all be sent packing. And then this extortion! The left hand over there doesn't know what the right is doing. There is no longer a single contact person left holding office with whom we negotiated during the Shah's time."

"This chaos is exactly what's going to prove our salvation," I said.

We drove back in silence.

* * *

Saturday, July 21, 1979, 10 a.m.

A hushed quiet prevailed in the hospital—dead quiet. At first, Kraftwerk Union employees had still been coming in to have someone attend to their emotional troubles. They expected me to join with them in their appalling, whiny rage against their cruel employer who was so disgracefully letting them die in the desert. Or they wanted to hear that an aircraft was about to descend from the heavens to spirit them all away from here. Neither wish was fulfilled by me, and it quickly got around that I would abruptly rebuff anyone who didn't have a serious medical problem.

I decided to drive into the village, attired in my doctor's outfit, to wander through the market and glean a picture of the situation in Bushehr for myself. What was the prevailing mood? Were more men or more women out and about on the streets? Were all the women really wearing the chador? How well were the Revolutionary Guards represented?

Freddy ran up to me as I was driving to the camp exit, which was always well guarded.

"Say, I'm taking a quick drive into the village. Want to come along?" I asked him. Freddy didn't seem too enthusiastic about the idea, but he swung himself into the passenger seat, presumably out of pure boredom. The market, I had been informed, was located around twenty kilometers away from the construction site, at the northern end of the Talequani highway leading to the airport. It was impossible to miss, if for no other reason that the road ended there, at the sea.

With our hair wafting in the breeze, I was cruising along at a leisurely forty kilometers an hour over the empty road, until suddenly, parallel to the runway's southeastern end, a powerful jolt tossed us both out of our seats a little. I immediately jammed on the brakes, pulled over slowly to the shoulder of the road, and stopped. We got out to inspect the VW jeep all around. Freddy cast a critical look at me.

"You've gotten lucky again—you didn't shear off the entire axle! These 'silent guards' get more and more frequent the closer you get to the center of town."

In fact, I had overlooked a speed bump that had been inconspicuously embedded in the roadway. Paying a great deal more attention and opting for a commensurately reduced speed, I continued driving towards the market. Arriving in town, I drove once around a block of houses. The speedbumps recurred every couple hundred meters, and it was obvious that they were distributed throughout the entire village. Any escape or hot pursuit would be impossible here.

Standing in front of the market entrance were three sand-colored military trucks. Before them stood an enormous crowd of people, primarily children, adolescents, and elderly.

"What's going on here, anyway?" I asked. Freddy shrugged his shoulders cluelessly. I parked in the shadow

294

of a date palm, and we struggled to clear a narrow path for ourselves through the crowd.

When we had gotten close enough to the trucks, we saw their cargo: weapons, weapons, and still more weapons! Primarily Heckler & Koch G3 assault rifles with stick magazines and NATO rounds, but also Kalashnikovs with banana magazines, as well as handguns. The Revolutionary Guards were handing them out to anyone who wanted them.

"Is something here being given out for free? Does anyone around here speak English?" I asked.

A Revolutionary Guardsman grabbed me roughly by the upper arm and led me—with Freddy in tow—to his superior, a thin officer around 1.95 meters tall with a gaunt face, a well-groomed black beard, and a typically Persian hooked nose. Speaking perfect English, he asked me, "Who are you? What are you doing here?"

"My name is Dr. Dagobert Dussmann. I'm the new doctor at the nuclear plant construction site. I just wanted to have a bit of a look around the market and the village," I said naively, not having the remotest idea what kind of horrific consequences this statement would have in just a day or two.

The man nodded, but didn't introduce himself—which was rather unusual for Persians.

"Can anybody here pick up a weapon for himself?" I asked, glancing at the numerous children and teenagers, who were eagerly stocking up on assault rifles, pistols, and ammunition.

"Every Iranian man!" the man verified. "Our great leader, Ayatollah Khomeini, has proclaimed the motto *All Power to the People!* He has decreed that once the Revolutionary Guards have been supplied, all excess weapons are to be handed to the people. Everyone should be able to defend himself and Islam!"

"Against whom?" I asked.

"Against the enemies of our religion and against the enemies of our people! – It is better if you go now," the officer advised me with an unequivocal look.

Freddy and I walked quickly—albeit not *too* quickly— back to our vehicle. On the ride back, our construction site guard and security officer told me, "I know a few of the boys who were there. A couple of them work for us in the cleaning crew, and two weeks ago I nabbed one of them—his name is Arasch—breaking into our metal- working shop at night. He was filching tools."

"What did you do with him then?" I wanted to know.

"I took the tools away from the kid and simply warned him never do it again. He's fourteen. Should I have sum- moned the Revolutionary Guards, perhaps? They would have probably laughed in my face and even encouraged him to just take whatever he needed. Sometimes I really wonder what I am supposed to do here in the first place! – By the way, this Arasch character is pretty smart. He speaks better English than almost any other Iranian at the construction site, and a little German, too. He can even curse in Bavarian."

"Did he learn that from you?"

"No, of course not!" Freddy said, grinning.

* * *

Sunday, July 22, 1979, 7 a.m.

I had slept poorly, dreaming of children firing machine guns all over the place, and resolved to doze another

296

quarter of an hour. Then my walkie-talkie squawked: "Doc! Dagobert! Come in!" It was Freddy's voice.

"Good morning!" I answered.

"There's been some shooting going on! Grab your medical bag and come over to Behrens's house, fast! It's right next to mine. The door's open. But be careful!"

"I just have to get dressed quickly. Be right there!"

Behrens! Behrens? I thought to myself as I jammed my shirt into my pants. *Wasn't that the man who ran the vehicle fleet? Early fifties, blond, beard, eyeglasses, a bit chubby?*

I grabbed my medical bag and ran to the described house, which could be reached faster on foot than with my jeep. I probably hadn't dreamed the shots, but instead actually heard them while half asleep!

Freddy was waiting for me in front of the house's open front door.

"Chop, chop—can't you hurry up?" sounded a voice from the house.

Freddy and I nodded to each other and went inside simultaneously.

In the living room stood three boys between eight and ten years old, giggling embarrassedly. Each of them was carrying a G3 rapid-fire assault rifle on his shoulder. And their leader—Arasch!

The little kids were having difficulty stretching themselves tall enough to prevent their weaponry from scraping over the floor. Arasch, on the other hand, was aiming his weapon—loaded and with the safety off—directly at Behrens's head. Beads of sweat were running down the man's forehead as he crawled around on the floor, cleaning it. The fear of imminent death was written all over his face.

"I never able do right for Mr. Behrens," Arasch began, by way of an explanation, when he saw us. "Never was clean enough for him. I must do every cleaning job twice, even when everything already clean. Always he say, dust on refrigerator or still something other. Now he show how good *he* clean!"

"But I've already cleaned the entire house twice," whined Mr. Behrens.

Arasch fired a burst at the ceiling. Plaster crumbled and fell down.

"Now make corners good and clean again! But real clean! Just like I have to make clean, real clean!" Arasch shrieked at his victim, who was as pale as a corpse.

"Take it easy, Arasch," said Freddy, attempting to deescalate the situation using his calm, sonorous voice.

"You be next, Freddy! You force me to return tool. Tool no belong to you at all. Tool belong to us, the Iranian people! Everything belong to us! We pay for!" Arasch said.

I was mindful enough not to mention that the company still had a number of unpaid outstanding invoices in the nine-figure U.S. dollar range.

Arasch finally let Behrens go. Now he jockeyed Freddy into his house, keeping the G3 at the ready. The three kids and I followed.

"You clean only corners. Corners are most important! Take rag and then get on knees!" Arasch ordered. This time, though, he spared himself the intimidating rifle salvo. He was also handling the assault rifle more carelessly now, aiming the barrel at the floor.

Freddy was inwardly fuming. For him, trained as he was in hand-to-hand combat, disarming Arasch would have been an easy matter. Then I would have had to take care of the three children immediately before the situation spiraled out of control. But it would be better not to let things go that far.

"Please, Freddy! Just do what he says!" I asked him as a precaution. And so Freddy dropped to his knees and did the cleaning.

When Arasch was finally satisfied, he and his "followers" strolled around in front of the door and invited me to a shooting contest—just for fun! The new doctor was supposed to show what kind of stuff he was made of!

Arasch fired three short salvos from his hip at the hospital direction sign, which stood about fifty meters away. A couple of the shots hit their target. Then he took a rapid-fire assault rifle from one of the kids and handed it to me.

"Now you, Doctor!"

It was clear to me that he could have blown me away. Simple as that. Either from pure homicidal range or because I had a different religion. It would look even better if I were holding a weapon in my hand. Then, to cap it all off, he could falsely claim self-defense as well.

"I don't know how to shoot," I lied, refusing to accept the weapon, "but if you accidentally shoot yourself in the leg, I can provide you medical treatment."

At this very moment, out of nowhere, a pickup truck containing three Revolutionary Guardsmen roared up. Most likely, they had been notified by the gate watch. Sitting in the passenger seat was the lanky officer with whom we had spoken at the market the previous day, the one who had not introduced himself. Jumping out of the pickup, he spoke fiercely to Arasch in Farsi.

299

The youth and the three children climbed onto the pickup's bed and took their seats while the officer got back in. Then they all sped off.

Freddy and I went to Behrens, who was sitting on his sofa, completely despondent. I offered to give him a shot containing an ampule of valium to calm his nerves, but he preferred Freddy's offer: a shot of gentian liquor from his secret stash.

* * *

Tuesday, July 24, 1979, 8 a.m.

Word of the Arasch incident had spread throughout the entire camp, intensifying the we-want-to-get-out-of-here-right-now mood.

Then, suddenly, it was back: the pickup with the three Revolutionary Guards and the remarkably tall officer who had never introduced himself.

"We need you, Doctor!" the man said, instructing me, his G3 rifle at the ready, to climb into the bed of the pickup truck.

"Don't be afraid. We've got to blindfold you," he told me in English, instructing his people in Farsi to tie a black blindfold around my head.

The whole thing was making me queasy. I definitely had a worse gut feeling than I'd experienced a couple of months ago when the Kurds had blindfolded me to prevent me from memorizing the route to Sheik Akar Ahmad. Back then, I had voluntarily sought out the contact; this time, I was being forced to journey into the unknown. Flashes of thought went through my head—people being driven to their execution were blindfolded.

And, of course, they were never told where they were heading. But why should they kill me? Perhaps one of their child soldiers had injured himself while playing around with his weapon. But then why didn't they bring him into the clinic? I didn't even have my doctor's bag with me.

The fact that the pickup kept braking sharply, bouncing over speedbumps, then accelerating led me to conclude that we were driving into the village. After a while, the pace picked up through the desert; presumably we were leaving the village again.

We had finally reached our destination. The blindfold was taken off me. We were standing at the periphery of a bellowing mob, exclusively male, many of them in uniform. The tall, lanky officer led me through the crowd to an open spot. I saw a person's upper body, wrapped in a white cloth and buried in the ground up to her upper body.

The officer said, "We must stone this woman to death."

Shocked, I asked, "What did she do?"

"She refused to wear the chador and was distributing a leaflet calling upon other women to refuse as well. Inciting the violation of God's laws must be punished by death!"

The woman was sobbing abjectly.

"Who handed down the judgment?" I wanted to know.

"The qadi! He's actually entitled to cast the first stone, but has commissioned me to represent him. Next up are the witnesses who saw the leaflets being distributed and reported it. Then everyone else. You know what it depends upon."

"What does it depend on?" I asked.

"The stones mustn't be too small, and under no circumstances too large. They have to inflict pain upon the sinner for as long as possible. And meanwhile, you will report to me how long she still holds out. Now we begin!"

The lanky officer addressed the crowd in a few brief words and threw an initial, relatively small stone at the condemned woman's upper body. Five men from the first row followed suit, then all the others pressed forward to get their chance.

A ghastly sensation came over me. Never before had I ever witnessed anything this gruesome. The crowd's mood heated up, and the men sank into an outright blood frenzy as the white cloth over the woman's head gradually turned red. With every stone that struck, the condemned woman shrieked loudly—death shrieks! The louder she screamed, and the redder the cloth around her head became, the more stones went flying. Throughout, her tormentors yelled with every ounce of their strength: "*Allah uh akbar!*"– God is great!

I would have preferred to just as loudly yell, "*Allah uh saghir*" – Your God is small, if he allows this! But then, surely, they would have lynched me on the spot.

Gradually, the victim's shrieks weakened and grew fainter. The lanky officer ordered everyone to pause. A few men, who had run out of stones, were allowed to restock themselves using the ones that had already been thrown and were lying all around the victim. I was supposed to assess the young woman's condition. If I attested it was stable, the crowd would continue with the smaller to medium-sized stones, in order to protract the woman's suffering for as long as possible. If I declared the doomed woman unconscious, then they would deploy the larger stones, which would rapidly ensure her death.

"The way she's wrapped up, I can't check her pulse or respiration or examine her pupils' reaction. I can't assess her condition," I said.

The officer, who had never introduced himself, looked at me maliciously and shoved me aside without comment. At his signal, the mob now threw increasingly larger stones. Even when the woman was long since dead—her skull must have been smashed to smithereens—the men kept throwing. The stones, by now the size of peaches, kept coming, one after another, harder and harder, striking the slumped, blood-drenched head and torso. It was only with some effort that the officer was able to halt the grotesque spectacle.

Blindfolded, but with only a single guard, I was brought back to the camp. Just as we passed the main entry gate and the blindfold was removed, the Huey flew past us, droning away. Once again, I had missed the visiting hours at the offshore drilling rig. But after this experience, I could have hardly enjoyed the flight anyway.

The next day, I learned from an Iranian worker at the construction site that the woman stoning victim had come from his neighborhood. She had been just seventeen years old. Most of the stones had been thrown by the sinner's close relatives, by her own father, her three brothers, and her cousins.

How cruel can people actually be? Can religious delusion alone drive people to bestially torture and slaughter those who, just a day before, had been their own beloved flesh and blood?

* * *

Saturday, July 28, 1979, 6:20 a.m.

The nerve-wracking sound of nonstop car honking woke me out of a half-sleep. My alarm clock had actually not been set to go off until seven.

I slipped on my white doctor's pants and a white T-shirt, grabbed my keys, and ran out of the house to the honking car standing in the street between the clinic and my bungalow. It was the VW jeep towing the kitchen-equipped trailer.

Helmut Fischl, one of our two German cooks—a hulking, generally agreeable fellow who weighed over a hundred kilos—was clutching the wheel, panting.

"I've been shot!" he gasped. "I think the bullet's gotten lodged in my lung. Hurts like hell!"

Blood was flowing down Fischl's back, and enormous beads of sweat studded his forehead. The vehicle had bullet holes in the windshield, on the passenger seat, and on the trailer. One of the trailer's tires had been shot through. More and more construction workers had been woken up by the honking and were now coming out of their houses, dressed in pajamas, bathrobes, or only in their underwear.

Freddy, fully clothed in his black uniform, was the first to reach me. We linked arms with the cook left and right and brought him into the clinic, which stood only a few meters away. Then we went directly into the operating room, followed by curious, worried camp residents.

"Freddy," I yelled, "seal off the OR—better still, the entire clinic, at the front entrance! Patient care has top priority. At eight, everyone in the canteen is going to find out what went down. Mr. Wiesenthaler should also be present, if at all possible."

Freddy, as the first on the scene, would of course have known what had happened. He nodded silently, and did as I had requested.

After stripping off Fischl's shirt and undershirt, I asked him to sit upright. A shot through the lung, coupled with a fully involved pneumothorax, was potentially life-threatening.

"Breathe in and breathe out, deeply. Again, deeply, in and out, and again," I told the patient several times. As he complied, I used a stethoscope to listen to his lungs from both the front and back. His lung sounds were normal, without any rattling or rustling. Also, the maximal exhalation rate, as measured with a peak-flow meter, indicated values in the normal range. From an anatomical standpoint, the circular entry wound on the patient's back was positioned in the lower third of his left shoulder blade. A steady rivulet of blood was trickling out of the wound on Fischl's back. To prevent everything from flowing into his pants and underwear, I immediately placed a sterile compress over the wound. I explained to the patient that his lungs appeared to be fully unimpaired. I let him sit there and collect himself, while I asked what had happened.

"Like every morning," Fischl began, "I wanted to go into the village, to go to the market. My colleague and I take turns driving, to buy fresh vegetables, fruit, eggs, and poultry. As I was driving off and heading for our camp's main gate, I saw a huge throng of people there, twenty or more. Normally there are just two or three guards standing there. As far as I could tell at that distance, they were all Revolutionary Guards. At least, they were all carrying rifles. I drove very slowly.

"Right before the gate, I started getting a bad vibe

about the whole thing, so I turned around. Then they suddenly began firing at me. I drove faster, and I noticed that they had probably hit one of the trailer's tires—the trailer was thrashing around behind the jeep like a cow's tail. I threw myself down against the passenger seat. A shot whizzed past me and smashed through the windshield from behind. Suddenly I sensed stabbing pains in the upper left part of my back. I couldn't breathe for a moment. The bullet had probably ripped through the arm of the passenger seat and gone into my back. After the barrage of gunfire had let up for a while, I drove to your house as fast as I could and began honking," the cook reported.

"You did the right thing," I praised him, "and on top of that, you had a hell of a lot of luck! If you want, I can operate and remove the bullet."

"What do you mean, 'if I want'? What happens if I don't want to?"

"Then it'll just stay in there," I replied.

"Is that also an option?" asked Fischl.

"Yes, it is. But it's possible that at some point, the bullet will start to migrate and damage your lungs or pleural cavity. Then it can become dangerous."

"All right, go ahead and do it!"

I asked the cook to lie prone on the operating table, then I removed the provisionally applied compress, adjusted the lamp, disinfected the area around the entry hole, and asked him, "With or without local anesthesia?"

"I'm no hero. But perhaps we can try it first without, and if I can't bear it, then you can give me a shot," Fischl proposed.

"Then that's exactly how we'll proceed," I confirmed.

306

Cautiously, I attempted to use a pair of sterile forceps to probe the depth of the channel made by the projectile. After barely a centimeter or so, I struck something hard and metallic—the bullet! Since the cook was quite a stocky fellow and had at least about a four-centimeter layer of fat over his shoulder blade, the operation wouldn't be a problem. Even when I first touched the bullet, Fischl screamed like mad!

Not exactly bearing the pain like an American Indian, I thought to myself, and heavily injected the affected area with lidocaine. I waited a while for the local anesthetic to take effect.

Then I attempted to grasp the bullet with the forceps and extract it. But the attempt didn't work, at least not as easily as I had hoped. Even a somewhat greater pair of forceps proved unsuccessful. Finally, I had to use a small, sharp spoon to pick out the deformed projectile from its crooked channel. It was almost like nose-picking. Presumably, the bullet had become deformed when going through the back of the passenger seat, losing a great deal of its kinetic energy at that point, so that only a small fragment had penetrated into the patient's shoulder.

I decided not to suture the hole, which was circular with a diameter under ten millimeters. The wound ought to heal from the inside out, especially since some bacteria had surely made their way in there along with the bullet.

Since nothing suitable was on hand in the OR, I rummaged through the dentist's room for an antibiotic strip I could place into the wound to stop the bleeding. I found something there. Sterile compresses, sticking plaster—done. Fischl had endured everything without so much as a peep.

"Breakfast is in half an hour. People are then going to want to know what happened. Do you want to tell your story yourself? Or would you rather go to bed and first recover a bit from the shock and the operation?" I asked the cook.

"No, that's all right. In any event, there won't be any eggs for breakfast today. And I wasn't able to purchase anything for lunch either," Fischl told me.

Freddy had invited everyone to an emergency meeting in the canteen to be held at eight that evening. Like everyone else, I found out about it only shortly beforehand, via word of mouth.

"People, we've got to do something!" Freddy opened by saying. "Nobody has gotten out of here for three months. We've had no beer for a month, and starting today, no more food either. And now they're shooting at us. Mr. Wiesenthaler, can you perhaps tell us how we're supposed to continue this way?"

Mr. Wiesenthaler rose to his feet and told us, "Kraftwerk Union certainly won't leave us in the lurch. The problem is that everyone wants to get out at the moment, and the airlines and administrative authorities are completely overwhelmed. So I have to keep asking you for a bit of patience!"

"Patience is all well and good," said Freddy angrily. Ordinarily so level-headed, he was now in a rage. "Patience is fine for a couple of days or weeks. But not for over three solid months! And conditions have been steadily deteriorating. Things really got popping four weeks ago when they destroyed an entire container filled with 1,000 crates of the best Munich Augustiner beer—right at our own construction site. And it doesn't help that some of you have been leaving flowers over the beer-bottle graveyard behind the supply warehouse! The beer is gone! Simply evaporated in the sun! And a couple of days ago, Mr. Behrens and I were threatened with G3 assault rifles. We had to crawl around on the floor and clean it. And today Mr. Fischl was fired at, so the kitchen is non-operational. I've had it with patience! We've got to *do* something!"

Freddy received roaring applause. People clapped, cheered, stomped their feet, whistled, and shouted their agreement.

After Mr. Wiesenthaler didn't budge, I stood up and said, "We're going to find a solution. And soon!"

Freddy—the only person in the camp with whom I was on a first-name basis—now attacked me brusquely: "You haven't got a clue! You haven't been here even two weeks, anyway!"

"Okay, people. First of all, we want to ensure that we've got something to eat again starting tomorrow morning. And does anybody have any information yet about the reason behind today's shooting? Can we even leave the camp without getting fired at?" I asked the group.

Mr. Wiesenthaler took the floor and said, "A couple of hours ago, that tall Revolutionary Guardsman approached me and declared that the shooting was an accident. He claimed the driver was at fault for pulling a U-turn and driving off fast. That made his men think the driver had something to hide and was attempting to escape."

Laughter, cursing, shouting.

"Quiet, please!" I called out. "Is there anyone from the kitchen staff who would be ready to buy groceries at the market early tomorrow morning?"

Nobody raised a hand.

"Could someone else step in? I mean, there must be someone who's familiar with what has to be bought, the quality, and where to get everything."

Nobody raised a hand.

"Do we have anything in the deep freezer for emergencies? And by the way, what happened to the Italian Parma ham and semi-mature Gouda I brought along two weeks ago?" I asked, directing my question at the kitchen crew.

"Our supply of deep-frozen meat and vegetables is enough to last exactly three days. I've held onto your Parma ham and the Gouda for a special occasion," replied our second cook, the one who had taken charge of the special delicacies upon my arrival.

"Then kindly defrost the supply on hand. *Now.* Tomorrow morning, serve up the treats I brought," I insisted.

"Can you decree that so easily?" asked the cook. "After three days, we're all going to starve if nobody goes shopping again!"

Naturally, he didn't know that in three days he and the other Germans, if everything went according to plan, would already be dining aboard a Lufthansa aircraft. I nodded to Mr. Wiesenthaler.

"Do what our doctor said!" the construction site manager confirmed curtly.

"As far as our departure is concerned, I would suggest that we take all of Sunday to work out a couple of proposals for a solution, in a small group. Then we can present them to you for a vote at this hour on Monday evening, here in the canteen. The working group should consist of a maximum of three people. I was thinking of

Mr. Wiesenthaler, Freddy, as well as myself. If you don't agree with our proposals for a solution, then of course everyone is free to contribute their own," I said.

Murmuring and grumbling, the assembled group broke up. I had bought exactly the amount of time I needed.

* * *

Sunday, July 29, 1979, 2 p.m.

Mr. Wiesenthaler, Freddy, and I met at the beer-bottle graveyard, a place I hadn't known about before. It seemed suitable to me. After swearing Freddy to 100% secrecy, I revealed everything to him:

"At 0830 on Tuesday, a Lufthansa aircraft is going to be landing at the Bushehr airport. It's going to pick up all the German nationals from the camp, and it'll take off at 0930."

"Why didn't you tell me about this before?" Freddy asked.

"Part of the plan is that everyone concerned is to be informed no earlier than twelve hours prior to departure. That's supposed to ensure that no communication occurs with Tehran which could jeopardize the plan. Besides the three of us, nobody knows anything, and it has to stay that way until tomorrow evening!" I replied.

"And who's going to take charge of customs and processing at the airport?" Freddy pressed.

"Mullah Haschemi and his people!"

"But then he'll be able to communicate with Tehran, and they won't let us out," Freddy pointed out.

"No, he won't be able to do that. He doesn't even know yet how lucky he is. I'll talk with him tomorrow, after evening prayers."

Freddy shook his head.

"If only that works out!"

The construction site manager fell silent and appeared lost in thought.

"It'll go smoothly," I reiterated, deftly adding, for Freddy's benefit, "Sorry for not taking you into my confidence earlier. But now that you know, you're getting yet another special assignment!"

"No thanks, I don't need any more special assignments around here," Freddy said, declining.

"Oh, you might like it!" I said, whetting his curiosity.

"All right, then tell me," said our security officer.

"The Boeing 737-700 has a maximum carrying capacity of 139 people, plus the crew. But we've got 141 passengers. That's why I've twisted the pilot's arm to get him to reduce the complement of stewardesses by two. In exchange, one selected passenger and I will handle the onboard service. Imagine the exhilarating feeling when you serve your colleagues their first beer, high over the clouds, after all this enforced abstinence!"

"Provided the very first beer gets poured down my gullet, I'll do it!" Freddy laughed.

CHAPTER 12

The Biggest Coup

Monday, July 30, 1979, 7 p.m.

I was familiar with Mullah Haschemi's annual income and his corruption index. I also knew all about his alcohol addiction and his overall health. But what kind of man was he? Was he well connected? Did he even know that the Atomic Energy Organization of Iran, in Tehran, had blocked the Germans' exit? I had deliberately picked the hour after evening prayers for my visit with him. In exchange for some baksheesh, the ancient servant at the mosque's entrance willingly announced me to his boss and brought me to him.

"Thank you for receiving me, Your Excellency!" I said in greeting, merely to suss out how Haschemi reacted to the "Your Excellency" form of address—to which, actually, only heads of state, ambassadors, and bishops are entitled.

"Doctor! How are you?" answered the mullah, visibly flattered.

"I'm well. Better, in any case, than our cook, on whom I had to operate two days ago, to remove five bullets from his back. One of them had penetrated his lungs. But now he's out of danger," I said, shamelessly exaggerating.

"I heard about that," the mullah said. "The man turned around at the gate. He was trying to evade being checked by the watch, then he fled. They had to open fire."

"It was a stupid affair. It should never be repeated," I replied.

This time, a handful of Revolutionary Guards were lolling on the elegant divan in the mullah's study. These crude barbarians completely clashed with the educated holy man, and with what's called in Persian a divan—this splendid study, lined with Middle Eastern ornaments. And they certainly didn't complement the big, gorgeous, plush sofa—known in the West as a divan. Besides that, these gentlemen didn't fit into my plan. I therefore requested a private audience with "His Excellency." With a brief hand gesture, the mullah dispatched the Revolutionary Guards from the room, and had the elderly servant bring two glasses of tea.

"Who is actually the qadi here in the village?" I asked.

The mullah made a dramatic, pregnant pause before answering, "The qadi—that's me! Far and wide, I'm the only person around here who has studied Islamic law. And what's more, at the Theological University of Qom, our great leader Ayatollah Khomeini's alma mater, albeit many decades before me. Since the founding of the Islamic Republic a few months ago, I'm not only the local theologian and qadi, I'm also simultaneously serving as mayor, chief of police, commander of the armed forces, and director of the airport. Can you imagine how much work that is?"

"No, Your Excellency. But you enjoy my great respect!"

With all my strength, I thrust down the thought that I was now effusively currying favor with a man who a few days earlier had decreed the brutal stoning of a seventeen-year-old girl. Neither bringing the girl back to life nor rewriting Sharia law would be possible for me to accomplish. And right here and now, I had another goal to pursue.

314

We both drank a sip of tea and looked one another in the eye before I said, "I have a matter of great urgency, Your Excellency. And I believe that you are the only one here who can help."

"Let's hear it, Doctor. What can I do for you?" asked the mullah.

"You're aware of how difficult it is to obtain flights to Germany right now," I began. "That's why the construction management in Germany has been trying to charter an aircraft. The Lufthansa plane is landing tomorrow at 0830. It's supposed to take on as many of the Germans as will squeeze on board, then get tanked up and take off again an hour later. Can you organize everything with customs processing and passport checks?"

"Impossible!" replied the Mullah. "For tomorrow, that's cutting it too close. I would need at least three days' runup time for that. Why didn't you tell me about this earlier?"

"I simply had too much to do," I lied, "but also, we don't have any telephone connections to Germany, so we can't postpone the flight. It's a one-time opportunity! If you can manage to process the flight early tomorrow morning, I may be allowed to permit a small donation to be deposited with Your Excellency, in the name of Kraft-werk Union."

The mullah avoided my inquiring look, glancing off to the side and obviously wrestling with himself as to whether he ought to repeat his rebuff or at least listen to my offer.

"How small?" he inquired.

"What?" I said, responding to his question with another one.

"How small would the donation turn out to be?" asked the mullah, reformulating his question more precisely.

I held off answering until our gazes met again, then said, slowly and solemnly, "$100,000 U.S. And two bottles of your personal medicine!"

For a moment, the mullah was caught breathless, before he asked, "Where did you get hold of so much money?"

"I brought it along with me from Germany," I said, which was the truth, as far as it went.

"If you can count out the money to me right here on my desk before today's out, and if you also bring along my medicine, I'll see what I can do," the mullah told me.

"I cannot hand over the donation until it is certain that you will process all the German passengers tomorrow morning. I will deposit the money and your medicine in the drugs cabinet—the white safe in my treatment room. You remember it from the time Dr. Zimmermann treated you. As soon as all the passengers are sitting in the aircraft and it's fully tanked up, I'll hand you the keys to the safe," I proposed.

"Fully tanked? Absolutely not! We aren't permitted to issue any additional fuel beyond what's needed for the aircraft to reach Mehrabad Airport in Tehran. The pilots can calculate that amount. Once you get there, you'll have to pass through customs and passport checks again. That's the rule currently in force for all international flights. If I'm supposed to drive into the camp first, count out the donation, then drive back to the airport, the passengers will then have to remain sitting in the aircraft for three or four hours until I can issue clearance for take-off," the mullah estimated.

"We can tank up with the smaller amount proposed by Your Excellency. It'll suffice if we can get as far as Tehran and top off the fuel there. But there's another problem that has to be solved with the donation. We have almost no more vehicles left at the construction site. How are we going to transport our people to the airport?" I asked.

The mullah shrugged, at a loss.

"Do you have a bus available, perhaps?"

"Only an old American school bus, the one that's used to pick up the children around the area to take them to the Koran school in the mornings," the mullah recalled.

"How many seats does that bus have? And when is it needed for the pupils of the Koran school?" I asked.

"The bus has exactly seventy-two seats. And it runs at eight in the morning," Mullah Haschemi explained.

"From the construction site to the airfield, it's just about a half-hour's drive. Then the bus is going to have to shuttle back and forth twice, in order to pick up the first seventy-two passengers at 0500 and the rest an hour later. If you begin customs and passport processing at 0630, or check the first busload even earlier, can the passengers then board the aircraft right after it lands at 0830?" I asked.

"Not so fast, my dear doctor! I'll need a couple of people for that, so I'll also have to organize everything first. And I'm not inclined to do it as long as the donation has not found its way over here yet," the mullah informed me.

"Would Your Excellency commence the organizing immediately if I were to drive to the camp right now and return with half the donation in around an hour and a half? Your Excellency can then pick up the other half from the drugs cabinet after the processing," I proposed.

The mullah thought it over for a while. Then he gave me a friendly nod. As I was leaving, he called after me,

"When you come back, bring the full stock of medicine right away!"

It was 1950. I would no longer make it to the canteen on time for the assembly. When I entered the room twelve minutes late, the mood quickly began to really boil over.

"We're just getting jerked around and fucked over! We're not going to stand for it anymore!" yelled one of the men.

Mr. Wiesenthaler and Freddy were really on the hot seat, because they weren't supposed to discuss the outcome of our "working group" in my absence.

"Calm down! Good news! Very good news!" I shouted across the room, to drown out the tumult.

"There is one—but only one single chance! And I implore all of you to seize it! And without any debating or ifs, ands, or buts! And what's more, I cannot and will not discuss today why none of you were informed earlier. Tomorrow morning at 0500, a school bus is going to pick up the first seventy of you in front of the canteen and drive to the airport. The remaining seventy will be picked up at 0600. The mullah and his people will be taking charge of passport and customs checks. He has just promised me personally. At 0830, a Lufthansa aircraft will be landing. It's going to fly you all to Frankfurt Airport. Each person will be allowed twenty-five kilos of checked baggage and a small carry-on. There won't be any tickets or baggage claim checks."

I bent over to Freddy and asked him whether he would take charge of dividing up the two busloads. He nodded.

"The seventy people who want seats in the first bus at 0500, please register with Freddy. The others can sleep an extra hour," I proclaimed, knowing full well that almost nobody was going to get a wink of sleep tonight.

A hush had fallen over the room. In all likelihood, people had to digest the news first. I had neither the time nor the inclination to answer stupid questions that might crop up—like, "So who's going to water my cactus?" or "How am I supposed to get three years of my life in camp down to twenty-five kilos of luggage?" I whispered to Freddy, "I've still got to get back to the mullah!"

Then I left the meeting, charged into the treatment room, opened up the drugs cabinet, counted out half the donation, and grabbed the religious leader's special medicine, wrapped in metallic blue Christmas paper. I stowed the lot in my doctor's bag, in which I had cleared sufficient space. To better cushion the medicine, I stuffed a couple of compresses and packages of bandages on top, then shoved my stethoscope and blood-pressure cuff into the bag.

At our camp's gate, one of the two watchstanders, a very young, especially eager Revolutionary Guardsman, instructed me to get out, then began searching the VW jeep. Now that was all I needed!

"It is very urgent that I get to Mullah Haschemi! He is ill and needs my medicine," I said. But the young man didn't understand anything except his leader's name. When he wanted to reach for my doctor's bag, I recalled the acting training I had enjoyed at the CIA, and I staged the best pantomime of my life. Loudly I shouted, "Mullah Haschemi!" Then I clutched my heart, collapsed on the ground as though unconscious, and stood up again lightning quick. I opened up the doctor's bag just a crack, took out the stethoscope and blood-pressure cuff, and began measuring the stunned Revolutionary Guards-man's blood pressure. Then I performed steering move-ments with my hands, pretending to hit the gas pedal, to show how much of a hurry I was in. Again I shouted, "Mullah Haschemi!" clutched at my heart, and rolled my eyes—and right before I was about to dramatically col-lapse to the ground a second time, the Revolutionary Guardsman uttered just a single word: "Go!" – Exactly what I wanted to hear!

"Have you got everything with you?" the mullah asked as I entered his study with my doctor's bag.

"Yes, I do! And has Your Excellency arranged every-thing?" I asked back excitedly.

"The bus will arrive in the camp to pick the people up, once at 0500 and again at 0600. The head sentry has also been informed. At 0700, I'll be at the airport with five of my people, and I'll take charge of the processing. We had better not find any alcohol, pornography, or work-related materials. Tell the passengers!" the mullah explained.

"I'll do that," I replied, placing the bundle of money on his desk, along with two cans wrapped in metallic-blue Christmas paper.

While the man of God was counting the money, I pondered what kind of needs a mullah could have, and what he would likely set about doing with his wealth. Renovate the mosque? Travel abroad, just once? Import the forbidden "medicine" through illicit channels? Or would he even let a couple of attractive girls from his congregation, quite discreetly, doff their chadors—and perhaps a bit more?

When the mullah was finished counting the money, I couldn't refrain from commenting how I would be glad to share a belt of his exquisite medicine with him on a day like this one.

Mullah Haschemi went first to the main entrance, then to the back one, bolting from the inside both access points to his rooms. Then he lit an oil lamp on his desk, shut off the electric lights, and disappeared for a while. The light from the oil lamp exuded a heartwarming mood in the ornately paneled study. Almost like Christmas!

The mullah returned holding two tea glasses, each of which was about one-third filled with the best single malt Scotch whisky on the rocks. He handed me one, lifted his glass and nodded to me. We savored the way the fine liquid slowly bathed tongue and palate, lubricated the esophagus, and warmed the stomach.

Driving back to camp, I didn't have to worry about any security checks for alcohol because in Iran there was absolutely no alcohol—officially. When I arrived in the camp at around one in the morning, the lights were still burning in most of the houses. Still, I didn't want to convene another meeting just to tell people what must under no circumstances be found in their suitcases. Freddy and Mr. Wiesenthaler were supposed to communicate this information prior to the departure of each bus. I paid them both a visit in their houses. I also wanted to hear that everything really was proceeding as planned. Freddy would accompany the first bus, while Mr. Wiesenthaler and I would be aboard the second one.

My suitcase was packed quickly. I tried to snatch three hours' sleep, and had a wonderful dream: alcohol, in the form of tiny hand grenades, was streaming through the mullah's brain. The grenades were exploding precisely at the places were particularly brutal punishments under Sharia law were stored. These brain cells were destroyed, and the punishments eliminated from the holy man's memory.

Suddenly, I was torn from my dream by banging on the door and the sound of screeching cats. When I opened the door—clad only in my underwear—three middle-aged women stepped into my house. Presumably they were the wives of German construction workers.

Each of the women had a cat under her arm, and one of them spoke up, saying, "Doctor, you've simply got to help us! The Iranians—especially the children and the Revolutionary Guards—they all torture animals! They've often thrown stones at our cats. They'll torture and kill them once we're gone. Your predecessor, Dr. Zimmerman, promised us that he'd put our cats to sleep once we get out of here. Now you've got to do it!"

"Do I have to?" I asked, a slight smile on my lips, as I put on my white doctor's pants and reached for my shirt.

I went to the clinic with the women, courteously ushering them into the OR along with their mewing patients. It would be better if they didn't see what was stored in the safe in the treatment room when I removed the highly potent anesthetic.

Since cats, as everybody knows, have nine lives, I administered each animal a fair portion of fentanyl, a very powerful pain medication, overdoses of which induce respiratory arrest. As the three sobbing ladies were departing with their euthanized pets, they notified me that a dog owner was on her way with her mutt. I absolutely had to spare the dog too, they said, from the fate of a stoning. Of course I had to!

Now there was no further thought of sleep. I drove my car over to the canteen to watch the passengers who were slated to leave at 0500, and to accompany them at least as far as the gate. It was a good thing I was present, because the Revolutionary Guardsman on duty didn't know a thing and didn't want to let the bus pass through. The guard was discomfited by the bus driver's entreaties that Mullah Haschemi had personally commissioned him to make the journey. Then, when I helped grease the skids a bit with some baksheesh, the gate barrier was raised.

An hour later, Mr. Wiesenthaler and I accompanied the second bus on its trip. I asked the construction site manager whether it was really absolutely certain that every German national was out of the camp. His eyes welling up with tears, as though he had just attended his own burial, he replied, "Yes, every employee is gone. The camp and the construction site are dead!"

At 0700 on the dot, the mullah and his people began inspecting everyone's luggage. The holy man personally took charge of my suitcase. He let me open and close it again without so much as a glance inside. Mr. Wiesenthaler, who was next in line to have his suitcase inspected, wasn't as lucky. The mullah, rooting around in the gold and silver jewelry, removed an ornate box decorated in turquoise and mother-of-pearl, and even found two small hand-knotted silk rugs that had been rolled up together. Like many of the Germans, the construction site manager had blown his overseas allowance at the bazaar. All that, however, didn't interest the mullah. But when he discovered a pair of work gloves, he confiscated them, declaring, "No work materials are allowed to leave the country!"

It was the sole confiscation during the entire luggage inspection. Mr. Wiesenthaler could handle it.

0830: the Lufthansa aircraft's scheduled landing time. Nothing was stirring. No aircraft was to be seen or heard for miles around.

0835: still nothing. The tension rose by the minute.

0840: I was growing uneasy. Had I misunderstood something? Had there been engine damage or an unforeseen event that would now jeopardize the entire mission? How often, during our final meeting at the Kraftwerk Union office, reiterated in the pilots' presence how important the exact timing would be during this mission?

0842: I thought I could make out a tiny dot on the horizon, visible to the naked eye. Or was I just imagining that?

0847: the Lufthansa Boeing 737-200 touched down on the runway, and after a gentle landing and a deafening reverse thrust, taxied directly in front of our waiting area.

The mullah assigned me one of his men to monitor loading the aircraft. I delegated this task to Freddy.

When the gangway was pushed up to the aircraft, the front door opened and the first Germans entered the plane, I handed the mullah the keys to the clinic and to the drug cabinet. Not only had he now enriched himself by a pile of dollars, but by two offices: *he* was now boss of the clinic, and on top of that, of the world's largest abandoned construction site!

I asked Mr. Wiesenthaler to do a post-boarding head count to ensure that everyone was accounted for, and to check them off the roster of bus passengers one by one. Then I burst into the cockpit.

"Am I glad to see you!" I said, greeting the captain and the co-pilot, both of whom I knew from our last meeting in Offenbach.

The captain instructed the stewardess to close the cockpit door and to leave us undisturbed.

"Sorry for being late," he said, "but fueling up in Ankara was delayed somewhat. The tower here asked me to land using visual flight rules, which is extremely unusual. Do you think it's possible that the radar here isn't working?"

"Quite possible," I replied. "But it can also be that there simply aren't any personnel able to operate it. If the former air traffic control staff were known as Shah loyalists, now they've simply gone underground."

"The tower has just inquired as to whether we've got enough fuel to make it to Tehran, and I confirmed that we do. Actually, we'll also make it all the way back to Ankara. We still have both the options that we discussed in Offenbach. One is that we fly to Ankara, disregarding all instructions. If we do, we'll still be in Iranian airspace a full eighty-five minutes after take-off. Or, after five minutes, we can fake an elevated oil temperature in the left engine. Then, as the flight manual requires, we would have to shut the engine down after fifteen minutes. In that case, we could veer off to Kuwait and request an emergency landing there. We would then be out of Iranian airspace in ten minutes. But it could take hours—in the worst-case scenario, even days—until we get out of Kuwait. What do you think?"

"Naturally, the decision is yours, Captain! I've got the impression that everything here has descended into pure chaos. Neither air traffic control nor any of the authorities nor the military are properly organized or coordinated. They do know that every international flight has to be routed through Tehran. However, I can scarcely imagine that anyone in this country is capable of ordering a military interception, insofar as hardly any military pilots have defected to the new regime. Maybe in a year, but not now," I told him.

"That jibes exactly with the assessment given to us by German Intelligence before our departure today. We're taking off in fifteen minutes—officially, heading towards Tehran, unofficially, as the three of us know, wherever the journey takes us!" the pilot said.

As I was exiting the cockpit, Mr. Wiesenthal was standing before me, somewhat at a loss. "Freddy's missing," he said. "But every passenger seat has been occupied. Even if he shows up, he won't have a seat."

"We are *not* flying without Freddy!" I resolved. "But the seat isn't any problem. Freddy and I can use the jump seats next to the stewardesses," I explained to Mr. Wiesenthaler.

The gangway was still standing against the aircraft, and the door was open.

"We're missing one passenger! Keep waiting until I've found him!" I called into the cockpit.

Just after I'd run down the gangway, intending to hunt for Freddy, he came towards me, totally exhausted and out of breath.

"I've tallied up all the suitcases three times. There are only 140 of them, but we've got 141 passengers. I can't imagine that one of us is traveling without luggage," Freddy reported despairingly.

"Forget the fucking suitcase, whoever it may belong to and whatever the hell might be in it. We are taking off *now!*" I shouted against the racket of the revving engines.

We boarded the plane, and a stewardess closed the passenger door. The gangway was rolled back. The door to the hold was shut.

"Every man's aboard! And the women too, of course!" I shouted into the cockpit.

While the aircraft taxied into position for take-off, I introduced Freddy and myself to the head stewardess and requested instructions as to where we could sit and how we could lend them a hand with the on-board service a bit later. We had to sit down and buckle ourselves into a couple of rather uncomfortable jump seats. The sight of six lovely feminine legs clad in black nylons nicely compensated us for any inconvenience, though.

Once we had reached cruising altitude and the fasten-seatbelt sign had been turned off, Freddy asked me, "So where's the beer?"

I turned to the head stewardess—a tall blonde with a thickly braided plait of hair bouncing over her right shoulder, and bright-red lipstick—and explained the importance of the first beer to the passengers as a symbol of their regained freedom. I also mentioned that I had promised Freddy the first can.

"No alcohol is permitted to be served in Iranian airspace!" the cool blonde stated.

"Can't we make just one exception today?" I asked the lady, deploying my most charming smile. "I think it's extremely improbable that some Revolutionary Guardsman is suddenly going to peek through the window at 10,000 meters and run a check on us."

"Any exceptions can be authorized only by the captain," came the curt answer.

I quickly obtained the captain's approval to make an exception. Freddy got his first beer, then we assisted the three stewardesses as well as we could with distributing the beverages and the subsequent in-flight meals.

After about seventy minutes, I went into the cockpit and asked the pilots whether everything was running according to plan.

"The departure from Bushehr wasn't problematic," the Captain told me. "The man in the tower spoke only rudimentary school English, and whatever training he might have had as an air traffic controller, it definitely wasn't up to international standards. Probably good for us. But now the Turks are causing us problems!"

"How come?" I asked, astonished.

"Ankara Control is complaining that they don't have a flight report from us. They haven't received a transfer from Tehran Control or a flight plan from us out of Bushehr. Obviously, I couldn't very well submit a flight plan in Bushehr stating Ankara as our destination," the pilot explained.

"What do we do now?" I asked. "Surely Türkiye can't refuse us flight entry into their airspace and the right to refuel in Ankara, can they?"

"Theoretically, they can. But I don't think they'll do that. I've just submitted a flight plan over the radio and asked for permission to enter Turkish airspace and to land in Ankara."

"Is submitting a belated flight plan by radio also possible?" I asked.

"On flights subject to the Instrument Flight Rules— and our flight is an IFR one—normally, no. But I justified it by citing the special situation at our departure airport and in Iran. Now we've got to wait and see how they answer," the experienced flight captain suggested. In contrast to his visibly nervous co-pilot, the captain was radiating calm and optimism.

In the cockpit, the tension-filled minutes ticked by, in a drama to which everyone in the passenger cabin was blissfully oblivious.

Then came our salvation, in the form of a radio message out of Ankara:

"Flight entry into Turkish airspace and landing in Ankara authorized!"

The joy in both pilots' faces was unmistakable! Five minutes later, the captain made an announcement for all the passengers to hear: "We have just exited Iranian airspace and are now flying over Türkiye!"

Cheers broke out among the passengers. Most of them understood what the announcement meant. And I too was happy and relieved! What, now, could still go awry? Maybe they wouldn't give us any jet fuel in Ankara? Would they ship us back to Iran? Impossible! The battle had been won! Almost, in any event. I wouldn't really believe it, though, until after we'd landed in Frankfurt.

In Ankara, we had to endure a wait of more than three hours in sweltering heat, with the aircraft's air conditioning shut off. The arrival of the refueling tanker alone took a full two and a half hours.

After another three hours and forty-five minutes, we landed at Frankfurt am Main Airport at 1855.

After disembarking from the aircraft, before getting even as far as passport inspection and customs, I was received by two well-known faces: Messrs. Schmitt and Krause from German Intelligence. Their curt congratulations certainly could have been a bit more effusive! Instead, the first thing they did was take my passport and hand me back my old one. Henceforth, I was no longer Dr. Dagobert Dussmann, head of a small hospital on the Persian Gulf, but rather Michael Müller, a nurse at Munich-Schwabing municipal hospital. While waiting at the baggage carousel, Freddy and I exchanged telephone numbers.

"Whenever you're in Munich, just give me a call! Then we'll go for a beer. And don't be surprised if you hear a 'Michael Müller' answering the phone," I told him in parting. Freddy was one of the people I definitely wanted to see again in my future life.

"Who is Michael Müller?" Freddy asked.

"I'll explain that to you when we meet!" I replied.

The baggage carousel emptied out. Behind it, people were lining up before each of the ten telephone booths. Many of the returning passengers lived in the greater Frankfurt area and wanted to get in touch with their families and relatives or get picked up.

At some point, Mr. Schmitt, Mr. Krause, and I were the only ones standing in front of the baggage carousel, which now stopped. On the way to the baggage claim inquiries desk, I realized, seething, that one suitcase had already been missing at departure—and it could have only been mine! The suitcase with the false compartment and all the money in it! I had been so proud of myself for hanging onto most of it: out of the $500,000 U.S. entrusted to me, I had spent only $100,100, namely, $100 for the taxi ride from Shiras to Bushehr and $100,000 for Mullah Haschemi. The mullah must have purloined the suitcase for himself! But how had he known that so much money was in it? The sole explanation I could find was that he *didn't* know! The old fox had simply surmised from the whole transfer business that maybe I had

330

brought even more money from Germany and had stashed it somewhere in my suitcase.

With my head drooping dejectedly, I reported to Messrs. Schmitt and Krause my conjecture, nay, the certainty—that my suitcase would never arrive. Any baggage-claim inquiry would have been totally pointless, especially since the facts were unambiguous. This flight didn't even have baggage tags anyway.

The two gentlemen from intelligence community notified me that the crisis staff had been waiting for our return all afternoon, and at 1800 had adjourned until 1400 the following day. The two intelligence agents would now chauffeur me to the Intercontinental, where a room had been reserved for me. It was requested that I appear at Kaiserlei punctually at 1400 tomorrow to make my report.

A trifle reluctantly, Mr. Krause lent me twenty Deutschmarks so I could get something to eat and take the subway to tomorrow's meeting. In fact, he never saw the money again. I put dinner on the hotel's tab and used Krause's money to treat myself to a couple of beers—I hadn't drunk a drop of alcohol on the plane, by the way—in the neighborhood around Frankfurt's train station. There, quite satisfied with myself, I contemplated the past fourteen days. The business with the missing suitcase was the only thing that annoyed me a little. But nobody was hurt—just some paper burned. Money that had never been mine in the first place. And I would have never put the mission at risk, even if I had known, prior to our departure, that the mullah had the suitcase.

In the large meeting room of the Kraftwerk Union tower at Kaiserlei, in Offenbach, once again the entire crisis management staff was represented, exactly the way it had been at our last meeting around three weeks earlier: besides me, the Undersecretary of State, the woman keeping the minutes, the Kraftwerk Union board chairman, both gentlemen from German Intelligence, and the two pilots were all present. The only additional person in the room was Mr. Wiesenthaler.

Undersecretary of State Lautenschlager thanked me expressly "in the name of the Federal Republic of Germany" and described me as "one of the many unsung heroes who have rendered a great service to their country and will nevertheless always remain anonymous." The Kraftwerk Union board chairman also thanked me for my successful mission.

Every participant in the rescue mission was now supposed to provide as detailed a report as possible about how the recent days and weeks had unfolded. I went first and told them about everything, about my observations at the Shiraz airport, and Dr. Zimmermann's transferring the clinic to me, the mood in the camp, the distribution of weapons in the village square, the Germans' humiliation by armed children and adolescents, the cook who was shot, and finally, the negotiations with the mullah. I omitted the part about the rather complicated operation I performed on the child who had slipped and fallen from the date palm. The same went for the stoning of the young woman, an experience that I'll never forget for the rest of my life. Both of these stories were irrelevant to the extraction mission.

Nodding, Mr. Wiesenthaler confirmed everything I said, adding only the part about the effrontery with which the Revolutionary Guards had confiscated half the vehicle fleet shortly after my arrival. The pilots described the progression of the inbound and returning flights, from their perspective.

Last but not least, I had to disclose the matter of the lost suitcase containing almost $400,000 U.S. of German taxpayer money. After confessing this setback, I felt released from a burden! Strangely enough, the story didn't seem to interest anyone much, not even Mr. Lautenschlager.

At the meeting's conclusion, the undersecretary of state issued me an order check in the amount of 240,000 Deutschmarks, solemnly handing it to me with only a single, but thoroughly weighty word:

"Tax-free!"

Shouldn't it have been for an additional 1,000 Deutschmarks? A fixed fee of 100,000 Deutschmarks for the 141 passengers, plus 1,000 Deutschmarks for every German citizen who arrived in West Germany uninjured, counting me in, of course, ought to have been a total amount of 241,000 Deutschmarks. I probably wasn't allowed to factor myself in. But then they should have had to include Dr. Zimmermann, who was also a German citizen and was able to leave Iran only due to my work in Iran. But in light of the overall handsome sum, I didn't want to be petty, so I courteously thanked them.

The board chairman got me a Lufthansa flight to Munich for that same evening and bade me a very fond farewell. From his firm handshake, along with the beaming expression on his face, I could clearly sense how relieved he was.

Without any luggage, but with a big fat check in my jeans pocket, I caught a flight out of Frankfurt. After the plane took off, I closed my eyes, satisfied, and let myself dream about the future a little.

First and foremost, I had to come clean with Birgit, my great love. How could I reconcile with her? With a big bunch of long-stemmed Baccara roses? With a princely dinner at Tantris, the city's finest restaurant?

I visualized going to the local branch of my savings bank at Kurfürstenplatz to deposit the order check. How would the treacly little female teller, who was always a bit snippy, act upon accepting a check for an amount that she surely didn't see every day?

Besides the 240,000 Deutschmarks I had just earned, I still had $50,000 U.S. from my last CIA assignment, distributed into various envelopes jammed under my mattress. Now I felt truly rich! What could I do with so much money? A few possibilities danced around in my mind:

1. Purchase a nice little house on the outskirts of Munich—debt-free, too, plunking the cash right on the table! I would still have a nice fat chunk of dough left over. I would start a family with Birgit and sire a couple of rugrats. I could really devote plenty of time and love to the children and consciously enjoy every phase of their development. For this adventure—the greatest of all—I would be ready to give up my agent work anytime!

2. Obtain my high school diploma, at long last, and eventually enroll in medical school? Possessing a solid financial foundation, I wouldn't have to hold any part-time jobs while attending, and afterwards I could purchase an existing practice or start my own.

3. Go into business with Gustl Harry Lechner and establish the first American factory manufacturing gummy bears—in the process, becoming a millionaire or perhaps even a multimillionaire?

4. Purchase a small piece of property behind the parachutists' packing area from Larry, the owner of Skylark Airfield at Lake Elsinore in Southern California. I could set up a bunkhouse there, a kind of hostel for skydivers, with inexpensive bunkbeds, washing machines, a billiards room, a bar, and a small movie theater for parachuting films, where the legendary greats of the parachuting world living there—Carl Boenish, Ray Cottingham, and Rande DeLuca—could show their films. That was exactly what I had missed in the world-famous cradle of parachute formation jumping. I could use the revenue from the hostel to go skydiving every day, from sunup to sundown. Always 12,000 feet high, always sunny, always in huge formations, always new world records—in a word, unlimited freedom!

5. Establish a company involving parachuting, helicopter flight, medicine, or, ideally, combining all three fields.

Dream over! The Lufthansa aircraft was approaching Riem Airport in Munich for landing.

I drove to my apartment in Schwabing, took the somewhat crumpled check from my jeans pocket and placed it in an envelope under my mattress. Then I looked in the drawer of my nightstand for our vacation tickets. Had Birgit perhaps gone off alone, or with a woman friend?

The tickets were gone! In their place was a slip of paper, which read: *I'm dating Hannes now, so I'll be taking the trip with him. Birgit.* Next to her name was a sloppily drawn heart.

That hurt! That really, really hurt! Hannes was also a nurse. I had even been introduced to him at the clinic and gotten him excited about parachuting. He and Birgit had been my best students.

Yes, Birgit had threatened to leave me if I ever again went off on another sudden trip. And the fact that this time around, I had even ruined our dream vacation— that was indeed a tough row to hoe. Also, in my despair, I had given Birgit the tickets, telling her she could do with them whatever she wanted. But this was something I hadn't reckoned with—*Hannes!*

CHAPTER 13

How Everything Turned Out

My mother, who, during my childhood, burdened me with the accusation that I was a nail in her coffin and even stood to blame for her early death, is now ninety-five years old. Numerous attempts of mine at reconciliation foundered miserably. All the same, I am unbelievably grateful to her because she did accomplish something terrific: she brought me into the world!

Gustl Harry Lechner, sometime after sales of his sand paintings at Venice Beach dropped off, returned to Munich, borrowed some money, and flew to Bangkok, where he bought himself a motorcycle and spent two years driving all over Thailand. Back in Munich, Gustl— who so dearly loved beer—slipped and fell while buying a bottle of milk, of all things, and broke his leg. That proved to be his death sentence: during the operation he became infected with multi-drug resistant hospital-borne germs and died a short time later while convalescing.

The seasoned pilot **Barry Winslow Meeker** died on April 16, 1982, in a helicopter crash in a Bell 222, forty miles west of Oklahoma City. At the time, the press speculated that he had been murdered by the CIA because he knew too much (according to Munich's *tz*, a daily newspaper, dated April 20, 1982), and perhaps talked too much, too. I regard that as a conspiracy theory. But not every conspiracy has to be wrong …

After returning from Iran, **Freddy** obtained a highly paid job for a few years as a personal bodyguard for one of Germany's richest men. Later, until finally going into retirement, he became the head of a security company at Munich's airport.

The **Bushehr nuclear power plant**, even today, is still a major factor in global politics—especially the question concerning the extent to which the spent fuel rods, once they've been reprocessed and enriched, could bring Iran one step closer to building a nuclear bomb.

In 1980, Iran brought a lawsuit against Kraftwerk Union at the International Court of Justice, demanding that the company either return the money they had already received or complete construction of the nuclear power plant—and won. The German Federal Government, however, prohibited Kraftwerk Union from continuing work on the plant, not least due to pressure from the United States, whose embassy in Iran was being occupied at the time. In addition, it was questionable whether the corrosion that had meanwhile formed in the buildings would even allow safe completion of the project in the first place. Independent expert committees from India, Switzerland, and Germany placed this in doubt. In the course of the Iran-Iraq war, the construction site was repeatedly bombed between 1984 and 1988. In 1996, Russia declared itself ready to complete one block of the plant within four and a half years, using its own technology. This block was finally connected to the electricity grid in 2013.

I used **my bonuses** for the Bushehr mission to establish a successful company. Afterwards, I went abroad for the

CIA and for German Intelligence to the Middle East and Central America a couple of times. At some point, I started a family and didn't take on any more jobs, no matter how high the tax-free payment or how tempting the missions themselves would have been. Family and the life of an agent do not get along well. With a family, one is subject to blackmail and extortion. And one has responsibilities—so you can't very well simply die or bid everyone farewell to spend a couple of decades behind bars in a foreign country.

I had a lot of luck in my life, earlier with my agent's work—which often didn't lack an element of danger—and later, by correctly choosing my great love, who, right down to the present day, is always at my side, and gave me the gift of three wonderful children.

Glossary

Aeromedical evacuation (medevac)
Originally (since the Korean War, 1950–1953), the evacuation of wounded soldiers by helicopter from battle zones, as well as ambulance flights out of war zones. Medevac helicopters and aircraft are designated with visible red crosses on a white background. Later, the term was also extended to refer to civilian air rescue operations.

Ayatollah Khomeini (Sayyid Ruhollah Musavi Khomeini) (1902–1989)
Iranian political and Shiite Muslim religious leader who, in 1978, called for Islamic revolution in Iran while living in exile in France. After Shah Mohammad Reza Pahlavi was toppled and driven out of Iran, Khomeini returned to his home country on 1 February 1979, where he invoked the Islamic Republic of Iran on 1 April 1979. From then, until his death ten years later, Khomeini was Iran's Head of State.

AK-47, AKM, AK-74
see *Kalashnikov*

American breakfast
Most typically, American breakfasts consist of thick pancakes, hash browns (shredded fried potatoes), eggs, bacon, pork sausage links, toast, orange juice, a glass of

ice water, and "bottomless" coffee, meaning unlimited refills of coffee at no extra charge.

For the eggs, the restaurant guest usually has the option of requesting them scrambled, sunny side up (fried on one side only, with the yolk clearly visible), or over easy (fried on both sides).

Amon Düül II
A psychedelic rock band popular in 1970s Munich. Their bestselling albums included *Phallus Dei, Yeti,* and *Tanz der Lemminge (Dance of the Lemmings).*

Application for naturalization
Application for receiving American citizenship, with U.S. Government form N-400.

ARVN (Army of the Republic of Vietnam)
Pronounced "Arvin." Designation for the U.S.-backed South Vietnamese Army during the Vietnam War. Allied countries included the United States, South Korea, Australia, New Zealand, Thailand, and Taiwan. After the end of the Vietnam War in 1975, the ARVN was dissolved.

Atlas vertebra, first thoracic
The uppermost vertebra, as the part of the spinal column closest to the skull, supports the entire head and is therefore sometimes known as the "Atlas vertebra."

Baksheesh
A Persian-derived term (literally: gift, dispensation, boon) used in the Balkans and the Middle East to refer to both gratuities and bribe money.

Bell UH-1/Bell 205

Also frequently called *Huey* or *Iroquois*. With about 16,000 built, this turbine-powered helicopter is the world's most produced. It was originally conceived for the evacuation of wounded soldiers. Its greatest range of deployment came in the Vietnam War, where it was used for medevacs and troop transport, as well as on the battlefield. In Vietnam, the American military deployed 7,000 Hueys, of which only 2,000 were brought back to the United States after the war. This helicopter—unmistakable thanks to its signature sound, which was often likened to someone beating a wool rug—was also used by the Bundeswehr for SAR (search and rescue) operations until late 2016.

Bell 206 Jet Ranger/Long Ranger

The light, multi-purpose Bell 206 helicopter is both the most widely built and the most commercially successful civilian helicopter in the world. The Jet Ranger (Bell 206B, which seats five including the pilot) had its inaugural flight back in 1962. The longer version, the Bell 206L Long Ranger (a seven-seater), was capable of being outfitted with a litter and was also used as an ambulance and rescue helicopter in Germany when air rescue was first introduced.

Bugs

Term commonly used for any small listening devices that can be placed in rooms, under carpeting, lamps, or furniture, or hidden in the mouthpieces of old-style landline telephone receivers, for the purpose of secretly eavesdropping on conversations.

C-9A Nightingale
McDonnell Douglas C-9A, a twin-engine, narrow-bod-
ied aircraft specially built starting in 1968 for the requirements of the U.S. Air Force as an aeromedical evacuation
aircraft for wounded soldiers in the Vietnam War. The
C-9A was capable of transporting up to forty litters of
wounded. The twin-engine, low-wing aircraft flew at a
cruising speed of 504 miles per hour/438 knots (811
km/h). Depending on how the aircraft was equipped, it
had a range of about 2000 to 2600 miles (3200 to 4200
kilometers).

Cadi
see Qadi

Chador
A large cloth, cut in the form of a semi-circle, that women
in Iran wind around their heads and bodies and wear
over their mostly Western clothing. The everyday chador
is dark, usually black, while the prayer chador is light
and usually bears faint patterns. From December 1936
until December 1978, the chador was forbidden in Iran.
However, since early 1979—the beginning of the Islamic
Revolution—wearing the chador, or a similar veiling,
has been mandatory.

CIA
The Central Intelligence Agency, established in 1947, is
the foreign intelligence service of the United States. The
CIA's headquarters are located in Langley, Virginia, a
suburb located northwest of Washington, D.C. The name
'Langley' is often used to refer to the CIA itself. Its agents
operate worldwide. The CIA's training center, known

among insiders simply as "The Farm," is located in Camp Peary, near Williamsburg, Virginia, about 150 miles (250 km) south of Langley. Under the prevailing interpretation of American law, the CIA is permitted to conduct covert operations abroad using illegal means.

Confucius (c. 551 – c. 479 BCE)
A Chinese moral philosopher whose teachings, grounded in tradition and beliefs, emphasize the role of political and administrative virtue along with the importance of family bonds. Confucianism continues to be a mainstay of East Asian culture.

Dead drop (dead letter box)
Hiding place for the purpose of transmitting secret messages, e.g., a hole in a branch or wall, or the casing of a ball-point pen.

Deciphering
Cryptoanalysis, code-breaking, decoding of secret messages.

Deep Purple
An English hard rock band, founded in 1968 and one of the most commercially successful rock bands around the world. Their bestselling studio album, *Machine Head*, came out in 1972.

Detachment
Military unit, often subdivided into A-Detachment, B-Detachment, and so forth.

Diogenes of Sinope
Greek philosopher (around 400 B.C.E.) said to have voluntarily chosen a life of poverty and to have lived in a barrel, renouncing any and all worldly needs.

Deutschmark
Deutschmark, also known as the DM, DEM (for banking transactions), Deutsche Mark, D-Mark, Mark, or German Mark, was the official currency of the Federal Republic of Germany from 1948 until 2001, when it was replaced by the Euro. In 1972, the exchange rate between the mark and the U.S. dollar averaged about 3.20:1 (equivalent to about 1.64 Euro). However, in that year, the purchasing power of both currencies was about seven times today's.

Dust off
Radio call sign for Huey helicopters tasked with evacuating the wounded.

Effendi
Polite Turkish form of address, roughly equivalent to 'Mister.'

Exophthalmos
Physiological condition in which the eyes seem to project unusually far from their sockets. Commonly referred to as 'bulging eyeballs.'

Farsi
Persian language linguistically belonging to the Iranian branch of the Indo-European family of languages. It is the official language in Iran and an officially recognized one in Afghanistan.

Feldjäger (Bundeswehr)
Military police of the Germany Army (Bundeswehr).

Fentanyl
A synthetic opioid and powerful pain reliever used as an anesthetic, among other applications. In sufficient doses, it leads to respiratory paralysis.

Freelancer
In aviation, refers to pilots without a permanent job.

Feet/meters
In aviator jargon, vertical distances are generally stated in feet. One foot equals 30.48 centimeters; thus, an altitude of 1000 feet is the equivalent of approximately 305 meters.

G3, HK G3
The G3 (short for *Gewehr 3*, literally, "Rifle 3") is a rapid-fire rifle developed and produced by German weapons manufacturer Heckler & Koch. The box magazines can be loaded with five, ten, or twenty cartridges with a caliber of 7.62 x 51mm (NATO ammunition rounds). Since 1967, Iran has manufactured the rifle under German license.

Gadget
American slang for any small, technologically clever object or device possessing a particularly high degree of functionality and usefulness.

GI
Abbreviation for 'government issue' or 'galvanized iron'—popular designation, dating back at least as far as

World War II, for soldiers serving in the United States Armed Forces.

Greyhound Lines
Oldest and largest long-distance bus company in the United States.

HALO-jump
High altitude – low opening military parachuting was a military operation in which free-fall parachutists made their jumps at extremely high altitudes and opened their parachutes at low altitude. In this way, the drop plane was able to evade capture by enemy anti-aircraft defenses. Today, HALO jumps are no longer the usual practice, having been superseded by HAHO jumps (high altitude – high opening) following the development of square parachutes.

Hamam
Middle Eastern steam bath (sex-segregated), offering cleanses, massages, and fresh water.

Helms, Richard
Director of the CIA, 1966–1973. As a young journalist, Helms—who spoke fluent German—interviewed Hitler. Later, he became the first spy to hold the office of CIA director. His era encompassed the publication of the Pentagon Papers (June 1971), the break-in at the Watergate complex (June 1972), as well as the groundwork for the military coup in Chile (1973). At the end of his tenure as director, he ordered the destruction of the majority of the CIA's records pertaining to Project MK-Ultra (see below).

Hover
Helicopter maneuver in which the pilot utilizes the ground effect to maintain the aircraft in a consistent, stable, low-altitude position. Hovering is considered the most challenging skill for a helicopter pilot to master.

Huey
Popular term for the helicopter type Bell UH-1 (see above).

Ikebana
Japanese art of flower arranging.

Intelligence
Umbrella term encompassing information services, intelligence services and agencies, and secret and/or classified information (see also CIA and military intelligence)

Iroquois
Popular term for the helicopter type Bell UH-1 (see above).

Jet Ranger
see *Bell 206.*

Kalashnikov
Mikhail Timofeyevich Kalashnikov was a Russian weapons designer. The eponymous AK-47 assault rifle (*Avtomat Kalashnikov* 1947) is the world's most widespread assault rifle, with around 100 million units produced, including the AKM, AK-74, and other variations. The AK-47 is typically characterized by its curved, 30-round magazine.

KIA
Killed in Action (American military terminology for military personnel killed in combat).

Knots (air travel and sea travel)
Speed measurement used in aviation and seafaring, based on the nautical mile, a unit of distance. One nautical mile measures 6,076.1 feet or 1,852 meters (1.151 land or statute miles). In turn, one knot corresponds to one nautical mile per hour, i.e., to 1.151 land miles or 1.852 kilometers per hour (it is therefore inaccurate to speak of "knots per hour.") A speed of travel of 100 knots is thus the same thing as a speed of 114.9 land miles per hour or 185 kilometers per hour.

Khomeini
see Ayatollah Ruhollah Khomeini.

Krav Maga
A type of martial arts, originating in Israel, which combines elements of boxing, wrestling, aikido, karate, and judo. It is taught primarily to special units and intelligence services.

Kreiswehrersatzamt (district recruiting office) (KWEA)
From 1956 through 2011, when the Federal Republic of Germany still maintained conscription, KWEA offices around the country held responsibility for recording and physically screening all male citizens who had reached eighteen years of age. The KWEA decided whether draftees were fit for military service and whether they could be deployed.

M16

Primary assault rifle issued to the infantry by the United States Army starting in 1964. The M16A1 (1967–1982) had an effective firing range of 300–400 meters (max. 2000 meters). It could fire between 700 and 950 rounds per minute, and its standard magazine contained thirty rounds. Its nicknames included "Sweet Little Sixteen" and "Mattel," after the American toy manufacturer, due to the rifle's plastic pistol-grip plates.

M60

Fully automatic multi-purpose machine gun nicknamed "The Pig," used by, among others, aerial gunners aboard Huey helicopters. The M60 could be equipped with ammunition belts containing between 100 and 250 cartridges.

Makarov pistol

Popular 9-millimeter Russian pistol. The magazine holds eight cartridges. This self-loading pistol is milled completely out of steel and has been in continuous production since 1952.

Medevac

see *Aeromedical Evacuation*.

Melange

Mocha with a large quantity of milk, a popular Austrian coffee beverage.

MIA

Missing in Action, term designating a soldier missing after hostile actions, with regard to whom it remains

unclear whether he was killed, wounded, or captured—
or whether he has defected.

Michael Müller, pseudonyms

Michael Müller, a German, was naturalized in the United
States and took citizenship under the name *Michael
Miller* (using the typical American pronunciation of the
first name). Miller was sent to fight in the Vietnam War
and later deserted, during which time he assumed the
identity of his comrade-in-arms Bill McPherson and of
Washington Post reporter Mike Love. Subsequently, he
received training by the CIA under the assumed name of
Martin Cooper, which he used for the rest of his life
under CIA direction. As a sleeping car conductor, he
worked under the names Hans Gruber and Hans Schultz.
During Miller's operations in Iran, he first assumed the
identity of Thomas Freeman, an English reporter for
Reuters, and later Dr. Dagobert Dussmann, a German
physician.

Military Intelligence

The process of collecting and analyzing information to
furnish direction and guidance to assist field command-
ers in sound decision-making. Ideally, MI provides an
assessment of data from a range of sources relevant to
mission requirements or as part of operational or cam-
paign planning.

MK-Ultra Project

CIA research program employing psychoactive sub-
stances for the purpose of finding a truth serum. The
program ran from the early 1950s until the beginning of
the 1970s. The program encompassed human experi-

ments on thousands of uninformed, non-consenting test subjects. In 1973, CIA Director Richard Helms, at the end of his tenure in office, had nearly all the project files destroyed.

MTA
Medical-Technical Assistant.

Nap-of-the-earth flight
A flight maneuver in which the pilot flies at extremely low altitude during military and intelligence operations, in order to prevent detection by aerial surveillance radar.

NCOs (non-commissioned officers)
Strictly speaking, a military officer who has not pursued or obtained a commission, although generally, the term *officer* is used to refer solely to personnel who hold a commission. Noncoms, as non-commissioned officers are called, typically earn their position of authority (such as sergeant, petty officer, etc.) via promotion from the enlisted ranks, starting with private (in the Army and Marine Corps) seaman recruit (in the Navy) or airman (in the Air Force).

NGOs (non-governmental organizations)
Non-governmental organizations involved in humanitarian activities, e.g., the Red Cross, MHD, UNICEF, UNHCR, Amnesty International.

NLF (National Liberation Front of South Vietnam) and the LASV (Liberation Army of South Vietnam).
The National Liberation Front of South Vietnam, along with its military arm, the LASV—generally known as the

Viet Cong—was a guerilla organization during the Vietnam War that pursued armed resistance against the South Vietnamese government and the United States. The NLF was founded in 1960 and dissolved in 1977. Its most significant allies included China and the Soviet Union.

PAO
Public Affairs Officer.

Pentagon Papers
Study commissioned in 1967 by Robert S. McNamara, then the United States Secretary of Defense, which documents the preparations and decisional processes for the Vietnam War. An informant, Daniel Ellsberg, leaked the Pentagon Papers to the *New York Times* in 1971. The United States Government sought to prevent the publication of the study because it showed how the American people had been lied to about the reason for the war and the initiation of it. The *New York Times* and the *Washington Post*, however, won the lawsuit before the Supreme Court of the United States, and in 1972 they published excerpts from the 7,000 documents. The publication of the Pentagon Papers caused worldwide outrage and massively bolstered opponents of the war.

Pinch-hitter flight training
Term adopted from baseball terminology: a pinch hitter is someone who steps in or represents another. In pinch-hitter flight training, a passenger is supposed to be capable of flying and landing an aircraft in the event that the pilot becomes incapacitated. The training encompasses, among other things, navigation to the nearest airfield as well as radio and transponder operation.

Pitch control
Lever in a helicopter that controls pitch; at first glance, it resembles a handbrake. It is operated by the pilot's left hand and adjusts the main rotor blade's angle of attack, in turn influencing the helicopter's ascent, descent, and speed.

Platoon
Army hierarchical unit; in the United States Army, a platoon consists of between sixteen and forty soldiers and is generally comprised of two or more squads, sections, or patrols.

Private
Lowest enlisted rank in the United States Army, encompassing the period immediately following enlistment and for a certain amount of time thereafter.

Private First Class (PFC)
Soldier who has completed Basic Training, roughly equivalent to the Bundeswehr rank of *Obergefreiter* or the NATO OR-2 designation.

Qadi
From the Arabic *al-qadi*, meaning 'decision-maker' or 'judge.' An Islamic legal scholar who pronounces judgment in accordance with Sharia law.

Radio Free Europe/Radio Liberty (RFE/RL)
During the Cold War era, a CIA-financed radio propaganda station headquartered at Munich's English Garden. Initially, RFE broadcast in Czech, providing the Western viewpoint in political matters. Soviet jamming

constantly disrupted the news broadcasts on a massive scale. There were numerous deadly attacks by Eastern Bloc agents against the station's employees and facilities. Today, the station has its headquarters in the United States, in Wilmington, Delaware and its primary facility in Prague. It broadcasts in twenty-six languages, primarily for listeners in the Middle East and Asia.

Reverend
In the United States, this term designates a person who may lawfully perform marriages. A Reverend usually, but not inevitably, belongs to a particular religious community. No training or education is required for this occupation, merely a licensing or registration in the given state.

Sannyasa
A Yoga practitioner who has renounced worldly possessions. In the 1970s, the term was also adopted by Maharishi Mahesh Yogi's acolytes, who wore dark orange clothing. The great master was the founder of Transcendental Meditation, captivating followers numbering in the hundreds of thousands.

Shah Mohammad Reza Pahlavi
The autocratic monarch Shah Mohammed Reza Pahlavi (1919–1980), of the Pahlavi Dynasty, was the final Shah (King) of Persia. With the assistance of the CIA, he ascended to the Peacock Throne in 1941, and until 1979 ruled with a strong hand and using SAVAK, his highly organized, merciless secret police. On 16 January 1979, the Shah was forced to leave the country as a result of the Islamic Revolution. After brief sojourns in the United

States and Panama, the dethroned monarch, now ill with cancer, died in exile in Egypt on 27 July 1980.

Sharia
Body of law, a kind of Islamic law book, which governs Muslim life on the basis of the Koran. The punishments derived from it are severe and inhumane. It calls for the death penalty for adultery as well as for "apostasy from the faith." Public scourging, stoning, and hangings based on Sharia law have been daily occurrences in the Islamic Republic of Iran ever since its founding in April 1979.

Shiite
Islam's second-largest denomination, after the Sunnis. About 98% of the Iranian population are Shiites.

Specialist
U.S. Army enlisted rank (E-4, equivalent to corporal) that can be obtained by means of special skills and qualifications. Besides the military, police forces, the FBI, and intelligence services in the United States have Specialists for nearly every special assignment imaginable. Specialists are distinguished by high levels of skill and competence in their respective fields.

Stick
Control stick aboard a helicopter, operated by the pilot's right hand; changes the inclination area of the circle described by the rotor, thereby determining the direction of flight.

Sweet Little Sixteen
see *M16 assault rifle*.

The Star-Spangled Banner
National anthem of the United States of America since 1936. The lyrics were actually composed over a century earlier, by Francis Scott Key in 1814, to express his joy at the American victory over the British in the War of 1812. The third and fourth verses, due to their militantly anti-British tone, are always omitted. An unforgettable version, definitely worth listening to, is Jimi Hendrix's electric-guitar rendition at the Woodstock festival in 1969.

Time designations
In civilian life, Americans state the time in twelve-hour cycles, adding a.m. (*ante meridiem*, i.e., before noon) or p.m. (*post meridiem*, after noon). Thus, for example, '11 a.m.' refers to 11 o'clock in the morning, while '11 p.m.' refers to 11 o'clock in the evening.

In the military, however, the 24-hour clock is used exclusively. Two zeros at the top of the hour are spoken as "hundred." The Army adds the term "hours," whereas the Navy and Marine Corps do not adopt this practice. Examples:

0800 is spoken as "zero eight hundred (hours)" (8:00 a.m. to American civilians).

2000 is spoken as "twenty hundred (hours)" (8:00 p.m. to American civilians).

Türkiye
For decades, *Turkey* was the name of the Turkish Republic. Because the word *turkey* can also refer in common parlance to a species of poultry, a flop, or a foolish person, the Turkish government demanded that the country's official English-language designation be changed to

Türkiye. The United Nations officially implemented the new name on 3rd of June 2022.

Unimog 404
The Unimog (from the German *Universal-Motor-Gerät*, literally, "Universal Motor Device") Model 404 was a small, versatile truck produced by Mercedes Benz between 1955 and 1980. It was outfitted for a payload of up to 1,500 kilograms (3,307 pounds).

United States Army (U.S. Army)
Ground forces of the United States of America. In the Vietnam War, its allies included the Army of the Republic of Vietnam (ARVN), South Korea, Australia, New Zealand, Taiwan, and Thailand.

USPA (United States Parachute Association)
American parachuting club, which, among other activities, regulates the licensing of its members.

Viet Cong
see *NLF*

Vietnam War (1955–1975)
Also known as the Second Indochina War, the Vietnam War was a proxy war between the superpowers during the Cold War. After the partition of Vietnam into North Vietnam and South Vietnam in 1954, the Communist North was supported by the Soviet Union and China while the South was backed by the United States, Australia, New Zealand, South Korea, Taiwan, and Thailand. The number of Vietnamese casualties, both civilian and military, is estimated to have ranged between two and

five million. A total of 58,220 American soldiers died, as well as 5,264 soldiers from the countries allied with the United States.

VW Kübelsitzwagen, Type 181
Literally, "bucket-seat-car," in essence the German counterpart to the Willys Jeeps and their successors used by the American forces. The Type 181 (1969–1980) was an all-terrain military vehicle manufactured by Volkswagen, initially for military purposes only. However, due to its elegant simplicity and usefulness, it quickly became in great demand by businesses and civilian consumers as well. The civilian version was marketed as "The Thing" in the United States during the 1970s.

Watergate
The Watergate Affair was triggered by the failed break-in by five alleged CIA agents into Democratic Party headquarters in the Watergate hotel complex in Washington, D.C., on 17 June 1972, followed by the investigation of the underlying events by *Washington Post* journalists Bob Woodward and Carl Bernstein. Their legwork revealed that the American people had been lied to by the government and by Republican President Richard M. Nixon. These revelations eventually led to Nixon's resignation from the Presidency on 9 August 1974.

West Point graduate
Graduate of the United States Military Academy at West Point (USMA). Perhaps one of the most prestigious universities in the United States, USMA was founded by the government in 1802 to train a professional officer corps for the United States Army. Located in West Point, New

York, about fifty miles (eighty kilometers) north of Manhattan, the USMA campus lies on a scenic bluff overlooking the Hudson River.